PRAISE FOR BRI~~T~~
BO~~C~~

"Brittainy Cherry has the ability to shatter our hearts and heal them in the same story."

—*The Bookery Review*

"This is not just your ordinary romance. It is completely addictive and intensely consuming. Heartbreakingly real in all its entirety."

—*Kitty Kats Crazy about Books*

"Full of heartbreak and loss and pain. But also so full of love and hope and sweet and happy moments. I adored every single word in this book!"

—*BJ's Book Blog*

"As usual Brittainy wrote a stunning story that will touch your heart and stay with you."

—*Mel Reader Reviews*

"I'm speechless and completely overwhelmed by the beauty of this story."

—*Two Unruly Girls*

"As always Cherry aims straight for our hearts and hits a bull's-eye!"

—*Book Bistro Blog*

"*STUNNING!* Brittainy Cherry has once again blown my mind with another one of her beautifully written stories. There is no doubt in my mind that readers are going to fall just as madly in love with this story as I have."

—*Wrapped Up in Reading Book Blog*

"You don't just read a Brittainy Cherry book—her books, her words, devour you. Landon and Shay's story is positively magnificent, and the best part is we're only halfway through it."

—*Passionately Plotted*

"There is so much emotion throughout, so many beautiful words, and I could not get enough. I laughed, my heart broke, and I felt everything the characters felt."

—*Bibliophile Ramblings*

"*Beautiful*, heart-achingly real, and *one of the best books I have ever read.*"

—*Elle's Book Blog*

the
WRECKAGE
of US

OTHER TITLES BY BRITTAINY CHERRY

The Elements Series

Other Titles

the
WRECKAGE
of US

BRITTAINY
CHERRY

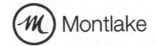

Published by Montlake, Seattle

www.apub.com

Amazon, the Amazon logo, and Montlake are trademarks of Amazon.com, Inc., or its affiliates.

ISBN-13: 9781542017862
ISBN-10: 1542017866

Cover design by Hang Le

Printed in the United States of America

To the ones who struggle but never give up on love

1

HAZEL

"I think you're in the wrong spot," Big Paw said as I sat across from him in his office. "You have to go down to the Farmhouse restaurant to apply for a waitstaff position."

Sitting across from a man like Big Paw made a person feel smaller than small. Obviously, his name wasn't really Big Paw, but that was what everyone in town called him. He was an older gentleman in his eighties and quite a force to be around. You didn't live in Eres without knowing about Big Paw. He lived up to his name too. He was a big man, both in weight and in height. He had to be well over six foot five and around 250 pounds, easily. Even at his age, he didn't slouch over much, but he moved a bit slower. He always wore the same thing, too, day in and day out. A plaid shirt with a pair of overalls, his cowboy boots, and a trucker hat. I swore, his closet must've had a million plaid shirts and overalls, or his wife, Holly, did a lot of laundry.

Eres, Nebraska, was a place unknown to most of the world. We walked on dirt roads, and most of our pockets were dirt poor. If you had a job in Eres, you were a lucky one, though it probably didn't pay you much of anything. You worked paycheck to paycheck if you were fortunate. If you weren't lucky, you'd probably take a loan out with Big Paw, who wouldn't ever expect you to pay it back, even though he'd tell you that you owed him on the regular. Old Man Kenny down at the auto shop still owed Big Paw $50,000. That debt had been held up since 1987, and I doubted that debt would ever be paid off. Still, during every town gathering, Big Paw brought it up with a grumpy look glued to his face.

Big Paw was pretty much the godfather of Eres. He ran Eres Ranch, which was the centerpiece of the whole town. From his crop fields to his cattle, Big Paw had created something no one else seemed to have been able to do in Eres—he'd built something that had lasted.

Eres Ranch had been running strong for over sixty years, and most of the people who worked in town worked for Big Paw. They worked either on the ranch or at the Farmhouse.

I definitely wasn't sitting in his office in hopes of a waitstaff position, even if I looked like I wasn't made out for the ranch.

"With all due respect, Mr. Big Paw—"

"Big Paw," he corrected. "No 'Mr.' crap like that. Just straightforward Big Paw. Don't go on making me feel older than I already do."

I swallowed hard. "Yes. Sorry. Big Paw, with all due respect, I am not interested in a position at the restaurant. I want to work on the ranch."

His eyes darted up and down over me, taking in my appearance. Sure, I was certain most girls my age didn't want to be getting down and dirty in the pigpens or horse stables, but I needed that position, and I wasn't going to walk away until I'd secured it.

"You don't really look like my regular crew." He huffed and grimaced. I didn't take it personal, though, because Big Paw was always huffing and grimacing. If he ever smiled at me, I'd feel as if it were a death wish.

"Don't know if you have what it takes to work in the barns," he explained, shuffling through the paperwork. "I'm sure Holly can get you a nice position at the resta—"

"I don't want a restaurant position," I argued again. Then I paused and swallowed hard, realizing that I'd cut off Big Paw. People didn't cut off Big Paw. Or at least they didn't live to tell the story. "Sorry, but I need a position at the ranch."

"And why's that?" His eyes were so dark you felt as if you were staring into the biggest black hole as he looked your way.

"It's no secret that the ranch hands make double the amount of the employees at the Farmhouse. I need the money."

He pulled out a cigar from his desk drawer, placed it between his lips, and leaned back in his chair. He didn't light it, but he chewed on the end. He almost always had that cigar in his mouth, but never once had I seen him light it up. Maybe it was just an old habit that he held on to. Or perhaps Holly had scolded him and ordered him to stop smoking. She was hell bent on making Big Paw take care of his health, even if he didn't want to, and I swore that man would do anything to make his wife happy. Holly was probably the only soul alive who ever received his smiles.

"You live down at the trailers, right?" he asked, brushing a thumb against his upper lip.

"Yes, sir." He cocked an eyebrow at the word *sir*. I cleared my throat and tried again. "Yes, Big Paw. That's right."

"Who's your kinfolk?"

"Just my mother, Jean Stone."

"Jean Stone . . ." His brows pushed closer to one another as he tapped his fingers against the desk. "She's attached to Charlie Riley, ain't that right?"

My stomach turned a little at the mention of Charlie. "Yes, si—*Big Paw*."

For a split second, Big Paw didn't look grumpy. He almost looked sad. He chewed on his cigar and shook his head. "That boy ain't no good. He causes a lot of trouble in our town, bringing in that crap that messes with people's bodies and heads. I ain't got no place on my staff if there's any kind of drug use going on. I don't have time for that mess."

"I swear, I don't use. I actually hate it with a passion." Almost as much as I hated Charlie.

Charlie was Mama's husband—my dear ol' stepfather—and he'd been in our lives as long as I could remember. I'd never known snakes could be people until I'd grown up to find out the type of person Charlie was. He was the dark spot in Eres, a toxic infection that spread throughout town. He was the biggest drug dealer and the main cause of the meth habit that had taken over.

Charlie Riley was trouble—and he was too damn good at his job to ever get caught.

There were many reasons to loathe that man, but my main reason was based on the person he'd turned my mother into.

Mama always said she loved Charlie, but she didn't like him that much. At least not when he was drunk, and if there was anything Charlie was good at, it was being drunk. Sometimes, Charlie would get so drunk and so loud he'd throw things and hit Mama until she started crying and apologizing for things she'd never even done.

Once I'd asked her why she wouldn't leave him, and she'd told me, "Everything we have is because of that man. This house, the clothes on your back, the food you eat. Don't you see, Hazel? Without him, we are nothing."

I didn't understand that. I didn't get why someone was allowed to hurt you just because they gave you things. Maybe she was right about Charlie giving us stuff, but if we had nothing, that would've meant she'd have no black eyes either.

She'd told me to drop the conversation and not bring it up again, because she loved Charlie and she'd never leave him.

It'd been three years since we'd had that conversation. I was now eighteen years old, and it seemed like day in and day out, Mama was beginning to side with Charlie over me. I knew it wasn't her true thoughts, though. Charlie had poisoned her body and mind to the point that Mama hadn't a clue which way was up. She was a slave to his control and his drug supply. When I looked into Mama's eyes nowadays, I hardly saw my real mother looking back at me anymore.

I would've moved on completely if it weren't for the fact that Mama was four months pregnant. I felt somewhat responsible for my soon-to-be sibling. Lord knew Charlie wasn't looking after Mama's care.

I needed the job at Eres Ranch in order to save up money for my sister or brother. I needed money to buy prenatal vitamins for Mama. Money to make sure her fridge was full. Money to make sure that somehow the baby could come into the world with a little bit more than I had.

Then, with the rest of the money, I'd buy a one-way ticket and leave Eres and never look back. Somehow, I'd convince Mama to come with me, too, with the new baby. The last thing she needed to do was raise a child with Charlie around.

Mama was right—we did have a roof over our heads because of Charlie. But just because someone gave you four walls to stay in didn't mean they weren't a prison. I couldn't wait for the day that I collected enough money to get myself my own four walls. Those four walls would be filled with love, not threats. With happiness, not fear.

And the name Charlie Riley would be a distant memory.

Big Paw rubbed the back of his neck. "We were looking for ranch hands, not some girl who's probably too afraid to get her hands dirty."

"I'm not afraid of that at all. I'll get down and dirty with the rest."

"You have to be able to lift over sixty pounds."

"I'll lift seventy."

He cocked an eyebrow and leaned forward. "You have to be here before the sun rises, and if you don't finish the task, you stay after dusk, and there ain't no overtime. You get paid by the daily tasks being completed, not by the hours you spend here. If you get done early, you can leave early. If you get done late, you're stuck here late. Also, I don't believe in three strikes. I believe in one. Mess up, and you're gone. You understand, girl?"

If anyone else called me "girl," I'd slam my fist straight into their nose to show them just how much of a girl I was, but hearing it come from Big Paw wasn't an insult. He called it as he saw it in a straightforward way. He'd call any man younger than him "boy," too, because he could. I was sure people who identified differently would be offended by the title Big Paw would give them, but he was too old to bother correcting himself.

Old dog, new tricks and all.

"I understand." I nodded. "I'll be the hardest worker out there, I promise."

He grumbled some more and rubbed his beard. "Fine, but don't come complaining to me when you ruin your favorite pair of shoes in the pigpens. You report to the stables tomorrow at noon sharp for training with my grandson, Ian. He'll be in charge of getting you up and running."

I sat up a bit straighter as my stomach tightened. "Wait, Ian is training me?" I frowned. "Are you sure Marcus or James or someone can't take me on?"

"No. Those boys are already training a few other ranch hands." He raised his brow once more. "You aren't already making yourself difficult, are you?"

I shook my head. "No, sir—er—Big Paw. Sorry. That is fine. Noon tomorrow. I'll be there."

The idea of being trained by Ian Parker made me want to gag. He was known as the playboy rock star of Eres. Ian had graduated three years before me, and I'd been the lucky girl with my locker right beside his during my freshman year. Which meant I'd had a front-and-center viewing of him swapping spit with whatever small-town groupie was wrapped around his pinkie at the time.

I was shocked that mono wasn't being spread around more due to Ian Parker and his manwhore ways. Nothing said *I hate you* more than having to wedge my way between him and blonde-chick-of-the-week to get into my locker. Now, he was responsible for training me at the ranch.

I doubted he even knew who I was, seeing as how I'd spent a good amount of my time in high school trying hard to not stand out. My wardrobe consisted of black on black with a sprinkle of black. It matched my charcoal hair, inky-black nails, and deep-green eyes. The darkness of it all went with my personality. I was a loner and found life a bit easier that way. Most people called me the solo goth of Eres and thought me unworthy of their time. Though a good handful of girls had muscled up the energy to bully me through the high school years, as if I'd been some bully charity case. *Oh? Look at Hazel Stone minding her business—let's make her stand out more by throwing food at her during lunch. That's the attention she's craving.*

If I disappeared, no one would probably come looking for me. Not to be overly melodramatic, but it was true. Once I'd run away from home for two weeks, and when I'd come home, Mama had asked me why I hadn't done the dishes. She hadn't even noticed I was missing, and if my own mother wouldn't notice, I doubted anyone else in Eres would. Especially someone like Ian. He was too busy with his hands either wrapped around a woman or strumming his guitar.

The next day, I showed up at the ranch two hours before I had to meet with Ian. I hung around the stables, wasting minutes before it was time to get to work. I didn't have a car to get to the job, so it had taken me nearly thirty minutes to walk from Charlie's place. The sun stung against my skin, forcing sweat to trickle down my forehead. My underarms were Shrek's dreamland based on the swamp-like moisture attacking them. I held my arms away from my body, trying to stop the sweat stains from deepening, but the summer sun in Eres was unapologetic to the mere human beings it attacked.

When two hours had passed, I headed to the ranch office, where I was supposed to meet with Ian. I sat there for thirty minutes. Then forty-five minutes. An hour went by.

I hadn't a clue what I should do. I'd checked my watch about five times, making sure I hadn't blacked out and missed my appointment with Ian.

After waiting over an hour, I began walking around the ranch, hoping to cross paths with Ian or someone who could lead me to Ian. The more time that passed, the more nervous I grew, thinking that if Big Paw found out I wasn't being trained, he'd cut me loose before I even had a shot at nailing the job.

"Excuse me, can you help me?" I asked a guy carrying a stack of hay on his back. He turned to me with an exhausted look. It had to be around fifty-some pounds of hay resting on him, and I felt bad for even interrupting him, but I couldn't lose my job.

"Yeah?" he breathed, beaten to his core. I'd seen him around school too. He was James, Ian's best friend. James was much less of a manwhore than Ian. He smiled a lot more, too, even with heavy hay about to break his spine. The two guys were in a band together called the Wreckage, and even though Ian was the lead singer, James was the heart of the music. People craved Ian, while they wanted to be James's best friend. He was that nice of a guy. James wore a white T-shirt with the sleeves ripped off the arms and a backward baseball hat. His shirt looked like it'd seen better days, covered in dirt and rips, but still, he found a way to smile at me.

"My name is Hazel, and I'm supposed to be meeting with Ian for my training. It's my first day."

James arched an eyebrow before dropping the hay down to the ground. He brushed the back of his palm against his forehead and cleared his throat. "You're working here?" he asked, sounding more baffled than I would've liked.

"Yes, I am. It's my first day," I repeated.

His eyes moved across my body, and he shook his head, making every insecurity I could've ever had come to the surface. It was funny how a simple look could light up one's diffidence so easily.

James must've picked up on my discomfort, because he gave me one of his free smiles and leaned against the stack of hay. "You're going to die out here, dressing in all that black. Black denim jeans and a long-sleeve shirt? Are those combat boots?" He laughed. "Are you sure you're not supposed to be at the Farmhouse?"

His laughter wasn't insulting. It was coated more with confusion, but still, I didn't like it. "I'm not worried about my wardrobe. I just want to get to work."

"You should be worried about your wardrobe, seeing as how the sun on this ranch doesn't let up. Heatstroke is a real thing."

"Do you know where Ian might be?" I asked through gritted teeth. I hadn't come to the ranch for fashion criticism. I was there to work.

"Knowing Ian, he's probably off in the office outside of the horse stables. But a little heads-up—" James started, but I cut him off.

I didn't have time for a heads-up.

I was already almost an hour and thirty minutes late.

"Thanks," I said, hurrying off in a jog toward the small office attached to the stables. Had Big Paw mentioned I was supposed to meet Ian at the horse-stables office? Had I misunderstood him by showing up at the main office? Oh crap. I only had one strike, and I'd already messed that up.

The moment I got to the office, I swung the door open, already having my apologies sitting on the edge of my tongue. "Hi, Ian, I'm Hazel, and *ohmygosh*!" I blurted out, looking up to see a girl on her knees in front of a half-dressed Ian. His white T-shirt was still on, but his blue jeans and boxers were wrapped around his ankles as a woman's lips were wrapped around his—

Oh my lanta, was it supposed to be that big? How was the girl not choking to death on the dynamite stick resting in her mouth? The way the veins bulged out of his penis made me think that thing could've exploded any second, and the girl on her knees had no problem with that outcome happening between her lipstick-coated lips.

I turned to look away, stunned at what I'd walked into. "I'm sorry, I'm sorry!" I shouted, shaking my hands around in a fright.

"Get the fuck out!" Ian barked, his smoky, gruff voice dripping with irritation and pleasure all at once. Who knew you could be annoyed and pleased at the same time? Any man getting a blow job interrupted, I supposed.

"Sorry, sorry!" I repeated, hurrying out of the room. I shut the door quickly behind me and took a deep breath. My hands were shaky, and my heart pounded against my rib cage. That was the last thing I'd expected to happen inside the horse-stables office at one in the afternoon on a Wednesday. Leave it to Ian to give me quite the view that afternoon. A view I wished I could bleach from my mind.

I stood there like a complete moron for a few minutes before I checked my watch.

How hadn't they finished yet?

Now, I wasn't a blow job expert, but based on the size, the veins, and the determination of said woman on her knees, Ian should've been close to completion.

Still, I didn't hear that happily-ever-after groan fall from his lips, and the day was passing on.

I knocked on the door.

"Piss off," Ian's voice hissed.

Still that charming fella I remembered from high school.

"I would if I could, but I can't. You're supposed to be training me today."

"Come back tomorrow," he ordered.

"I can't. Big Paw told me I have to train today with you, no ifs, ands, or buts, and I refuse to lose this job opportunity. I need this."

"Save the sob story for someone who cares," he growled, making my anger build more and more.

Who did this guy think he was?

Just because he had found a glimpse of musical success on the internet and had every female—and some males—in Eres wanting his attention, it didn't mean he had the right to talk to people the way he did. I mean, hell, he was a rock star in the middle of nowhere, Nebraska. It wasn't as if he were Kurt Cobain or Jimi Hendrix.

I swung the office door open to find the two still in their same positions, and I placed my hands on my hips. "I'm sorry, you're supposed to be training me, so therefore this situation should probably be put on hold until later."

Ian looked at me and cocked the highest eyebrow in history, and for the record, I was working very hard to not take notice of the other cocked body part of his on display.

"How about you get a hint and realize he's busy with me?" the woman sneered, finally pulling herself away from her mouthful.

Good girl. Come up for a breath of fresh air.

"How about you not talk to me?" I snapped back. "It's my first day," I repeated, this time through gritted teeth as I stared at Ian. "And you are my trainer, so I expect to be trained."

His eyes pierced me. "Do you know who I am?"

Seriously?

Did he just use that cliché line?

Do you know who I am?

Again, not Kurt Cobain, buddy.

"Yes, I know who you are. My trainer. So if we could—"

"I'm not training you," he said. "So you can get lost."

"Yeah, get lost," the woman said.

11

"I'm sorry, is there a desperate echo in here?" I asked, shooting my stare to the woman, then back to Ian. "I'm not leaving until you train me."

"Well, please enjoy the view," he commented, placing his hands behind the woman's head to bring her closer to his member.

"Okay. I'm sure Big Paw will be fine to know what you were busy doing instead of training me," I threatened.

The woman released a catty chuckle. "As if Ian cares what Big Paw thinks." She went to lean in, but Ian's hands lightly moved her back.

"The mood's dead. We'll try again later," he commented.

She looked at him, stunned. "You're joking, right?"

He shrugged. "Not feeling it right now."

Those words were also known as *I'm scared shitless of my grandfather and don't want to get on his bad side.* Even the town's rock star had his own set of fears.

"I can make you feel it," she said, going to lean in, but he stopped her again.

"How about you take a hint and realize that he's busy with me?" I blurted out, mocking the words the woman had given me, feeling my sass level hitting an all-time high. I wasn't often a sassy girl—unless someone sassed me first. An eye for an eye and all.

She stood and smoothed out her sundress. As she pushed past me, she gave Ian a seductive smirk. "Call me later, will you?"

"Of course, Rachel."

Her eyes widened. "My name's Laura."

"That's what I said." Ian waved in a dismissive way. If he could be any more of a small-town asshole cliché, he'd be Jess from *Gilmore Girls*. Cocky and arrogant, with a whole lot of sexiness.

I wasn't attracted to him in any way, shape, or form due to his disgusting personality, but pretending Ian wasn't sexy was a waste of time. The man oozed sex appeal like black magic. It was as if he had sold his soul to the devil to look that good. Ink-black hair, tattooed body, arms that made it look like he deadlifted cattle during his downtime. And that freaking rock star smirk. You knew the smirk. The one that said, *I could probably get you to blow me right here and now if I wanted you to.* That same smirk I was sure he'd given to Laura earlier that day. We lived in the countryside, where most people's wardrobes were plaid shirts and jeans, sundresses, and cowboy boots, but where most people were more or less ordinary looking, Ian looked like a demigod who'd been placed in the wrong damn galaxy.

While he yanked up his boxers and jeans, I turned away, giving him a bit more privacy than I had a few moments before.

When he finished, he cleared his throat. I looked back at him, and he brushed his thumb against his nose. His lips were pressed together, unpleased. He definitely wasn't giving me his blow job smile. "Who the hell are you?"

Obviously, his new sworn enemy.

"Hazel."

"Hazel what?"

"Stone. Hazel Stone."

The minute I said my full name, Ian's brows knitted tightly together as a sneer fell against his lips.

"Your mother's Jean Stone?"

I swallowed hard. Anyone who knew my mother normally wasn't a big fan of hers, because they knew of her connection to Charlie—the big bad wolf of Eres. "Yes, that's her."

His hands made and released fists nonstop as the information settled into his head. "Does Big Paw know this?"

"Yes, he was made aware. I don't see what this has to do with—"

"He knew of this"—he cut me off—"and said I'm supposed to train you?"

"That's what he said."

There were moments of silence as Ian's fists tightened.

"One hour," Ian growled, appearing much more irritated now than he was when I'd walked in on his blow job. Did my connection to Charlie really have that big of an effect on people?

Who was I kidding? Of course it did.

"What do you mean, one hour?" I asked, not wanting to push the clearly annoyed Ian any further.

"I give you one hour before you run out of this place crying like a baby. You don't have what it takes to work here, to work under my watch."

"No offense, but you don't know what I have. I can handle working on the ranch." Was that a true fact? Heck if I knew. I didn't know anything about working on a ranch, but I did know determination, and I had that in spades. I didn't have room for failure.

"Oh, darling," he said, "you don't know what you just signed up for. Welcome to hell."

He brushed past me, sending chills down my spine. I wanted to punch him square in the jaw for calling me "darling." If there was anything I hated more than nicknames for females, it was condescending nicknames. *Baby. Sweetheart. Dollface. Darling. How about a hefty serving of* fuck off? I wanted to call him out for the stupid, belittling nickname, but he didn't give me a chance to snap back at him. He was already going on and on about the tasks we were going to cover over the next hour before I was apparently supposed to run away and quit like a sobbing child.

Pigpens. Horse stables. Chicken coops.

He kept going on and on about the shitty jobs I'd have to take on, which paired well with his shitty personality. I knew he wasn't kidding about it being hell, and with the venom spewing from his mouth, I was 100 percent certain Ian Parker was the devil himself.

2

IAN

Hazel Stone was Jean Stone's daughter, Charlie Riley's stepdaughter, and a person I had no damn desire to get to know—let alone train. Anything and anyone who was attached to the likes of Charlie Riley was no one I wanted in my life. That included Hazel.

The collar of Hazel's long-sleeve black shirt sat tightly pressed over her nostrils as we stood in the pigpens. I'd instructed her to start shoveling out one of the pens for cleaning, and she was struggling, just as I'd known she would be. She hadn't had the pleasure of becoming nose blind to the filthy aromas of pig shit, and the T-shirt covering her nose was proof of that. She should've counted herself lucky for that. Old Man Eddie had been working in the pens for so many years that he didn't understand why people gave him odd looks when he went into town smelling like manure. The poor schmuck couldn't even smell himself anymore.

Every now and again, Hazel made gagging sounds as if she were about to upchuck her lunch.

What in the goddamn hell had Big Paw been thinking when he'd hired Hazel to work at the ranch? Old age must've been getting to his good-decision-making skills, because nothing about hiring that girl made any sense whatsoever.

She looked as if she'd walked out of a vampire coffin five minutes before she'd entered the ranch, with all the black eyeliner she had plastered on her face. The dark wardrobe wasn't making her seem any less vampy. If darkness was a person, it would be Hazel Stone. Her clothes were baggy and oversize, and she didn't know how to smile. I couldn't fault her for the smiling thing. I didn't have a big smiling face, either, but what bothered me the most was how she had interrupted my time with Erica—er—Rachel? Hell, whatever the name of the chick was who'd had her lips wrapped around my throbbing cock. Now, I was suffering from a case of blue balls like no other. It wasn't as if I'd been planning on getting off from a blow job. That never really happened for me, but it was the foreplay before I would've laid the woman across my desk and fucked her until the cows came home—which happened around six in the afternoon.

Now, instead, I was walking around the ranch with Wednesday fucking Addams following me, telling her about what it took to be a ranch hand at Eres Ranch. News flash: She wasn't what it took. She was so far off from what it took to be a ranch hand that I felt like a damn fool for wasting my afternoon showing her around.

"Don't think anyone's going to give you an easier time around here because you're a girl," I ordered her as she shoveled soiled hay into the wheelbarrow.

"I'm not a girl," she barked, struggling to lift her pitchfork but not giving up.

I glanced back at her and eyed her up and down.

Sure, she wore baggy clothes, but beneath them I could see a set of globes somewhat highlighted behind her shirt.

Before I could comment, she shot her stare my way. "I'm a woman."

I huffed. "Barely. What are you, eighteen?"

"Yes. Which is exactly the age of becoming a woman. I'm not a girl."

I rolled my eyes so hard I was certain I'd lose my eyesight. "Woman, girl, chick, whatever. Just finish your job. You're going to have to move faster than that if you want to work here. You're wasting time taking so long on that one pen. There's seven more you got to get to cleaning."

She gasped. "Seven? There's no—"

"No what?" I cut in. "No way you can do seven pens?" I lifted a brow, and she noticed. A sinister smirk fell against my lips. It had only been forty-five minutes, and it seemed like little Hazel was already close to waving the white flag.

She rolled her shoulders back and stood straighter. "I can do seven pens. I *will* do seven pens. Even if it takes all night."

Judging by the speed she was going, it would take all night. Fine by me—I had rehearsal later that night at the barn house, so I'd be on the property late anyway. If Hazel didn't want to throw in the towel yet, then she could spend the rest of her evening in the pens if she wanted to.

It took her three hours to finish two pens.

Three damn hours.

It was way longer than it should've taken her, but I had to give it to her—she didn't punk out. She hardly even stopped for water breaks, except for when I forced her to do so. "It's ninety-six degrees out. Take a damn break. Otherwise I'll be dragging you out by your ankles and rushing you to the emergency room," I ordered.

Reluctantly, she'd take her breaks but then be back at it, working her ass off.

Around seven, I gathered my stuff from the office and headed to check in on Hazel one more time. "How many more?" I asked.

"Three." She sounded exasperated. "Just three more."

I nodded once. "I'm off to the barn house for band practice. Stop in there once you're finished, and get me to come check your work."

She didn't reply, but I knew she'd heard me. At least she better have, because I wasn't in the business of repeating myself, and if I didn't check her work by the end of the night, she'd be SOL on the job front.

I didn't even know why she was working for the ranch. I didn't understand why she'd put herself in the position that she was in. She could've simply gone to her piece-of-shit stepfather and joined the family business of drug dealing.

After a silent reply from her, I headed toward the barn house to meet up with the other guys. For the past five years, I'd been in the band the Wreckage, which consisted of me and my three best friends. We'd grown close many summers ago when we were all sixteen—except Eric, who was only thirteen—and forced to work on the ranch. I was forced by Big Paw, because he didn't want me out causing trouble during the summer, and the rest of the guys were forced by their parents to help their families with income.

If you lived in Eres and were sixteen, then there was probably a good chance you had a small job to help bring money into your family's home. A parent's salary wasn't enough to put food on the table most of the time.

The guys and I spent that summer shooting shit and forming a band to help pass time. In a small town, you did whatever you could to make time go faster. The summer days dragged, and the nights were boring. Music changed that for us. It didn't take long for us to actually give a damn about what we were creating, and over the years, we'd somehow found a touch of success. Not enough to quit our day jobs, but enough to dream of a life outside of Eres.

Plus, we all had enough talent to make our band stand out.

First, there was James, the people person. If there was a soul in need of love, James was right there to give it to them. He played the bass guitar and had such a warm personality that he could make a sworn enemy swoon at his feet. Not only was he a badass on the bass, but he was the smiling face on our social media accounts who brought in the fans.

Marcus was the drummer from the gods and the band's clown. He was the comedic relief whenever tensions began to build between us all—which happened when you had a group of artists who sometimes had differing views on creativity.

Eric, our keyboard player, was the wizard behind our social media. I swore his brain worked in code. He was the mastermind behind building a following for the Wreckage on all platforms. Even though he was the youngest out of us—he was Marcus's brother—he was such a key part of the band. It was very much due to him that we'd built up the fan base we had. Over five hundred thousand followers on Instagram, sixty-five hundred on YouTube, and a TikTok number I couldn't even say. Eric was always looking for a way to expand our reach, and that meant a lot of livestreaming of us in band rehearsals and working our small-town lives on the ranch.

It turned out people liked to watch rock musicians live really country lifestyles. I didn't get the appeal, but Eric was a professional at giving fans what they wanted to see. If there wasn't a camera in his hand or set up somewhere nearby, I would've been convinced he was terminally ill. Even when you didn't think he was recording, you should've known he probably was.

Then there was me. The lead singer who created the lyrics and carried the vocals. I was the one with the weakest personality, and I knew if it weren't for my band, I wouldn't have found the sliver of success that I had. I was kind of an asshole, overall. Not good with people, and even worse with social media. But I did love the music. Music understood parts of me that humans never got close enough to discover. Music saved me from some of the crappiest days of my life. I didn't know what I would've been without the Wreckage. Our daily rehearsals were what kept me grounded.

As I walked into the barn house, the guys were already debating about the next steps for the music.

"We have to put on a local show and livestream it on Instagram Stories," Eric clamored as he raked his hands through his red hair. "If we don't give the fan base a taste of the new music, we'll get trampled by people who are driving hard-hard-hard on social media. If we want to be the next Shawn Mendes to be discovered online, we have to push like we want it," he said.

"Christ, take a chill pill, E. I don't want you giving yourself a heart attack over this Instagram bullshit," Marcus grumbled, grabbing a beer from his six-pack. "How about we ease up on the social media aspect for a minute and create some good-ass shit?" Marcus had always been that way—more into the music, less into the fame.

"Ease up . . ." Eric began huffing and puffing as he paced the barn house. "What do you mean, ease up on social media? Social media is our one shot at this thing taking off, and you want to go back to just dicking around in the barn house? Our video views dropped by five percent over the past few weeks, and you all are acting like it's not Armageddon out there!"

I smiled at my extremely nerdy yet passionate bandmate.

If there was one way to ruffle Eric's feathers, it was by having Marcus tell him the social media aspect wasn't of importance. The two argued like the brothers they were.

"Maybe because it isn't Armageddon," Marcus said with a shrug.

Eric took off his glasses, popped out his hip like my grandmother after a hard day of cleaning, and pinched his nose. "Thirty-seven percent," he said.

"Oh, great. Here he goes with the statistics again." Marcus groaned.

"Yes, here I go with the statistics again, because they really fucking matter. Thirty-seven percent of United States citizens are on Instagram. Our biggest followers are in the United States, and do you know their age bracket?"

I joined the group and sat down on the edge of the wooden stage Big Paw built years back, listening, knowing Eric was about to take Marcus to school with the lesson.

"Please, do share," James said, obviously interested.

"Ninety percent is younger than thirty-five years old. That means we are dealing with a world of millennials and Gen Z, who have the focus of a puppy chasing its tail. If we don't capture their attention and give them a reason to give a damn about our sound and our brand, then they will be on to the next faster than a Kardashian moving through a basketball team. We need to focus. We need to think bigger. Otherwise, we'll lose the footing we've gained over the years."

Everyone shut up after Eric's words, because it was clear he knew what he was talking about. Plus, I agreed 100 percent. Lately, I felt stale. As if the music wasn't going the places I'd hoped it would go. I had massive dreams and goals, the same way the other guys had, but it felt as if we were stuck. I hadn't figured out how to break through to the next big thing. I knew Eric was right about the social media side of things, but if we didn't have the music, no amount of pushing was going to make us a success.

We needed hits, not just mediocre sounds.

"What about that new stuff you were working on, Ian? Maybe we could do some of those tracks for the livestream," James offered.

I cringed. None of the stuff I was working on was ready to be explored. My mind felt stuck, and when a mind was stuck . . . "I'm still working through some things with it."

"But until that's ready, we have to push forward. We'll play our best tracks within the next few weeks. Invite all of the townspeople and livestream. It will at least get traction going again," Eric offered.

"Good deal. So how about we run through a set list and rehearse that?" Marcus offered. "Make it shiny and neat and shit."

We finally all got on the same page and began doing what we loved—making music.

Hours passed as we rehearsed with only a dinner break, where Eric shared the knowledge with us that pizza was the most Instagrammed food—sushi and chicken taking second and third.

I swore, the amount of information in that guy's head was destined to be used on *Jeopardy!* someday. You couldn't know that much stuff and not end up on some nighttime game show.

When the barn house doors opened, I was shocked to see Hazel walking in. She looked a complete mess. Her hair was pulled up into the messiest bun I'd ever seen, her eyes were flashing exhaustion, and her clothes were tattered, torn, and covered in shit—literally. Her combat boots were destroyed, and her spirit was clearly broken, but she still stood there. Battered, but not ruined.

"Sorry to interrupt, but I'm done with the pigpens," she said to me, nodding once. "If you want to come and check my work."

I stuffed a piece of garlic bread into my mouth and rubbed my grease-covered hands against my jeans. "Took you long enough. I'll head over there in a few."

She didn't say a word, just turned around on her heel and walked away.

James cocked an eyebrow. "You didn't really make her clean those pigpens all on her own, did you? You know Big Paw normally has three guys on that task."

"Hell yeah, I did. I figured if I broke her down now, I wouldn't have to waste my time for the rest of the summer."

"I would've thrown in the towel," Marcus commented. "It looks like she's got a lot more heart than you think."

After enough hardships, hearts had a way of giving in. Maybe Hazel had made it through the day, but over time I'd break her down.

I said good night to the guys, and as I started toward the pens, James chased after me. "Ian, hold up."

I turned toward him and crossed my arms. "Yeah?"

"That Hazel girl—she's Charlie's stepdaughter, right?"

I nodded. "Yup."

James blew out a cloud of hot air and shook his head. "Listen, don't be too big of a dick to her because of that. She's not Charlie. You can't put your resentment for that asshole on her shoulders."

"Anyone who's kinfolk with that man is an enemy of mine."

"But Hazel didn't get your parents hooked. She's not responsible for what happened with them."

I clenched my jaw and nodded toward the barn house. "How about you make sure everything's locked up. I'll deal with Hazel the best way I see fit."

He didn't argue, because he knew I was a stubborn asshole and there wasn't much getting through to me. Like I said, James was the peacekeeper.

Me on the other hand? Not so much.

I headed to the pens, where I found Hazel leaning against one of the gated areas, still looking as if she'd lifted the whole damn moon on her shoulders that evening.

I walked around the pens, and to my surprise, they were fucking perfect. She'd handled every task I'd given her and somehow managed to do better than any of the guys who normally took care of the stables.

Color me shocked.

I wasn't going to let her know of her job well done, though. I was still convinced she'd screw up somewhere down the line. "It's a mediocre job," I told her.

Her jaw dropped. "Mediocre? I worked my ass off in here, and it looks great."

"How would you know? I doubt you've ever spent time in a pigpen before."

"That doesn't mean I don't know what looks good. This place looks the best it can."

I shrugged. "Whatever. Be back by sunrise tomorrow for more work."

"That's it?" she snipped. "Just a 'be back by sunrise' comment? No 'job well done' or 'great work, Hazel'?"

"I'm sorry. I didn't know I was in the business of handing out compliments for employees just doing their jobs. If you need applause for every task, then you're in the wrong place. Now, if you could get a move on so I can lock this place up and get on out of here."

She pushed her purse strap higher up on her shoulder and walked toward the front door. "Eight hours."

"Excuse me?"

She looked over her shoulder toward me. "Eight hours. I lasted eight hours longer than you thought I would." She gave me a "fuck you very much" smile, and I swore the girl almost curtsied toward me in the most sarcastic fashion before walking away.

Why did I get the feeling that girl was going to be a pain in my ass?

3

HAZEL

Every single inch of me ached, and when I said every inch, I meant every single freaking inch. From the top of my head down to my toes. I hadn't even known toes could ache until I'd worked a day at the ranch. By week's end, I was certain my body was going to rebel against any form of movement. But I kept at it, falling asleep around midnight and waking before sunrise to trek my way to the ranch.

Ian hadn't been letting up on me either. I was certain he was determined to break me, and truthfully, I wasn't sure why. It couldn't have been all because of the blow job, because if it was, that made Ian the pettiest man in the history of the world.

I was certain his anger and grumpiness came from a deeper place than that. I just hadn't a clue how to figure out where. Truth was, I didn't really care to figure it out. As long as I did my job well, I didn't have anything to worry about.

He couldn't get rid of me if I didn't showcase any reasons for him to do so.

After walking home after yet another physically draining workday, I found a trashed house. Since I'd begun working, Mama hadn't picked up the chores that I normally handled. The sink was piled high with dishes, and the laundry was backed up. There were cigarette butts throughout the house, tossed around like the humans who lived there had never heard of an ashtray, and empty beer cans were scattered everywhere.

Mama sat on the couch watching TV. She'd fallen asleep on that couch the night before, and I couldn't help but wonder if she'd moved from that position since then.

"About time you made it home," she commented. "Charlie said you need to clean this place up before he gets home."

A cigarette sat between her lips, and that made my stomach turn. "Mama, I thought we were going to work on you giving up smoking for the baby."

"I am giving it up. I've been cutting back. Don't come on in here judging me."

"I'm not judging. Just making sure you're taking the best care of yourself." Which she wasn't, of course. Mama smoked a pack a day. Her cutting back wasn't very likely.

"I am. Plus, I smoked like a chimney with you. You turned out decent."

"Well, thanks, Mama," I said, rolling my eyes. I pushed up my sleeves and walked into the kitchen to start working on the dishes. It was stupid that I was in charge of cleaning up the house even when I didn't mess it up, but I wasn't interested in getting on Charlie's bad side. It worked best if I did the household chores and kept my mouth shut. Cinderella had two evil stepsisters and an evil stepmother; I only had an evil stepfather and an uninterested mother. I could've had it worse.

After I finished the dishes, I tossed in a load of laundry and headed back to the kitchen. I swung the refrigerator open and noticed the lack of food. It seemed that if I didn't go grocery shopping, it didn't happen. I was sure Charlie was out picking up food along the way for himself, but Mama hardly left the house. If there wasn't food in the fridge, she probably wasn't eating, which was a problem. Especially when she was supposed to be eating for two.

"Mama, did you eat dinner?"

"Charlie said he was bringing Chinese."

I glanced at the time on the microwave. It was already past ten. Knowing Charlie, he could've been out for hours. Who knew when he'd bring the food for Mama?

"I can make you a grilled cheese," I offered.

She accepted, and when I finished, I walked into the living room and joined her on the couch. She looked too skinny to be carrying a baby. She was almost five months but was hardly showing. Mama had always had a small frame, but I worried that she wasn't getting enough nutrition throughout the day. When I received my first check, making sure the refrigerator was stocked up would be at the top of my list.

"Are you done cleaning?" she asked, biting into her sandwich.

"Yup. I just have to dry the load of clothes; then we're all set."

"Good. That means we can talk now before Charlie gets home." She placed her plate on the coffee table and took my hands in hers. "Charlie and I think it's best if you move on."

My heart caught in my throat. "What?"

"He said all your stuff needs to be out by today. He doesn't like how it feels as if you're always judging our way of life, and you don't really keep the house together. You're always running around to God knows where—"

"I work, Mama."

"Sounds like an excuse to me. Anyway, you can't stay here anymore. There just isn't enough room with the new baby coming and all. Pack up your things and go."

"But I don't have anywhere to go, Mama." Did she really have me clean up the whole house before she kicked me out? Was that the woman I called my mother?

She pulled out another cigarette and lit it. "You're over eighteen, Hazel. It's time for you to fly the coop. We're not going to support you forever. So get a move on."

I wanted to argue with her and tell her how I'd done more for her over the past few years than she'd done for me. I wanted to yell and shout that if anyone had been acting like a burden, it was her and Charlie. I wanted to cry.

Gosh, how I wanted to fall apart. My mother was all I had in this world, and she was pushing me away without a split second of guilt or remorse. She was back to watching the TV, blowing smoke from between her lips.

When Charlie walked through the front door, my stomach churned. It was a good thing I'd made Mama a grilled cheese, because that man had no Chinese food to speak of.

His eyes darted from Mama to me and back to Mama. "I thought I told you to have her out by the time I got back."

"I did. The girl's hardheaded like her father," Mama blurted, blowing out a cloud of smoke. She hardly ever spoke of my father. I didn't even know his name, but whenever she brought him up, it was to insult him. I couldn't really back him up much, seeing as how he meant nothing to me.

"I have nowhere to go tonight," I said, standing from the couch.

"Tough cookies. When I was eighteen, my parents kicked me out too. It's called being an adult. If I figured it out, you can too," Charlie ordered. "I'm done with you being a moocher and not contributing to the house. Get your shit out in the next hour and move on. Gotta turn that room into a nursery."

"It's already past midnight."

"I don't give a damn," Charlie replied as he lit up a cigarette. "Just get out."

Mama didn't say a word. She was back to watching television as if she hadn't just taken part in crushing my soul.

I swallowed hard and walked toward my bedroom. I didn't know where I was going to go or what I was going to do. All I knew was I had sixty minutes to gather up my life and leave.

There was something so unnerving about realizing your whole life could fit inside two garbage bags. I walked out of the house without any send-off and fought the tears that were pushing at the backs of my eyes.

My first thought of places to go was Garrett's trailer—my on-again, off-again boyfriend. He was also Charlie's nephew and his right-hand man in their family business. Garrett's big dream was to take over for Charlie at some point down the line. He idolized his uncle, which was a major flaw in my mind. I couldn't imagine why anyone would want to be like Charlie. He wasn't someone to look up to at all.

Garrett's and my relationship was currently off, due to the fact that he had a way of sleeping with women who weren't me. He said it was my own fault, because I wouldn't have sex with him, but that was idiotic. I'd never understand how a cheater could blame anyone other than their unfaithfulness, but then again, I was the dummy who went back to him time and time again.

It was amazing how low self-esteem could make you fall into the wrong arms.

As I approached Garrett's place, I was reminded of a trait I'd inherited from my mother: dating assholes.

"You can't stay here, unless you get on your knees," Garrett said, blowing out a cloud of smoke from his cigarette. He wore a plaid top and jean shorts that were too big for his slender frame. A ratty old belt held them up on his hips.

"Don't be gross, Garrett. Listen, Charlie kicked me out. I need a place to crash for tonight at least."

"Like I said, on your knees, or you can find another place to crash."

"Are you joking?"

"Am I laughing?"

Just then, a girl walked up behind him, and I recognized her right away. Megan Kilt—the same girl who Garrett had said was just a friend. Back then I'd known better than to believe him.

The moment Megan saw me, a wicked grin fell against her lips. "Well, if it isn't gothic Barbie," she cooed. "Really, why do you wear so much eyeliner? It's overkill."

I flipped her off and looked back to Garrett. "Just let me crash on your couch tonight, and you can do whatever you want with bimbo Barbie," I offered. "I'll even wear earplugs."

"Sorry, Hazel. Charlie told me to not take you in. Said you needed some tough love."

There was nothing loving about what Charlie was doing to me. It was cruel.

"Charlie won't have to know."

"Charlie knows everything. Even the shit that you think he doesn't."

I hated that it was true. It was as if Charlie had eyes in the back of his head and was able to be a step ahead of everything and everyone.

Garrett blew another puff of smoke, and Megan wrapped her hands around his shoulders, as if she was trying to make it clear that he was now her play toy. Fine by me. I'd always known Garrett wasn't the one for me. He was just the one who was always there.

Except when I needed him the most.

Garrett was the bad boy that romance novels made you think you wanted, though, unlike the novels, he didn't have a turning point. There wasn't a moment when he said the right thing or spoke to me in such a poetic way that I fell more in love with him each day. He didn't make sacrifices for our relationship or surrender himself to our love.

He was just Garrett, the boy who was there when no other guys would look my way. I wished that I could've said I was strong enough to look away, but sometimes loneliness made you crave any kind of connection—even from those who sucked your soul dry.

The only difference between him and Charlie was the fact that Garrett would never put his hands on me. He was an asshole, but he wasn't physically abusive like Charlie.

Still, that didn't make him someone worth worshipping.

Sometimes I wished Garrett was a fictional character.

I would've killed to see his growth.

"Hazel, before you go, how's your mom? With the whole pregnant thing?" he asked, stomping out the cigarette. "Is Charlie treating her right? Making sure she's eating and shit?"

I shook my head. "You know Charlie only has a one-track mind. And it's not on my mother. I was the one making sure she was being cared for, not him. And somehow he managed to have her turn on me."

Garrett pulled out another cigarette and lit it. I swore, the guy smoked like a chimney. "I'll check in on her for you, to make sure she's not missing her vitamins and shit."

Well, that's nice and extremely out of character.

"Thank you."

"Yeah. My mom will probably want to make sure she's good too."

Garrett's mother, Sadie, had been Mama's best friend through the good and the bad. Sadie wasn't a bad person. She'd just been placed in bad situations.

Like a lot of people, I supposed.

Garrett flipped his lighter on and off in his free hand. "You should get lost, though, before Charlie finds you here and gives you and me hell."

I left, passing teenagers being rowdy on the streets and adults being rowdier inside Carl's Bar due to the freedom of Friday night.

I kept going even though my feet burned from walking so much. I couldn't wear my combat boots, seeing as how I'd ruined them in the pigpens, so I was stuck wearing stupid, uncomfortable flip-flops that I'd taken from my mother without her knowing.

Without much thought, I found myself back at the ranch. It seemed like the only place I could think of going. The barn house was lit up with music blasting, probably from Ian's band, and for the most part it sounded amazing—minus the crappy lyrics.

Don't get me wrong; Ian could sing. The lyrics were just piles of crap.

Behind the barn house, through the wooded area, was a small abandoned shed that I'd found a few days ago while trying to release a cramp in my hip. I walked in that direction and opened the door.

There wasn't much inside, but there was a beat-up old rug that I rolled out. It would serve well as a bed for the night. "It's just like camping, Hazel. Just like camping," I told myself. There was a big hole in the roof of the shed that showcased the star-filled sky. Whenever I looked up at the sky, I felt at peace. The galaxy made me feel small, and oddly enough, that made me feel better about things. Almost as if there was so much to the world that my current situation wasn't too dire. Things would turn around. They had to at some point. Life wasn't meant to be this sad, and I was certain I'd find my way out of this godforsaken town sooner or later. I'd hoped that Mama would join me, but it was clear she'd chosen her side and I was no longer on her team.

I laid one of the bags with my clothes in them on the rug and used it as a pillow. I stared up through the hole toward the sky and listened to the Wreckage create sounds that were worth hearing. I may have hated their lead singer, but it was no lie that as a whole their sound was breathtaking.

Now, if only those lyrics were better . . .

I closed my eyes that night to the sounds of Ian Parker's voice, and I tried my best to not think about anything else.

Tomorrow would be better, and the sun would rise again.

History seemed to be on my side, because the sun did rise the following morning. I was having a hard time shaking off the feeling of betrayal from Mama, but at least I had work to keep me busy. Even though I was supposed to have the day off, I still showed up to work around the ranch. If I was working, I couldn't think about my current homeless situation. When you were shoveling manure, it was hard to think about anything other than the fact that you wanted to vomit.

Plus, now that I was squatting in the broken-down shed, I didn't have to walk thirty minutes to and from work every night. Silver linings.

"What the hell do you think you're doing?" a raspy voice boomed as I sat in the stables, brushing Dottie, the most beautiful horse I'd ever set my eyes on. Dottie and I had shared an apple not too long ago, and since then, we'd been engaging in girl talk, because my life was now at the stage where I talked to animals to feel less alone.

Groovy.

Truthfully, animals were a lot kinder than humans, so I counted my newfound friendship with Dottie as the ultimate win.

"I thought I'd stop in to help around today," I replied to the Grumpy McGrump Ian standing in the doorframe.

I wondered if he knew what a smile was . . . I was certain he had more reasons to smile than I did, and still, I found enough reasons to do it.

"You aren't on the schedule," he scolded.

"I know. I was in the neighborhood."

"Well, get out of the neighborhood."

"Why does it matter? The guys hardly brush Dottie and the others the way they should be brushed. If anything, you should be happy that I'm helping."

His brows lifted. "You don't get paid for this."

"I didn't punch in. I know how jobs work."

"Clearly you don't, because showing up to said job on your day off isn't how this goes."

I stopped brushing Dottie and let my hands collapse to my lap as I stared at Ian. "Why are you so grumpy toward me?"

"Why do you do idiotic things to make me grumpy?" he barked. His hair was wild and untamed as he stood there with his arms crossed

33

tightly across his toned body. If his biceps could wave, they'd probably flip me off.

"Just ignore me," I offered. "I'm not in anyone's way, and Dottie is enjoying my company."

"She's a horse. She can't enjoy people's company."

"It's kind of silly to think that just because she's a horse she doesn't have feelings. When was the last time you asked her how she was feeling?"

"For the love of . . . ," he murmured, before running his hand through his hair. "You can't be on the property while you're not working. That's called trespassing. It's against the law."

"What? Are you going to call Sheriff Cole to come arrest me for brushing Dottie?"

"Don't test me, Hazel," he said through gritted teeth. "Are you trying to push my buttons, or does it come naturally to you?"

"Like breathing air."

He grumbled some more and brushed his thumb beneath his left eye. "If I hear about you getting in anyone's way, you're out. And I don't just mean for today, but I mean *out* out. Fired. Do you understand?"

"I hear you loud and clear, Coach."

"Stop the sarcasm."

"That comes naturally to me like breathing air too."

Before he could bark his annoyance at me, a woman walked into the stables and looked toward Ian. "Are you ready to go, Ian? I only have such a short lunch break if we are going to . . . you know." She glanced over to me and looked away, growing a bit red in the face.

Oh, trust me, sweetie, we all know.

If I had a dollar for every woman I'd seen approach Ian in the past few days, I wouldn't even have to work at the ranch anymore. I'd be Kylie Jenner–level rich. I could've probably made a whole makeup palette based on the eye colors of the females that crossed his path and made it into his office.

Emerald green. Midnight blue. Black shadows.

Ian looked at me as if he wanted to scold me some more, but his desire to take that girl to his pen was higher than his want to boss me around. I was pleased when he left me alone. Dottie and I had more to catch up on.

4

IAN

"She's a pain in my ass," I complained to Big Paw after a few weeks of training Hazel. Day in and day out, that girl kept showing up in her black wardrobe and messed-up combat boots, ready to work. No matter the task I gave her, she completed it. Sometimes she'd stay late into the night to finish, but she always left her work completed, giving me no reason to fire her. Even though I really wanted a damn reason to let her go.

Plus, on her days off, she was still lurking around. It was as if she had no fucking life outside the ranch. Her favorite pastime was talking to the livestock as if someday they'd talk back. I knew Dottie well enough to know that she didn't care a lick about what Hazel was saying—she just wanted those damn apples.

All the other guys on the ranch seemed to be fine and dandy with Hazel wandering around like a lost dog. James said she stayed out of the way and even came in handy when he needed an extra pair of hands. Marcus and Eric found her equally helpful, and I swore Old Man Eddie had kissed Hazel's cheek when she'd offered to help him in the chicken coop.

It seemed I was the only asshole who didn't want her around, and I knew damn well that it was because of my personal issues with her connections to Charlie.

Seeing Hazel every day reminded me of Charlie, and thinking of Charlie reminded me of my parents. I tried my best not to think about them. I worked hard to keep them buried deep in the back of my mind, but seeing Hazel made that near impossible.

I didn't know the girl, but the taste she left in my mouth made me sick. If she was connected to a snake like Charlie, no good could come from her working around the ranch. She came from a world of toxicity.

"And you're a pain in mine," Big Paw replied, sitting at his desk in his home. He scratched at his overgrown beard that Grams had been trying to get him to shave down and yawned without covering his mouth. "She's been working harder than half the blockheads out there. Every time I've passed by the ranch, I've seen her working hard, struggling sometimes, sure, but working. Unlike half your team that I find slacking off and shooting the shit."

"Yeah, but . . ." I groaned, knowing I didn't have a leg to stand on but still wanting a fucking leg to stand on. "Did you know she's Charlie's stepdaughter?"

"You think I don't do my research before hiring hands? Of course I knew that."

"And you still brought her on?" I asked, flabbergasted. "You know that Charlie is the reason Mom and Dad—"

"Don't start, boy," Big Paw sneered, his voice coated in annoyance. He flicked his finger against the bridge of his nose. "I don't got time for you bringing up this issue. Hazel Stone is working at the ranch, and you will be the one overseeing her work. End of story."

"But—"

"I said end of story!"

How could he push it away so fast? If it weren't for Charlie, Mom and Dad would've never gotten hooked on meth all those years ago.

They wouldn't have run off in a drug haze, chasing their next high. They would've still been the parents I needed in my life.

So fuck Charlie, and fuck everyone who was attached to him. He ruined lives—including mine.

I wished I hadn't known my parents before the drugs slipped into their lives. I wished I hadn't seen their good side, but I had for thirteen years of my life. I had a slew of memories in my brain that reminded me of what Mom had been like before meth. I remembered how she'd loved to help Grams garden. I remembered her laugh, her rose-scented perfume, her smile. During the summers, Dad would let me go down to the dump and use the forklift out there to help him move around busted-up automobiles.

The worst part of having parents who developed a drug habit over time was remembering that they hadn't always been so fucked up. If they had always been tragic people, I would've had an easier time when they'd left.

"You should think about letting her go. Or at least having someone else look after her," I offered. That would've made it less annoying for me—if I didn't have to look after Hazel.

"I can't let her go. I owe it to someone close to her to give Hazel a shot."

"Who? Who could you possibly owe?"

His brows knitted, and he avoided my question. "How much are you paying for rent at the property on the ranch?" he asked, his question loaded, and I knew exactly what trap he was setting up.

"Big Paw—"

"Easy question, boy. Now answer it."

I slumped down in my chair. "Rent-free."

"I was talking to Tyler down at the marketplace the other day, and he was telling me that ranch house was easily worth over two hundred thousand. He asked me if it was up for sale. I'm debating if I should take him up on that offer."

"Okay, I get it."

"I don't think you do." He clasped his hands together. "I could be making money on that ranch house, but I don't because you're my grandson and I knew you wouldn't be able to find a nice spot on your own without the help. I lend the barn house to you and your bandmates to rehearse in, even though I could be making a profit from renting it out to others. In a town where so many people are struggling, you're living like a goddamn king, and you have the nerve to come into my office whining like a baby because you don't like a girl who works harder than most people? Well, tough cookies. If you want her to have a new trainer, then quit. But Lord knows you'll be losing everything that comes with your comfortable life."

I didn't say another word, because Big Paw was right. I was being a little shit and throwing a fit because I wasn't getting my way.

"You were given a good shot at life, Ian. A few crappy things happened to you with your parents leaving, but overall, you've been gifted with blessings that most people in town would kill for. Don't let your ego get so big that you don't think others deserve a shot at that same blessing. Hazel hasn't done a damn thing to prove herself to be anything like Charlie. She was just dealt a shitty hand. Let her play her cards the best she can, and stop being a whiny little dickhead about it."

Leave it to Big Paw to help you realize that you and your idiotic opinion were invalid and void.

"On second thought, I have an even better idea," he said, leaning back in his chair. "That spare room in the ranch house—give it to Hazel."

I choked on my next breath. "Excuse me?"

"I get the feeling she's in need of a place to stay."

"What makes you think that?"

"The fact that I've caught her snoozing in that broken-down shed the past few nights. I've been sleeping in my pickup truck nearby to make sure nobody bothers her. I know some hoodlums sneak into the ranch when they are bored and cause a ruckus, and I didn't want them bothering Hazel. I wanted to offer her a place to stay, but I get the feeling she'd be too embarrassed to admit her struggles, so I want you to offer it to her."

"Psh, yeah, right. She'd never take a handout from me."

"She would if you offer it up to her in a nice box with a fancy bow on top."

"How am I supposed to do that?"

"I don't know, Ian. Get creative."

I narrowed my eyes, knowing my grandfather was setting me up to make it impossible to not offer Hazel the ranch house. "And if I don't?"

"Well"—he chewed on the end of his cigar like it was bubble gum—"I guess I'll have to see how much Tyler is willing to offer for the house."

Figured.

I scratched at the slight stubble on my chin and grimaced. "Why is she even sleeping in that shed?"

"Don't know. It's none of my business, but I get the feeling it's probably due to the same asshole you're hating her for. Make friends with her."

"*Friends?*" I bellowed. "She and I ain't got nothing in common."

"Don't say 'ain't' like you're uneducated. That's part two of the deal. Give her a place to stay, and make her feel welcome. Befriend her. She ain't got nobody, so you might as well give her someone to turn to when she needs it."

I would've sassed him for saying "ain't," but I knew no good would come from it. The last thing I needed was an eighty-year-old kicking my ass.

Befriend Hazel Stone?

I didn't know the first thing about being a friend to a girl like her. We had nothing in common outside of the fact that we both worked at the ranch. How would I make a connection with someone who was the complete opposite of me?

Plus, I wasn't really in the market for a roommate, let alone a friend. The only friends I needed were my bandmates, and sometimes that felt overwhelming.

I brushed my hands through my hair, knowing that there was no way I'd be able to get Big Paw to let up. When he made up his mind, there was no changing it, unless Grams was the one pushing for the change.

I grimaced. "I'll do my best."

"Do better than that," he ordered. "It's supposed to rain in a few days, and I don't need no girl dying on my farm from pneumonia."

Before I could reply, Grams poked her head into the office. She was wearing oven mitts on her hands and had the same caring smile she'd always worn plastered against her face. "Are you two done being blockheads? Because dinner's done, and I don't have a problem eating it without you."

"Woman, can't you see we're talking in here?" Big Paw hissed, throwing a hand of dismissal at Grams. That only made Grams walk farther into the room.

"Harry Aaron Parker, if you ever talk to me like that again, I will shove this oven mitt so far up your butthole you'll be wondering why your mouth tastes like poop. Now, apologize," she ordered. My grandmother was a little woman, but boy, was she fierce. She didn't take crap from no one, especially Big Paw.

And like always, Big Paw lowered his head and put his tail between his legs. "Sorry."

"Sorry what?" Grams scolded.

"Sorry, my lovebug."

I tried to hold my laughter in at the nickname. Leave it to Grams to soften the old man's heart. The two of them were sassy and intense

41

and filled with so much love. If I ever found the time to fall in love, I'd want a love story like theirs.

"That's what I thought," Grams said, walking over to Big Paw. She smacked him on the back of his head with the oven mitt. "Now, get to the dining room before I change my mind and take the dinner to the church for their Bible study tonight."

That made us both shoot to our feet. My definition of cooking was sloppy joes. Sometimes I was fancy as hell, and I'd even toast the hamburger bun, but that was the end of my cooking expertise. That and ramen noodles. I could make a badass pot of ramen. Chicken flavored—obviously.

Outside of that, I counted on leftovers from Grams. She was pretty good at keeping me full.

As we walked to the kitchen, Grams complained about the creaking wooden floors. "We need to call someone in to fix those," she grumbled.

"Hush, woman. I'll get around to them when I get a chance," Big Paw said.

"You've been saying that since 1995. I'm not holding my breath."

"Maybe if you held your breath, you wouldn't be able to sass so much," he replied.

She shot him a look that could kill, and Big Paw smiled a little. It took a lot to make that man smile, and Grams controlled them. "Sorry, my lovebug."

"You'll be even sorrier on the couch tonight," she said in return.

I couldn't help but snicker at my grandparents' dramatic conversation. Real love was funny, and I loved that my grandparents didn't take their insults too seriously.

After stuffing my face at my grandparents', I headed to my place with enough leftovers to get me through the next few days.

Thank God for that.

No sloppy joes this week.

As I reached my place on the ranch grounds, a huge knot sat in my gut. The shed Hazel was apparently crashing in was a dump. Unsafe too. Leave it to her to do something so idiotic.

Stop being an asshole. You don't even know the girl.

I couldn't shake off the fact that she was connected to Charlie, even though I knew Big Paw was right. So I went ahead and swallowed my pride, pulled up to the shed, and knocked on the door.

I heard someone shuffling around for a minute before it went silent. I cocked an eyebrow. "Hello?" I called out. More quiet shuffling. I knocked on the door. "Open up, Stone. I know you're in there."

More silence. Less movement.

A weighted sigh rolled through me as I flung open the door and saw Hazel sitting up against the far corner of the shed with those wide green eyes of hers. She looked as if I were coming to attack her, which was all the more reason that she shouldn't have been staying in the damn shed. She was lucky it was me walking in on her as opposed to some town drunk crossing her path.

"Wh-what are you do-doing here?" Hazel asked, her voice shaky.

"What am *I* doing here?" I shone my phone light in her direction. "No. What in the goddamn hell are *you* doing in here?"

She got to her feet and blinked her eyes a few times. I hadn't a clue what she'd been up to, but her hair was dripping wet, as if she'd just taken a shower. A few of her clothing pieces hung on the shelves, including her cotton panties, which had unicorns printed on them. She hurried over and snatched the panties from the shelf and shoved them behind her back.

"You're living in here?"

"No!" she quickly replied.

I cocked a brow. "You're living in here," I repeated, this time as a statement.

She sighed. "Only temporarily."

"You can't live in this shed."

"Why not?" she asked. "It's not like anyone was using it."

I groaned. "That's not the point. The point is you can't live in a damn shed like an animal. Half the roof is missing, Hazel!"

"I like to look at the stars."

"It's drafty at night."

"I like the breeze."

"Are you always this stubborn?"

"Are you always this bossy?" she countered, and holy shit, I couldn't imagine living with someone as annoying as that girl right there.

"I'm only bossy to people who act like children."

"I'm not acting like a child. I'm acting like a person who needed a place to stay for a little while."

"Yeah, well, you can't live here," I said matter-of-factly. "This isn't a home. It's a broken-down shed. On private property, may I remind you. You can't be a squatter here."

For a split second, the hard exterior of Hazel cracked, and I saw a flash of worry race through her. The hard shell that she wore on the daily was to protect her from getting hurt, and in that split second, I saw her truths slip out through her eyes.

Shit. Maybe we had more in common than I thought.

My hard shell was made of the same material.

"You'll stay at my house," I said with a stern voice. I crossed my arms and nodded once. "You can take the spare room."

"There's no way I'm living with you!" she gasped, surprised that I was even offering her a way out of the shed.

"Hell yeah, there is. You can't fucking stay here, Hazel. It's stupid and not safe. I have a free room. Take it."

"I don't need your handout."

"Says the girl literally living in a shed."

"I hate when people say the word *literally*. It's a stupid word that people use when they can't come up with a better phrase."

"Literally, literally, literally," I blurted out. I gestured toward her garbage bags of things. "Grab your unicorn undies, and let's go."

"I know you're probably used to women dropping everything to give in to your demands, but I'm not one of those girls. I said no, and I meant no. I am not going to take a handout from you. I don't want or need your help."

What in the goddamn hell was the matter with this girl? She was being offered a place to stay for free and turning it down because of her goddamn pride? How was I supposed to do what Big Paw wanted if she wasn't willing to budge an inch? I'd never met such a stubborn woman in my life.

"You know what? Screw it. Fine. Stay out here with your creepy-crawlies and rodents. I'm not going to waste my time on someone who is choosing to suffer. Have at it."

5

HAZEL

Ian left in a huff, cursing under his breath as he slammed the shed door shut. The whole space shook, and I swallowed down the knot that formed in my throat.

Jeez. That man sure knew how to make me feel uneasy. I was so confused by the whole interaction between us. It was as if he was still his rude, grumpy self but also . . . nice? Offering someone a place to stay seemed nice, but I couldn't help but think that it came with strings attached. I'd vowed to never take something from a man. That way he'd never be able to hold it over my head. For years I'd watched Charlie throw in our faces the fact that Mama and I lived in his house. Ate his food. Slept in his beds. Nothing we had was our own, and I hated how he used that against us, making it seem like we were worthless without him.

From here on out, whatever I had, I'd get on my own.

Well, except for the shed I was squatting in. I'd have to pay Big Paw back somehow for the time I was spending in Betsy.

Yup. That was right. I'd named the shed Betsy. And boy, oh boy, if those walls could talk, I bet they'd have a lot of stories to tell.

Christ. I was getting so lonely that not only was I making friends with horses, I was making friends with objects.

I needed to stop being a loner as soon as possible.

I hadn't always been this way—lonely. When I was younger, I'd had a best friend named Riley—not a horse or a shed. An actual living, breathing person. Riley was the daughter of one of Charlie's clients. Sometimes they'd come over to the house for business, and the adults would kick us girls out into the backyard to get us out of their hair. Some days during those times, Riley and I would pretend we were witches and created magical potions to take us to magical worlds. Other times, we'd pretend we were an all-girls band, and we'd make up our own lyrics and sing to the squirrels.

Riley was so good for me. She was my best friend and the first person to make me feel as if I belonged in Eres. When her father finally got clean and moved away, Riley wrote me for a bit of time, but the letters began getting shorter and shorter until they completely stopped. I supposed she'd found a world outside of Eres, and I couldn't fault her for it. Once I got away, I wasn't planning on ever looking back either.

One in a million.

That was what Riley's friendship was to me. I'd never made that connection with anyone else, and it broke my heart to think that a friendship like hers was a one-in-a-million type of situation.

I was certain I'd never find that level of connection with another again—besides Garrett. But to be honest, what Garrett and I had wasn't a friendship. Sure, we'd dated for a while, but we didn't talk about things. We'd mostly just make out, and I'd watch him get high and play video games for hours. Nothing to write a love story about.

So that left me with talking to walls and hoping that the wood was thick enough to hold all my secrets.

When I woke the next morning, I walked out of the shed and found a basket filled with a few goodies. Bottles of water, a toothbrush and toothpaste, a box of cold cereal, and a small jug of milk with a spoon and a bowl. Beside that was a twin-size air mattress with a set of sheets and a comforter.

There was also a note that read:

If you want to be stubborn, then be stubborn.

But don't sleep on that damn floor without a bed.

—Ian

PS: Stop being a fool and take the fucking spare bedroom.

Never in a million years had I thought it would be Ian Parker who saved me during some of the hardest days of my life.

I had a bit of free time before I had to head into the stables that morning. I sat cross-legged on the inflatable bed eating a bowl of cold cereal while I wrote in my journal. I'd been writing every day of my life since I was eight years old. I used to write spells and other stupid kid stuff in the books with Riley, but over time it had just become a collection of things on my mind. Poetry and prose. My hopes, wishes, and dreams were all in one place.

One of my biggest dreams was getting into college. It was my dream to achieve a life the complete opposite of the one I was raised in, and college seemed like the first step to that future. I was going to do everything in my power to make that dream come true too.

I can't become my mother. I can't become my mother.

I didn't want to turn into the person my mother had become. I wanted more. I wanted to get away so bad that my bones ached from the idea of staying in Eres forever. If I stayed, there was a chance I'd end up as sad and depressed as my mother was, in a relationship with a man who had no respect or love for me, losing every shot at living that was brought my way.

As I wrote in my journal, I thought about Ian. The grumpy boy who'd given me a bed. I couldn't help but wonder what his angle was or why he was helping me. Truthfully, I was a bit surprised he hadn't kicked me out of the shed and fired me on the spot when he'd found me squatting. I knew he'd been looking for a reason to let me go, and trespassing seemed like a stellar reason to send me packing.

During the day at work, Ian didn't sass me like he usually did. He didn't push me harder than he pushed the others and didn't scold me for mediocre work. What was his deal? Why was he not treating me the way he had been for the past few weeks? Ian Parker went out of his way to make me feel terrible, but now, if I didn't know any better, it seemed as if he was being . . . nice. No, not nice. That would be ridiculous. But he was being much tamer than usual. It made me both pleased and uncomfortable. It was a warning sign when someone went from cold to hot so quickly.

I tried my best to not overthink his shift, even though it was so blatantly obvious that a change had occurred.

That night, on the blow-up mattress, I fell asleep after spending hours looking up at the stars, and my back didn't hate me come morning.

—— ❧❧ ——

The next day, I woke to the sound of hammering outside the shed.

I hurried outside and found Ian standing at the top of a ladder, placing planks of wood on the roof to cover up the giant hole.

"What are you doing?" I asked, confused by his fixing the rooftop and a bit dazed by the fact that he was shirtless. His body was sculpted by the gods, and seeing him shirtless made chills race throughout my body, even though I didn't find him attractive in the least.

Nope, not at all.

So ugly, Ian Parker.

The lies we told ourselves to keep from being turned on by men we were supposed to hate.

"What does it look like? I'm fixing the roof."

"You don't have to do that for me."

"Who said I'm doing it for you? I'm in charge of this ranch, and it's my job to do tasks," he said with sweat dripping down his chest, and oh my gosh, how was watching a man sweat an instant turn-on?

I'd been single for most of my life, minus my mundane, passion-free relationship with Garrett, and obviously I'd passed the deadline where you got turned on by extremely awkward things, like sweaty men. What was next? Was Ian going to lick an ice cream cone, and I'd moan while watching him?

Chill out, hormones. We'll watch a Chris Hemsworth movie soon enough and get all these feelings out.

Ian kept doing things like that. Fixing up the shed. Moving things around. Leaving food and supplies outside the door. I couldn't keep up with him helping me, and every time I called him out on it, he'd make it clear as day with his Grumpy McGrump butt that he wasn't doing it to help me at all. Whenever I felt like saying *thank you* to him, he'd say something catty and rude, which would turn my *thank you* into a *fuck you*.

Being around Ian was a weird thing. I'd never met an individual who was both hot and cold, all within two minutes. He was confusing for my brain, and I felt as if I were going into overdrive trying to keep up with his mood swings.

When payday came, I knew exactly where the first part of my check was going to go.

"What is this?" Ian asked as I handed him one hundred dollars.

"Money."

He grumbled and rolled his eyes. "I know it's money, but why are you giving it to me?"

"It's for the stuff you've been leaving outside of the shed for me. I don't take handouts and wanted to pay you for it all. I'm not sure how much the blow-up mattress cost you, so if you need more, let me know."

"I didn't give it to you in hopes of being paid back. I figured you didn't have enough to get yourself that stuff, seeing as how you were sleeping on that beat-up rug."

"Well, now that I got my paycheck, I'm able to give you the money for it."

"I don't want your money."

"And I didn't want your help, but here we are."

He pinched the bridge of his nose. "Why can't you take people helping you?"

"Because I know that they can throw it in your face down the road."

"Have you honestly been burned that bad?"

I swallowed hard, and my silence was his answer.

He narrowed his eyes and looked at me—and I mean really looked at me. He stared as if he was trying to uncover my secrets, and I looked at him the same way, as if I could tap into the words Ian often felt and never showcased. He might've been a grumpy man, but that anger came from some source, and I couldn't help but wonder where exactly. What root of past struggles fed his grumpiness? Who or what had made him that way?

And why in the hell were women attracted to him at all?

I couldn't ever imagine being intimate with someone as cold as Ian. There couldn't have been any heart in their interactions—he didn't seem the type to give too much of himself to anyone.

Then again, being intimate with him would mean he was shirtless, and that wasn't such an awful idea to me.

"Listen, it's supposed to downpour over the next few days. You can't stay in that shitty shed. Even with me fixing up the roof, it's still not sturdy. Everything you own will get ruined, and you'll probably get real sick. Just take the room at my place. I'll even stay somewhere else if you're uncomfortable with me being there."

"Why would you want me to stay with you? It's clear you can't stand me."

"It's also clear that you've fallen on hard times. If you need the place to crash, the door is open to you."

"No, thank you."

He released a weighted sigh and shook his head. "You're so damn stubborn. It's not safe around these parts at night, all right? Just because we live in a small town doesn't mean there aren't some creeps around. I've caught one too many wandering on the grounds in the past."

"It's fine. I can protect myself."

He huffed as if he didn't believe me. "Whatever you say, darling."

Darling.

Way to make me gag.

He started to walk away and said, "But I bet showering with the water hose outside the stables isn't the most pleasing sensation."

I showered with that water hose extremely early, and the idea that Ian had caught me made my stomach turn. "How did you know I was showering with the hose?"

"Because that's what I would've done."

He left me standing there in the open field with a million thoughts I wanted to decipher. Instead of wasting more time trying to understand the mind of Ian, I went to work. Thank goodness for the hard work at the ranch. It gave me zero time to overthink things.

——— ✥ ———

It's just a stray dog; it's just a stray dog.

Those were the words I kept on repeating to myself as I heard rustling outside the shed.

Or maybe it's a chicken who got out of the coop. Or a cow roaming around. Maybe Dottie is here for girl talk.

Or perhaps it's a psychotic mass murderer who's here to skin me alive and make a stew out of my body parts.

It was funny how during the day places could feel like the safest places in the world, but then when the sun set and the shadows of night took over, everything became horrifying.

I pulled my comforter up to my chest as the rain hammered against the shed and water leaked inside through a variety of holes that Ian hadn't managed to cover. For the most part, I'd managed to stay dry, thanks to him ignoring me when I told him he didn't have to fix the rooftop.

Note to self: thank Ian for not listening to me.

I heard more movement outside, and my stomach sat in my throat as the sound of voices became audible over the pounding rain. There were people outside. People talking around the shed, near me.

"Rumor has it there's a chick crashing in here," a voice said, forcing me to my feet. Then there was a pounding of a fist against the shed.

I looked around the space for something I could use to protect myself. Anything at all to beat off whoever was outside my door. I picked up a flashlight that Ian had left me a few days ago and held it tightly in my hands. I wasn't certain if I was going to blind the people to death or beat them over the head. All I knew was the only thing currently protecting me was that metal flashlight.

Note to self: thank Ian for the flashlight.

"Let's go get the others to check it out," one said.

I waited a few seconds and listened to them hurry away. The moment I thought they must have departed, I swung the door open, dashed out of the space, and ran like Dottie across the field straight to Ian's house. I rang the doorbell repeatedly, shivering from the rain and my dang nerves as I glanced over my shoulders in a panic again and again, terrified that there was someone following me.

I began pounding against his door as my heart rose to my throat. I tried my best to swallow it down, but my mind was spinning too quickly.

Knock, knock, knock.

Open the freaking door, Ian!

The moment it swung open, I released a breath of relief and rushed into the space without an invite of any kind. "Okay, you win. I'll take the spare room," I said, my voice shaky as I began pacing in his living room. His . . . very nicely furnished living room. His very nicely furnished and very warm living room.

Warmth.

Oh gosh, that felt so good.

"Uh, can I help you?" a voice asked. I finally turned around to see the person who'd opened up the door, and it was definitely not Ian. It was a woman wearing his clothes, though. At least I assumed they were his clothes. Otherwise she was wearing things fifty times too big for her body. I shouldn't have assumed, though. I supposed I did the same thing.

"Oh, sorry. I thought . . ." I scrunched up my nose and rubbed my forehead. "Is Ian here?"

"What's going on in here?" a deep, smoky-as-sin voice asked, making me snap my head toward the hallway. There he was in all his glory. A towel sat wrapped around his waist, his hair was dripping wet, and his body gleamed with water droplets as if he'd just walked out of a waterfall cover shoot, and oh my gosh, I was staring at the bulge beneath his towel as if his member were singing siren songs toward me.

I wondered if his lower half could hit the same high notes as his vocals.

Wait.

No.

I didn't wonder that at all.

I spun on my heel away from him and covered my eyes with my hands. "Oh gosh, I'm sorry. I didn't know you were otherwise occupied. Jeez. That's gross. Okay, I'll be going now," I said, trying to walk away but bumping into a table, sending a lamp crashing to the ground. I peeked through my fingers and cringed. "Oops? Sorry about that."

I looked over to Ian, and he was still in that dang towel and still giving me his displeased expression.

"What are you doing here?" he asked, raking his hand through his dripping hair.

"I thought—" I started.

He held a hand up to me. "Not you." His eyes darted to the other woman. "You. What are you doing here?"

His eyes pierced into her as if he was beyond annoyed. He looked at her with even more hatred than he gave me—which said a lot.

She ran her hands over her outfit and gave him a sly smile. "Yes. I figured we could try to have that night together that we missed a few days ago."

"You mean the night where I found out you had a husband?" he murmured.

"Listen, it's complicated. My husband and I aren't even intimate anymore."

"Don't care. Not my problem. The minute a spouse is revealed, I'm out. I don't have time for your drama. Take it elsewhere. I don't know how you got into my place—"

"The front door was unlocked," she commented. "And I heard rumors that if the front door is unlocked, women can walk right on in."

"Bullshit. So go ahead and walk right on out. Take off my clothes and leave them here too."

Well, this is uncomfortable.

I stood there frozen during the most awkward situation of anyone's life. The woman looked defeated as she moseyed over to her clothes and switched into them quickly before heading outside into the rain.

If I were a turtle, I'd be an awkward one standing there.

Ian brushed his hands against his face and released a weighted sigh as I counted the water droplets still rolling down his toned chest.

One, two, skip a few . . .

Each water droplet cruised down his abs to hit the top of the towel, and there I was, staring once again, at his crotch.

I shook my inappropriate thoughts away and cleared my throat. "Do you often have random females crashing into your house uninvited?"

"You'd be surprised to know it happens a lot more often than not. Now, what are you doing here?"

I bit my thumbnail and tried to control the nerves rocking inside of me. "I was wondering if that room was still available for me to take on?"

He cocked an eyebrow. "What? You get spooked out there or something?"

"No," I lied, crossing my arms. "Your roofing skills just aren't as impressive as they should've been." *Gah, Haze. Stop being so sassy and sarcastic. He offered you an olive branch. Don't piss on it and end up back in the shed with the psycho killers.* "Sorry. My instant reaction is sarcasm."

"It's fine. My instant reaction is asshole."

"Well, as long as we both know who we are, rooming together should be fine. But I do have a few rules about us living together."

"Why doesn't that surprise me one bit?"

I smirked a little and kept my arms crossed. "I pay rent. Whatever you're paying, I'll pay half of it."

"Done. What else?"

"I like to cook, and if there are leftovers, you can have them. I hate leftovers."

"Okay. Any more things, darling?"

"Oh yes. Don't call me 'darling.'"

"Chicks love being called 'darling,'" he countered.

"Women don't like being called 'chicks' or 'darling.' Really, for a rock star, you sure are ignorant to what women want."

He took a few steps closer to me and lowered his brows. His deep-chocolate eyes pierced me and forced my stomach to flip upside down and sideways. The stubble on his chin was so perfectly groomed, and his lips looked soft enough to kiss. He slid his teeth slowly against his bottom lip before brushing his thumb against it and raised a brow. "And what exactly is it that women want, Hazel Stone?"

The way he used my full name made me dazed and confused. Gosh, I hated him. I hated how cocky and confident and moody and sexy he was all at once.

"Th-they w-w-want to be called anything in the world other than 'chick' or 'darling.'"

He eyed me up and down and placed his hands against the top of his towel, securing it in place. "Duly noted. Any more rules?"

"Yes, and this one is important."

"I'm all ears."

"We lock the door at night. The last thing I need is some Amber, Reese, or Sue sneaking into the house, looking to find you for a round of sexual escapades, then taking a wrong turn and ending up in my bed."

A wicked smirk hit his lips. "That doesn't sound so bad to me. I could always head over and join in on the party."

I felt my face flush and tried my best to shake off the nerves. "I'm serious, Ian. I don't want some random person walking in. That makes me nervous."

He rubbed the back of his neck, still staring at me as if he was trying to dissect my mind. Then he moved away from my side and walked over to the front door and locked it.

A whispered breath left my lips. "Thank you. Do you want to show me which room is mine?" I asked, taking a step toward the hallway, but his hand landed on my shoulder.

"Now hold on there a minute. You're not the only one with house rules. I got some of my own."

"Oh? And they are?"

"You can't judge me on the number of women I bring in and out of this household. We all got our hobbies, and mine happen to involve a lot of intimate moments with different women."

"Ignore your manwhore ways. Got it. What else?"

"I'm more music than man. When I'm inspired, I might start playing or singing at odd hours of the night. If I don't get it out, I'll drown. I don't want no noise complaints."

"Makes sense. What else?"

"This is the most important one of all. I'll stay out of your affairs, and you'll stay out of mine, but if Big Paw asks you—you and me? We're friends. Good ol' pals."

"Why would it matter if Big Paw thought we were . . ." My words trailed off, and I arched an eyebrow. "Did he tell you to befriend me and to let me move in with you?"

His quietness told his truths.

"Unbelievable." I sighed. But then again, was it really that unbelievable? Of course there was a reason Ian wanted me to crash at his place. I was well aware that he hadn't liked me from the jump, so the complete one-eighty of him inviting me to stay with him made no sense whatsoever. "Why would Big Paw do that?"

"He found out you were staying in the shed and didn't want you doing something like that, seeing as how it's idiotic and unsafe."

There was the Ian I knew and loved. Mr. Charming.

"So he told you to let me stay with you?"

"Yup."

"And if you didn't?"

"He'd sell the house, and I'd be living in a damn shed too. Look, I know this isn't ideal for either of us, but we both got a dry place to put our heads at night. So let's just make the most of it, and if Big Paw asks, we're buddy-buddy. Okay?"

"Okay. I can handle that. How much do I owe for rent each month?"

"Free ninety-nine. I don't pay rent, so half of that is nothing. I'm going to get ready for bed, but your room is down the hallway to the left. I left you some spare clothes if you need them."

"Please don't tell me they are the clothes other women have worn of yours."

"Don't worry; they are freshly cleaned. If you need anything else—don't."

He turned around on his heel and took his grumpy and somewhat sexy ol' butt to bed.

"Good night, best friend," I called out, tongue in cheek.

"Don't push it, Hazel Stone."

I couldn't help it. Pushing Ian Parker was becoming one of my favorite pastimes.

I headed to my bedroom and found a bathroom attached to it. I had my own bathroom. One I didn't have to share with anyone other than me. Never in my life had I thought that would ever be a thing for me. I grabbed the clothes on the bed, headed straight to the shower, and turned it on steaming hot.

Warmth washed over me as I scrubbed my body clean with a very masculine-smelling soap—probably the same soap Ian used against his skin.

I'd forgotten how great it felt to stand inside a tub and have hot water racing across my body. The water hose outside the stables was always freezing cold. After the shower, I tossed on Ian's clothes and looked a little too much like the woman who'd left earlier that evening. I would've complained about it if the clothes were not so freaking comfy and dry.

When it came time for bed, I thanked the heavens above for an actual mattress and a pillow to lay my head against. Tears formed in my eyes from Big Paw's kindness. The fact that he'd seen me struggling and forced his grandson to help me was the truest form of kindness. I had nothing to offer Big Paw. I pretty much had nothing to my name, and still, he'd chosen to help me.

I owed him everything and more.

I had been without a home for two and a half weeks, and they were the toughest few weeks of my life. I couldn't imagine what it felt like for people who lived that life on the regular.

Even though all the pieces of my messy puzzle weren't together, I was thankful, because I knew somewhere out there, men and women were sleeping in dangerous corners of the world without a Big Paw to bring them in for the night.

That night I promised myself that whenever I received the chance to help someone, I'd pay it forward in a heartbeat.

6

IAN

What in the hell is that smell?

I woke up to an excruciating scent filling the house, and the moment I sat up in my bed, I knew exactly what the smell was—pig shit.

I pulled myself out of bed and headed toward Hazel's bedroom. I knocked repeatedly against her door, and she opened it, still tired in the face, but freshly out of the shower. She was wearing a pair of shorts and a tank top and not a drop of makeup.

She looked . . . different.

Completely different than I knew her to be. Hazel had a much smaller frame than her oversize clothes would've led one to believe, and her skin was perfectly smooth, with small freckles dancing across her nose.

Her green eyes shone so much more without those pounds of makeup sitting against her face too.

She was beautiful.

Fuck me sideways and call me Jim—Hazel Stone was breathtaking.

She cocked an eyebrow as I cocked another body part. "Can I help you?" she asked.

I tried my best to shake off my moment of confusion and cleared my throat. I started sniffing the air and looking around her bedroom as I scratched at my messy hair. "It smells like pigs in here."

"If you think telling a girl her room smells like pigs is your way of making a girl feel good about herself, then you are very off track."

"I thought you were a woman, not a girl."

"Girls, women, chicks, darlings—either way, we don't like being told we smell like pigs."

I almost smiled. "I didn't say you smell like a pig. I said your room does."

I walked inside uninvited and kept searching, kept sniffing the air, and then my eyes landed on the pair of torn-up combat boots sitting in the corner of the room. "Haze! You can't just leave those sitting in here. They're gonna stink up the whole place. Then you'll go nose blind to pig smells, and your life will undoubtably go horribly from that point on."

I went to pick them up, and she jumped in front of me, holding up her hands to halt me. "No, stop!"

"Listen, if it's about the shoes, I'm sure you can get a new pair."

"I don't want a new pair. These are mine."

I raised an eyebrow and studied her. She looked as if she was on the verge of tears over some dang combat boots. "What do they mean to you?"

"Everything."

"Why?"

"They were the last thing my mom bought for me," she confessed, and for some reason that confession seemed so out of character for her to share with me. "I love those boots. Sure, they're dirt cheap, have holes in the soles, and pinch at my toes, but they're mine. And they hold a special memory."

I couldn't argue with that. I still had articles of Mom's and Dad's clothing sitting in a box in my closet. But dammit, those boots smelled so bad.

She cleared her throat and crossed her arms. "During one of Mama's stints of getting clean and away from Charlie, she took some cash from him, and we stayed in a motel for two weeks. It was the best two weeks of my life. We crashed the vending machines daily, watched *Pretty Woman* on repeat, and laughed about anything and everything under the sun. It was the longest amount of time I ever had my mom to myself. One afternoon, she took me shopping, and we came across those combat boots in the Goodwill store, and I fell in love with them. She said if they fit, they were mine. I remember sliding them on, wishing and hoping they were mine.

"When they moved up my legs, I gave Mama a big smile and spun around in them. They were crushing my toes, but I didn't want to tell her that. I wanted those shoes too much to pass them up. She bought me the boots, and I've worn them every day since then. That was over three years ago and the last thing Mama bought for me. Those boots stand for happiness to me, and now they are coated in pig manure, which seems like an appropriate metaphor for my life. *Happiness is shit*," she joked.

I gave her a lopsided smile. She probably didn't even notice, because her eyes were fixated on those boots.

Damn.

That was a good enough reason to keep shitty boots around.

I didn't say anything. I left her room, collected a few items, and returned to her with a pile of things in my hands.

"What is this?" Hazel asked.

"Plug-in air fresheners and air freshener spray. If you're going to have those in here, then you're going to need all the help you can get." I started plugging them in around her room, and then I gave the space a nice spritz of lavender air freshener. I left again and came back with two pairs of shoes.

"You can go with the white or the black running shoes. I'm sure both pairs will be way too big for you, but it's better than crap-covered shoes." I smiled, and I think she noticed because her lips curved up, too, and who fucking knew? Hazel Stone had a beautiful smile.

She reached for the black ones and took them.

I chuckled. "I had a feeling you'd go for the black ones."

"I have an image to uphold," she joked. "I can't really be sporting white shoes when my soul is black."

Why did I get the feeling that there was nothing black about her soul? It felt more like her soul was simply battered and bruised—something else we had in common.

I turned to leave her space and paused when she called after me. "Thank you, best friend," she said with a hint of sarcasm and a dash of gratitude.

Whenever the Wreckage held a concert at the barn house, everyone in town showed up. There weren't many opportunities for people to get together and eat and drink for free, but this was one of them—thanks to Big Paw providing food and beverages. Before a show, I'd always get a stomach of nerves, and they wouldn't go away until I set foot on the stage and fell into the character of Ian Parker—the rock star. There were so many days I felt like an imposter, and I was always waiting for the other shoe to drop before me.

Eric finished setting up the livestream equipment, and right before the band went on stage, Grams came out and introduced us. I swore, there was no one in the world more adorable than my grandmother. She had a smile that could make the grumpiest men happy—Big Paw and I were living proof of that fact.

"Now, I just want to say how proud I am of these boys right here. For the past few years, they haven't missed one practice, and they show up day in and day out to make their music. Now, maybe I don't get the music of today—I'm more of a Frank Sinatra kind of gal. Oh, and Billie

Holiday. And, oh, let me tell you about this one time when I went and saw Elvis in Mississippi and—"

"Grams," I called from the side of the stage, knowing she was about to go into one of her big monologues that would last all night if possible.

She smiled and smoothed her hands over her floral dress. "Right. As I was saying, please welcome the Wreckage!"

The crowd went wild, and every fear I had evaporated as my bandmates and I rushed to the stage. Performing felt like the biggest high I'd ever chased. I wasn't into the drug scene. I knew what they'd done to my parents, and I chose to not go down that line in life no matter what. But when I sang in front of a crowd, it felt like the best natural high I'd ever received.

Watching people lose themselves in the music made me want to fucking cry like a damn baby. They were rocking side to side, singing my songs, and that blew my damn mind. I remembered a time when the only people showing up to that barn house to watch us perform were Grams and Big Paw. Now, all of Eres was standing in front of us, singing, dancing, and getting happy drunk. Also the fact that thousands of fans were tuning into Instagram Live was fucking insane.

Every song we performed made the crowd excited. Watching them swallow up our performance should've made me the happiest man alive, and trust me, I was happy, but still, there was something sitting in the back of my mind that kept me from truly feeling completely euphoric.

There was a spark that was missing from the performance, and I couldn't put my finger on it. I needed to tap into it, though, if I'd ever be able to figure out the next steps of the Wreckage's career. Something was missing, and I was going to do whatever it took to pinpoint that missing piece.

"That was fucking amazing!" Marcus exclaimed, tapping his drumsticks against his thigh after we finished our final song for the night. Eric checked and rechecked all our social media accounts with a huge smile on his face, showing he was also pleased.

James was already mingling to thank everyone for showing up, and still, I felt off.

It was a good show, but it wasn't great.

Why wasn't it great?

"Ian, oh my gosh, you were sooo good," a girl said, wandering over to me with her best friend's arm looped through hers.

"Yeah, like, you are sooo good and sooo hot," the other girl giggled.

I gave them a half smile, somewhat living in the moment, somewhat overthinking the performance that'd taken place. "Thanks, girls. Means a lot that you came out to see us."

"We'd love to see a little bit more of you on a one-on-one basis," the first girl said.

"Or even two on one," the other added, giggling.

On a regular night, I would've taken them up on the offer, but my mind was a bit more on the show than it was on the women. I wouldn't be able to think about anything else until I pinpointed what had gone wrong. Unfortunately, that meant a sexless night for me.

The girls huffed and puffed but finally headed off to get more drinks. The party in the barn would keep going on for a few more hours until Big Paw shooed everyone away. People would get drunk, hook up, and make bad decisions that felt good.

A typical Eres Saturday night.

I wandered the ranch with a notebook and pen in my hand. I kept scribbling down lyrics and crossing them out before trying again to create something better, stronger—realer. I ached to unlock the pieces that I was missing. As I paced back and forth, a voice broke me away from my mind.

"It's the words."

I looked up to see Hazel sitting in the rocking chair that Big Paw built for my mother years ago. I used to sit in Mom's lap as she read me stories before bedtime all those years back.

There'd been times I'd thought about getting rid of the chair in order to forget that memory, but I hadn't found the strength to let go just yet.

"What do you mean, it's the words?" I asked, walking up the steps of the porch. I leaned against the railing facing her.

She blinked and tilted her head in my direction. "Your words are trash."

"What?"

"The lyrics to your songs. They are complete garbage, filled with clichés and bubble gum. Don't get me wrong, the music style and tempos are brilliant. And even though it pains me to admit, your voice is so solid and soulful that you could be a star in a heartbeat. But your lyrics? They are pig shit."

"I think the saying is *horseshit*."

"After spending weeks in a pigpen, *pig shit* seems to truly sum up my feelings about your music. But my gosh, your voice. It's a good voice."

I tried to push off her insult and tried to ignore her compliment too. But it was hard. I had an ego that was easy to bruise, and Hazel was swinging her punches while also speaking words of praise. It was as if every bruise she made, she quickly covered with a soothing cream.

Insult, compliment, insult, compliment. Wash, rinse, repeat.

"Everyone else seemed to enjoy the performance," I replied, tense with my words.

"Yeah, well, 'everyone else' are morons who are drunk off their minds."

"Oh? And you think you could do better?"

She laughed. "Without a doubt."

"Okay, Hazel Stone, master of lyrics, give me something to go with."

She gestured toward the other rocker beside her—the one Dad used to sit in.

I sat down.

She pressed her lips together. "Okay. Give me one of your songs. One that you know is crap but are pretending isn't crap."

"They aren't—"

"Lying isn't going to get us far tonight, Ian."

I narrowed my eyes and murmured a curse word before I began flipping through my notebook to find a song for Hazel to magically make better. "Fine. We can do 'Possibilities.'"

"Hmm . . . what is it about?"

"A new relationship forming. I want to showcase those beginning feelings, you know? The fears and excitements. The nerves. The unknown. The—"

"First chapters of love," she finished my thoughts.

"Yes, that."

She took the pencil from behind my ear and took the notebook from my grip. "May I?"

"Please. Go for it."

She began scribbling, crossing things out, adding things in, doing whatever came to her mind. She worked like a madwoman, falling into a world of creativity that I hadn't thought she held inside of her. The only thing I knew about Hazel Stone was where she came from and the clothes she wore. I hadn't known anything else, but now she was pouring herself out on the page, and I couldn't wait to see what the hell she was scribbling.

She took a breath and handed the notebook back to me. "If you hate it, no harm, no foul," she said.

My eyes darted over the words. *It's possible this is forever ours. It's possible we'll reach the stars. We'll fight for this; we'll make it real. Is it possible, possible, to show you how I feel?*

"Shit." I blew out a breath of air. "Hazel . . . that's . . . fuck. It's like you crawled into my head and read the thoughts I couldn't decipher. That's the chorus. That's it."

"You really like it?"

"It's kind of perfect. Help me with the next verse? 'Too late to go, too early to stay, just want to find out what brings a smile to your face. Is this fake, or is it real? The beating of my heart . . .'" I paused. "The beating of my heart . . .'"

"'The beating of my heart and the shivers down my spine. Just let me know if you'll be mine,'" she tossed out, as if it came easy as ever to her. She did it over and over again with my other lyrics too. Adding the missing pieces that I'd been in search of for years.

What in the goddamn hell was happening? How had Hazel managed to tap into a source I hadn't ever been able to find?

"How do you do that?" I asked. "How do you just . . . get it?"

"Easy." She shrugged. "I'm not a brick wall like you."

"What the hell is that supposed to mean?"

"It means exactly that. You're a brick wall. You don't get in touch with your emotions, which means your lyrics come out bland and unauthentic. There's no heart in them, because you don't have any heart to give."

Those words felt like a personal attack.

I tensed up. "Bullshit. I feel things."

"No, you don't."

"Stop talking like you know me."

"I'm not talking like I know you, because I'm pretty sure I don't know you. I doubt many people know you at all, because, again, you're a brick wall. You don't let people in, because you're too afraid."

I couldn't believe this girl. She was going on and on about how I was cold and closed off, but she didn't know what the hell she was talking about. And to think I'd given her my black shoes! My chest tightened, and I pushed myself up from the rocking chair as I snatched the notebook from her grip. "I don't need you telling me who I am or what I'm afraid of," I snapped, feeling a bit unsettled at how she seemed to see me in a way no one else had.

"You can be pissy about it, but I know you are just because I'm right."

"You're not."

"Am too."

"I don't even know why I'm wasting my breath with you," I grumbled and released a weighted sigh. "I got better things to do."

"Like write worse lyrics?"

"What the hell is your problem?" I asked, feeling a fire burning in my chest. It had been a long time since anyone had managed to get under my skin, yet there Hazel was, clawing her way into my irritations.

"My problem is that you are talented enough to get out of this town but you're too stubborn to reach deeper. I would kill to have the gift of music that you do. Your vocals are amazing, and you're seconds away from your breakthrough, but you're too afraid to push for it."

I didn't want to listen to her anymore, because she was annoying and judgmental and fucking right.

I turned on the soles of my shoes and headed toward the front door. As I opened the screen, Hazel called after me. I didn't turn to face her, but I did pause for her words.

"You can't write the truth if you're lying to yourself."

She was right, and I knew it, but I'd been lying to myself for a majority of my life. Over time the lies almost seemed real.

7

HAZEL

Ian and I'd gone a few days staying out of one another's way. Ever since I'd told him about his lyrics, he'd been doing his best to avoid me like the plague. I couldn't blame him—I hadn't been the nicest about it. But I'd listened to enough people blowing smoke up Ian's butt after his performance that I'd figured he could use some tough love. It had been clear he wasn't feeling fully confident about his performance, either, based on his pacing.

On Tuesday evening, he came to my room, cranky as ever, and stood in my doorway. "So you're telling me you're able to write lyrics like that because you're in touch with your damn feelings?"

I nodded. "Yes, exactly."

"And you think I can't because I'm closed off?"

"Yes, exactly."

His eyes were narrowed, and a crease ran across his nose as he stood there in deep thought. He scratched the back of his neck and murmured something under his breath before looking at me once more. "That's the stupidest thing I've ever heard."

"Yes, well, it's also true."

He didn't like that reply, so he continued to ignore me.

It wasn't until late the following Friday that Ian peeked into my bedroom. "Hey, are you awake?"

He seemed much calmer than before. His eyes not as harsh and distant.

"Oh yes, Ian. I am such a loser that I would go to bed at nine on a Friday night," I responded sarcastically. Even though I was definitely about to go to bed at nine at night.

He flipped me off in response to my sarcastic tone. I flipped him off in return. We were clearly becoming best friends.

"What's up?" I asked.

"Nothing. I was supposed to rehearse with the band, but Eric came down with the flu or a cold, or he was going out of town or something."

"We need you to work on your communication skills."

"You're probably right. Anyway, I was going to invite another friend over if that's okay . . . ?" He sounded timid, embarrassed even.

"You're asking me if you can have a friend over?" I laughed. "You do know this is your house, right? And wasn't one of the ground rules that I wasn't allowed to judge you for your manwhore ways?"

He ran his hands through his hair and bit the corner of his mouth. "Yeah, I know, but well, it's your place right now, too, and I don't want to, like . . . I just want you to feel comfortable."

"Ian . . ." I looked down at my attire, which was footie pajamas. "I'm wearing a onesie. I've never been more comfortable in my life, and if you are really asking if it's okay for you to bring a woman back and have sexual intercourse with her, then yes. Balls to the wall, best friend."

He cringed. "Do you know how awkward you are?"

"I am fully aware."

"We have to work on your communication skills," he mocked. "Okay, well, have a good night. If you need anything"—he paused—"don't need anything tonight, okay?"

I chuckled and nodded. "Okay. Just make sure to not play her any of your music during sex. It's like an instant turnoff," I joked.

He flipped me off with both middle fingers this time.

I returned the gesture. *Obviously.*

A few hours later, I was awakened by a panicked Ian standing over me, shaking my shoulders. "Hazel, get up!"

I sat up straight in my bed and rubbed the sleep from my eyes. "What the hell are you doing?"

"Shh," he whispered, placing his finger against my lips. My eyes moved to his finger, and his eyes moved to his finger. We stared at our touch for moments, which felt a little like eternity, before he slowly removed his finger from my mouth. "Sorry. But I need your help."

"It's still dark outside, Ian," I muttered, trying to push myself back to my pillow, but he wouldn't let me.

"I know, I know, but I need you. Please." He sounded really desperate.

I sighed and sat up straighter. "What is it?"

"Remember I said I had a friend coming over?" he said.

"Yes."

"Well, I need her to leave."

I looked over to my clock. Four in the morning. I cocked an eyebrow. "You want me to scare her off? At four in the morning?" He nodded. "You do see that it's a really crappy thing to kick a girl out of a house at four in the morning, right?" He nodded again. But he stopped making eye contact. I took the time to really wake up and stared at him. His hands were closed in fists, and his face was flushed. His foot nervously tapped against the floor nonstop.

It looked as if there was something really bothering him, eating at him under the surface, but he wouldn't say. I didn't know him well enough to ask, so I climbed out of bed.

"Do you want me to be mean or nice?" I asked.

He didn't reply, yet he dug his hands into the side of the mattress and kept tapping his feet. Now the taps didn't seem nervous.

Mean it was.

When I woke up the next morning, the house was empty. I brushed my teeth, wondering if my interaction with Ian last night had been real or only a weird dream. Moving to the kitchen, I glanced out of the window to the backyard, where I saw Ian chopping away at pieces of lumber. His white shirt wasn't on his body but was tucked into the side of his jeans as he swung the ax through a piece of wood.

His arms were muscular and tan, as if he worked most days in the sun. I grabbed myself a cup of water and went out on the small back porch. There was a porch swing that I gladly sat on, still in my footed pajamas. I swung back and forth, and I watched his body react to the sound of the swing squeaking as it swayed with me on it. He knew I was there, but he didn't turn my way.

After opening and closing my mouth a few times, I finally built up the nerve to ask him a question. "Do you want to talk about last night?"

He swung the ax up and then snapped another piece of wood in half. "Nope."

He still hadn't turned to look at me.

I wished I could crawl into Ian's head and see what he was thinking. Even though he and I joked a lot about him sleeping around, I knew that his issues were much deeper than he let on. I should've let him be, allowed him to have his alone time, but something in my heart was telling me to not leave. Something in my heart was asking me to stay.

"You don't have to be so closed off all the time."

"I know, but I want to be."

"Nobody wants to be closed off."

"I do."

"Why?"

"Stop pushing," he ordered, slicing into a piece of wood, but I couldn't help it. I had a feeling that most people other than his grandparents didn't push Ian in any way, shape, or form.

"I'll stop pushing once you open up."

"Well, you'll probably be here forever."

"I don't work today, so that's fine."

He sighed as he hefted the ax and slammed it into the piece of wood in front of him. "Dammit, Hazel. What the hell is wrong with you? Why can't you just leave me be?"

"Because you want to be more." I shrugged. "And last night something happened to you when you asked me to get rid of that woman. Something ate at you deep down inside, and I'm just letting you know you don't have to keep it to yourself. I grew up keeping things to myself. I know how hard and heavy that can be on one's chest."

"Yeah, well, you and me aren't the same."

That was the truest statement ever spoken.

I stood from the porch swing and nodded once. "Okay. Fine. Be that way. But don't blame me when it all becomes too much for you."

"What makes you think it will become too much?"

"It always becomes too much, until your emotions go into over-drive and you break down."

He huffed. "Personal experience?"

"Something like that."

I turned around to walk inside and paused when I heard Ian release the most dramatic sigh in the history of sighs. "She brought up my damn parents. Called them junkies and went on and on about them as if she knew them. It takes a lot to get under my skin—like you said, I have brick walls built—but the comments about my parents always get to me."

Looking back toward him, I saw the heaviness in his eyes as he rested his hands on the handle of the ax. "And why's that?"

"Because the comments always seem to be true. My parents were junkies. My parents did abandon me. My parents did choose their fucked-up habit over their own child. They left this place and left their kid with his own set of fucked-up issues. Okay? That's why it bothers me."

My chest tightened listening to Ian talk about his parents. I knew there was a drug problem in Eres, and I knew a lot of that problem was caused by one man in particular. "Was Charlie their dealer?" I asked, the words stinging as they fell from my tongue.

He brushed a thumb against the bridge of his nose and nodded. "Yes."

"And that's why you hate me?"

"No." He shook his head. "I don't know you enough to hate you. I just don't like what you stand for—the memory of what happened to my parents."

I understood that concept. Maybe more than he could've imagined. "I don't like what I stand for either."

"What do you mean?"

"I also lost a parent at the hand of Charlie. It's because of him I was living in that shed. My mama kicked me out because he wanted me gone, and if it weren't for her drug habit, I doubt she would've done that. She used to be my best friend, but drugs had a way of changing that. I wished I hadn't known her before the drugs because it just . . ." I sighed as my words fumbled away. I wasn't even sure how to explain it, but Ian seemed to understand.

"It just makes it harder, remembering a time when drugs weren't an issue," he finished for me.

"Yes. Exactly."

He started swinging the ax again, huffing and puffing as he spoke. "It pisses me off," he confessed. "How parents could just allow something like drugs to separate them from their children."

I looked at Ian—really looked at him—and saw the broken kid that lived in his anger. There was something so raw and real about how he chopped the wood, swinging that ax with all the pent-up aggression in him.

I walked into the house and came back outside with a pen and paper in my hand. I took my seat back on the porch swing and gave the sweaty, exhausted man a smile. "Okay, let's do it."

"Let's do what?"

"Use your anger to create music."

He grumbled a bit as he pinched the bridge of his nose. "Not interested."

Before I could reply, he walked off, leaving me looking like a silly girl who'd wanted to break down the wall made of stone.

8

HAZEL

It'd been four weeks since Mama and Charlie had kicked me out, and I hadn't been able to really come to grips with it all. Each day, I still worried about Mama's health and well-being. Each day, I thought about her and prayed that she was okay. When it all became too heavy on my heart, I headed for their house to check in on how she was doing after I finished my work shift.

I knew there would be hell to pay if Charlie caught me stopping by, but I didn't care.

I showed up with groceries for Mama's fridge, and when I knocked on the door, I heard her shuffling around.

"Who is it?" she called out.

"It's me, Mama. It's Hazel."

The movements sounded more hurried, and when she opened the door, I gasped at the sight of her. The groceries in my hand crashed to the ground as I stepped forward. "Mama! What happened to you?" I breathed out, taking in her battered and bruised face. Her left eye was almost sealed shut, and her wrists were black and blue.

"Don't make a fuss," she warned, waving me off. "Charlie and I just got into an altercation. I made a mistake with his business, and I should've done better."

"What? No," I said, barging into the house. "No matter the issue, he has no right to put his hands on you, Mama. It's not right, and we really should get you checked out. Let me take you to the hospital."

She shook her head. "No. I'm not going to the hospital. I'm fine."

"We need to make sure the baby is okay, though, Mama. Please."

She lowered her head, and I saw the hurting in her heart. There was a struggle going on in her head. I couldn't imagine what was going through her mind, though. Every now and again, I saw flashes of regret in her eyes that matched mine. My mother had lived a life of struggles, and I saw her battling against her pain every single time she blinked.

"I don't have that kind of money for a doctor appointment . . . ," she started. "I ain't got no insurance, and Charlie will be upset if a bill comes through for it."

"I'll cover the cost. Really, Mama. Let me help you."

She was seconds away from agreeing. Seconds away from doing the right thing for her and for the baby, but before she could speak, Charlie walked up behind me. I turned to see his eyes widen when he saw me, and he then glared at Mama.

"What the hell is going on here?" he barked.

"I'm taking Mama out for a little bit," I said, trying my best to not showcase the fear that sat in my throat. Sure, Charlie didn't look like a threatening man, but I knew the harshness that lived inside him. It wasn't the first time I'd noticed Mama's body being bruised at the hands of Charlie, but I'd figured ever since she got pregnant, he wouldn't hurt her.

I'd been too hopeful believing that Charlie was not the biggest monster.

"Where?" he demanded. "You shouldn't even be here."

"I'm allowed to see my mother," I shot back. "Come on, Mama. Get your things, and let's go."

"She isn't going anywhere with you. Go ahead and make me a pizza, Jean," he ordered Mama, which made my irritation skyrocket.

"She's hurt," I scolded. "I'm taking her to get checked out."

He cocked an eyebrow and looked at Mama. "You going to a hospital?" he asked, his words low and controlling. "What the hell you going to do, Jean? Turn me in? Say I hurt you?"

She hesitated as she fidgeted with her fingers, looking down at the floor. "Of course not, Charlie."

"Because I didn't hurt you, did I?"

The way his words slithered off his tongue made the hairs on my skin stand straight up. Gosh, I hated him so much and despised how he used his authority to control Mama's thoughts.

"No, you didn't," she lied. She blinked her eyes shut and shook her head back and forth. "I tripped. You know I'm clumsy, Hazel."

No, Mama.

Don't let him control you like this.

"Even still, you should get checked out because of the baby," I offered, trying to tame the anger rushing through me. I needed to get her out of there. Out of that house, out from under Charlie's control. Because I knew if she stayed any longer, she'd end up six feet under due to him taking it one step too far.

Maybe if we ran away together, she'd be able to get her mind clear again. Maybe she'd realize that we didn't need Charlie. That we were better without him, that—

"She's not going anywhere," Charlie cut in. "The baby's fine, and so is she. And you are not welcome here anymore. So get out."

I stepped toward my mother, guarding her from Charlie. "I'm not leaving without taking her with me."

He rolled up the sleeves of his shirt and stepped toward me. "Get out, Hazel."

"No," I sternly stated. "I'm not going anywhere."

He grabbed me by the arm and started dragging me toward the front door. For a small-looking guy, his grip hurt.

"Let me go!" I shouted. I tripped over my feet as he yanked me, and the second I found my footing, I shoved hard against his chest, making him stumble backward.

Before any thought, I felt the sting of his fist slamming against my face. I fell straight to the ground.

Holy crap.

The stinging sensation that overtook me made me want to vomit. He hadn't just slapped me; he'd punched me. He'd sent me flying backward and crashing to the floor as if he hadn't a care in the world for his actions. Was that what he did to Mama? Did he punch her repeatedly like she was a rag doll and not a person?

My head began pounding, and tears fell from my eyes as the pain engulfed my entire system. I went to stand, but Charlie came barging toward me, and he shoved me back down.

"I told you to fucking leave," he hissed, his voice dripping with hatred.

"Fuck you," I cried.

He raised his fist to hit me again, but Mama rushed in and took his hand into hers. "Stop, Charlie. Please. She gets it. She's leaving and never coming back," she swore.

I stumbled to my feet as my right eye stayed closed. Wetness dripped from my face as I wiped it. *Is that blood?* Charlie's ring must've sliced into my skin.

"Right, Hazel?" Mama asked, looking at me with wide eyes filled with fear. She lived with that fear on a daily basis.

"Come with me, Mama," I begged, my chest rising and falling at erratic speeds.

"Again, she's not going anywhere. Now, leave before I take it out on the both of you," Charlie said.

It was clear he was a psychopath. He didn't have a twinge of remorse for his actions—quite the opposite actually. He looked as if he was ready to give me another blow any second now.

"Go, Hazel," Mama begged, tears welling in her eyes. "Please."

I wanted to argue, but I knew if I pushed Charlie, he'd push both me and Mama back. I couldn't handle the idea of him hurting Mama, so I left.

The ache in my chest had me feeling nothing but guilt for leaving her in that terrible situation. For a moment in time, when she'd grabbed Charlie's arm, I'd seen my mother. My real mother, not the drugged-up human she'd turned into over the years. She'd stepped in to protect me, and it killed my heart that there was no one to protect her back.

I headed to Ian's house, and as I walked, I tried my best to keep my head down and covered. A car horn blared at me, sending nerves straight up my spine. I kept my head down and kept walking. "Hazel!" a voice hollered from the car. I still didn't look up. "Hey, Hazel, it's Leah. James Scout's sister. He works on the ranch, and I'm heading over there to check in on the horses. Are you heading that way? I can give you a lift."

She pulled her car over, parked it, and hurried over to me. I'd known Leah for some time now. We'd graduated together, and she was the definition of royalty in our town. Leah Scout was beautiful. From her gorgeous blonde hair to her crystal-blue eyes. She had a smile that could've been used in toothpaste commercials, and she gave that smile to everyone who looked her way. She was just like her older brother, James, too—overly nice to anyone and everyone.

As she reached me, she gasped and placed her hands over her mouth. "Oh my goodness, what happened to you?"

"I, um, I don't want to talk about it." I started to walk, and Leah kept her pace beside me.

"Wait, Hazel. Who did this to you?"

"I don't want to talk about it," I replied shortly. "I just want to get home and clean up."

"Okay." She nodded her head and linked her arm with mine.

"What are you doing?"

"I'm walking you to my car so I can drive you home. You shouldn't be walking on these streets looking like this, and you definitely shouldn't be alone. James said you're staying with Ian for now, right?"

I nodded. "Yes. But you don't—"

"Don't be silly, Hazel. Us girls gotta look out for one another in a town filled with creeps. It's not a big deal. Come on, now. Let's get you home so we can clean up that wound."

When we got to the ranch house, I tried to get Leah to go on with her day, but she wouldn't leave my side.

"You can't go without cleaning up that eye. Otherwise, it will be swollen shut for a while. I volunteer at Dr. Smith's office. I can help you," she offered.

I didn't have the energy to fight her to go away. Plus, some odd part of me didn't want to be left alone.

I sat on the edge of my bed as Leah headed to the kitchen to get a wet cloth and ice for my eye. When she came back, she sat beside me and did her best to nurse me back to good health.

"Who did this, Hazel?" she whispered.

I shook my head. "It doesn't matter."

"Of course it does. People shouldn't be allowed to hurt you like this. They should pay for their actions."

I gave her a lopsided smile and remained quiet. I didn't need strangers knowing too much about my personal life. Even though Leah was nice, I hadn't the need to lay all of my hardships at her feet.

"I'm really okay," I lied.

She gave me a knowing smile. Then she frowned and shook her head. "Ian is going to lose his mind once he finds out."

I raised an eyebrow. "That's not very likely."

"Are you kidding? Of course it is. You're his roommate, and someone hurt you. He's going to care about it."

I snickered. "We really aren't that kind of roommates. We pretty much stay out of each other's way, unless he needs me to kick a random girl out at three in the morning."

Leah brushed her hand against her face. "I don't know, Hazel. This kind of stuff gets to Ian. His dad used to lay his hands on his mom before they left all those years ago, and it drove Ian crazy. He doesn't take well to women being abused."

Abused.

I didn't know why that word made me want to throw up. That word made Charlie's actions seem even more intense, but it was true. He did abuse me. He abused my mother. And I knew he wouldn't stop, because when it came to Charlie, abuse was second nature.

"Listen, I know Ian is hard around the edges, but he's really a good guy. I've known him all my life, seeing as how he's best friends with my brother. When his parents ran off, it did a number on him, but that kindhearted boy is still there."

"He's cold all the time. He doesn't have feelings."

Leah laughed out loud. "That's ridiculous. If anything, Ian Parker feels too much. That man has more feelings than most people in this world. He gets so overwhelmed by his emotions that he puts up that wall. But man, he cares. He cares so much that I think it drives him crazy."

I lowered my head for a minute and held the towel with ice against my face. I wasn't certain what else to say to Leah, so I shrugged my shoulders and gave her a small smile. "I'm getting a bit of a headache. I think I'm going to rest for a little while."

"That's a good idea. Take some ibuprofen for the pain, and keep icing that eye every few hours to help with the swelling, okay?"

"Okay, thank you, Leah. Truly, thank you." She didn't have to help me, but still, she did. That meant more to me than she'd ever know.

"Of course." She stood from my bed and gave me a smile. "And if you ever need some girl time, let me know. Hanging around these boys on the ranch would drive me mad. I'm always around visiting the horses anyway, so maybe some days we can grab lunch or something."

I gave her a true, genuine smile. "I'd love that."

"Rest, Hazel. I hope you're feeling better soon. And whatever you do, don't let the asshole who did this to you get away with it."

After Leah left, I locked the bathroom door as tears rolled down my cheeks from the pain shooting through me. The more time that passed, the more the punch to the face began to ache. The right side of my face was swollen and turning black and blue as each second passed. I looked like Mama, and that broke my heart so much.

Charlie had never laid a hand on me before . . . he'd never crossed that line because Mama would always take the hits for me. Now, I knew how she felt, what she'd been going through, the struggles she'd had.

The aching in my chest wasn't solely for me—it was for Mama. I wanted to get her out of there. I needed to get her away from that psychopath. Who knew what kind of lies he was poisoning her with? What kind of drugs he was pumping into her without her even knowing? Charlie was desperate to control people, and Mama made it so easy for him to reign over her, because she was too weak and scared to fight back.

That night, I couldn't think straight, because I was too fearful of what was going to happen with Mama. I stayed in my bedroom, not wanting Ian to see me in my current state. I couldn't eat, I couldn't sleep, and I couldn't stop crying. I kept thinking about how I had to get Mama out of that terrible situation, away from Charlie—or at least get Charlie away from her. I knew enough about Charlie from both Garrett and Mama to be able to set him up somehow. I could get him in enough trouble that he couldn't pull Mama down anymore. I didn't know exactly if my plan would work—but I knew I had to try. Otherwise, not only would Mama lose the child she was carrying, but she'd lose her own life too.

So, late in the night, I picked up Ian's house phone, and I called the police station.

"Eres Police. How can I direct your call?" a tired voice said through the line.

"Hi, yes, I'd like to leave an anonymous tip for a big drug trade that will be happening over the next few days."

The voice lowered on the other end of the line. "Connor, is that you? Are you pranking me again?"

"What? No. I really have a tip."

"*Ookay*," the person said, unbelievingly. "Out with it. What's the tip?"

"Once a month, Charlie Riley distributes his supplies to his men to take out to other towns. It happens right on the outskirts of Eres, at the old laundromat on Wood Street and Timber Avenue. It takes place around two in the morning, and it should be happening two days from now."

I was thankful for Garrett getting high enough to spill those beans to me all that time ago about where Charlie's supply came in and went out. He'd been so giddy about his uncle giving him more lead in the family "business" that he'd gotten drunk and high and told me all about it during one of his video game binges.

"And how do you know this?"

"Trust me, I just do."

"Yeah, okay, Connor, we'll look into it."

"I'm not Connor!" I argued, brushing my hand against my face. Did I really sound like a boy? What the heck? "Look, just trust me on this one. The laundromat is where Charlie's deals go through. You'll find everything you need there. Make sure you take backup too."

"Okay. Is that all?"

"Yes." I bit my bottom lip as my stomach flipped and turned. "That's all."

"Okay. Laundromat. Wood and Timber. Charlie Riley. Bad drugs. Got it. Good night, Connor."

The phone clicked, and I took a deep breath as my panic began to settle, and I thought about how things would be different for Mama in two days. In two days, she wouldn't have to escape Charlie's hand. In two days, he'd be dragged away on his own.

She wouldn't have to try to run from him ever again.

This time, we'd win.

Ten Years Ago

"Come on, Hazel, hurry up. Just grab a few things," Mama ordered as she pulled me from my bed. She had a suitcase sitting on my bed and was slinging some of my clothes into it.

The sky was still dark as I yawned. "What's going on, Mama?" The sun wasn't even awake yet, so I didn't understand why I was.

"We're leaving, sweetheart. We're getting the hell out of here, okay?" Her voice was so low, and she moved on her tiptoes, as if not wanting anyone to hear her sounds.

I knew it was because of Charlie.

Mama always whispered when she didn't want Charlie to hear her.

"Now come on, and be as quiet as you can, okay?" she asked.

"We're really going?" I asked, my voice timid.

Mama had talked about leaving Charlie before, but we'd never really packed our bags to go. I'd started to believe we'd always be under Charlie's control, no matter how much we wanted to go. He was mean to Mama, and I didn't like how he made her cry.

"Yes, honey, really. Now, grab anything you need, because we aren't coming back."

"Never?"

She bent down in front of me and combed the hair away from my face. She had tears in her eyes, and that made me sad. I hated when Mama cried, and she cried too much lately. "Never ever, baby. This is it. We are getting away and never looking back at this town. Okay? Just you and me. Just the two of us."

I grabbed my stuffed animal on my bed and hugged it close to me as I put my free hand into Mama's. "Okay."

"Ready?" she asked.

"Ready," I replied.

I'd been ready for so long that I couldn't help but smile at the thought of running away with Mama.

"Just the two of us," I murmured to myself as I walked off with Mama holding my hand.

That was all I'd ever wanted.

"Are you crying because you're sad?"

"No, honey. These are happy tears."

Happy tears.

I didn't know people could cry when they were happy.

When I found that out, I started crying too.

9

IAN

"Are you boneheads done rehearsing? If so, I can give you a lift home, James," Leah said, walking into the barn house with the same smile that was always plastered against her face.

"You can give me a ride home? Didn't you take my car today?" James asked. "Therefore, wouldn't it be me giving you a ride home?"

"Potato patahto. Come on. I need to binge *You* on Netflix and stuff my face with popcorn." She waved to me and the other guys. "You guys are sounding pretty good."

Eric nodded. "We could sound better. Are you following us on all social media platforms, Leah? We'd really love the support." Eric was like a social media hustler—always after that next like and follow.

"Sure am." Leah beamed and walked in my direction. She stuffed her hands into her shorts pockets and swayed back and forth in her flip-flops. "Hey, Ian. How's living with Hazel going?"

I shrugged. "We don't really cross paths that much."

"I graduated with her. She's a really cool person. Quiet, but nice. You know, I think she's pretty interesting once you get to know her. She was always really smart in school too. I bet she gets lonely sometimes."

My eyebrow arched at the overly sweet Leah. I knew she was getting at something; therefore, I wished she'd just spit it out. "What are you trying to get at, Leah?"

She smiled bright as always and shrugged. "I'm just saying—it wouldn't kill you to get to know her. She's been through a lot of terrible things. It would be nice if she had someone nice to talk to sometimes."

"I'm not a nice person," I told her.

She rolled her eyes in the most dramatic fashion and patted me on the back. "Yeah, okay, Ian, and I'm not addicted to the Kardashians. Don't think for a second I forgot who showed up for two weeks straight to play tic-tac-toe with my grandma when she was in the hospital after breaking her hip."

"What can I say? I'm a sucker for tic-tac-toe."

"Just be nice to her, dumbo. I get the feeling she could use a friend."

"Then you be her friend."

"That's in the works, but for the time being, she needs a roommate friend. Someone who's around her enough to crack open her shell."

I grimaced, still unsure, and Leah gave me yet another dramatic eye roll.

"Fine! Be a jerk, but just be a lesser jerk, okay? Stop being so hard on her around the ranch."

"I'm hard on everyone around the ranch," I muttered, a touch annoyed by what Leah was getting at. I treated everyone the same around these parts, and I didn't like how she made it seem as if I came down harder on Hazel than any of the other ranch hands.

Leah sighed, growing tired of my responses the same way I was growing tired of hers. "Whatever, Ian. You treat Hazel worse than the others. I've seen the way you boss her around when she's probably one of the hardest workers at this place. I mean, hell, she puts in more work than my bozo brother."

"Hey, leave me out of this!" James shot out as he packed up his things. "But she's not wrong. Hazel is a damn good worker, and you do sometimes come down hard on her."

Well, there was nothing as grand as being tag teamed by the Scout siblings. The shitty thing about it was that they were two of the nicest people around. So if they had issues with the way I was treating Hazel, they were probably spot on about it. True, my judgments based on Charlie might've affected the way I'd treated Hazel at the ranch, and having Leah and James point that fact out to me made me feel like a big ass. I'd do my best to keep it in mind to take it a little easier on Hazel.

Which meant I had to remind myself repeatedly that she wasn't the same type of person that Charlie was simply because she'd been raised by the devil himself.

"You should take it easy today. It's too hot out to be working that hard," I warned Hazel the following day as she was shoveling hay into the back of a pickup truck. The temperature was nearing one hundred degrees, and she was dressed in her usual all-black outfit, with her long sleeves. It was too damn hot for that type of wardrobe, especially when Hazel was working directly in the sun. She even had a hoodie on, with the hood up like a madwoman.

"It's fine. I got this," she muttered, her voice low as she shoveled the hay. She hadn't said much over the past few hours, which was odd. Normally, she'd have a rude, sarcastic comment to make toward me, but there was none to be heard.

She hadn't even mocked me the previous night about me burning dinner. Come to think of it, I hadn't even seen her at the house. Her bedroom door was closed, and even though I heard her moving around, she didn't step foot outside. When I woke in the morning, she was already off to work on the ranch.

"Don't tell me you're still pissy about me not wanting to open up to you about my feelings and crap that other morning?"

"Contrary to popular belief, not everything is about you, Ian Parker," she snapped.

I should've left it—and her bad attitude—at that. Still, watching that sun beat down on her was making me dizzy. Shit, I was seconds away from passing out for her.

"Come on, darling. Don't be stupid. Heatstroke is a real thing." I called her "darling" to try to get under her skin, and she didn't react whatsoever. Damn. What was with that girl?

She pulled on the edges of her hood and cleared her throat before going back to work. "It's fine. I'm good."

"At least head to the pigpens. I'll even help you in there. Or take a water break. It's too—"

"I said I'm fine!" she finally snapped.

The moment she turned toward me, my chest tightened. Her eyes were bloodshot red, as if she'd been crying for the past forever hours, and she was wearing pounds and pounds of makeup. Sure, she wore makeup on the regular, but she currently looked like she was auditioning for *RuPaul's Drag Race*.

I didn't even know why, but seeing that level of sadness in her eyes broke my cold fucking heart. "What's wrong?" I hammered.

She shook her head as tears proceeded to dance down her cheeks. "Nothing. I'm fine."

"You're lying."

"Drop it, Ian."

"Can't, darling."

She parted her lips to maybe sass me, which would've made me feel a little bit better about her current state. If she had enough in her to sass me, then she wasn't too far away from her regular annoying self.

But instead of her speaking, her eyes crossed, and she dropped the pitchfork in her grip. As it fell to the ground, I watched her body waver back and forth.

Fuck.

She was going to pass out.

Her eyes began to roll back in her head, and I rushed over to her, catching her just in time before she crashed. She passed out in my arms, her body going limp against me. I lifted her up and hurried off in the direction of the house and kept repeating the same words over and over.

"I got you, darling," I muttered. "I got you."

The moment we made it to the house, Hazel was coming to, and I hurriedly tossed her into the shower and ran cold water over her body. The sensation of the chill woke her up quickly as she squeaked in horror.

"Oh my gosh, that's cold!" she cried out, shivering from the ice droplets hitting her body. She rubbed her hands up and down her arms as she sat in the tub.

"Good," I grumbled. "I told you it was too damn hot to be out there in that sun."

She reached forward to shut off the water and shivered. "I'm fine."

"You're not. You need some electrolytes to recover from the heat. I have some sports drinks in the fridge. Here's a towel to dry off." I grabbed the closest one on the hook and held it out to her. She quickly began wiping the water from her face, and with the water went her makeup.

"What the fuck happened to your face?" I barked out, horrified by the bruises that were revealed as she removed the makeup.

Her eyes widened, and she turned away from me. "It's nothing."

I placed my hands on her shoulders and turned her back to face me. "Bullshit. That's not nothing. It looks like someone fucking punched you in the damn face."

The way her eyes watered made me realize that was exactly what had happened.

Holy shit.

Someone had punched her in the damn face.

"Who did this to you?" I asked, my voice tight with anger. I didn't even know who the hell I was mad at, but I was pissed. "Was it a man?"

She nodded slowly.

"Tell me who," I ordered.

The tears began falling faster than ever down her cheeks as she shook her head back and forth. "It's okay. I'm figuring it out." She went to get to her feet and stumbled a bit, still off balance, and I caught her in my arms. She gave me a broken smile. "You're good at that."

"At what?"

"Catching me."

"Well, it would be best if you'd stop falling."

"Trust me"—she released a weighted breath—"I'm trying."

I didn't know what to say to that, because it sounded so damn heartbreaking. I wanted sarcastic and rude Hazel Stone back. The sad one made me want to cry right alongside her.

"What can I do for you?" I asked, my voice cracking as I stared at her swollen eye. What kind of asshole laid his hands on a woman? What type of weak bastard would do such a fucked-up thing? I knew who—my father. I remembered watching him attack my mother in his drunken rage when I was a kid. I remembered Mom's bruises and how she'd tried to hide them with makeup—the same way Hazel had done.

I wanted to kill him.

I didn't even know who he was, but I wanted blood.

Hazel tried her best to keep smiling through her pain. "Well, first, sports drink," she said. "And then tonight, vodka."

I cocked an eyebrow. "Aren't you too young to be drinking?"

"Yes." She nodded. "But I had a pretty bad day."

Well, okay then.

Vodka it was. *After* the sports drink.

If there was an award for the world's biggest lightweight, it would go to Hazel. She'd taken three shots under my watch, along with a mixed drink, and was dancing around in circles in the living room. She hummed a tune that I couldn't quite place, but somehow it sounded perfect.

"Why don't you drink too?" she asked me, raising an eyebrow as she plopped down on the sofa.

"I'm not feeling up to drinking tonight."

"What? Of course you're feeling up to drinking tonight. Everyone should be feeling up to drinking every night. Drinking is fun," she exclaimed.

I sat on the opposite side of the sofa. "And how many times have you drank?"

"Oh, psh." She puckered her lips and blew out a heavy breath. "Counting today?"

"Uh-huh."

She held two fingers up, and then she studied her fingers with a dumbfounded stare. Then she dropped one finger. I couldn't help but snicker, because she left her middle finger up without even knowing.

Hazel Stone was officially partaking in her first ever drinking display, and she was officially shit faced.

"You know what I miss?" she asked, rubbing the back of her hand against her mouth.

"What's that?"

"The shed."

I laughed. "Am I that bad of a roommate that you'd rather live in a shed?"

"No." She giggled, and it sounded kind of beautiful. "I just mean I miss looking up through the ceiling at the stars and sky. I love the stars and moon. It makes me realize that there's so much more than my problems out there."

"Are you the type of person to wish on stars?"

"I'm the type of person to wish on everything." She tilted her head toward me. "Does it always feel this good? Being drunk?"

"Depends. I can't drink whiskey, because it makes me sad."

"What the heck do you have to be sad about? You sing like a god, you live rent-free, and your grandparents are freaking amazing! Plus, you're H-A-W-T. Hawt. Like, if I didn't know how many women you've put your penis in, I'd think about you putting your penis in me, too, you know, if I let people put penises in me."

The words tumbled off her tongue with such ease, and I knew if she were sober, she'd kick herself for saying those things out loud.

Didn't mean I couldn't have some fun with it.

"Oh. You think I'm H-A-W-T?" I asked.

"Yes, I do. If I had a lady boner, it would be erected all day every day when I'm around you. Even when you're mean to me."

I frowned. "I'm sorry I've been mean to you, Haze." The more I watched her in her drunken state, the more guilt hit me for being so closed off toward her.

"It's okay. I'm used to people being mean to me."

That made me feel like complete shit. I brushed my thumb against my nose and moved in closer to her.

"What are you doing?" she nervously asked.

"Checking your bruise. May I?" I asked, my hand hovering in the air.

She nodded slowly.

My fingers landed against her cheek, and she didn't flinch from the touch. She just kept humming to herself.

"Does that hurt?"

She shook her head. "I don't feel anything but good."

"Another side effect of booze."

"Why were you so mean to me?" she asked, her green eyes piercing me.

"Because I'm an idiot," I confessed. "I have a few issues with your stepfather."

Her fingers moved over the top of mine, which were still resting against her cheek, and she closed her eyes. "He's no father of mine."

"Did he do this to you?" I whispered, a little too afraid to say it any louder. I didn't know why, but the idea of Charlie hurting Hazel made me want to vomit.

She nodded slowly. "He's a monster."

"I know."

And I was going to kill him.

"Mama's bruises are worse," she softly said as she raked her hand through her charcoal-colored hair. "She has no escape from him, and he hurts her a lot more than he has ever hurt me."

"Why won't she leave him?"

"She's tried, time and time again. He always finds her and pulls her back in." Tears fell down her cheeks, and she shook her head as I wiped them away. "Can vodka make you both happy and sad?"

"It's possible."

"But I don't want to be sad anymore. I want to be happy."

"You will be," I promised. "Sometimes it just takes time to get to the happy lyrics."

"When are you going to write happy lyrics?"

I pushed out a chuckle. "I'm actually looking to hire a girl to help me on the lyrics end."

She pushed her tongue in her cheek and narrowed her eyes. "I bet she's really cute."

"She has no clue how beautiful she is," I gently replied. "With and without the makeup."

She sat up a little straighter, seemingly surprised by my words. "Thank you."

"Can I ask why you wear so much makeup?"

97

Hazel raked her hands through her hair again and shrugged her shoulders. "That's because of Charlie too. When I was younger, around fourteen, I used to always wear a tank top and shorts around the house. One night, when Charlie was drunk, he stumbled into my bedroom and made comments about how he wanted to touch my body. About how I was showing it off for him with my olive skin. So I started dressing in heavy layers of clothing and makeup to ward him off."

I felt sick to my stomach as she told me that. What kind of fucking psychopath was Charlie? If I'd had plans to kill him before, now I was raging with the need to strangle the bastard.

Such a softness fell over her as she looked my way. "Ian?"

"Yeah?"

"Drunk Hazel likes you a lot."

I snickered. "Let's work on getting sober Hazel to like me too."

"That's easy enough." She yawned in my face, not bothering to cover her mouth. "Just say hi to me sometimes, and it helps if you take off your shirt too."

Dammit to hell. How had I treated someone like Hazel so shitty for so long? If I'd pulled my head out of my own ass, I would've realized that there was nothing about her that mimicked Charlie. She was the complete opposite, actually. She was caring and funny and beautiful and kind.

Christ. What a fucking idiot I was.

"Hey, Ian?"

"Yes?"

"I'm going to vomit now."

I'd spent the last ten minutes holding Hazel's hair back as she upchucked into the toilet. As she murmured about how she was never drinking again, I smiled to myself, thinking about all the crappy drinking nights I'd had where I'd said those same exact words.

When she finished her violent attack on the toilet, she lay down on the ground and curled into the fetal position. "I sleep here," she mumbled.

I chuckled as I bent down to lift her in my arms. "No, you sleep in your bed."

"I sleep in your bed," she echoed, snuggling into my arms.

Not exactly right.

After I laid her down—in *her* bed—I placed a puke bucket on the floor, just in case, and then I tucked her in.

She reached her arms up and wrapped them around my neck, pulling me into a hug. "Thank you, best friend," she whispered, before plopping back down against her pillow. As I turned to walk away, Hazel murmured some more. "I have to help her."

"Help who?"

"Mama. I have to get her and the baby out of there. I have to help," she said with her eyes shut as she began to fall into a deep slumber.

I wasn't sure she knew what she was saying, but I said, "I'll help you help her, Haze."

"Promise?" she whispered.

"Promise," I replied.

10

HAZEL

What was that excruciating sound?

Was it a rooster? Was a rooster honestly screaming outside my window as my head pounded as if it were going to explode?

Why did my mouth feel so dry?

Why did I feel like death?

"Cock-a-doodle-doooo!" Mr. Rooster shouted, making me push a pillow over my face. I hated how awake and happy the guy was, as if he hadn't drunk all the vodka in the land the night before.

Vodka.

Ugh. Screw vodka.

My eyes warily opened as I sat up on my elbows. I groaned as my stomach flipped, skipped, and turned. Just then, the painful sound of the doorbell ringing went off. When it kept dinging, I dragged myself from my room to answer it, seeing as how Ian hadn't any plans of getting to the door.

I swung it open as the sunlight beamed toward me. I'd never felt more like a vampire in my life, and when I noticed a woman standing there with a basket of goodies, I instantly felt bad for hissing in her face.

She didn't frown at my insane reaction to the light, though. She smiled brightly and tilted her head to the left. "I've been meaning to stop by to meet you," she said, walking into the house. She set the basket of things down on the table and then turned back to me and held her hand out for a shake. "You must be Hazel. I'm Holly, Ian's grandmother."

The woman I'd just hissed at was Ian's grandmother.

What a great first impression.

I brushed my hand across my face and cringed a bit when I hit the bruise. I'd forgotten that was there, and now Holly was staring at me and my massively bruised skin. I held my hand out and shook hers.

"Sorry, I'm just waking up. Normally I'm better at first impressions." I smoothed my hands over my pajamas—pajamas I hadn't recalled putting on—and gave her a tight smile.

"Oh, honey, don't worry about it. You look beautiful." She smiled so brightly I couldn't help but smile too. I'd never seen such a genuine expression in all my life.

Holly was so beautiful in an effortless way. She had long silvery hair that was pulled back into a ponytail and eyes that matched Ian's. Though she was much shorter than Big Paw, she held her head high. She was slender and stood up straighter than most people my age.

If I didn't know any better, I would've assumed she was in her late sixties—not eighties.

"If you're looking for Ian, it seems he's not here, or maybe not up yet," I told her.

She shook her head. "Oh no. I know that. He's the one who called me. He's working at the ranch already and—"

My eyes widened in pure panic. "Oh my gosh, what time is it? I'm supposed to be at the ranch working!" I knew if Big Paw found out that I was late, I'd be out of a job in a heartbeat. "I'm sorry, Holly, I have to get going to—"

She placed a hand on my arm and shook her head. "No, it's fine. Ian said you weren't feeling well today, so he's taking over your tasks."

A ripple of relief and shock raced through my system. "Is he upset? That he has to take on those tasks?"

"Lord, no. He actually sent me over to check on you and make sure you had some food to eat and some coffee to drink." She raised an eyebrow. "You do drink coffee, right?"

I smiled, feeling relief fall over me as my anxiety was replaced with comfort. "All the coffee."

"Good." Holly walked over to her basket, pulled out a few ibuprofen and a water bottle, and handed them my way. "Now take these and shower up, and by the time you're done, I'll have some breakfast ready for you."

I thanked her for her kindness and headed off to hop in the shower.

I understood why people drank to forget. Last night, I'd felt free from the burden of Mama's struggles for a split second. I needed that break to stop feeling everything so strongly. But unluckily, I wasn't one of those humans who forgot everything that happened when they drank.

Nope. I remembered it all.

Especially the parts where I'd called Ian "H-A-W-T" and talked about the lady boner I had for him. Gosh. The next time I saw him, I was certain I'd be fifty shades of red from humiliation.

After my shower, I considered putting on makeup to cover my bruise, but since Holly had already noticed it, I didn't see much reason to do it.

The house smelled heavenly, as if a Top Chef had come in all on their own to cook up a meal for me. As I walked into the dining room, I found Holly setting up two plates that were filled with bacon, eggs, and home-style potatoes. My coffee cup was filled to the brim, and my stomach started doing somersaults of excitement.

"This looks and smells amazing," I commented as I took my seat.

She smiled as she slid into hers. "The best cure for a hangover is homemade cooking," she exclaimed. "I've had to cook plenty of these meals for Ian and his best friends throughout the years."

"He's lucky to have you."

"I'm lucky to have him. He and Harry are my two biggest headaches. Lord only knows how I've dealt with their grumpy exteriors, but deep down inside, those two are teddy bears. They build up walls to avoid getting hurt; that's for sure. I'm one of the lucky few who they've let see their gentle sides."

"So I shouldn't take their grumpy sides personal?"

"Heavens, no. It's just their wall of protection from getting hurt. After my daughter and son-in-law left, both Harry and Ian struggled. Having someone so important to them leave without a goodbye really damaged their hearts. My boys are sensitive. More than most people. They are terrified of being hurt, so they pretend that nothing stings them."

"That has to be lonely."

"Yes." She nodded. "I worry more about Ian. He's so closed off and doesn't let anyone in close enough to show him any kind of comfort— outside of his bandmates. But then he played me your song, and I saw a spark inside of him that I haven't seen in a while."

"What do you mean? What do you mean, he played you my song?"

"The one you helped him write. He came over and played it for Harry and me, and we were blown away. I hadn't seen him that invested in his music in so long, and those lyrics . . ." She pressed her hands to her chest and shook her head in amazement. "I haven't heard my grandson sing such beautiful words in all my life. So thank you for that."

"For what?"

"Helping him find his voice. He's been searching for years, and for the first time ever, it seems he's on to something, and I think it has a lot to do with you. You're truly gifted at the written word."

I felt my face grow flushed, and I wiggled around in my chair. "He's an amazing singer on his own," I said.

"Yes." She reached out and placed her hand on top of mine. "But what's a singer without beautiful words to sing? All I'm saying is you're good for him, even if he pretends that you're not. Plus, I think he cares about you, too, just from what he said when he called to ask me to stop by."

"What did he say?"

"To make sure you're okay. That he needed you to be okay."

And just like that, my heart skipped a beat from Ian Parker's words.

Holly leaned forward and placed her hands against my bruised face. "Who hurt you, sweetheart?"

I closed my eyes and took in a sharp breath. "Charlie, my mother's boyfriend."

"Does it hurt?"

"The bruise? A little less than before."

"No. Your soul. Does it hurt? Does it ache?"

I swallowed hard. "Yes."

She wiped away a fallen tear from my eye before smiling that kind smile my way. "My boyfriend before Harry used to use his hands against me. He'd bruise me in places where people couldn't see for a long time. From the outside, we looked happy. On the inside, I was dying. It wasn't until he left a big mark against my face that I knew I needed to stop the cycle of abuse. I felt humiliated. I wore so much makeup to try to hide the bruises; then I found a way to leave. Over time, the outer bruises healed, but the bruises on my soul took a lot longer. Then, when I found out my daughter's husband was doing the same to her, it broke my heart. No real man would ever lay a hand on a woman, except to show her his love. I hate that someone did that to you. I hate that someone hurt you."

"I worry so much about my mother," I whispered, my voice shaking. "She has so many bruises, both inside and out, and I don't see

104

them ever healing with her so wrapped around Charlie's finger. He's so abusive toward her, and I hate it. I hate how he hurts her, and I hate how she stays. I hate how she falls into drugs to cover her pain. We've almost gotten away so many times, but she always finds her way back to his toxic ways. I hate that she's so weak."

"No, no, no. She's lost, not weak. I've watched the drugs take over my Sarah; I watched how they changed her into someone that she wasn't. Your mother's mind is lost, and Charlie is using that fact to control her."

"What if she never finds her way home again?"

"We don't give up on people finding their way home. It's been years since my daughter and Brad ran off together, but you know what? Each night, I keep the porch light on, just in case they find their way home again. And I'd welcome them with arms wide open. You know why?"

"Why's that?"

"Because I've been lost before. Just because I didn't fall into drugs or anything, that doesn't mean I'm any better than them. Everyone deserves a home to find their way to at some point in their lives. It might not happen as soon as you'd like it to, but if their hearts are still beating, there's a chance it could happen."

"What do we do in the meantime?" I asked.

"Well, sweetheart, we pray for the lost ones." She gave me a tight smile. "And we leave the light on at night."

She cupped my face in her hands and kept grinning. Gosh, I'd never known a smile could heal until Holly looked my way. "But please know this. If Charlie ever lays a hand on you again, that will be the end of his life."

I chuckled and wiped my last falling tears away. "Why's that? Are you going to fight him?"

"No." She shook her head. "Those were Ian's words, not mine. He said if Charlie came near you ever again, he wouldn't live long enough to regret his actions."

Ian Parker was standing up for me, and that was enough to make the ache in my head slowly begin to fade.

"You covered for me today," I said as Ian walked through the front door after a long day at work. I knew he'd had a long day, because I knew the tasks that were on my to-do list.

"I did," he replied, rubbing the back of his hand against his forehead. He looked burned out and exhausted.

I gave him a smile. "I owe you."

"Well, actually, I owed you—for helping with the song a few days back. Even though you were sassy about it, you helped me a lot."

"It was mostly you to begin with. I just helped where I could."

"You changed it for the better, which brings me to the next issue at hand—and trust me, it pains me to say this: you were right."

"I was right about what?"

"Me having a wall and needing to break through it in order to tap into my emotions better for my music. The guys agreed after hearing the song."

A sly smile found my lips. "You performed the new song for your band?"

"Yes. They all loved it. So I need you to help me."

"Help you?"

He nodded. "I need you to help me create more music. Look, I know I'm an ass, and I've been an ass toward you from the jump, but hell . . . I'll do anything to have you help me with this emotions shit, because I don't get it, and it seems that you do."

My eyes narrowed as I crossed my arms. "And what do I get out of this deal?"

"I don't know. You can rub it in my face and mock me for the rest of forever?"

"Well, that does sound satisfying, but I want one more thing."

"And what's that?"

"You help me in the pigpens. You take half of them to clean yourself."

He groaned. "I'm more of an overseer of the pens. I haven't cleaned them in years." That was one of the perks of being a manager on Eres Ranch, I supposed. You handed out the jobs, but you didn't have to get your hands too deep in the dirty work. But if Ian wanted my help, he'd have to come down to my level.

"Well, that's my deal. I'll help you with the lyrics if you help me with the pens. How bad do you want that dream of yours, Ian?"

I could tell from his stare how bad he wanted it.

Really freaking bad.

I held my hand out toward him and smiled. "Do we have a deal?"

There was a moment of pause until he walked over to me and shook my hand.

"Deal. Just promise me one thing."

"And what's that?"

"No lady boners in the pens."

If my face could turn any redder, I'd be a dang tomato.

"Trust me, we'll be fine. But before we move on, can you say that one thing again?"

"What one thing?"

I pushed my tongue in my cheek. "That I was right."

He rolled his eyes so hard that I was certain he was going to damage his vision. "Shut up, darling."

Before I could reply to his comments, the doorbell rang, and Ian hurried over to answer it. "Can I help you?" he asked.

"Yeah, rumor has it Hazel Stone is crashing here," a deep voice said, making me look up toward the front door.

Garrett stood there in all black, looking moody as ever. My stomach flipped as the two of us made eye contact. A fire blazed in his eyes, and within seconds, he barged into Ian's place and gripped my arm. His embrace was tight. Too tight.

"What the hell, Garrett? Let me go," I hissed, trying to pull my arm free, but he wouldn't let it go.

"Heard the craziest rumor today," he sneered, his voice coated in anger and alcohol. "It seems someone snitched on Charlie. You wouldn't know anything about that, would you?"

My heartbeats sped up as I kept trying to rip my arm away from his hold, but I couldn't. "No," I lied, feeling my emotions building more and more with each second that passed.

My plan . . . it worked. It really freaking worked.

"Why do I feel like you're full of shit right now?" he asked.

"Let me go," I ordered once more, cringing at his tight hold against me.

"That was my uncle, my family. All of us were a unit, and you went and fucked that all up."

"He beat her! He beat my mom all the time, Garrett. He was going to kill her!" I cried, mostly from that truth, slightly from the pain of his fingers digging deeper into my skin. What was happening? Garrett wasn't like Charlie. Never once had he hurt me physically, only mentally; he'd never laid his hands on me. Not until now. Now, he looked so wild in the eyes that I hardly even recognized him.

"Yeah, well, sometimes a bitch needs to be handled."

Acid rose from my stomach and sat in my throat as I built up enough strength to shove him away from me. "Fuck you, Garrett."

"I did you a favor giving you a minute of my damn time. You think anyone else would've put up with dating your disgusting ass? And then you go ahead and screw over the only family you ever had. Only three people in this town outside of Charlie knew about the drop location." He grabbed both of my wrists in his hand this time and pulled me in closer to his body, pressing himself against me. His hot, intoxicated breaths brushed against my cheek as tears burned at the backs of my eyes. "Do you know what happens to snitches, Hazel Stone?"

It felt like a threat, but I knew it was more. Garrett didn't come from a family who offered empty threats. They always turned out to be more like promises.

Before I could reply, Ian rushed over and shoved Garrett, knocking his hold away from me.

"What the . . . ? Back the hell off," Ian ordered, his chest rising and falling.

Garrett stumbled back a little, taken by surprise. Yet when he regained his footing, he rolled up his sleeves and cranked his neck. "You know, I'm real sick of you preppy bitches thinking you own this town. Hazel and I were having a conversation that was none of your business."

"Yeah, well, it looked like Hazel wasn't really in the mood for talking, and seeing as how it's happening in my house, that makes it my business."

Garrett's hands formed fists, and he moved in closer to Ian. "Well, if she's not down for talking, maybe you and I should have a conversation, asshole."

Ian rolled up his sleeves. "I'd love to hear what you have to say."

"You guys, stop. Please," I begged, stepping between them both. "Just leave, Garrett."

He huffed. "Fine, but don't think we're done here, Hazel. You'll be hearing from me again."

That thought alone terrified me.

As he began to walk away, he turned back and flipped his lighter on and off in his hand. "Whatever your plan was with ratting Charlie out went sideways. He wasn't the only one busted, you dumbass. Your mom was there too. So congratulations. You got your mother locked up too."

11

IAN

"Do you want to talk about it?" I asked, knocking on Hazel's closed bedroom door. Since that Garrett guy left, she'd locked herself away in her bedroom.

I was still trying to piece everything together, but listening to Hazel sob on the other side of her door was fucking sad as hell. The past few days, her life seemed to be in complete turmoil, and I hadn't a damn clue how to help her.

But if she needed someone to listen, I was all ears.

"I'm fine," she sniffled. Her sniffles were enough reason for me to know she was lying. "I just need to get some sleep."

I didn't know her well enough to push her, but man, did I want to. I wanted to make sure she was all right and give her anything she could've needed to feel a tad bit better, but I had a feeling she wasn't going to leave that room anytime soon. So I gave her the only words I could think of.

"I would've done the same if it were my mom," I offered up. "I know whatever your plan was didn't go as expected, but I would've done the same thing. Think of it this way—as long as your mother is locked up, Charlie can't get to her, and she can't get into more trouble. It's a chance for her to get a restart."

I remembered when my parents used to go MIA, I'd hope that the cops would pick them up. That way, they'd have a place to sleep that night, and they couldn't get into more trouble.

"Haze," I sighed with my hands pressed against the wooden door, "if you need anything, I'm next door."

A soft thank-you was all I heard before I walked away to give her some space to think and reflect. I had a feeling she'd be up all night, thinking and reflecting too much.

I would've done the same thing.

When the door opened, I was surprised to see a puffy-eyed Hazel looking my way. I'd been convinced she wasn't going to come out until morning. "You know what would help take my mind off everything?"

"What's that?"

"If we made music together. I just need a distraction, and I think writing songs with you could help."

"Of course. We can hang out in the living room and start messing around with some stuff I've been working on—and failing at. I'll go grab my guitar and some pens and paper, and I'll meet you there."

"Okay, sounds good."

I began to walk away—and froze as I felt two arms wrap around me from behind. I looked over my shoulder to see Hazel holding on for dear life, and I raised an eyebrow.

"Sorry," she murmured, still holding on to me. "I just needed something to hold on to for a second."

"Go ahead." I turned to face her and pulled her in for a tight hug. "Hold on for two."

We stayed up well past two in the morning with one another, making lyrics that sometimes worked and other times didn't. Hazel asked me questions that were hard on my soul to answer—I wasn't one to dig deep with my emotions—but I tried my best to do it for her, because if anyone was having a shitty day, it was Hazel. She didn't need me being a hard-ass to her while she was trying to help me.

"What was the hardest day of your life?" she asked me, lying on the couch as I sat in front of her with a notebook in my hands.

"That's an easy one. When my parents walked out on me."

She tilted her head and stared at me with the most genuine eyes. "Tell me about it."

I swallowed hard. It was the worst day of my life, and I didn't like talking about it. Even though it had happened almost fourteen years ago, it still felt like yesterday. But again, for her, I'd try. "They said they were going out for food and I was old enough to stay home alone for a while. So I hung out all day, waiting for them to come home. When the morning came, I started getting nervous, but I still waited, because no matter what, they always came home." I scratched at my chin and cleared my throat. "Except this time, they didn't. I sat in that house alone for forty-eight hours before Big Paw and Grams came over and found me. I remember Grams falling apart and crying. They took me in right away, and my parents never came back."

"You were just left waiting alone? That had to be horrifying."

"It was. It's probably the reason I hate being alone, but oddly enough, I push people away so I am forced to be alone."

"Why do you push people away?"

"Because then they can't leave me."

She frowned, and damn, it broke my heart. "I'm sorry that happened to you, Ian. But you've done a pretty good job growing up."

I snickered. "I'm an asshole."

"Only on the surface. Inside, I think you're still that hurt little boy who's trying his best to survive."

Now it was my turn to frown as I tapped my pen against the notebook. "Hurt little boy . . . hurt little boy . . . like a lost boy. That's what I've felt like my whole life. Lost."

Hazel smiled, realizing that inspiration was coming to me. "I'd love to hear that song."

So I began writing it. It was hard, it was painful, and it was raw, but the whole time I wrote it, Hazel was right there, cheering me on and holding my hand through the emotions that were overtaking me.

For the first time in a while, I didn't feel alone.

The following day, I was more than ready to help Hazel in the pigpens. Sure, I was more than willing to get to work, seeing as how I wanted to tap into our lyrics sooner than later, but mainly my goal of the day was to make sure Hazel was all right.

She tried to deny my help at first, but I refused to back down from our handshake deal.

"Okay, if you want to start on the pens to the far left, I'll do these ones over here," Hazel said as we walked into the pens. "I'll pull in the hay after we finish, and you can leave early."

"I'll help you with that."

"I can do it on my own."

"The whole point of having a partner is that you don't have to do it alone, Hazel."

She didn't reply. I had the feeling she wasn't used to getting help from people. She had such an independent way about her.

We started cleaning the pens, and Hazel didn't say a word besides some grunting and grumbles when she stepped in a not-so-nice spot. Luckily, Grams had given her a pair of boots for ranch usage only; therefore, no more shoes would be sacrificed in the name of pigs.

Music was playing on my phone, but still, it felt uncomfortably quiet.

I couldn't stop overthinking what had gone down with that Garrett guy the night before. I couldn't stop thinking about Hazel and the state of her mind.

"Want to play confession time?" I asked her, trying to break up the awkwardness of it all.

She tilted her head in my direction. "What?"

"Confession time. James and I play it when we clean the pens to help time move faster." Okay, that was a lie. Confession time was something I had made up on the spot, because I wanted to know more about Hazel, and I knew she wasn't trying to give me any details on her own. "It's like, I say a confession, and then you give one too."

She narrowed her eyes. "What kind of confessions?"

"Anything, really. For example, I wet the bed until I was ten years old."

She grunted. "That is a confession you should've probably kept to yourself."

"True, but the more embarrassing or deep the confessions, the better. It makes the game more interesting."

She suspiciously said, "And what were some of the confessions that James shared?"

"Oh no." I shook my head. "Confessions that happen in the pigpen stay in the pigpen. So come on." I rested my head on the top of the shovel handle in my hand. "Out with it. What's your confession?"

She grimaced as if the game was the last thing she wanted to be taking part in. "I, uh, put ranch on my spaghetti."

"*Boooring,*" I hollered. "Try again."

"Jeez, tough crowd." She placed her pitchfork down and rubbed her hands against her thighs. "Okay. When I was thirteen, I stole a sheet cake from the grocery store for my birthday."

I whistled low. "We have a rebel without a cause here."

"I had a cause. My mom forgot my birthday—*again*. And she forgot to have food in the house—*again*. I shared the cake with a few kids in the neighborhood around mine, and we had a party. It was lame, and the gifts they gave me were like rocks and sticks and crap, but it was the best party. One of my favorite memories."

"How did you steal a whole sheet cake?"

She snickered a little and shook her head. "I knocked over a whole shelf of tomato sauce. While they were distracted by that mess, I snatched the cake and ran. I probably have some bad karma coming for me over that."

"You shared the cake, so I'm sure that evened out the karma."

"Is that how it works?"

"I hope so, because I've done some crappy things in my past as a stupid kid, and I hope doing a few good deeds nowadays would balance out the karma scale."

"Like giving a girl a place to stay."

"Yeah, well, I figured I owed you for being an asshole."

"Never truer words spoken. What's your next confession? Make it good too."

"I, uh, I don't think I like sex."

Her eyes widened. "What? Everyone likes sex, Ian. Especially you, I think, based on the number of women I've seen you with."

"Yeah, but . . . I don't know. I mean, it feels good, but it doesn't feel important. Not as important as everyone builds it up to be."

"Doesn't live up to the hype, eh?"

"Not at all."

"Then why do you keep hooking up with different women?"

I shrugged. "Just hoping to stumble into the mind-blowing sex people talk about, I guess. Just looking to feel something deeper."

"How old were you when you lost your virginity?"

"Fourteen."

"Holy crap. When I was fourteen, I was mixing potions in my backyard, not thinking about sex at all."

"Potions?"

"You know . . . making magic. Thinking about sex wasn't on my mind. It still isn't, really." She looked up to me, and her color rose high on her cheeks. "Confession time: I'm a virgin."

"What? No way," I said, pretending that she hadn't already revealed that fact during drunken-Hazel night.

"Total way. Not that I haven't had opportunities, because I have with my ex-boyfriend, Garrett—the guy you had the pleasure of meeting yesterday. It's going to sound stupid, but I didn't want to end up like most of the people in this town. I didn't want to end up like my mother—a pregnant-teenager statistic. I didn't want to have the chance of getting knocked up before I got out of this hellhole."

"That makes sense. My mom got pregnant with me when she was fifteen. I couldn't imagine having a kid at that age."

"Fifteen? And she left when you were how old?"

"Eight. She and Pops skipped town, chasing a high."

"I couldn't imagine doing that . . . walking away from my child after that many years."

"Yeah, well, you'd be better than most in this town."

"I'm sorry that happened to you. I never knew . . . it makes sense why you were so cold to me when you met me, seeing as how I had a connection to Charlie."

"Doesn't make it right," I countered.

"No, but it gives a bit of clarity."

I smirked and brushed my hand against my forehead. "Confession time, I have a fear of people abandoning me. Guess that's why I don't date. I can't get left behind if I don't let people close enough to abandon me."

She set her pitchfork down and walked over to me. She tilted her head sideways and studied me up and down. "Confession time . . . I knew there was more to your story than the grumpy man you presented yourself as."

"I'm still working on trying to not be an asshole and come off so hard."

"You're doing pretty decently, if you ask me. One step at a time."

"Any tips on room for improvement?"

"Just keep up the good work." She smiled, and fuck, my chest did some weird tightening thing. What the hell was that?

"Okay, I gotta ask you something, and I don't really care about the answer. Because, shit, it doesn't matter, and it's really none of my business, but curiosity killed the cat and all that crap . . ."

"What is it?"

"Are you really a witch?" I blurted out. "You mentioned potions and crap, so I just wanted to know."

She snickered. "Why? Nervous that I'm going to put a spell on you or something?"

"Nah. I mean. Maybe. But really. Are you into that kind of stuff?"

She shook her head. "No. I did it as a kid to escape the crappy world I lived in. I'd write spells in hopes it would change my future. In hopes that it would save my mom from her own tragedy, but at the end of the day, there's no such thing as magic. I was just a stupid kid who wrote stupid chants that didn't change a thing. But I do have a strong love for nature. For the stars and the moon. I feel like there is a healing connection to the elements of the world. As long as we slow down enough to appreciate our surroundings."

She was so much more complex a human than I'd ever given her credit to be. The more I learned, the more I wanted to know.

"Now, come on. Get to work, or we're going to be here all freaking night," she ordered.

I wouldn't have minded staying there for a few more hours getting a few more confessions out of her. I could've thought of a million things that would've been worse than spending an evening in the pigpens with Hazel.

"Wait, I have one more confession," I told her.

"What's that?"

"I think what you did to protect your mother was the bravest thing a person could ever do."

Her eyes softened, and she stilled her movements. "You really think so?"

"I do."

"Thanks, Ian," she whispered with a timid voice.

"No problem, best friend," I joked.

She smiled again, and I felt fucking privileged to witness the curve of her lips.

12

IAN

Hazel held up her part of the bargain. Every night after work, she'd sit up with me in the house, and we'd create music with one another. Some nights, we'd work for so long that the sun would start peeking through the sky.

She pushed me to open up, to dig deeper with my thoughts and my emotions, and it was working. Everything was pouring out of me in a way it never had before. The music felt realer with her help. It felt authentic. It felt as if Hazel Stone was the missing piece to my dream coming true. She was the muse I'd been praying for, and I hoped she'd keep helping me cowrite the songs that would change my life.

"What do you think of that, Hazel?" James asked her as she sat in on yet another one of our rehearsals. The same way she was growing on me, she was growing on the bandmates. Hell, I couldn't count on my hands the amount of times I'd found them around the ranch, talking about our music instead of doing their work. Eric and Marcus were addicted to going to Hazel for advice on their sounds, and she was more than willing to help them out.

"I think it sounds great. Maybe a bit longer of a guitar solo." She winked toward him, speaking directly to his soul.

"I can do that!" He beamed, picking up his guitar and strumming at the chords.

She did that for all of us—she made us feel excited about the music, and it seemed like a long time since we'd had that level of joy over our creations.

As the days went by, the guys and I worked harder than we ever had to create the next tracks. Eric was quick to post samples of the new sounds all over social media, and the response across the board was mind-blowingly better than anything we'd ever discovered in the past.

"Over three hundred thousand views in twenty-four hours!" he exclaimed late Friday afternoon. "Holy shit! And that was only a twenty-five-second clip! Just wait to see what happens when we release the full clip!" he breathed, sounding shocked as ever.

"This is it," James said, cheesing like a damn fool. "This is going to be our breakthrough."

"Remind me to kiss the hell out of Hazel Stone when I see her again," Marcus joked, and it wasn't fucking funny.

"Stay the hell away from her," I warned, sounding more serious than I should've. But the idea of Marcus kissing Hazel made my blood boil.

Why, though?

Why did that thought piss me off so much?

Marcus tossed his hands up in surrender. "Just joking, man. You know I don't kiss where my best friends are interested."

"What? It's not like that. I'm not interested in Hazel. I just don't want to kill a good thing by having you break her heart or something. I need her to keep helping me with the tracks."

"Right." James smirked. "And it has nothing to do with you developing feelings for the girl."

"Feelings?" I huffed. "For Hazel?" I huffed again.

No way. I didn't do feelings—except for when it came to the newest lyrics of my songs. In those, I felt everything. But in real life? Still stone cold. Yup. My heart was still closed off from feeling things on a deeper level for anyone.

"Sure, Ian." Marcus walked over and patted me on the back. "Keep telling yourself whatever it takes to help you sleep better at night, man."

I would, because what I was telling myself was true. I didn't have feelings for Hazel Stone.

She was just a girl who helped tap into the music in me.

"Confession time, I need your help," Hazel said early one Saturday morning as we were taking care of some housework tasks. Her hair was pulled back into a high ponytail, and she wasn't wearing makeup. She never wore her dark makeup on the weekends, only when she was working on the ranch and around other people, as if the heavy eyeliner and deep eye shadows were some kind of shield for her.

The dark, oversize clothing remained, though. Black on black with a splash of black.

I cocked an eyebrow and stopped folding the basket of laundry in front of me. "With what?"

"I need you to take me somewhere today." She brushed her left hand up and down her right arm.

"Where do you need to go?"

Her eyes darted away from me, and her stare fell to the ground. "To visit my mom in prison. It's a few hours away, and I have no other way of getting up there."

I nodded once, tossed on a pair of shoes, and grabbed my keys. "Let's go."

We rode the whole way almost in complete silence. Hazel kept fidgeting with her hands and chewing on her thumbnail with her back slightly to me. I didn't know what to say to her, because I wasn't good at knowing what the conversation should be like when you were driving to see your mom who was locked up in prison due to a call you'd made. Kind of a buzzkill, if you asked me.

So I turned to the one and only thing I really knew: music.

"Any tunes you want to listen to?" I asked Hazel.

She shrugged her shoulders and kept looking out of the passenger window. "Doesn't matter."

"Wrong answer. All music matters. So there has to be something you like. Anything, Haze. You name it, and I'll play it. As long as it's not complete trash."

"Really, it doesn't matter."

"Again—all music matters. Who's your favorite?"

She glanced over at me, and I swore I almost saw a little redness to her cheeks.

She had adorable cheeks . . . I didn't know people could have adorable cheeks. But they were the kinds of cheeks that you wanted to lean in toward and repeatedly kiss.

I wanted to kiss Hazel Stone's cheeks.

If that wasn't the craziest realization I'd had in a while, I didn't know what was.

"You can't laugh," she said warily.

"I promise."

"What does a promise from a boy like you mean to a girl like me, Ian Parker?"

"Everything," I confessed. "It means everything." I didn't know why, but I had the strange urge to do whatever it took to make that girl happy. She had so many sad moments in her life; I wanted to bring her some bright ones.

Her lips kind of curved up a little, but she turned back toward the window so I couldn't see the bashfulness resting against her mouth. "Shawn Mendes."

"Seriously?" I choked out.

She shot me a harsh look and pointed at me. "You promised!"

122

"No, it's fine. I just . . . I didn't expect a girl like you to like something so pop sounding like Shawn Mendes."

"What did you think I'd be into? Slipknot or the Grateful Dead?" she asked. "Because of how I look and dress?"

"Honestly? Yes."

She rolled her eyes. "You know what happens when you put people into boxes?"

"What?"

"They break out of them, proving you wrong time and time again. I'm more than my exterior."

I almost told her how I wanted to know about her interior more than anything, but I didn't want to sound like a complete needy moron.

I grabbed my phone and put on one of Shawn's albums. Hazel couldn't hide the smile that fell against her lips as she began mouthing the words to every song that played. Her fingers drummed against her thighs, and her head nodded to the beat. When the song "Perfectly Wrong" played, tears rolled down those cheeks of hers that I'd been thinking about kissing. I wanted to wipe them away. Shit—I wanted to kiss them away, but I knew it wasn't my place to put my hands against her skin without her permission.

She sniffled a little and wiped them away on her own.

"I like them, too, you know," she softly said. "Slipknot and the Grateful Dead. I'm a girl with many facets."

I was learning that second by second. She was a complicated woman, and day by day, I wanted to know all about her complex sides.

When we arrived at the prison, I had to park in a designated area. Hazel was constantly rubbing her hands against her jeans as she took in deep breaths.

"Want me to go in with you?" I asked.

"No. I have to do this alone. I don't know how long it will take, so if you want to head home, I can try to find another way back."

I cocked an eyebrow at her, baffled at her words. "I just drove you over three hours to get here. Why the hell would I leave you now?"

She shrugged. "The kind of people I knew would've left."

"I encourage you to meet better people."

"I think I'm on the right path," she murmured, almost so quiet that I missed it. Or maybe I made it up completely in my head and just wanted those to be the words that left her lips. Either way, I hoped I was on that path she was speaking of.

"I'm not going anywhere," I said, giving her my word and a small grin. "I'll be right here."

She smiled back and didn't even try to hide it from me. "Thanks, Ian."

"Welcome. Good luck in there."

She nodded once and walked away, with fidgety hands the whole way to the entrance.

As I waited, I played Shawn's song "Perfectly Wrong" again, letting the lyrics sink into my system. Letting a part of Hazel fall into my soul. You could learn a lot about a person based on the songs that made them cry.

It played on repeat a dozen times, and by the thirteenth play, my chest ached a little too.

13

HAZEL

Walking into a prison always felt so terrifying to me. They searched the visitors as if we were the prisoners. We went through metal detectors, then were scanned with another device. A thorough pat down followed. The first time I'd experienced that kind of procedure was when I was eleven years old and Mama had taken me to visit Charlie with her. It had scared me pretty badly, and I remembered having heavy nightmares after the process.

When I showed up now, the nerves still rumbled in my stomach the same way they had at age eleven. Only this time, guilt struck me too.

Up next was all of the paperwork I had to fill out in order to see my mother. As I scribbled down my information, I tried my best to not overthink my emotions. I kept trying to convince myself I'd done the right thing too.

I stuck a name tag onto my shirt and headed to the meeting area. I went through a gate and sat down at a table where I'd wait for a security guard to bring my mother out from the back. As I sat there, I drummed my fingers repeatedly against my thighs, taking in sharp inhales. Around me, there were other tables where inmates were conversing with their family members. Some laughed, others cried, and some didn't exchange words at all. They just sat in silence, staring at one another as if their stares said all the words for them.

When a guard brought Mama out from the back, I got to my feet, still fidgeting with my hands. I couldn't stop moving my fingers against one another if I wanted to. My nerves were too intense.

Mama's hands and ankles were shackled, and that broke my heart. She looked skinnier than she had before she'd gone in, which was very concerning, seeing as how Mama was already skinny to begin with. She was skin and bones minus the baby bump. I wondered what they were feeding her. If they were looking after her, seeing as how she was probably going through withdrawal from her drug usage too. She looked bizarre in the face. Dark circles sat under her eyes, and her skin was paler than normal, as if she'd been sick for days. Her hair was wild, tangled and knotted as if she hadn't cared enough to run her fingers through it, and her lips were chapped and split open.

Did they not have lip balm for the inmates? Not even petroleum jelly or something?

Oh my gosh. What had I done?

I'd thought turning Charlie in was the safest option for her, and after she'd gotten busted, too, I'd tried to convince myself that her being locked up was good for her, because she couldn't get into any more trouble. I'd thought she'd look a little better than when I'd last saw her, battered and bruised from Charlie's hand. But truthfully, Mama looked even worse than before. She looked broken in a way I hadn't known humans could crack. She was shattered to her core.

And it was all my fault.

It wasn't supposed to go like this.

She sat down across from me, and when her eyes locked with mine, tears flooded my stare. She looked so dead in the eyes—as if any light that was left inside her had been drained away.

"Hey, Mama," I whispered, my voice pained as I watched her skinny fingers fidget together, same way mine had. I wiggled around in my seat and tried my best to push out a broken smile. "How are you doing?"

What a stupid question, though I wasn't sure what else I could've said to her. What did you say to the woman you loved more than life, yet who you were also responsible for locking away?

She huffed at my question and looked away, picking a corner of the table to focus her stare on.

"Craziest shit," she murmured, shaking her head. "I've been trying and trying to figure out how we got caught, you know? Nobody knew about the drop location except Charlie, me, Garrett, and . . ." She turned her stare back to me and tilted her head in a knowing way. "Garrett stopped by and told me that you had something to do with this."

Tears burst out of my eyes, and I covered my mouth as her eyes pierced into me. "I'm sorry, Mama," I cried, feeling every rush of emotion shooting through me. "I didn't think you would be there. I thought it would only be Charlie."

"Why would you do that to him?"

"Because he's a monster. He was going to kill you. He was going to kill you, Mama."

"He would never hurt me," she sneered, shooting me looks of hatred.

Hatred. My mother, the only woman I'd ever loved, stared at me with so much hatred that I instantly began to hate myself.

"But he did, Mama. He hurt you time and time again, and I couldn't keep watching it happen. I couldn't let him do it to you." I sniffled and brushed my hand beneath my nose. "I know this isn't perfect, but after this, when you're done with your time, we can start over. You'll be clean, and I've been saving up some money for us to get our own place. We can go anywhere in the States. We can start over, Mama. We can build a new beginning and—"

"I took the fall," she whispered, making me raise an eyebrow. "What?"

"For all of it. I took the fall for Charlie. He'll be out soon, and I'll be in here for much longer."

My heart began shattering into a million pieces. "What? No. Mama, you can't do that! You can't take the blame for—"

"He's my soul!" she barked my way. "Everything I am is because of him, and I'd do anything to protect him."

That made my heart shatter completely. She was so warped in her mind about what love was and how it looked, how it worked, that she truly would go out of her way, give away her own life, for a man who didn't give a damn about her at all. She was right about one thing, though. Everything she was was due to that man. Her messed-up mind, her jaded lifestyle, it all existed because Charlie had poisoned her soul with his toxicity.

"But Mama—"

"I hate you," she sneered, the words hitting me like bullets to the chest. "I hate everything you are, and I never want to see you again. I wish I would've had the abortion when I had the chance. Being your mother has made me miserable. You're no daughter to me."

"No." I shook my head. "You don't mean that. I know you're upset and hurting, but Mama, I love you. I did this for you, to protect you."

"You ruined my life. You ruined me, and I hope your life from here on out is a living hell. I hate you."

Tears streamed down my cheeks at an impossible speed, and I didn't even bother wiping them away. I reached across to her to grab her hands in hope of her feeling my warmth, feeling my love, feeling me.

She pulled away before I had the chance.

"Guard, I'm ready to go back." She got to her feet and gave me a harsh glare as her hands fell to her stomach. "At least this time, the baby will take after her father," she stated, making my mind flip sideways.

"And Charlie will be able to take care of the kid once it's born, no thanks to you. Maybe this one won't be such a disappointment."

"Mama . . . let me help you somehow. Let me—"

"It's a girl," she cut in as she rested her hands against her stomach. "I always wanted a real daughter."

That cut me deeper than anything ever had before.

"I can help with the baby," I offered.

"Don't you think you've already done enough?" she asked as the guard walked over to lead her away. "I never want to see you again, and when karma catches up to you for what you've done, I hope it burns."

She was guided away, leaving me standing there with a hole in my heart and an ache in my soul. And the burning of said karma? It happened instantly. My entire being was set to flames.

14

IAN

When Hazel came back, she was in a frenzy, wiping fallen tears from her eyes at a rapid speed. I hopped out of the truck and raised an eyebrow at her. "Hey, you okay?"

She didn't say a word, probably because her emotions were too heightened. She toppled toward me as I caught her in my arms. She began to sob into my T-shirt, tugging me closer to her, and I allowed it. She was breaking, and I was the only thing keeping her from crashing to the ground.

I didn't know how long I held on to her. Five minutes, maybe ten. All I knew was I stayed as long as she needed me to be there for her.

When we started our trek back home, Hazel remained pretty quiet, and I didn't push her to talk. I knew she'd speak up when she was ready, and she did when the time came.

We were about two hours into the drive home when she cleared her throat. "She's taking the fall, so he'll get out before her and be able to raise the kid once it's born . . ." She cried harder. "It's not right. No kid should be raised by Charlie. I've been through that. It's not a good thing. And that kid won't even have my mom by their side . . . even though she struggled, she was still a mom sometimes. That kid will only have the monster."

"Shit . . . I'm sorry, Haze. I don't know . . . maybe there's a way it can be proven that Charlie can't have the kid . . ."

"I asked to help her, but she doesn't want my help." She shrugged and looked down to her hands. "She said I was a mistake. She said I was the biggest fuckup she'd ever made in her life and she wished she would've aborted me when she had the chance."

Her head lowered, her tears returned, and I hated the fact that I was now on the freeway and couldn't reach over to hug her again.

"That's a messed-up thing to say to a person. You didn't deserve it."

"Maybe I did. What I did was awful. And now she's going to be there longer, because I didn't think it all through."

"What you did saved your mother's life."

"I don't know . . . each night I've been having nightmares. I twist and turn in bed at the thought of what I did. I wake up in a panic, because I can't breathe. Then I can't fall back asleep. I don't think I deserve to sleep comfortably while she's in such a terrible place. Why should I be able to sleep peacefully when she couldn't do the same? I mean, what kind of monster would do that to their own mother? I figured she'd end up free . . ." She sniffled and wiped her sleeve beneath her nose. "I just didn't want her to die."

I parted my lips to speak, but she shook her head. "Can we just listen to music? I don't think I need comfort right now. I want to feel like shit for a while."

I agreed to her request and turned on Tool's second album, my favorite one.

We drove the remainder of the way in silence, even though I wanted to keep telling Hazel that the world was better with her in it. Even if it kept showing her reasons why she shouldn't have belonged.

I parked the truck in the driveway, and Hazel hopped out. She turned to me and gave me a smile, but it wasn't a happy smile or anything. I didn't know smiles could be sad until I saw the one resting on her lips.

"Thanks, Ian. Sorry you wasted your day."

"It wasn't a waste. I'm glad I could help you. If you ever need anything at all, I'm around."

"Thanks again." She snickered to herself and brushed her finger across the bridge of her nose. "I thought seeing my mom today would've brought me a little bit more comfort with today being the day that it is."

"What's today?"

She rubbed the palms of her hands over her tired eyes. "My birthday."

"Shit," I muttered. What a shitty birthday. What a shitty life. "Happy birthday, Haze. Sorry it was so crappy."

"It's okay. At least I didn't end up spending it alone."

Later that night, I heard her tossing and turning in her bed again. It made it impossible for me to fall asleep knowing she was in such distress. So without an invitation, I tiptoed into her bedroom. I quietly closed the door behind me and moved over to the distressed girl, twisting and turning in her sleep.

"Haze. Hazel, wake up," I whispered, nudging her in the arm. She sat up, alarmed and terrified.

"What?" she screeched, covered in sweat.

I shook my head a bit. "You were having a nightmare."

Her breathing became more controlled as she combed her hands through her hair. "Oh."

"Here, move over."

"Why?"

"When I was a kid, I used to have nightmares after my parents left. Grams would lie with me every now and again, and on those nights, the dreams weren't as bad. It helped to have someone lie beside me."

Warily, she scooted over and lay against the wall. I climbed into bed beside her.

As I lay beside Hazel, her body was trembling with nerves or fear or sadness. One of those things. Maybe all three.

I wrapped my arms around her body and held her against mine.

My eyes drifted closed after she felt safe enough to shut her own.

15

HAZEL

"Hey, can you come help with something in the barn house?" Ian asked, popping his head into my bedroom as I was writing in my journal. "Big Paw has this big log he wants moved, and I can't do it on my own. Meet me there in five?"

"Sure." I tossed on a pair of shoes to hurry off to help him. It had been a week since I'd gone to visit my mother, and for the past seven days, Ian had crawled into bed to lie beside me. I didn't understand why he'd been so nice to me, but having him lying beside me made it much easier to sleep at night. Whenever I'd wake in a panic, he'd be right there, soothing my troubled heartbeats.

I headed over to meet Ian at the barn house, opened the door—and gasped when I saw it decked out with decorations. Balloons, streamers, and a huge hand-painted banner that read, *Happy Birthday, Hazel Stone.*

There was a table set up with a huge cake and minicupcakes around it. Along with pizza and snacks.

"What is this?" I asked, my voice shaky as butterflies filled my stomach. Big Paw and Holly stood next to the table of food with smiles on their faces. Well, Holly smiled. Big Paw sported his grumpy face, which was one of my favorite looks on him. Beside them was Leah, looking as cheerful as ever.

"Can't you tell? It's your birthday party. We even went all out and got you a band," Holly said.

Leah raced toward me and wrapped her arms around me. Over the past few weeks, she and I had been spending a lot of time together. I never thought I'd be one to have a girlfriend as cheerful as she was—but it was turning out that Leah was a light in my dark world. Laughing with her had become effortless.

"Do you like it, Hazel? I did all the decorations myself, even though the boys tried to put in their input on it all. But I told them to stay in their lane and prepare their gift to you."

"Their gift to me?"

Leah grinned ear to ear. "Oh my gosh, Hazel. You're going to love it. It's really special."

Before I could reply, Ian and his three bandmates walked out to the barn stage. My eyes were wide as they picked up their instruments.

Ian wrapped his hands around the microphone and gave me a half smile. "The Wreckage has been together for years now, but we hadn't truly tapped into the depths of our music until a girl dressed in black came around and helped open us up to the possibilities of what we could create. Hazel, without you, these songs wouldn't exist. Without you, I would've never delved deeper into the music. These songs are for you; these songs are because of you. Happy birthday, Hazel Stone. I hope it's as special as you."

He looked to his bandmates, and the four of them held a conversation with no words, and then Marcus began on the drums.

It only took seconds for me to realize they were playing the songs Ian and I had been crafting over the past few weeks. They felt so unique and complete due to the way the band had pieced together the instrumentals. The passion they had for their music was showcased as I watched those four men fall deeper in love with their creation, and every inch of me belonged to Ian's voice. He moved on the stage as if it were made solely for his talent. His voice dripped with charm, smoothness, and sex appeal. Oh, how he looked so good up there, singing those words that he was delivering straight to me.

If I had a favorite day, it would've been that one. It was a memory I'd replay over and over again when my days got hard and my emotions overpowered me. I'd go back to that moment in time when Ian sang his songs solely for me.

That band was going to skyrocket someday soon, and I knew I'd be their biggest fan.

When the show concluded, everyone dived into the food and dessert.

"Why did you do this?" I asked Ian as he stuffed his face with another piece of pizza.

"Because you deserved a party. You deserved a good birthday. Sorry it's a week late."

"It's right on time."

"Oh! I almost forgot your presents." He dropped his pizza onto his plate and hurried to the corner of the room, where he grabbed a wrapped—terribly wrapped—box and held it out to me. "Wrapping isn't my strength, but it will do. Go ahead. Open it."

I raised an eyebrow and began unwrapping the package. When I opened the box, my eyes watered, and my chest tightened. There they were staring back at me—my combat boots. Clean as a whistle, as if they'd never stepped foot into the pigpens.

"How did you . . . ?" I asked.

He smirked and shrugged. "A lot of toothbrush scrubbing at first, until I found a shoe-cleaning shop. They did the hard work once I realized I couldn't handle it myself. I know it's kind of stupid and a cheap gift to give you something that was already yours, but—"

I shut him up by wrapping my arms around his body. "Thank you, Ian. You don't know what this means to me. What this all means to me."

"You deserve this, Haze. You deserve good things happening to you."

The party continued, and I received more gifts from Big Paw and Holly. They'd given me a cell phone so I would be able to get in touch with them at any time.

"I think cell phones are the devil's work, but Holly was determined to get you one," Big Paw huffed. "And whatever the lady wants, she gets, so happy birthday."

I thanked them, feeling very undeserving of everything that family had done for me. At the end of the night, after the party came to an end, Ian pulled me out of the barn house for one last surprise.

"You've already done enough," I said, feeling so unworthy.

"I haven't done nearly enough, but I hope you like this last one the best," he said. "Now, close your eyes." I did as he said, and he led me toward the final gift. "Okay, you can open them now."

When I did as he said, I gasped as I looked at the formerly broken-down shed that had been fully remodeled.

"What is this?"

"Well, it's your she-shed," he explained. "I figured you could use a nice place to create. I know writing is a big deal for you, so I thought it would be nice. Plus, if you ever need a safe place to take a break and look up at the stars . . ." He swung the door open, and I gasped as I walked inside. The ceiling was glass, and I looked up to see dozens of stars in the sky. There was a nice twin-size bed that I could lie on if I wanted to, and two Shawn Mendes posters sat against the walls, making me laugh.

"This is too much," I said, shaking my head in disbelief.

"You deserve it."

"I can't thank you enough." I turned to face him. "But I have this awkward fear of staying out here alone after all those weeks ago when these guys were outside the shed."

Ian bit his bottom lip and stuffed his hands into his pockets. "Confession time—that was me and James trying to spook you to get you to come stay at the house with me."

137

My jaw dropped, and I batted his arm. "Ian Parker, are you kidding me? You scared me to death that night!"

"Which was the plan . . . listen, to be fair, you were stubborn as ever, and if I didn't get you in that house, Big Paw was going to kick me out sooner than later. So, desperate times . . ." He shrugged. "Trust me when I say this shed is safe."

I narrowed my eyes. "I want to be mad at you, but also, this is the best thing I've ever seen, so I'll forgive you for now."

I moved over to the twin bed and lay down to look up at the stars. I patted the spot next to me, and Ian joined me.

The bed was tiny, and our bodies were pressed together just to keep Ian's big, broad frame from falling off the mattress.

"Here, let me see your cell phone," he said, reaching for it. He programmed his cell number into it and then sent himself a message. "Now I can send you annoying text messages that make you roll your eyes."

"Oh joy," I joked, but secretly I loved the idea.

I took the phone from him and laid it down. Seconds later, my phone dinged.

Ian: Haze?

Hazel: Yes?

Ian: I hope you had a good birthday.

Hazel: The best one yet.

Ian: I have a secret to tell you.

Hazel: What is it?

Ian: I stole the cake from the grocery store.

I burst out laughing and covered my mouth to shield my chuckles as I turned to face Ian. Jeez, how corny were we? Texting while we were right beside each other.

"You didn't steal it!" I whisper-shouted.

"Okay, no. I did think about it, but there wasn't a good pasta sauce display going on."

"You're a dork."

"You're beautiful."

What?

My eyes fell to his lips to make sure those words had escaped him. My pulse heightened as I became unable to think straight. What had he said? And he'd said it to me? No way. I'd been called a lot of things in my life, but *beautiful* hadn't ever been one of them. I had to have imagined it. There was no way Ian would've ever said those words and directed them toward me.

"I hate myself, you know," he whispered, "for the way I treated you when we first met. I was a complete dick, and you didn't deserve that, Haze. I judged you without knowing you, and that was a shitty thing to do."

"You don't have to keep apologizing for that. We both came in with our thoughts on one another."

"Yeah, but you only responded to my idiotic ways. You didn't come in swinging the way I did, and for that, I'm sorry. I'm going to keep apologizing, too, no matter what. So just let it happen."

As we lay in bed together, he moved in close, keeping me warm and keeping my heart racing. In the past few nights, I'd felt his hardness pressed against my behind when we'd cuddled, and I was beginning to fully understand why women seemed addicted to finding their way into Ian's pants. A pool of heat flooded my center, and flutters attacked my stomach. I tried my best to not think about it as his warm skin pressed against mine.

"Ian?"

He yawned. "Yeah?"

"You're my new favorite musician."

He snickered. "I bet you say that to all the boys who throw you parties, build you she-sheds, and clean shit out of your boots."

I laughed.

"I like that," he whispered. "Your laugh is my new favorite sound."

Butterflies, butterflies, oh, the butterflies.

I turned toward him and looked into his brown eyes. Then I looked down to his lips. His lips that had small breaths falling from them every few seconds. His lips that had a perfect Cupid's bow and were flesh colored. His lips that looked so soft.

So very, very soft.

"Ian?" I said once more.

"Yeah?"

"I love the new songs. They are perfect."

"It's all because of you. Those songs only existed because of you." He gave me a sleepy smile, picked up his phone, and began typing.

Ian: Good night, Haze.

Hazel: Good night.

He fell asleep before I did that night, because for the first time in ages, being awake didn't feel like a nightmare. I stayed frozen in place as his body warmed mine, and I tried to collect all the information of what had gone down over the past week.

Number one: Ian had slept beside me to help keep my demons at bay.

Number two: he'd built me a freaking she-shed so I could look up at the stars.

Three, four, and five: he'd watched over me, he'd shared his secret confessions, and he'd listened to mine.

Lastly, there was number six: the butterflies he left floating in my gut.

Oh yes.

We couldn't forget about the butterflies.

16

HAZEL

"Two words for you: *Bon. Fire*," Leah gleefully expressed, waving her hands in the air with excitement. She'd been stopping by the ranch to visit me—and the horses—almost every day since she'd picked me up on the side of the road. I would've tried to push her away, because I had a fear of letting people get close to me, but Leah was like a burst of sunshine on the cloudiest day. I couldn't keep her away if I wanted to.

"I think *bonfire* is one word," I joked, feeding Dottie an apple.

Leah rolled her eyes. "Don't be a smart-ass, Hazel. Two words, one word—it doesn't matter. There's the annual bonfire happening this weekend at the lakefront, and you need to be there with me."

"Are there going to be a lot of people?"

"Tons of people!"

"Partying and dancing?"

"So much partying and dancing!"

"And you said a ton of people, right?"

She grinned wider, as if she were going to explode from the excitement of it all. "Yes, yes! Pretty much everyone in town goes to the summer bonfire—one word, not two."

I laughed and shook my head back and forth. "Then go ahead and count me out."

Her mouth dropped open. "What? No way. You have to come, Hazel. It will be so much fun."

"I'm not really a big people person, so being around all those people seems somewhat like a nightmare to me. The only kind of people I really like hanging out with are fictional and live within the pages of a book."

Leah rolled her eyes and began brushing Dottie. "You're being crazy. There will be boys there. Hot, hot boys who are tan and buff and delicious. Oh, Haze, you have to come! You just have to do it. Think about it—bathing suits, drinks, and great music all night."

I knew Leah was new to what it meant to be my friend, so I'd give her the benefit of the doubt for misunderstanding everything about me, but the last thing I wanted to do was hang out with strangers in bathing suits.

Leah must've seen the resistance in my stare. "Come on, Hazel. You work so hard at the ranch, and you never really give yourself any days off. You think I don't see you working on your days off? You're a youthful workaholic, which is an oxymoron if I ever did hear one. So let your hair down and come to the bonfire with me."

"I don't know, Leah . . ."

She sighed and tossed her hands up in defeat. "Fine, fine. It's just too bad. The Wreckage is performing, and I figured you'd like to see them."

I straightened up a little. "Ian and the boys are performing?"

"Yeah. They've been the performers for the past few years. It's tradition." She gave me a knowing grin. "Wouldn't you like to see Ian perform in front of a crowd? I mean, I know he performed for you at your party, but seeing him in front of a bigger crowd just makes him larger than life."

"You mean wouldn't I like to see the whole band? Not just Ian."

"Well, the way your cheeks turn bright red when I mention him gives me the feeling you care more about him than my brother and the other two." She arched an eyebrow and leaned in toward me. "So is it true?"

"Is what true?"

"Do you have a crush on Ian?"

"What? What? No! No way! A crush on Ian? On Ian Parker? No way." Oh my gosh, every inch of my body was on fire, as I sounded so far from convincing when it came to my feelings for Ian. I couldn't count the number of times I'd caught myself daydreaming about his eyes, his lips, his smile, his dic—"We're just roommates," I pushed out, wanting to fan my face from embarrassment.

She wiggled her eyebrows. "A roommate with benefits is probably something you're interested in, huh?"

"No, Leah, not at all," I lied like the freaking liar I was in that moment. "Besides, even if I did have feelings for Ian—*which I don't*—he's so far out of my league I couldn't even imagine him ever giving me a chance."

"I'm sorry, but are you stuck on stupid?"

"What do you mean?"

"For a smart girl who knows that *bonfire* isn't two words, you sure are stupid, Hazel. Ian is crazy about you."

"Come again?"

"I see him all the time checking you out around the ranch, and when you aren't at their band rehearsals, he goes on and on about you as if you're every star in the sky. He's obsessed with you."

I laughed. "He's not. Trust me, if Ian was obsessed with me, I'd know."

"Really? So you think a man who spoons you every single night and builds you a she-shed isn't into you? I mean, I have a boyfriend and can hardly get a good-morning text, and you're getting whole sheds built in your honor! He's, like, in love with you!" she exclaimed.

"Shut it, Leah; he's not." But he had built me a she-shed. Did that mean something more than just a roommate being nice? Did Ian . . . ?

No.

No way did he like me. I wasn't his type. I'd seen his type. The tall, curvy girls who always smelled like expensive perfume. I wasn't the kind of girl who caught Ian's attention. I was more the girl who hid in the shadows, not the limelight, and Ian dated limelight girls.

"Just come to the bonfire and see for yourself. Now that I've awakened you to the fact that Ian is crazy about you, you'll notice it yourself. Trust me. A blind dog couldn't miss the connection between the two of you."

I hesitated before tossing my hands up in defeat. "Fine. I'll go, but it's only to prove to you how wrong you are about this Ian situation. He doesn't see me that way."

"Yeah, okay, wink-wink, nudge-nudge. You'll see, Haze. But there's one thing we need to do before the bonfire this weekend."

"And what's that?"

Leah's giddiness intensified times a million as she tossed her arms into the air in celebration. "A makeover!"

The bonfire was still a few days away, but thanks to Leah, I found myself watching Ian's every move around the ranch, and I'd come to one massive realization: Ian was hot. And sexy. And hotly sexy. I hadn't a clue what had come over me over the past few days, but whenever I was around him, my lady boner went full force. My eyes danced across him as if he were the best cooked steak in the world and I wanted to devour every single inch of him.

It didn't help that a few nights I'd wakened up from the dirtiest of dreams about him taking control of me. Every night when we'd sat down to work on lyrics, I'd had to force myself to not reach over and, oh, you know, accidentally swipe right on his penis.

If there was a dating app for Ian's body parts, I'd swipe right until the cows came home.

Calm down, lady boner; he's just your friend.

I kept telling myself those words, but it was growing more and more hard to believe them every night he crawled into bed with me and pressed his rock-hard abs against my body. Just watching him work around the ranch was making me hot. I wouldn't have thought seeing a shirtless, sexy man brush a horse could be so exciting.

Sure, it didn't sound as if it was an act of sex appeal, but my gosh, was it the sexiest thing I'd ever witnessed in my life.

"You want to ride?" Ian asked, glancing my way.

"Oh God, yes," I muttered in a deep whisper as my eyes danced across his figure in a hypnotic way. I shook my head, shaking myself from the daze I was residing in, and tried to keep the heat of my skin at a tame level. "I mean, what?"

He smiled my way, seemingly unaware of my current state of desperate need to slide into his pants. "Do you want to ride the horse?" he asked, patting Dottie's back. "I mean, it seems that the two of you are the best of friends, but I've never seen you out giving her a ride."

Oh.

The horse.

He wanted me to ride the horse.

Of course that was what he meant.

"I, er, I've never ridden a horse, and if I'm honest, that sounds pretty terrifying."

He laughed. "It's not as bad as you'd think. Come on; I'll help you out. We can ride together."

"You want to ride me?" I blurted out, then mentally slapped my forehead. "I mean, with me. You want to ride with me?"

"I'll ride beside you and make sure Dottie treats you well." He walked past me, brushing his arm against mine, and needless to say, I almost melted into a pile of mush. Every time that man came near me, my body reacted intensely. All I could do was pray that he never noticed.

He grabbed a saddle for me and then led Dottie out to the open field for a ride. He came back to the stables and picked Big Red to be his riding partner for the afternoon. As we walked outside toward Dottie, Ian helped me learn how to mount the beauty.

"Okay, so we have our stepping block set up for you to use to help you get on Dottie. Place your left hand on her mane, and then place your right hand on the other side. Place your left foot in the stirrup, and then swing your right leg over the saddle."

Yes, yes, Ian. Talk horsey to me.

As he said all of this, he helped me by placing his hand against my lower back. Once I was seated on top of Dottie, I felt as if I'd just achieved the ultimate life goal—I'd climbed onto a horse while Ian had assisted me, and I'd lived to tell the story.

"Well, this isn't so bad," I said, sitting on top of Dottie without a clue what to do next. Ian headed over to Big Red and saddled up like the hot rock star cowboy that he was. *Rock star cowboy* seemed like an extreme oxymoron, but I was wholeheartedly into it.

"Okay, hold on to your straps and move slowly," Ian said, pulling Big Red next to Dottie and me. He was close enough that if I needed his assistance, he'd be able to help me out. We started out very slowly, which was exactly what I needed, because the second Dottie began to move, my fears came rushing back to me.

"Are you sure this is safe?" I asked, feeling terrified by the whole situation.

"One hundred percent safe. Trust me, darling, you're in good hands. Just talk to me to get out of your head. Keep your mind light and your movements light. You're doing great."

"Okay, okay. Talk, talk. What do we talk about?"

"Anything. Tell me whatever you want. How about your name? How did you get the name Hazel?"

I snickered a little, thinking about that. "Funny story. When I was born, I had big hazel eyes. Mama said she fell in love with them right away, but she hadn't a clue that when a baby was born, her eye color could change over time. So she named me for my hazel eyes, even though down the line they'd become green."

"I like your green eyes," he commented, and I hoped to God my invisible lady boner wasn't poking into Dottie.

I gave him a tight, awkward smile, because I didn't know what else to say to his comment. I didn't know how to take compliments, especially compliments from Ian. If someone had told me the man I'd met weeks back who'd been getting a blow job from some random woman would tell me he liked my eyes, I would've laughed in their face.

Now, I was stuck blushing like a fool but hoping that the sunbeams were enough excuse for the redness of my cheeks. Unluckily for me, that wasn't the case.

"Do you always blush when someone gives you a compliment?"

"I don't know. I haven't received many throughout my life."

He eyed me up and down as he scrunched up his nose. "It makes you uncomfortable, doesn't it?"

"Times a million." I laughed. "I don't know how to react when nice things are said to me. Not enough practice."

"Well, shit. That makes me want to say more nice things to you to make you uncomfortable, because you're cute as shit when you don't know how to take a compliment. The color in your cheeks heightens, and it's adorable."

My cheek color probably heightened some more. "Shut up, best friend," I murmured, knowing I was redder than a Red Delicious apple.

"You have a beautiful face, Hazel Stone," he mocked. "Your eyes remind me of the stars. You have a perfect-shaped nose, and I've never seen a pair of ears that were sexier."

I laughed as I flipped him off. The moment I let go of the strap with my left hand, Dottie must've been freaked by something, because she took off at a crazy speed, sending me into a full-blown panic.

"Oh shit," I heard Ian mutter as he started off in our direction.

I grabbed the strap that I'd dropped to give Ian the finger and held on for dear life. "Stop, Dottie!" I hollered, hoping my soon-to-be-ex–horse friend would slow down her movements.

I flew up and down against the saddle as Dottie proceeded to lose her freaking mind, and that, my friends, was how Hazel Stone broke her vagina. Once I'd managed to get Dottie to halt, Ian rushed over and helped me slide off the saddle. Every inch of me was battered and bruised from Dottie's random burst of energy, but nothing, and I mean nothing, ached more than my vagina.

"Holy shit, are you okay?" Ian asked, his voice strained with worry. "I've never seen Dottie ever do something like that before. It's like she lost her mind for a second or something. Fuck. Are you okay, Hazel?"

I couldn't reply right away, because I was too busy bending over and holding my hoo-ha in my hands. You know what I always wanted in my life? A bruised vagina from horseback riding.

"Dang, did Dottie smack you down south?" he asked.

"Way below the border." I nodded. "One nice bump sent this vanilla bean straight to hell."

Ian raised an eyebrow, and a wicked grin fell to his lips. "You know what we have to do, right?"

"No, I don't," I groaned, still bent at the waist in pain.

"We have to ice it."

"Ice what?"

"Your vagina."

"My vagina what?"

"We have to ice your vagina."

The redness from my furious pain shot straight to a new form of redness from embarrassment as I stood up. "You're not icing my vagina, Ian Parker!"

"I'm just saying it's the best way to get the pain down, and you don't want swollen, um, you know . . . lips . . ." Now it was his turn to blush a little. Who knew that the playboy of the century could get shy from talking about my inflamed vagina?

"Well, if anyone's icing me down below, it's going to be me."

"No, I can definitely do it. That's what roommates are for, anyway," he joked.

I laughed in agony. "Roommates are for icing each other's private parts?"

"I mean, only the best roommates. Think of it as a roommates-with-benefits situation."

"And the benefit is holding an ice pack to my lower region?"

"Yep. It's a tough job, but somebody has to do it."

I shook my head. "And that someone will be me. Now, if you'd excuse me, I'm going to hobble over to the ranch house and swim in a pool of my own tears."

"Don't be silly. I'll carry you."

"You will do no such—Ian!" I remarked as he scooped me up into his arms. "Put me down!"

"I will, once we reach the ranch house." He waved over to another ranch hand and instructed him to put the horses back in the stables for us.

"No, do it now!" I argued, but secretly in my head, my thoughts were more like, *Oh yes, Ian. Carry me back to our dungeon and ice my hoo-ha and tell me I'm pretty and sing into my ear as you feed me dark chocolate.*

Had I mentioned Ian's pecs?

Hey, Rock? Meet Hard.

I grumbled as if I were irritated the whole walk back to the ranch, but truly I was wondering if that roommates-with-benefits situation was a real thing. Because once my vagina wasn't in a flurry of pain, it was going to take Ian up on that offer.

When we entered the house, Ian laid me down on the sofa. "I'll get you something for your situation. Stay here," he said.

I didn't argue, because I was pretty certain I couldn't move, even if I wanted to. My hand slightly massaged my lower region while he was gone, as I groaned in pain. When he came back, he had a pack of frozen peas in his grip and gave me a sloppy smile. "Sorry, this was all we had."

I held my hand out, not even caring. I grabbed the vegetable bag from him and slammed it against my lower half in unbelievable pleasure. "Oh my gosh, yes," I moaned in excitement from the coolness hitting my lower region. *Sweet dreams are made of peas.*

Ian sat down on the coffee table directly in front of me. He still had a smile plastered to his lips. "Is that enjoyable?"

I closed my eyes and nodded. "You have no clue. I never thought I'd dream of the day when I'd be able to place peas against my vagina."

"If you want, I can hold them in place," he said, tongue in cheek. I opened my eyes to see his mischievous smirk. "You know, just a helpful roommate."

"Well, aren't you just the roommate of the year?"

"I take my roomie duties seriously," he joked, eyeing the peas. Or, well, eyeing my vagina. It was hard to tell at this point. "You were doing pretty good riding until Dottie lost her mind."

"I know, right? I really thought Dottie and I were friends. Needless to say, we aren't on speaking terms for a while."

"I'd never seen her do that before. Maybe she was trying to be a wingwoman to help get me to ice you."

I laughed. "She could've found a better way to do it."

"Are you okay, though? I feel shitty, because it was my idea to get you riding. I figured it might've been a nice break from the day-in-and-day-out ranch work. Plus, you and I haven't had a chance to hang out outside of working with the band and working on the ranch."

He wanted to hang out with me outside of work and music?

Well, that was surprising to hear.

I combed my hand through my hair and gave him a weak smile. "Maybe next time we can just go out for ice cream," I joked.

"I'll keep that in mind. Damn . . . the guys are going to give me a hard time once they hear I put you on Dottie and she treated you bad. You wouldn't believe the hell they gave me once they heard I pretty much treated you like shit when we first met. They love you. It's like you're a manager to them or something. I swear, sometimes they come up with music ideas when you aren't around and say, 'We should run it by Hazel first. She'll know if it's good or not.' I don't know how you did it, but you got them all wrapped around your finger."

I smiled. "And what about you? Are you wrapped around my finger too?"

His dark brows lowered, and he leaned in toward me. As he pierced me with his stare, every hair on my body stood up with nerves. "I'm wrapped so tightly around that finger you could tell me to go dive into the pigpens, and I think I would."

I bit my bottom lip while my hand stayed placed against the peas. "I know I joke about us being best friends, but we are friends, right? Like, we're not just roommates and coworkers, right?"

"Right. You're my friend, Haze. I don't deserve to be your friend, but I'm happy I am."

Just friends, though? I thought to myself, but I didn't let the words leave my mouth. I shifted around on the sofa and cleared my throat.

Ian looked from my eyes down to the peas. "Are you sure you don't want my help icing your vagina? I'm pretty sure that would make me the best of friends, helping you out like that."

I smirked and shook my head. "I'm sure you have enough women that you could be icing down south if you wanted to, even though you haven't brought anyone home in a while."

He grew a bit somber and shrugged. "I don't find the need to hook up with random women anymore."

"Oh, and why's that?" I asked, somewhat terrified of the answer.

He narrowed his eyes in confusion, as if I were the slowest person alive. "Come on, Haze," he whispered, running his hands through his hair. "You can't really be asking that, right? I think you know why."

I blinked. "Maybe, but—"

"Because of you," he said, cutting me off, making it clear as day. "I don't want any other girl to try to give me inspiration. Because I have you."

No words left my mouth, because I wasn't certain if I was dreaming or having delusions due to my throbbing lower half. Did Ian just confess to having some kind of feelings for me? Did he just open up in a way that I hadn't expected him to do?

Did he like me in the same way I liked him?

He gave me a small smile and got to his feet. As he turned to walk away, I called after him. "Where are you going?" I asked.

"I think we've got some broccoli for your vagina. Maybe if I'm lucky, you'll let me hold that against you."

Oh, Ian.

You can broccoli my vagina anytime.

152

17

IAN

There were a lot of things that I didn't like about small-town life, but one of the best parts of Eres was our summer bonfires. We held a big festival each summer with a shit ton of bonfires going on around the lakefront. Every youthful person in town came to the bonfire festival, where they'd dance, drink, and be merry. The night sky lit up with fairy lights that I was certain a bunch of girls twisted around the tree branches, and music was blasting through the speakers whenever the band and I weren't performing. It was the best feeling in the world—summer nights and bonfires.

People seemed so free and lighthearted at the event. It was almost a guarantee that most people would end up in the lake, too, drunkenly splashing and celebrating summer. Even though our town had its issues, we didn't miss a chance to celebrate in the lake with beers in our hands.

"Who in the hell is that with Leah?" Marcus exclaimed as Leah and a group of her friends pulled up in the parking lot for the bonfires. They all looked pretty standard to me, but there was one girl wearing short yellow shorts and a white crop top that stood out in the crowd. Her dark hair was pulled back into a high ponytail, and she was laughing and smiling with the other girls as if she belonged, and holy shit, it was Hazel.

Her face wasn't plastered with makeup, and I swore her skin was glowing. She looked like she was floating on a cloud, and her confidence was out of this world.

"No way," Eric said, staring in the same direction as the two of us. "That can't be Hazel."

"It is." My jaw was pretty much on the ground, and the hard-on in my jeans was going to be a fucking problem, but holy shit, she looked breathtaking. I wanted to take her into my arms and slam my mouth against hers more than she'd ever know. I also wanted to press my body against her to showcase how hard she'd been making me lately.

I couldn't count the number of times I'd awakened with a boner against her back. There were times I had to sneak out of bed to go stroke myself to my happy ending, with thoughts of Hazel on my mind.

She looked amazing that night, but she always looked amazing. Only that night, she was wearing color. Yellow shorts, to be exact. Short shorts. And her ass looked amazing in yellow. Yep. She should've definitely added more color to her wardrobe.

"What are we all looking at?" James asked, following our gaze. "Holy crap!" he remarked.

"I know, right?" Eric said.

"How the hell did my parents let Leah leave the house in those short-ass shorts! I'm going to kick her ass!" he hollered, obviously not noticing the same thing us other guys were taking in.

The girls began walking our way, and Marcus patted me on the back. "You might want to close your mouth before she sees you gawking at her like a damn predator."

I shut my mouth, but not before telling him to piss off.

"Hey, you guys." Leah beamed brightly. "What's going on?"

"What's going on is you're going home to put on a sweater and sweatpants," James ordered his little sister.

Leah rolled her eyes. "It's like eighty degrees out, James. I'm not covering up. Besides, I'm over eighteen. I can wear what I want. Just like Hazel," she said, shifting the conversation over to the quiet girl who I hadn't been able to take my eyes off. "Doesn't she look great tonight?" Leah smiled.

"She does," I commented, eyeing Hazel up and down. I watched as her cheeks blushed from my stare dancing over her, but I couldn't help it. She looked fucking amazing.

"Come on, guys. Let's go get some drinks. While we're doing that, how about Ian and Hazel go grab us one of the bonfires to sit around," Leah said, sounding exactly like the matchmaker I needed in my life.

I wanted alone time with Hazel, but not the kind that was spent sitting next to a fire. I wanted to take her back to our place and introduce her to the hardness in my pants.

I gave Hazel a half grin and tried my best to stop thinking about how I wanted to own her body. As everyone began walking away, I nodded toward her. "You look beautiful."

She bit her bottom lip, and fuck me sideways, I wanted to bite it too. "Are you doing that compliment thing to make me feel uncomfortable?"

"Not this time. Just speaking the truth."

She smiled, and I loved it. "Let's go get some seats."

The rest of the night was spent with me gazing over at Hazel every chance I got. I didn't know why, but for some reason I felt like a damn fool around her. I tripped over my words and came off corny as ever without even trying. That woman drove me crazy, and I didn't think she even knew it.

Luckily, the band didn't give me too much alone time with Hazel to keep embarrassing myself. We sat around the bonfire taking in the smell of summer nights in Eres.

The boys had grown pretty attached to Hazel over the past few weeks, looking at her as if she were the mother hen of the band. They'd begun calling her "momanager" not too long ago. The Kris Jenner of the Wreckage.

Every now and again, Hazel would shout out, "You're doing great, sweeties," and the guys would blush like damn fools at getting her approval.

Hazel had that characteristic to her: she took care of people. She always went out of her way to help Grams whenever she needed it and to go above and beyond at the ranch for Big Paw. She worked harder than most of Big Paw's employees. Once I asked her why she pushed herself so hard, and she replied, "I want to work hard for all your grandparents have given me."

We spent the night around the bonfire, trading embarrassing stories about each other to see who could make Hazel laugh the most.

"I shit you not," Marcus exclaimed, taking a swig straight from the bottle of vodka, "Ian set Big Paw's hand-carved mailbox on fire while stoned, and when he realized Big Paw's prized possession was going to go up in smoke, he pulled out his junk and tried to pee out the flames."

Hazel was cracking up in laughter at the story.

"Luckily he'd downed a ton of soda, because I swear it seemed like he peed for ten minutes straight before realizing it wasn't gonna be enough to stomp out the fire. I swear, he waved his little Peter Pan back and forth like he was in search of Tinker Bell." Marcus chuckled.

"And Big Paw still doesn't know it was Ian?" Hazel asked.

"Nope. We made a pact to never tell. The Wreckage has a handful of secrets we aren't allowed to tell people," Eric stated, holding his camera in his hands. He looked down at it and turned it off. "I mean, I'll edit those secrets out."

Hazel laughed. "You always have a camera in your hand, don't you?"

Eric nodded. "If I didn't play the keys, I'd probably be a videographer or in the computer world in some way, shape, or form. I'm lucky I get to do all this stuff and play the keys, though. Just think, with all the footage I have, I'll be able to make a badass documentary for us down the line someday that Netflix will pick up. You see, with the way I do my recordings—"

"Stop talking nerdy to her, Eric! You're going to bore her to death," Marcus commented, taking a swig of vodka.

"Oh, no way! It's not boring. I think it's interesting," Hazel said, staring at Eric with the biggest smile. I wished she were looking at me with that smile. With those lips, with that tongue that sometimes grazed against her bottom lip.

Fuck, those lips. I wondered what they tasted like.

I shook my head and tried to control the hard-on that was determined to grow with the thought of Hazel's lips. I focused more on how happy and relaxed she seemed that night at the bonfire. Most of the time, Hazel was overthinking life. She wrote letters to her mother every week and never received a reply. She overthought how Jean was doing in prison and counted down the days until the baby would be born.

"She's probably around six months by now," she told me the other day. "In a few months, I'll no longer be an only child. Isn't that crazy?"

The heaviness of her words saddened me, because guilt dripped in her tones. So whenever she found a way to laugh, like she was doing that night, I took it in. She was so beautiful when she smiled, and I didn't think she had a clue how hard it was for me to not want to be around her every single second.

"Holy shit!" Marcus exclaimed, hopping up from the folding chair he was sitting in. His cell phone was glued to his hand as he stared wide eyed with shock. "Holy shit!" he repeated, making everyone turn his way.

"What is it?" James asked.

"Max. Fucking. Rider. Just. Emailed. Us," Marcus said, making James, Eric, and me sit straight up.

"Holy shit!" we shouted in unison, leaping to our feet.

Hazel sat still with a confused look. "Who is Max Rider?"

"It's not Max Rider," Marcus remarked. "It's Max Fucking Rider. The manager known for taking everyday, average artists and making them megasuperstars. He's like the godfather of music. He makes masterpieces."

"What did he say?" I barked as my chest tightened.

Marcus cleared his throat and began reading the email. "'Max here. The Wreckage, huh? Neat name. Came across and listened to some of your tracks on YouTube and Instagram. I think you got something. I know it's short notice, but I got some free time in my schedule next Friday in Los Angeles to meet up. Can you bring some new stuff to listen to? I cc'd my assistant on the email. She'll pass on more information on location, date, and time. Chat soon. MR.'"

"Oh my God, I just creamed my fucking pants," Marcus sighed, holding his hand over his heart as if he were going to have a heart attack.

"Holy crap," James coughed out, pacing back and forth. "We have to go! This is it. This is the kind of shit that makes and breaks people. We're going to LA next week come hell or high water."

Hazel celebrated just as wildly as us guys, because she could tell how much it meant to us.

"This is it," I said to her, pulling her into a hug. Pulling everyone into a hug. "This is the moment that changes our lives."

We proceeded to get shit faced and danced the night away as we slammed on the drums and howled at the moon like the freaking animals we were that night. After the guys headed home, Hazel and I stumbled into the house, and she kept singing the lyrics to my song, swaying side to side. Hazel Stone made the cutest drunk girl in the world, and when my lyrics fell from her tongue?

Instant fucking man boner.

As she stepped into her bedroom, I followed, not even walking to my own room to change.

She quickly turned toward the door. "Hey, Ian," she hollered, not knowing I was steps behind her. She crashed into my body and giggled, covering her mouth. "Sorry. Didn't know you were so close."

I moved closer.

She didn't step away.

"Sorry," I murmured.

"Sorry," she replied.

We didn't even know what we were apologizing for. Maybe for our proximity? Maybe for our drunkenness?

Maybe for our hearts?

Shit, I wanted to kiss her so bad my chest physically hurt. I was drunk and high on life, and Hazel Stone was the most beautiful human in the whole goddamn world, and I wanted her lips against mine.

She placed her hands on my chest and looked up to meet my stare.

Did she feel it?

Did she feel my heart beat and how it was beating for her?

"I'm so proud of you, Ian. You deserve this. You deserve all of this."

"I want to take our songs," I confessed. "I want to play for him the songs you helped me write." Over the past couple of months, Hazel had helped me create dozens of songs. Being around her, working with her, came so naturally. To the outside world, the two of us probably seemed like polar opposites, but to me?

To me, we made perfect sense.

She inspired me in ways I'd never been inspired. She pushed me to create songs in a way I'd never considered. She challenged me; she coached me. She was my muse. She was the music.

She was . . . closer.

She was so much closer than she had been mere seconds ago. Had I pulled her toward me? Had she moved in on her own? How did my

159

hands land against her lower back? Why didn't she try to pull them away?

"Confession: I want you," I breathed out, knowing that rejection was a possibility, but I felt drunk and brave enough to not care.

"Confession"—she swallowed hard—"I want you too."

"You're drunk," I whispered.

"I am," she replied. "You're drunk too."

"I am."

Her stare shifted away from my eyes to my lips and then back up again. "Play those songs. They're yours, after all."

"They're ours," I disagreed. "They are ours."

"But it's *your* future. I'd give you every lyric that lives inside of me to make your dreams come true, Ian."

My stare shifted away from her eyes to her lips. My stare stayed there. "The only dreams I have right now involve kissing you, Haze. I want to lie with you in that bed and kiss you until the sun comes up in the morning."

"Sometimes I wake up and you're still sleeping, and I think about leaning in. I want you more than I've ever wanted anything, Ian, and that scares me. I never wanted to kiss someone as bad as I want to kiss you."

"Me too," I confessed. "And well, now we're drunk and saying shit we probably wouldn't normally say, so there's that."

She smiled and I loved it. Fuck, did I love it. If the only thing I could ever stare at again was Hazel Stone's smile, I'd be the luckiest bastard alive.

"Maybe we should sleep," she said, nodding toward her bed. "Sober up a little and see how we feel about things in the morning."

"Yeah, okay."

I slipped off my shirt and pants, staying only in my boxers. I turned my back to her as she slipped into her pajamas.

We climbed into bed, and our bodies melted together as if we were meant to be fused as one. I kissed her forehead without much thought. I let my lips linger there too. My lips against her skin, swallowing in the small taste I was being allowed.

Her eyes closed as she moved in closer, twisting our legs together. Our foreheads rested against one another, and her small breaths brushed against my skin.

"You're my best friend," she said softly, her words piercing me. "I know your bandmates are yours, and I know I can't take their spots, but to me, you're it, Ian. You're my best friend. I've never had a best friend before, but I want you to know that it's you, and I'm so proud of you for your dreams coming true. This is just the beginning. You're going to be huge someday. You're going to be a star."

"You are the stars," I whispered, our mouths so close that if I moved an inch in, we'd be pressed against one another's lips. Fuck, that was corny, and fuck, I didn't even care. Hazel made me want to be the corniest asshole alive. "You've been my light, my muse, my inspiration. Haze . . . you are every star in the goddamn sky. You are my galaxy."

Her lips fell into a smile, and her eyes closed as she moved a bit closer to me and rested her head against my chest. As I inhaled and exhaled, I couldn't stop thinking about how I felt so alive with her in my arms. My heart, which I'd thought had died the day my parents had walked out on me, was fully functioning once more, all because of a girl who wasn't afraid to push me enough times to wake me back up.

We fell asleep that night, drunkenly entangled in a sea of wishes and hopes and dreams.

What if Hazel and I were meant to be together? What if our puzzle pieces fit seamlessly together? What if everything we'd ever wanted was right there on the other side of our fear?

"Ian. Ian, wake up," Hazel whispered, nudging me a little.

I squinted my eyes a bit and noticed a small pool of light coming in from her window. My head ached thanks to the large amount of drinking that had taken place. "What's up?" I grumbled, still tired. I looked toward the window, and the sun wasn't completely up.

Then I turned to Hazel, who was looking at me.

"Are you still drunk?" she asked, biting her bottom lip.

"No. Just a bit of a hammering headache."

"Yeah, me too."

I raised an eyebrow. "Did you wake me to tell me you had a headache? Want me to get you ibuprofen?" I started to stand up, and she placed a hand on my arm.

"No. I woke you because, even though I'm now sober, I still want to kiss you."

That got me to sit up a bit more. A sleepy, goofy smile probably appeared on my lips. "Oh yeah?"

"Yeah. What about you?"

"Haze . . . I've been wanting to kiss you for weeks now. With alcohol, without alcohol, shit . . . I just want to—"

She cut me off by leaning in toward me and placing her mouth against mine. Sure, she began the kiss, but I took the lead from there. My hands wrapped around her body, and I pulled her closer to me as I kissed her hard with lust, with want, with need. I parted her lips with my tongue and slid inside of her mouth, tasting every part of her and hoping I wasn't in some fucked-up dream, because I needed this to be my reality.

Her kisses tasted so sweet as warmth filled my chest. She pulled me in more, kissing me harder, allowing her tongue to dance with mine.

I felt her need, her want, and that only made me yearn for her more. Our bodies were pressed up against one another, and I was certain she felt the hardness of my cock against her thigh, but she didn't push it away, and I didn't try to hide it. I wanted her to know what she did to me, how she made my body react to her touches, to her kisses, to her.

If heaven was a kiss, it lived against Hazel's lips.

She pulled back slightly and nibbled gently on my bottom lip before lying back down against her pillow. I lay down facing her, and both of our breaths were heavy. Her eyes were dilated and wild, and she refused to look away from me.

Her cheeks blushed, and she combed her hair behind her ear. Her mouth parted, and she nodded once. "Again?" she whispered.

Fuck, yes . . .

Again.

18

Ian

"I'm going to fucking vomit," Marcus groaned as we walked toward Max Rider's house. We'd landed in Los Angeles the night before, and I swore not one of us had been able to sleep a wink. It felt like we were five-year-olds waiting for Christmas morning—waiting for our dreams to come true.

My mind was dazed and confused as we walked up the pathway to Max's front door. We were literally meeting the star maker at his freaking mansion to have a meeting about our music. What was this life? How did us dumb small-town boys end up having a meeting with Max Fucking Rider?

Grams called it destiny.

Hazel called it talent.

Big Paw called it hard fucking work.

Whatever it was, I was thankful for it. All I prayed was that we didn't blow the opportunity when we stepped inside of that house.

Max's assistant, Emma, welcomed us into the house. She led us to the studio, because Max Fucking Rider had a freaking studio in his home. We waited for a while, maybe an hour or so, and we were quiet as damn mice. It was almost as if we were afraid if we made a sound, *poof!*—the dream would be gone.

"Is anyone else sweating like a sumo wrestler?" Marcus muttered, loosening the tie that Eric made us all wear. "I swear, my balls are swamp-level moist. My dick feels like a sticky Slip 'N Slide."

"Too much of an awful visual, Marcus," James commented.

"I thought it was tastefully stated," a voice said from behind us, making us all turn around.

There he was in all of his glory. Max Fucking Rider, walking in on a conversation about Marcus's swamp ass.

If that wasn't a great first impression, we were screwed.

We all leaped to our feet with our mouths hanging open. Then, like freaking morons, we all started greeting the man at the same time, rambling on and on about how excited and honored we all were and bullshit.

"It's so great to meet you!" James said.

"We're so lucky you're taking the time out of your day," Eric commented.

"You have no clue how much this means to us," I tossed out.

"Dope fucking shoes," Marcus swooned.

Couldn't take Marcus anywhere.

"Okay, okay, enough ass talking. Let's just get down to business." Max took his seat in his oversize swiveling chair in front of his sound system, and he turned to face us. He clasped his hands together and nodded once. "I think you got something."

OhmyGodwehavesomething!

"Not saying that it doesn't need work. From what I heard, it was good, but not . . . great. It's missing magic. I asked you to come out here for two reasons. One, to see if you would actually make it happen on such short notice. To work with me, you have to want the dream."

"Oh, we want it!" Marcus exclaimed. "More than fucking anything."

Stop cussing so much, Marcus.

"Good. And two . . . I do better hearing bands live. Anyone can sound good online with all the whistles and bells, but to be able to perform live, as a unit, that is what takes the ordinary and makes them extraordinary. So go ahead." He gestured in front of us, where a set of drums, a bass guitar, a keyboard, and a microphone were waiting for us. "Show me your music. And not those same tracks I heard before. I asked for better. Give me your best. Impress me."

We all took a breath and walked toward his equipment. Before walking to our locations, we huddled together, and we had James lead our pep talk. We did it before every small-town performance, and if ever there was a time for James's hippie mumbo jumbo, it was when we were about to perform in front of Max Fucking Rider.

We held each other's hands and bowed our heads.

"We want to send out waves of love, light, and energy to the universe as a thank-you for bringing us all here today. This place, this experience, has been nothing but powerful to us all. This is more than we could've ever asked for and more than we deserve, but we swear to do good with this gift. We'll give our music so it can heal. We'll give our music so it can challenge. We'll give our music as a way to make this fucked-up world a little better. Yesterday, today, and tomorrow. Until forever," James said.

I squeezed the two hands that I was gripping, and they squeezed back as we all said in unison, "Until forever."

It was the pact we'd made since we were kids. To always be there for one another, until forever.

Then we took our rightful spots, I gripped the microphone, and we began to play. We played five songs for Max. It was hard to tell if he was into it at all, because he had a stone-cold expression as he listened, and his eyes were hidden behind sunglasses. Whenever we finished a track, he'd wave his hand in the air and say, "Next."

When he finally held up a halting hand, we all took a breath, exhausted, but more than willing to play all night long if need be.

"All right, come on out."

We were dripping with sweat and excitement as we stood in front of Max. Still, it was almost impossible to read him. I couldn't tell if he liked what he heard or loved it. Up until he took off his shades and gave a half grin.

"Where the fuck did that gold music come from?" he asked.

My heart exploded, and I hoped he couldn't see it happen.

"That was nothing like the recordings I heard on Instagram. This shit is magic. It's passion. It's the living, breathing, doing kind of music that I crave. What changed?"

James smirked and nudged me in the arm. "Ian got himself inspired by a girl."

"It's always a fucking girl," Max muttered, shaking his head. "I'm not one to bullshit or to waste my breath, so believe me when I say you got the 'it' power. Even your little cheesy family group pep talk before performing was important. You don't try to overshadow each other. You all shine because you work as a unit. You're tight, something most bands can't say about each other. You can easily be the next Maroon 5."

We all glanced at one another, feeling a little deflated by those last few words.

The next Maroon 5.

I knew what all of the bandmates were thinking, so I cleared my throat to speak up. "With all due respect, Mr. Rider, I don't think we want to be the next Maroon 5. We want to be the first Wreckage."

He grimaced a little, his brow low and moody. If there was anyone in the world who was hard to read, it was Max. Fucking. Rider. If he was pleased, you couldn't tell it. If he was pissed off, there was no way to know. His brain moved quick, and when he made up his mind, he made up his mind.

I felt sick thinking that I'd just shot myself in the damn foot by disagreeing with him about our future. If he wanted us to be the next Maroon 5, then we should've been fucking ecstatic about the fact. My answers should've been, *Yes, Mr. Rider. Whatever you say, Mr. Rider. We will suck your dick if we have to, Mr. Rider.*

I would've been willing to make the same ultimate sacrifice as the brave men of the Fyre Festival, and I would've gotten down on my knees and blown Max Fucking Rider if it called for it.

Take one for the team, Ian.

I shifted in my shoes and nervously coughed.

Max put his sunglasses on and stood up. "I think that's a wrap for today, boys."

He started walking away, and I felt as if I'd been sucker punched.

"Wait, Mr. Rider—" I started.

"I hope you're okay leaving the small-town life," he cut in. "Because we're going to be busy starting as soon as possible to make you the first Wreckage."

And just like that, our dreams came true.

19

IAN

"Tell me again," Hazel said through the phone as I sat in bed that night, reciting to her everything that had gone down with Max Fucking Rider that afternoon. The other guys were in the second hotel room, celebrating the successful meeting we'd held.

Max wanted us to come out in two weeks to be ready to work our asses off. Everything was moving so fast, and I hardly had a grip on what was coming our way.

It felt like an odd dream, and I was terrified I'd wake from it any second now.

I chuckled into the phone. "I've already told you three times."

"I know, but I love hearing the excitement in your voice."

I couldn't wait to get back to Eres to kiss her. Whenever I wasn't thinking about music, I was thinking about Hazel and those full, thick lips of hers. It had to mean something, the fact that when the good news came to us, she was the first person I wanted to share it with. She was the first person who came to mind. She was . . . my person.

"You are my best friend," I whispered, chills racing through me as the words rolled off my tongue.

More chills hit me as she said it back. "You are my best friend."

I didn't say the next words that crossed my mind, because I knew it would've been too confusing and too much, but I loved her. I loved her so much, and I didn't know if it was just a friendship kind of love or a romantic kind of love, but it didn't matter to me whatsoever.

Because love, no matter what kind it was, was a good thing. She'd taught me that through making me explore my emotions . . . she'd tapped into the love that still lived in me, even though I'd thought it was all gone after my parents had abandoned me. Love was a good thing, and Hazel Stone was a good fucking thing for me. She was the best thing, and I loved her so much it scared me a little.

The last people I'd loved that much were my parents, and they'd walked away and never looked back. Love felt so good, but in the back of it was the fear that it could someday slip away. I wouldn't tell her yet. I'd keep the love thing to myself and hold on to it as long as I could.

"Confession time," she said, as I lay against my pillow with one hand resting against the back of my head. "I didn't sleep that well without you next to me."

"Confession time. I've been hugging my pillow each night thinking it's you."

"Confession time. I miss your smile."

"Confession time. I miss your laugh."

"Confession time . . ." She took a deep inhalation and released it slowly as each word fell from her lips. "I . . . miss . . . you."

"I miss you more."

"Not possible."

"Always possible."

"When you get back, can we kiss some more?" she asked.

I chuckled. "Hazel, when I get back, all we are going to do is kiss. In the pigpens. In the house. In the barn house. In the streets. I'm going to steal so many kisses from you to save up for while I'm gone in Los Angeles."

She went quiet for a second. "You're really moving to LA, huh? This is really happening."

That was the first moment it hit me that we were really moving on to Los Angeles. That our lives were truly about to change forever. Shit.

"You realize how big this is, right, Ian? This is the biggest opportunity of your life, and it's Max Fucking Rider," she dramatically exclaimed, somehow sounding more excited than I did.

We stayed on the phone that night until Marcus and James came back to the room to crash. After they were asleep, I asked Hazel if I could call her back. She said of course, and I slept with the phone pressed against my ear. We were going to fall asleep with one another, even though we were miles apart.

When I heard her small snores, I let my eyes go heavy too.

20

HAZEL

While the guys were in Los Angeles getting the keys to their dreams, I was back in Eres trying my best to stomp out my nightmares. I'd been writing Mama letters nonstop, looking to get an idea of how she was doing. I assumed they took care of the pregnant inmates to some extent, but based on the knowledge I had on the subject—a.k.a. watching prison documentaries on Netflix and crying real tears during every single one—I had a heavy set of fears.

Was she getting her vitamins? Was the baby healthy with her past drug usage? Would the child really go to Charlie once he got out?

As far as I knew, Charlie was still locked up, and I was thankful for that. What I wasn't thankful for was the fact that I had no way of knowing how my mother was doing. If she was being cared for, if she was scared.

Of course, she had to be scared. How could she not be?

When my thoughts became too loud and every terrifying thought passed through my mind, I built up enough courage to take myself to my old neighborhood and to knock on Garrett's door.

I wore one of Ian's oversize hoodies and had the hood up. I'd been sleeping in his hoodies each night since he left. I liked how they still smelled like him. It almost felt as if he were there with me each night.

My eyes kept darting around the trailer park with hopes that no one would notice me being there. Garrett's past words kept playing in my head.

You know what happens to snitches?

When he came to the door, he grumbled as he pushed the screen open. A cigarette hung from between his lips, and he huffed out a cloud of smoke. "You got a lot of fucking nerve coming over here," he muttered.

"Yeah, I know, but I couldn't think of what else to do. I've been trying to get in contact with my mom, but she won't reply to any of my letters. I'm not allowed to go visit anymore, and I'm worried about her."

"Oh yeah? You're worried about the mother you got locked up? How fucking thoughtful of you," he sarcastically remarked, blowing more smoke directly into my face. He looked wrecked—as if he'd been using more than normal. When we were together, he'd never looked as strung out as his current state. He'd lost a lot of weight, it seemed, seeing as how his jeans were sitting so low against his hip bones. Had he been eating? Was he taking an inch of care of himself?

I swallowed hard and did my best to push the thought away.

Not my concern anymore.

I grimaced. "I just want to know that she's all right. Have you been in contact with her?"

"Like I'd ever tell you shit."

"Please, Garrett," I pleaded. I wasn't above begging. I needed answers to the questions shooting through my head day in and day out. "I only want to know that the baby is okay and what will happen when it's delivered, since I don't know if Charlie is going to be out of prison to take care of it. Do you know any of that, Garrett? Do you know anything?"

Garrett gave me a smirk that sent unnerving chills down my spine. "Maybe I do."

"Please," I begged again. I sounded so desperate, but I didn't care. If he wanted me to drop to my knees in front of his freaking trailer, I'd do it and grovel at his shoes.

"You need to get the hell out of here before I let people know you're back around these parts," he threatened, making my chest tighten with fear.

I took a step back. "Okay. But please . . . can you just make sure the baby is okay? I know you hate me, and I can't blame you for that. I hate myself enough for the both of us. But if you care anything about that child, please make sure it ends up cared for. You know what it's like growing up in these parts, Garrett. You were luckier, because your mom is actually a good mom, but you know the lives that most of the kids in these parts grow into. You know the world I grew up in. This child deserves more than that. It deserves more."

I left it at that and started walking away.

"Hazel." The sound of my name made me turn around. Garrett stood tall, still smoking that cigarette that was dangling between his lips. "It's a girl."

A small breath fell from me as a wave of emotions rushed through me. "I know. She told me."

He put his cigarette out on his railing and tossed it toward the graveled road. "She hates being pregnant, and fuck, it looks like it's doing a number on her, but she's all right. My ma and I went to see her last week."

"Does she need anything? Money? Supplies? Lip balm?" I blurted out, my heart racing faster and faster each second.

He shrugged. "Everybody needs that shit. If you want, you can drop it off to me in two weeks, when Ma and I go visit her again. And Ma's going to take in the baby for the time being."

Sadie was taking in the baby.

The baby girl.

My little sister.

That was good. Sadie had her fair share of flaws, but being a bad mother wasn't one of them. I remembered being young and wishing my mom did some of the things Sadie had done for Garrett. Taking him to the park. Driving out to go on movie dates. Buying him Christmas gifts every single year. It might've been iffy how she got the money to do all of those things, but every cent she'd ever had went to that child.

So much comfort fell over me knowing those details.

"I'll bring the stuff in two weeks. Thank you, Garrett."

"Whatever. Get lost, will you?" he said, reaching into his cigarette pack and pulling out another one to light up. "I'm tired of seeing your fucking face."

I didn't argue his request. I hurried away with a bit of calmness to my heart as I headed back to Ian's house. Garrett's words flew through my head on repeat as I walked.

When I reached the house, I saw Ian's pickup truck sitting in the driveway, and I rushed inside the house.

He was home! Ian was back, and I had so much to tell him, so much to share. So many kisses to make up due to lost time. I searched the whole house and didn't find Ian anywhere.

I headed up to my room to change, and as I opened my bedroom door, a smile fell against my lips as I saw Ian sitting there on my bed, waiting for me.

"Hi," he said, getting to his feet.

"Hi," I replied.

"Again?" he asked, raising an eyebrow. I knew exactly what he was referring to too.

I walked over to him, wrapped my arms around his body, and stood on my tiptoes to reach his lips, and I kissed him.

Again.

I wished I had a remote control that was able to freeze time. To pause on beautiful moments, to rewind those same seconds to replay the best parts. The next two weeks of my time with Ian and the rest of the band flew by too fast. I tried my best to be present in every situation, but the weight of it all changing in a few days was more than I could handle.

I wished things were different. I wished I had more time to hold philological conversations with James. I wished I had more time to talk to Eric about his passion for social media. I wished I could've listened to more of Marcus's bad jokes.

I wished I had more kisses with Ian. More everything with him, really.

If there was a world where the both of us stayed in place, I'd be completely his by tomorrow. Yet the sad truth of it all was we didn't have a tomorrow. We only had that day.

Big Paw and Holly were throwing the guys a going-away party in the barn house, and everyone in town came to it. They were known for hosting big events, and since it came with free food and drinks, every-one always showed up.

Their parties were a breath of fresh air in a very toxic town.

I'd been wandering around the party, looking for Ian, for the past twenty or so minutes.

"You're not going to find him in here," a voice said, making me turn around.

I smiled to James, who was holding a soda can in his hand. "Where is he?" I asked.

"Waiting for you."

"But where?"

He smiled. "The same place we scared you out of all those weeks ago. Sorry about that, by the way."

I laughed.

The shed.

James placed a hand on my arm and gave me another grin. "Hazel, thank you for everything you've done for this band, for Ian. I don't even know if we would've had this opportunity if it wasn't for you."

"You guys were good enough without me."

"Yeah, but you made us better. You made him better. So thank you for that. I'd never seen him really love a girl before. It looks good on him."

My heart skipped a million beats.

Love?

Ian loved me?

James must've seen the panic in my eyes, because he shifted his stare away from mine and tried to backpedal. "I mean, er, like, he has love for you. I mean, what I meant to say . . . ah, shit. Foot in mouth. Anyway, Ian's at the shed."

"Thanks, James."

"No problem. And Haze?"

"Yes?"

"Can you keep it on the down low about the fact that Ian loves you? I didn't mean to spoil it before he said it to you. Shit. I don't want to ruin that moment for him telling you whenever it happens."

"Maybe it won't happen," I argued.

"Trust me"—he shook his head—"it will. Just wait and see. And hell, act surprised, will you? But not too surprised. The normal amount of surprised. Not too much and not too little."

I chuckled and nodded. "Will do. Did he tell you that he loved me during your confession-time game?"

James lowered his eyebrows, perplexed. "Confession-time game?"

"You know, the game you two play in the pens when cleaning them. To make time go faster."

"Uh, I have no clue what you're talking about."

He seemed completely thrown off by my comment, and those butterflies came flying back to me in an instant.

Oh, Ian. You and your lies to get to know me.

21

IAN

People always said you'd miss home the minute you left it, but I didn't believe that. I wasn't going to miss that place—not for a minute. I wouldn't miss working in the pigpens or going around town with small-minded people. I wouldn't miss manure or moving hay. I wouldn't miss the mosquitoes that were out for murder. I wouldn't miss the things that made up Eres, but there were people I'd miss.

Three, to be exact.

I'd miss Grams and her homecooked meals. I'd miss how she'd still come over to my place and fold my laundry, even though I'd tell her I could do it on my own. I'd miss her hugs and comfort. Her wise words. Her positive persona. Her daily doses of love.

I'd miss Big Paw too. I'd probably even miss him chewing out my ass over stupid things. I'd miss his hard-knock style of parenting. I'd miss his almost smirks, when you did something to make him proud. I'd miss his attitude and tough love.

Then there was Hazel. I'd miss every single thing about her. Even the things I had yet to discover.

I sat inside the shed as I stared at the stars in the sky. A few hundred feet away was the barn house, where an energetic party was taking place. I'd told my grandmother that the boys and I hadn't wanted a going-away party, so of course she and Big Paw had thrown us a going-away party.

"Are you going to sit in here all night reflecting, or are you going to come down to this party of yours and celebrate breaking free?" a voice asked.

I glanced up to see Hazel wearing one of my hoodies and black shorts. Her thighs looked smooth and thick, and fuck, I wanted to bury myself between them and stay for a while. She was wearing her favorite pair of lucky black shoes. My shoes. There was no denying that they looked better on her than they'd ever looked on me.

"You know I don't give a damn about that party," I answered. "I'd rather have my last night hanging out with the people I care about the most."

"Like who?"

I gave her a knowing grin. The color on her cheeks heightened as she returned the smile.

Those fucking kissable cheeks.

"How about you come outside and hang out with me. I feel like swinging on the tires."

I did as she said and met her outside of the shed.

She started wandering off in the direction of the old tire swings set up against the two big oak trees on the ranch. Right behind the tire swings was a wishing well that had been out of commission since before I was born, but still people would come around and toss their coins into the well in hopes that their dreams would come true.

Hazel reached into her back pocket and pulled out two coins. "Do you believe in magic?" she asked.

"Ever since you, I'm starting to a little more each day."

She handed me a coin. "Then make a wish. Make it a good one. I've heard about this wishing well. How people have wished for money and babies and marriage. Then all of their wishes come true."

179

I went to toss the coin into the well, and Hazel leaped in front of me. "Wait, Ian! You can't just toss it in. You have to take your time and make sure your wish is clear as day. You only get one shot at getting the wording right. Make your wish count."

I gave her a sloppy smirk and flung my coin into the well.

She frowned and held her coin close to her heart, closed her eyes, and tilted her head up to the moon. It was a crescent moon. If you had asked me months ago if I knew the difference between a full moon, new moon, and crescent moon—both waxing and waning—I would've called you crazy.

But that was the type of crap I knew now, all because of Hazel and her intriguing mind.

She brought the coin to her lips before opening her eyes and tossing the coin into the well and then swung around on her heels to face me. "I bet my wish comes true before yours, since I took my time with it."

"What did you wish for?"

"You can't tell people your wish, otherwise it voids it out." She narrowed her eyes. "What did you wish for?"

"Oh no. You're not screwing up my wish."

Once we reached the swings, we didn't talk much. Hazel would look up to the stars with such wonderment in her stare. Sometimes she'd close her eyes, and I swore she was making more wishes.

"You hear that song, Ian?" she asked, swaying back and forth on her tire.

"Yeah, I hear it."

"It's one of my favorites."

"Oh? What is it?"

She shrugged. "Don't know, but I can tell it's going to be a favorite from the beat."

I laughed. "You're weird sometimes."

"I'm always weird." All of a sudden Hazel leaped up from her seat and held her hand out toward me. "Come dance with me."

"What? No. It's a slow song. I don't dance to slow songs."

"Do you dance to fast songs?"

I paused. "Well, no."

"Ian Parker, if you don't get off your tailbone and dance with me, then I swear I'll tell everyone you were the one who set Big Paw's mailbox on fire."

I cocked an eyebrow. "You wouldn't dare."

She pushed her tongue in her cheek and placed her hands on her hips. "Try me."

"That goes against the wolf pack rules."

"Luckily I'm not a part of the wolf pack."

I laughed. "After these past few months, I think you're more a part of the wolf pack than I am. You wouldn't really tell Big Paw."

"You want to bet on it?"

I narrowed my eyes at her, and she narrowed hers right back.

She's bluffing.

She has to be.

I shook my head. "What does it matter? I'm leaving this town come morning, anyway."

"You think Big Paw won't track you down to kick your ass for ruining his mailbox?" she asked.

Well, yeah.

I knew he would. He'd carved that mailbox by hand over twenty-five years ago. That mailbox was older than me, and it had probably pissed Big Paw off a lot less than I did.

I stood up from my tire and pointed a finger her way. "If I dance with you, you can't hold the mailbox thing over my head again."

"I won't."

"Promise?"

She took her fingers and made a cross over her chest. "Cross my heart, hope to die."

If she weren't so annoying right then, I would've thought she was cute.

Who was I kidding? She was beautiful.

"I get to lead," I told her.

"Wouldn't have it any other way," she replied, holding her hand out.

I reluctantly took her hand into mine, and we began to dance to the slow song that she hadn't known but was certain was her new favorite.

"*Ouch!*" She jumped back seconds after I stepped on her foot.

"Sorry," I muttered. "I told you I don't slow dance."

She regrouped and moved in close again. "It's fine. You can only get better with practice."

We danced back and forth, and Hazel laid her head against my shoulder. As we swayed, she hummed the song as if she knew every word.

"See?" she whispered. "Isn't this nice?"

I didn't reply, but truth was I didn't hate it. I hated a lot of things about small-town Eres, but slow dancing with Hazel wasn't one of them.

"Are you scared, Ian? About leaving home?"

"Not at all," I quickly replied. There was nothing scary about leaving town and going off to Los Angeles to chase my music career. The only scary thing to me was staying in a small town and never reaching my dreams.

If I didn't leave Eres tomorrow, I was almost certain I'd never get away.

"Then I'll be scared for you," she commented, holding me tighter, and I allowed it, because all I wanted to do for the next fifteen hours was hold her close to me. "I just don't want you to lose yourself, you know. People often go chasing after this big Hollywood dream, and they lose themselves."

"What do you know about people chasing their Hollywood dreams? Nobody we know has ever done what my band and I are doing."

"I know, but I've seen enough movies to know that Hollywood changes people."

Maybe.

Not me, though.

I just wanted to play my music for a bigger crowd than the old folks down at the barn house.

"I'll be fine," I told her.

"Good, because I like you the way you are. You know what, Ian?"

"What's up?"

Hazel looked up at me with teary eyes and shook her head a little. "Sometimes I think about you not being around anymore, and my heart hurts a lot."

"Come on, Hazel. Don't get too emotional. I'll be back."

"No, you won't," she whispered, laying her head back against my shoulder.

I didn't reply, because I knew she was pretty much right, and by the time I came back, she'd probably be gone chasing her own dreams.

"I'm going to miss you so much, Ian," she confessed.

We kept dancing between the tire swings, Hazel kept smiling my way, and jeez, *I'm going to miss that smile.*

The song shifted to a faster one, but we kept our slow speed going.

She looked up at me and gave me another smile. This time it was sadder. "Again?"

I kissed her.

I kissed her slowly and gently and let my lips linger, because I was too afraid to pull away from her.

"Haze . . . ," I whispered, looking into her eyes. I felt everything for that girl. I wanted to tell her about the words flying through my head. I wanted her to know how love was racing through every fiber of my existence and that love belonged to her. But I was scared, because come morning, I'd be gone. Come morning, I couldn't do anything about said love.

She looked at me and nodded. "I know, Ian," she softly said, as if she could read my thoughts and my messy mind. "Me too."

Her head fell back to my shoulder, and we swayed for the remainder of the evening. Then I took her to her bedroom and held her one last time.

As we lay in bed, I began to close my eyes but stopped once I felt a hand slightly stroking against my boxers. If there was anything that would wake a tired man up, it was a hand moving against his cock.

I tilted my head to look her way, wondering if the slight touch was a sleepy mistake, but her stare was fully focused on me as she did the act. She fingered the band of my boxers before pulling it away from my skin, making enough room for her to slide her hand inside. As she gripped my cock, she began stroking it up and down slowly, keeping full eye contact with me as she did so. Then she added a small bit of pressure to her strokes, making me moan in pleasure from the slight sensation she delivered me.

She pulled her hand out of the boxers for a second and licked the palm, then sucked on each of her fingers, getting her hand completely lubricated, before sliding it back in and making her strokes a tad bit faster. My cock grew in her hand as she turned me on, gliding her hand over my head and moving it down to the shaft. Every time she stroked it, my mind wanted to explode.

"Haze . . . just like . . . that," I sighed, unable to keep my eyes open as the sensation of desire overtook me.

She sat up in the bed and began pulling my boxers down my legs. She tossed them to the side of the room and lowered herself so she was kneeling on the floor, right in front of the bed.

"Rotate your body," she ordered. "Come closer to me."

I did as she said, my heart pattering like I was a fucking child on Christmas morning as she kept her strokes going strong. She moved her mouth closer to my dick, and her hot breaths brushed against my inner thighs as she kissed my skin lightly. Her tongue slid out of her mouth, and she circled the tip, making chills race down my spine.

Fuuuuck.

Fuck, fuck, fuck.

Then she took me all into her mouth, sucking my cock long and hard, allowing her hand to glide up and down along with her mouth. Her tongue made fucking figure eights against the base, and fuck me sideways, I had to cover my face with my hands to keep from shouting out in pleasure. She kept up the pace and swallowed me whole, allowing the intensity of the blow job to overtake me. She placed her free hand right below my stomach and lightly pushed down against me, and fuck, I was going to come in Hazel Stone's mouth if she didn't stop any second. My feet started tapping against the floor as my body began to lift off the mattress from being so close to getting off.

"Stop, stop, stop," I ordered, pulling her away.

She looked up at me with confusion in her stare. "I'm sorry. Did you not like . . ."

"Shit, Haze," I murmured, shaking my head. "I fucking loved it. But I want to taste you first." I pulled her up from the ground and laid her down against the bed. "I want to taste every single piece of you."

"Oh . . . ?" she asked as her cheeks reddened in an instant. "So what do you need me to do?"

"That's easy. I need you to take off your pants."

22

HAZEL

I'd never had a guy go down on me. All Garrett and I had ever done was make out, and I'd give him hand jobs and blow jobs every now and again, but he'd never do anything to me. He said it grossed him out a lot, and he didn't like being down there.

I never thought about it too much, because I didn't care. If I wanted to get myself off, there were plenty of ways to do it without a stupid boy who was too much of a child to please a woman.

But with Ian that night? There was no problem in the world. Ian pulled off my pajama pants and panties with such calmness. He stared at my body in a way that Garrett never had—as if he worshipped every crease and every curve.

He pulled my shirt over my head, and I sat there in my bra, almost completely naked in front of the first ever man to have full control over my heartbeats. Then he proceeded to run his lips across every single piece of me. All the parts I loved and the ones that brought about jaded insecurities. His tongue danced down my neck, across the curves of my chest, against the folds of my stomach, across my hip bones, against my inner thighs.

A pool of heat fell against my core as Ian spread my legs apart. He breathed against my sex as I lay back, anticipation making my inhalations and exhalations harder and harder to achieve. Then he took two of his fingers against my core and spread me open, creating a V with his fingers. And right between the V, he placed his tongue, licking me up and down, sucking against my clit as I cried out in pleasure.

Oh my gosh . . .

How did he do that with his tongue? How did he move it fast and slow, up and down, deep and deeper.

Oh my gosh, Ian was burying himself in me as my juices released from his wants, his needs, and his desires. He slid two fingers inside of me and made a hook motion against my core, bringing me closer and closer to an orgasm. I wasn't sure how much longer I could hold it in. I wasn't sure if I'd be able to control myself from fully letting go.

"All of you," he whispered, looking up to stare me in the eyes. He slid another finger in with the other two and worked them around like a magician, filling me with his mystical powers. "I want to taste all of you. Let go, Haze. Let go," he ordered before he returned his tongue to my sex and once again began fucking me hard and deep with his tongue. My fingers tangled up in the sheets as my hips pushed up from the bed and toward his mouth. My legs began quivering as he quickened his pace. In and out, in and out, long wet strokes of his tongue.

"Ian," I cried, but no words came out as I unleashed every single drop of me into his mouth. He licked and licked, sucking me as if he were a starving animal, not wanting to leave a single drop. As he finished his course, he sat back on his legs and smirked at me. His face glistened with my juices all against him, and I blushed as I watched him lick his lips clean. Then my eyes fell to the hardness of his cock, which he was slowly stroking up and down. My eyes became fixated on watching his hand move up and down his massive rod, and a flood of want came shooting back to me.

"Take me," I whispered, sitting up on my forearms.

He raised an eyebrow. "Haze . . ."

"Take me," I repeated, nodding. "Please, Ian. I want you so much right now, right here . . . please . . ."

He stood up from the ground and moved over to me. His body hovered over mine, and he kissed me hard, allowing me to taste myself against his lips. Our tongues danced, and he kissed me as if he were trying to tell me a secret that I would someday unlock.

"If we do this, we can't pretend we aren't a thing, Hazel," he warned. "If I slide into you, you're mine."

"And you're mine," I breathed against his lips, placing my hands on his chest. "You're mine." Truth was, he'd always been mine. I'd just been waiting for the day when I was his too.

He steadied himself over me and rubbed his hardness against my sex. "If it hurts . . . stop me, okay?"

"Okay," I lied. I had no plans of stopping Ian from sliding into me. I had no plans of keeping him from filling me up inside.

He reached to the nightstand and grabbed a condom from his wallet. As he slid it on, I watched in amazement. He pumped his hand up and down his shaft a few times before rubbing against me again. Then he slid into me.

My mouth gasped open as he found his way so deep inside of me. It surprisingly didn't hurt as much as I thought it would. It took a few seconds for me to get used to the new feeling, but as I settled into it and allowed Ian to push himself deep into me, I began to moan because it felt . . . so . . .

Good.

I already felt as if I was on the verge of another orgasm as his hips rocked against mine. He took my wrists into his hands and pinned them above my head as he drove into me hard and pulled out slowly, teasing me, making my desire grow more and more.

Each time he pulled out slowly and slammed back into me, my body trembled all over. Every muscle in Ian's body was highlighted in a new way as he pinned me to the bed.

"Ian . . . I'm going to . . . I'm going to . . ." *Scream.* I snatched my hand away from his and grabbed the closest pillow. I covered my mouth with it as I caught the moans from the best orgasm of my life. My whole body shook with nerves as Ian kept going. Harder, faster, deeper . . .

"Fuck," he groaned, "Haze, I'm going to . . . fuck, I'm gonna . . ."

"Please," I begged, wanting him to feel as good as I did. I wanted him to explode inside of me. I wanted him to lose himself. I wanted to be responsible for his eyes rolling to the back of his head from complete bliss.

And when it happened, when his body began trembling on top of me, I lost myself too. He shut his eyes as he came hard inside of me, and my heart raced with pride, with wonderment, with . . . love.

Oh my gosh, I loved him.

He collapsed on top of me, sweaty and out of breath. He didn't say a word for a moment, and then he slid himself out of me and rolled to the left side of the bed.

"Holy . . . ," he muttered.

"Shit," I finished, giggling a bit.

"You don't understand. That was . . . that right there . . . that was . . . shit . . ." He sighed again, rubbing his hand against his face. "I've never had it like that, Haze. It's never felt so fucking good." He leaned in and kissed my cheek. "That felt like more than sex. That felt deeper. That felt like making . . ." His words trailed off, and he caught himself before he said any more. Though I knew what he was thinking.

It felt like making love.

He gave me a lazy smile. "I liked when you screamed my name into your pillow."

"I liked when you did . . ." I paused and scrunched up my nose. "Everything."

He sat up and removed the soiled condom from his shaft and tossed it into the garbage can. Then he sat there naked on the edge of my bed, still trying to catch his breath. He took my hand to his chest and placed it over his heart. "You see what you do to me, Haze? You make my heart go wild."

I loved that feeling. I loved how he let me control him, and I loved how he controlled me in the same exact way.

We lay down beside one another, still naked and exposed, both our bodies and our hearts.

"I miss you already," he said, resting his lips against my forehead.

"I miss you more." I bit my bottom lip. "When you come back, can we do that again?"

He chuckled to himself. "And again. And again. You are, after all, mine."

And you are mine, Ian Parker.
All mine.

23

IAN

I'd gotten a total of three hours of sleep the night before due to how things had unfolded between Hazel and me. I wasn't bothered at all about that. I would've surrendered the three hours I had gotten if it weren't for the fact that she'd fallen asleep first.

My grandparents and Hazel helped me load my suitcases into the bed of Big Paw's pickup truck. When it was all said and done, I couldn't help but feel a knot forming in my gut. I didn't know how I was with goodbyes, mainly because I'd never had to deal with them before. I'd never had a chance to say goodbye to my parents before they'd run off, and ever since then, everyone I knew had a way of sticking around.

That was one thing about being in a small town your whole life— you never had to really say goodbye to the ones who meant the most to you, till death did us part.

But now, I had to do it. I had to say farewell to my family, and as it turned out, I wasn't ready. It felt like hands were wrapped around my neck, forcing my breaths to become harder.

"Well, I'll go first," Grams said. Her eyes were already heavy with tears. She walked over and wrapped me in a hug. "Don't forget to take your contacts out at night, all right? Otherwise you might go blind."

"Yes, ma'am."

"And floss. I know you probably don't even though I've told you to your whole life, but if you want to keep that smile of yours, you better floss daily. If not daily, every other day."

"Yes, ma'am."

"And for the love of the Lord, please separate your whites from your colors when you do laundry. And please, please, please, do your laundry. Don't let it pile up in the corner until you're down to your last pair of boxers," she ordered.

I snickered. "Yes, ma'am."

"And one last thing." She placed her hands against my face. "When you need us, you call. Day or night, you call home. Okay?"

"Okay, I promise."

She leaned in and kissed my cheek before patting her hand gently against it. It was how she "locked the kisses in place." "Okay, good."

I turned to Haze, who was standing back a little.

I rubbed my left shoulder blade. "You sure you don't want to ride with us to the airport, Haze? Or even come to LA?" I semijoked. I couldn't get the thoughts of our night together out of my head. All I wanted was more nights like the previous one. In the perfect world, I'd come home from a day in the studio, pull her into the shower with me, and make love with her under the steaming hot water. I'd make love to her in the kitchen too. In the living room. Dining room. In every single place possible, I'd make love to her.

"Don't tempt me," she said. "If I went to LA with you, I doubt I'd want to come back."

"All right, well, I guess we just say good—"

"Don't, Ian," she cut in, closing her eyes. "Don't say goodbye, okay? Just hug me, and get it over with."

I did as she said, and she held me tighter than she ever had before.

"Last night was perfect," I whispered into her ear.

"Perfect, perfect," she replied. She pulled slightly away from me. "You're going to call me," she ordered. "Whenever you get a chance."

"Will do. And you can use my truck while I'm gone to get around if you want."

I chuckled a little as I heard Big Paw ask Grams, "When did they get so close?"

"You're always sleeping through things, Harry. Missing the things right in your face," she said.

Big Paw grumbled a bit and scratched his beard. "We better get a move on if we're going to make it to the airport in a few hours."

It was a long, long drive to the closest airport, which meant we had to leave earlier than I would've liked.

A little more time with Hazel and Grams wouldn't have been awful.

How was I already getting homesick when I hadn't even left?

I nodded once toward Big Paw and then gave Grams and Hazel one last embrace.

I opened the passenger door of the truck and began to climb into my seat.

"Ian, wait!"

I looked to my left and saw Hazel come rushing toward me.

She leaped into my arms and pressed her lips against mine. I kissed her hard and deep, wishing I'd never have to let her go.

"I'm gonna miss you, Ian. When you make it big, don't forget about us small-town folks, okay?"

"I couldn't forget you if I tried. Besides, I'm going to be calling you each morning and every night," I swore.

She bit her bottom lip. "I don't know how that would even work, Ian. You're going to be so busy with your life and—"

"We make time for the things that matter," I said, cutting her off. "You're a thing that matters."

Her head lowered for a split second, and when she looked back up, she was wearing that smile I loved. I kissed her again. For the first time in my life, the music wasn't the only thing I truly cared about.

"Thanks, Haze."

"For what?"

"Teaching me how to feel again."

"What in the damn hell was that?" Big Paw barked.

Grams waved off his annoyed tones. "Oh, hush, you old fart. Let kids be kids. I remember a certain boy who used to kiss me like that too."

"Who was it?" Big Paw sneered. "I'll kick his ass."

Grams chuckled and shook her head. "Shh. Now, get a move on before you miss his flight and he'll have to come back and kiss Hazel again."

That lit a spark under Big Paw's butt, and he hurried over to the driver's seat.

I waved goodbye one last time before Big Paw put the truck into drive.

I watched the two ladies wave to me through the sideview mirror until they were out of sight.

The ride to the airport was pretty quiet. Big Paw and I weren't big on talking, and the silence didn't bother me at all. My mind was too busy thinking about the future and the past. When we pulled up to the airport, he helped me toss my suitcases out of the back. I grabbed my guitar case and sat it down on the curbside so I could say my final goodbye.

Big Paw kept scratching his beard. "Ian, look, I know I ain't good with words like your grandmother. She is much more emotional than most people, and well, she always says the right thing. That's not me, so I'm going to say what I need to say and get it out of the way."

He shifted around the baseball cap on his head before stuffing his hands into his pockets. He cleared his throat. "You've been a pain in my ass since you were a kid."

Not the goodbye speech I was hoping for.

"It's true." He nodded. "You've been a fucking pain in my goddamn ass. Throughout your whole childhood, you pushed my buttons. You acted out and gave me every gray hair on my head."

"Is this supposed to be an inspirational goodbye, because—"

"Just shut your hole and let me finish, all right?" he barked.

"Yes, sir."

He shifted his feet side to side before pinching the bridge of his nose. When he locked eyes with mine, his stare was filled with tears, and I swore I hadn't ever seen my grandfather cry. "I just want you to know that you got all those characteristics from me. The good, the bad, and the messed-up parts. You're a mirror of your old man, Ian, and I wouldn't want you to be anything other than who you are. So you go out to Los Angeles, and you give them fucking hell, okay? You be a pain in their ass like the damn devil you are. Push their buttons. Push the whole world's buttons until you get that dream of yours. You get that success, and you hold on tight to it. Don't you dare look back to this place until you truly need to, but when you need to look back, we'll be here waiting."

Damn . . .

Now I was crying.

I sniffled a bit and nodded. "Yes, sir. I promise."

"Good. Now come on. Let's get this mopey crap over with." He held his arms out toward me and pulled me into a hug. I held on to him, and I missed him before I even let go. "I'm proud of you, son," he softly said before letting me go. "Now go. Go be a rock star."

I picked up my guitar case and grabbed the handles of my suitcases. As I walked into the airport, a small part of me wanted to turn around and look back, but I didn't.

Looking back wasn't an option. From here on out, I only looked forward.

195

24

HAZEL

The colors of fall painted the leaves of Eres, and it wasn't long before summer moved out and autumn came crashing onto the scene. I spent the next few weeks trying hard to keep busy on the ranch.

When Big Paw called me to his office, I was just as nervous as the first day I'd met him. Even though over the past few months, we'd grown closer—in a Big Paw kind of way, which still felt not close at all—he still scared me a little.

"Sit down, Hazel," he told me with his gruff voice, chewed cigar hanging from his mouth.

I did as he said and cleared my voice. "If this has anything to do with the chickens getting out of the coop, I'll take full responsibility for that. The new guy left the gate open, but that was because I didn't tell him to shut it," I said, my words flipping off my tongue as the palms of my hands began to sweat.

"This ain't about no damn chicken coops," he uttered.

"Oh." I shifted my weight in the chair and wiped my hands against my legs. "Then what did you call me in for?"

"I saw your mother the other day."

"I'm sorry, what?"

He leaned back in his chair and rubbed his hand across his jawline. "I drove up to the prison to talk to her. To make sure she was doing all right. She said she's been getting your letters but felt bad answering them after her last talk with you. She was still detoxing her system, and I believe she said some things she didn't mean."

"How . . . wait . . . what? How do you even know my mother?"

His brows knitted as his hands clasped together. "Holly and I fostered kids in this town for as long as we can remember. Jean was nothing but a kid when she came through these parts. She was pregnant and scared—pretty much how she is right now. We took her in, and I did my best to care for her. Holly and I both did. She was a great kid. Quiet, but strong. She had dreams too. She talked about how she was going to go to college and get a degree. How she was going to make your life better than hers had been. How she loved you. She had dreams for herself and for you—but she came from a broken family. She had a lot of emotional bruises." The somber look that fell against his lips made me want to cry. "She, um . . . she grew close with my daughter—Ian's mother—which was the worst thing that could've ever happened to her, I believe. To this day, I blame myself."

"Blame yourself for what?"

"I didn't know," he whispered, lowering his head and removing the cigar from his lips. "Everything. I didn't know my daughter and her boyfriend were already getting into trouble. They had a three-year-old, and I figured they were just finding their way as parents. After you were born, you spent a few months at my house with your mother until your mother decided she wanted to move in with my daughter in the ranch house. That was when my Sarah introduced her to Charlie."

The air was knocked out of me as I sat back in my chair, completely taken aback by this revelation. I'd lived in that ranch house before with my mother? My mother had met Charlie because of Ian's parents?

My mind was moving a million miles per minute. I had so many questions, but I didn't even know where to begin. Big Paw must've seen the confusion on my face, because he sat up straighter in his chair, and for a moment, I thought I saw a flash of emotion hit his stare. A flash of guilt.

"I blame myself a lot for what happened to your mother over the years. If she hadn't gotten tied up with my daughter, who knows what your lives could've been? She would've had a college degree. She would've made something of herself. She would've never gotten involved with Charlie."

"Maybe." I shrugged. "Or maybe she would've ended up worse off. Maybe she would've ended up dead if you never took her in. Big Paw, you can't blame yourself for the choices that your daughter or my mother made. It's not your burden to carry."

"Then why does it feel so damn heavy on my back?"

I smiled and reached my hand across the desk and placed it on his. "Because your heart is so big you blame yourself for others' tragedies."

His eyes moved to my hand on his, and then he gave me a stern look. I pulled my hand away slowly.

Okay, we're not at the touching comfort stage of our relationship. Duly noted.

"All I'm saying is, my mother made choices that affected her life. You took her in when she needed a home, and that was more than most people would've done. On top of that, you took me in." I paused and narrowed my eyes. "Did you do that to make up for what happened to my mother?"

He slowly nodded. "I owed you. I wanted you to get the chance at making your life into something, like your mother wanted to do but never got the chance to tackle."

For a big, grumpy man, Big Paw had to be the sweetest person alive. I could see how Holly had fallen in love with him. Behind his big, mean exterior was the softest man alive. Ian must've taken after him. They were both like Warheads—extremely sour until the sweetness was revealed.

"I won't let you down, sir."

He cocked an eyebrow.

I cleared my throat. "I mean, Big Paw. I won't let you down, Big Paw."

"Good, which brings me to the next topic I wanted to discuss—you working here on the ranch. Do you enjoy your job?"

"Yes. More than I could ever express." For the first time in my life, I felt like I belonged somewhere. I'd never really had time to dream big, because I'd figured dreams were only for people who hadn't grown up in the world that I had, but working on the ranch had changed that for me. I'd never thought I'd be a girl who loved working on a ranch, but there I was, talking to horses and chasing chickens and loving every second of it.

"Good, good. I won't beat around the bush—your work ethic outshines everyone who has come before you, my grandson included. You go above and beyond with a smile on your face. You're quick to help others too. That's very important in my mind. I need good ranch hands who aren't afraid to help one another out. That's why I want to offer you a raise. I want you to take over Ian's manager position."

My eyes bugged out of my face. "What? Seriously?"

"Yes. I think you're a great fit and showcase great leadership skills. I think, if you're interested, you could keep climbing the ladder around here."

"I'm honored, Big Paw, and I swear I will work harder than ever to prove to you that you won't regret your decision."

"I believe that. There is one stipulation."

"And what's that?"

"You must enroll in a college program. You can take classes at the community college right outside of town, or you can do an online program, but either way, you need to attend college, Hazel. You are bigger than just being a small-town girl. You can get a degree toward your future. Don't worry about the costs either. Holly and I will take care of that. If running things like the ranch is something you might be interested in down the line, a business degree could go a long way. I want you to have all the possibilities that your mother missed out on. I want you to have more."

It was in that moment that I knew Big Paw truly cared for me, deep down in his soul. He believed in my future, too, which made tears well up in my eyes. I didn't cry, though, because I knew that kind of emotion would make him uncomfortable. You cried to Holly; you appeared strong in front of Big Paw. That was how it worked with Ian's grandparents. The grandparents of Eres.

I shook Big Paw's hand and stood up from my chair to get back to work. After I was done for the day, the first thing I'd do would be to hop on a computer and start researching colleges.

"Thanks again, Big Paw. This is life changing for me."

"I hope so. You're a good kid, Hazel. Don't forget that."

I smiled and turned to leave his office as my heart felt full from Big Paw's compliment. He called out to me.

"Wait, Hazel, two more things before you go."

"Yes?"

"Your letters to your mother . . . keep writing them. She's reading them. She just feels as if your life is better off without her and her sins, but those letters . . . I think they are helping her stay clear minded. Keep that up."

"Will do. And the other thing?"

His brows knotted as he clasped his hands together. "My grandson, Ian . . . you care about him?"

"Yes, sir—*Big Paw.*"

"Do me a favor, and do your best to not hurt him. It took him years to open up again after his parents left him, and I know that has a lot to do with you coming into his life. If you're in, stay in with him. I don't think he could handle another loss."

I gave him my word. The truth was the idea of things not working out with Ian—whatever it was that we were—terrified me. For the first time in my life, I felt as if someone had really been able to see my scars and still tag them as beautiful. Whenever I thought of Ian, my heart did cartwheels. The last thing I'd ever do was risk our happily ever after.

The busier I kept on the ranch, the less I had time to think about Ian no longer holding me each night. I kept sleeping in his hoodies, though, wishing it was his skin against my skin. Plus, he'd left his truck for me to use, which came in handy for when I needed to drive around to clear my head.

As promised, we talked every morning. Even with the two-hour time difference and Ian's insane recording schedule, he managed to fit in good-morning conversations and good-night talks.

We texted all day, every day too. I was certain his life had been a whirlwind. The group was getting more and more coverage. They'd officially released their first EP, which had three of their songs on it, and it was very well received.

I'd only followed five accounts on Instagram. Each of the guys and their main Wreckage page. I'd be lying if I said I didn't open and close the app a million times hoping for updates.

"So Rihanna is as amazing in person as she seems to be, and the rumors are true. She smells fucking amazing," Ian exclaimed late one night as I was curled in bed. It was already past two in the morning my time, a little after midnight for him. The guys had a crazy schedule of radio interviews and TV appearances for their upcoming new single. They'd been going nonstop until late in the evenings.

I laughed. "You should've asked her if I could get some of her new Fenty eyeliner. I've been dying to try it."

"You should've let me know earlier. I would've!"

I snickered. "And how again did you come across Rihanna?"

"We were leaving a recording studio as she was walking in for a meeting. Sure, she probably had no clue who we were, but she said hi. Hazel, let that settle in. Rihanna said hi to us. Things are getting wild."

I covered my mouth to yawn and turned the phone away from me so Ian wouldn't hear the sleepiness in my voice. Every time he heard me yawn, he quickened our calls.

"It looked like you had quite the groupies show up to the radio station. I saw the picture Marcus put up."

"It's crazy, right? Who would've ever thought these small-town boys would get that much attention. There were hundreds of people out there screaming our names."

"Just don't forget I screamed your name first," I joked.

"I can't wait to hear you scream it again. I want you to get so loud that all of the US hears you."

I smirked, thinking about how when we made love, I had to cover my mouth with a pillow. Then a strange ting of nerves settled into my stomach. "Looks like a lot of female fans."

"Yeah. Marcus and Eric are eating up the attention." He took a beat. "You're not . . . jealous, are you?"

I knew I didn't have the right to be. I knew I didn't need to be jealous. If anything, I trusted Ian. What I didn't trust was rabid fans who couldn't care less about the private life Ian had back home. To them, he was Ian Parker, the up-and-coming rock star who oozed sex appeal like a flowing river. But to me, he was my Ian. The small-town boy who spent his days shoveling manure with me and his nights performing in a barn house.

"You have nothing to be worried about, Hazel. I mean it. Sure, there are a lot of girls around, but all I really think about is how I want a break in my schedule to be back beside you. Our publicist is pretty hell bent on us going nonstop for the next few months, because we are up and coming. Max is getting down on us pretty hard about being one hundred percent committed to the music and the music only. No outside distractions. He said if he catches me on my phone in the studio one more time, he's going to break it."

I bit my bottom lip. "I hope I'm not distracting you. I'll make sure not to text as much."

"No. Please. Text me everything, all the things. It might take me a while to reply. But I will reply, Haze. I swear. I want to hear from you. You're kind of my compass. I don't want to lose myself in this world. You're my road map home."

I smiled at his words and pulled his hoodie to my nose to breathe it in. I'd been spraying it with his cologne every now and again. Jeez . . . I was addicted.

"Speaking of being my road map . . . today people paid me a lot of cheesy compliments that went directly to my head," he said. "So in an attempt to not get a big ego, I am requesting that you tell me a handful of my flaws."

I laughed. "Oh boy. Are you sure? We'll be here all night."

"Dive right in. Rip it off like a bandage."

"You fart in your sleep," I stated. "And they are smelly. Like rotten eggs in your face, worse than the pigpens, bad."

"Oh, wow. Okay, took you no time to get that one out."

"You don't always flush the toilet. You put the toilet paper on backward like a caveman. Sometimes you leave the bathroom so fast that I doubt you washed your hands, which makes me want to do the HCT."

"HCT?" he asked.

"Hand-check test. You know, when someone comes out of the bathroom and you shake their hands to see if they are wet or cold from washing them. You can smell them, too, to see if they smell like soap. Then you know they cleaned them well."

He laughed. "Don't tell me you go around smelling people's hands."

"Well, no. But don't be freaked out if I do it the next time we hang out."

"And where did you learn about HCT?"

"My mom used to do it when I was a little kid. I was obsessed with lying about washing my hands. So she created HCT to get me to stop." I paused for a second. My stomach tightened, and I tried my best to twist my memories of Mama away. There were so few good ones that whenever one popped into my head, it made me want to get emotional on the spot. Of course, I wanted to recall the good moments with Mama, but also thinking back on the good made me miss her even more.

"How is she doing?" Ian asked, probably taking note of my silence.

"Oh, you know. The best she can be. Garrett has shockingly been giving me updates on her. She should be delivering the baby in a few months."

"How are you feeling about it all?"

Too much. I'm feeling too much.

I curled into a tighter ball. "You snore in your sleep like a rhino. When you clip your toenails, you let the clippings fly anywhere, even if it's in the kitchen. Did I mention you hang the toilet paper the wrong way?"

He chuckled. "Okay, okay. Obviously, we're not talking about your mom anymore, but you're wrong about the toilet paper."

"No. You hang it with the paper facing over. That's wrong."

"No," he argued. "That makes it easier to pull. Easy access."

"Wrong, wrong, wrong." I yawned. It escaped me without thought, and I was quick to cover my mouth.

"Oh shit. It's almost three in the morning over there, isn't it? Go to sleep, Haze."

"I'm fine." I yawned again.

"Liar. I'll call you in the morning before you head out to the ranch. Sleep tight. And Haze?"

"Yes?"

"You snore like an elephant with a peanut caught in its nose."

204

I snickered. "Good night, Ian."

"Good night."

He hung up the phone, and a few minutes later, my phone dinged with a text message.

Ian: Here's a bit of reading material for the next time you're sitting on the toilet.

Following the message were five articles about how one was supposed to hang their toilet paper over versus under.

Hazel: I could find you an article online about how Bigfoot is real, too, if you're interested. And the truth about Santa Claus.

Ian: Big Foot is real. As is Santa Claus. You should really start believing everything you read on the internet. Like, right now there's an article going around saying I have a massive cock. Believe in that, Hazel.

Don't you worry, Ian. I have enough proof of my own on that subject.

Hazel: Massive is in the eye of the beholder.

Ian: I welcome you to behold it with your eyes when I see you again.

I smiled.

Hazel: Go to sleep, weirdo.

Ian: Haze?

Hazel: Yes?

Ian: You know what I'm thinking right now?

Hazel: Yes, and me too.

Ian: Good. Good night.

I knew his thoughts, even though he never said it straight out.

I love you too, Ian Parker.

Before I fell asleep, I turned on Spotify and put the Wreckage's songs on replay to help me fall asleep. Even though I didn't know when I'd see Ian again, I was already counting down the days until our reunion. And just like every other girl around the world, I pretended the love songs were written for me.

———— ⌾❦⌾ ————

The next morning, I awakened to my phone receiving a text message. I hurried to answer it, thinking it was Ian, but it wasn't. Garrett's name flashed on the screen.

Garrett: Kid came early. In something called NICU. Not looking so hot.

Mind spinning, I scrambled to my feet. My chest was rising and falling as I tossed on some clothes and headed out of my bedroom, writing Garrett back.

Hazel: What hospital?

Garrett: St. Luke's. About three hours from town.

Hazel: Are you and your mom there?

Garrett: Nah. Had no gas money this week.

Hazel: On my way.

Garrett: They probably won't let you near.

Hazel: She's my sister. I'm on my way.

Garrett: Figured you might want to know—we aren't taking the kid in.

What?

Hazel: What do you mean? Why not?

Garrett: Your mom decided to go with adoption.

No . . .

I read those words repeatedly, as if with enough willpower I could change them.

I rushed to Big Paw's house, where he and Holly were drinking their morning cups of coffee and fighting over a crossword puzzle.

"Hey, um, I—there's—my mom—" My gosh. I couldn't push any words out of my mouth without them coming up jumbled and messy.

"Slow down, honey. What is it?" Holly asked.

"My mom had the baby, but it's in the NICU. The hospital is three hours away, and I need to g-get there." My fingernails dug into the palms of my hands. "And I think I'm too shaky to go by myself."

Big Paw stood from the table and grumbled a little as he picked up his trucker hat and placed it on his head. "All right, let's go."

Holly stood up and moved to the refrigerator. "I'll pack you some snacks, and we'll get going." She pulled out a few pieces of fruit and some breakfast sandwiches she'd meal-prepped the other day. Then she walked over to me and gave me a big grin. "Don't worry, Hazel. Everything is going to be okay."

"How do you know that? How can you say that everything will be okay? She's in the NICU. I don't know a lot about the NICU, but I know that means it's not good. And . . . if Mama's not able to be there with her . . . she's all alone. She's there alone, and that breaks my heart."

"Yes. I know how that can all be a lot, but for the time being, I'm sure she has a lot of doctors caring for her. I'm sure there are nurses looking at her, monitoring her every movement. She's not alone, and soon enough her sister will be there too. So everything will be all right. You have to have faith."

I didn't say anything else to Holly, because believing in her faith was hard when I hadn't grown up in a world where faith really existed.

We drove in silence, with nothing but sports radio on. Every now and again Big Paw would mutter something to the talk show hosts as if they could hear his complaints about bad baseball plays the night before.

Holly sat in the front seat, knitting something she'd been working on for a while, and I sat quiet in the back, picking at my nails. Ian had texted me a few times, but I hadn't found the strength to reply yet. My mind was too busy overthinking.

How could Mama think putting my sister up for adoption was the right answer? I knew my current life situation wasn't perfect, but I couldn't imagine knowing that I had a sister out there who wasn't a part of my life. I needed to fight to keep her in my life somehow.

When we arrived at the hospital, by the grace of God, we were allowed to see my little sister. She hadn't a name yet and was hooked up to a million and one machines. Tiny tubes ran into her body, and her small breaths wavered in and out as her chest moved up and down.

"She's a fighter," a nurse told us as we stood close by. "She's been through some things, but she's fighting like heck to come back and be strong."

"She's so small," I whispered, staring at the newborn. She was beautiful. Even with all of the tubes and the distracting noise of the machines, I knew she was so beautiful.

I wondered if she started out with hazel eyes too. I wondered if she knew she wasn't alone anymore.

"Nurse, is it all right if we step outside and have a talk?" Big Paw asked, his voice heavy and deep.

"Of course."

The two stepped out of the room, leaving Holly standing with me. She placed her hands on my shoulders, feeling the trembling of my body.

"She can't be put up for adoption," I told her. "She can't. She's the only thing I have left . . . she's the only family connection I have, Holly. I've lost so much, and I can't lose her too. I can't lose my sister."

"Shh . . . sweetheart. It's going to be okay."

I wished she'd stop saying that, because it was looking so far from being okay. Everything was a complete mess, and I didn't see how any of these issues could've been cleared up with positive thinking.

We sat down in the room with the baby while Big Paw was off talking to the nurse. I couldn't stop shaking as Holly kept her arms wrapped around my body. My phone dinged a few more times as we waited.

Ian: Everything okay?

Ian: It's not like you to ghost.

I read his words over and over again before getting to my feet. "I'll be right back, Holly."

"Take your time, sweetheart. And tell him I love him," she commented, knowing I was off to call Ian.

I found a stairwell and stood there with the cell phone in my hand. I tapped in Ian's number, and a calmness settled over me when I heard his voice.

"Hey, Haze. What's up?"

25

IAN

"The baby came, and she's in the NICU. She's not doing too well, but the nurses seem hopeful she'll get a fighting chance at making a recovery," Hazel said, her voice low and controlled.

"Are you okay?"

I could tell from the sound of her voice that she wasn't. It all made sense that she'd gone radio silent that morning, because her world was taking a turn. She had a baby sister now who was busy fighting for her life.

"I don't know. My mom is talking about giving the baby up for adoption instead of having Garrett and his mom look after her. That breaks my heart. I know it sounds stupid, but this little girl feels like the only family I have . . . and now there's the possibility of her going to someone else."

"Don't overthink that now. Try your best to focus on the baby getting better. Okay?"

She sniffled a bit. "Yeah, okay."

"What's her name?"

"She doesn't have one yet."

"Okay, then tell me about her. What does she look like? Tell me the good, Haze. There's always some good in the bad parts of every story. What is the good?"

"She has a full head of hair," she said. I heard the energy of her voice shift a little as she began to search her mind for the good.

"Yeah?"

"Uh-huh. It's black as midnight. Thick too. Mama always said I was a bald baby and didn't get hair until I was around two years old. But my sister has it all in abundance."

"What else?"

"The nurse said her stats are looking up. With everything my mom did before getting pregnant, I'm surprised she doesn't have more issues. She's a fighter."

"She must get that from her big sister."

She chuckled lightly before she grew somber again. "What am I going to do, Ian? What will I do if they take her away?"

"Hey, come on. Everything's going to be okay."

"You're sounding a lot like your grandma right now."

"Over twenty years of life with Grams, and she has yet to be wrong about that fact. Just have a bit of faith. You don't need much. Just enough to get you through until tomorrow."

"Ian, what the hell? We need you inside," Max said, barging outside of the studio to find me sitting against the curbside talking to Hazel.

Shit.

"You said you were going to the bathroom, and I find you out here on that damn phone of yours."

Shit, shit, shit.

"Haze? I have to go. We'll talk later, all right?"

"Okay. Talk later."

I hung up the phone and turned to see an extremely irritated Max Fucking Rider standing behind me. "I'm sorry," I bellowed.

"You must not understand the opportunity you've been given here, Ian. Millions of people would kill to be in this studio, and here you are, wasting everyone's damn time and everyone's damn money, all because you had to take a freaking phone call to talk to some girl."

"It's not just some girl," I disagreed. "She's *the* girl, and she needed me."

Max eyed me up and down. "Come on, man. You're on the verge of your life changing forever, and you're risking it all for some romance? Wake up. There are three bandmates of yours waiting inside for you to give this thing the same amount of respect that they all are. You're the leader of this band, right?"

I grimaced. "Yeah."

"Then stop acting like a damn child, grow the hell up, and lead them. People aren't shitting you when they say this is a once-in-a-lifetime opportunity. Don't blow it because of some small-town girl."

My hands formed fists every time Max talked about Hazel as if she were nothing but a part of my past when I was trying to figure out how to pull her straight into my future. I didn't argue with him, though, because on the surface of it all, I knew he was right. The Wreckage was being given a chance that millions of people dreamed of, and Eric, James, and Marcus were counting on me to show up and give it my all, the same way they'd been doing.

"Sorry, Max. I swear, I'm committed."

He narrowed his eyes and stared at me, as if he wasn't completely convinced, but he allowed it. "All right. Let's get to work, then."

He held his hand out toward me.

"What?"

"Don't play dumb, Ian. Give me your cell phone. You're cut off during recording days."

We didn't get back to our apartment until well after midnight. I was certain Hazel was already asleep. When I received my cell phone from Max, I had a dozen text messages from her. She apologized a few times about getting me in trouble and taking up my time when she'd called earlier. She updated me that her sister was doing a little better, but they were keeping a close eye. And she also gave me a confession.

Hazel: Confession time. I wish you were here. I know that's selfish, and I know it's impossible, but I do wish that, Ian. I wish you were here to hold me tonight.

I texted her back and tried to push away the ultimate guilt that sat in my gut about not being there for her.

Ian: It's late, and I know you're probably sleeping. At least, I hope you are. But I wanted to say I love you, Hazel. I didn't want to say that via text message. I wanted to wait until we were eye to eye again and I was holding you in my arms, but it seems that life has a way of keeping you from the places you wish you could be the most. But I need you to know that I love you. I know your world is messy right now, and I wish I could take the hard parts and hold them on my own back. I wish I could hold you. I wish I could kiss you. I wish I could say I love you against your skin and wipe your worries away. For now, all I have are these messages. I love you, Hazel Stone. And everything is going to be okay.

When I hit send, I was surprised when I heard my phone start ringing. Hazel's name flashed across the screen, and I answered right away.

"You should be sleeping," I told her, falling against my own bed.

"You should be too," she argued. "But after reading your message, I knew I had to talk to you. I had to hear you say it to me . . . maybe not in person, but I needed to hear it from your lips. So please . . ."

She sounded so exhausted. As if she were already sleeping and speaking to me only in a dream state.

"I love you," I whispered. "I love you, I love you, I love you."

Her sighs were so gentle against the receiver, but my phone was pressed tightly against my ear as she replied to me, saying the words I'd hoped she would come to feel. "I love you too."

"Why do you sound so sad about it?"

"Because I've lived life long enough to know that sometimes love isn't enough. This is why I didn't want to start this to begin with. This is why I was so afraid to even cross that line with you. Your life is moving so fast, Ian, and it's all amazing things that are happening to you and the guys. You've worked so hard to get to where you are right now, and there's so much more coming. Everything is moving at warp speed, and I'm so happy for you, but I'm not in that world. Right now, my life feels as if it's moving backward, not forward. If anything, I'm frozen in time. We're on different timelines, and I don't want you to try to slow yours down to let me in."

I shifted in my bed. "You're overwhelmed and tired."

"Did you get in trouble for talking to me today?" she asked.

"Haze . . ."

She took a breath. "Maybe you're right. Maybe I'm tired. It's been a long day, and I should get some sleep."

"Yeah, okay. I'll call you in the morning."

"It's okay," she said. "You don't have to."

"I'll call you in the morning," I repeated. "I love you."

She released an exhalation. "I love you too."

It wasn't until that moment that I knew loving someone could feel so sad.

26

HAZEL

"I want her," I sternly said to Big Paw and Holly as I paced back and forth in the waiting room of the hospital. It was our third day there, and my sister was making a powerful recovery from all the trauma she'd gone through.

Ian's grandparents sat down in the metal hospital chairs with their hands clasped together and grimaces on their faces.

"It's not that easy, Hazel," Holly said, shaking her head. "There are rules and procedures . . ."

"Screw the rules and procedures. I want her. I want my sister. I can take care of her; I know I can. So do what you did for my mother all those years ago and for other foster kids. Or at least help me be able to take her in. I'll handle it all, I swear."

"It's not that easy," Big Paw said, repeating Holly's words, and that enraged me.

"Yes, it is."

"This situation is different. This is a newborn baby, Hazel. A child that the mother wants to give up . . ."

"She wouldn't if she knew I wanted her. She would want to keep us together. She wouldn't want to split up her girls."

"Hazel—" Holly started, but I cut her off.

"No." I stood tall and wrapped my arms around my body. "No. You promised. You swore that everything would be okay and that things would work out, so there has to be a way. There has to be some way to get that baby girl to stay with me. She's the only family I have. I can pay you for your help with getting in contact with the right people."

"You know damn well this ain't a situation about money, little girl," Big Paw barked, as if bothered to his core that I would assume such a thing. But how could I help it? My mind was spinning, and despair was swallowing me whole.

"Then what is it?" I cried out.

"It's *you*," he shot back, gesturing toward me. He stood from the chair, and then he was the one pacing. "It's you and your future, Hazel. You have the whole world right there in front of you." He snapped his fingers. "It's right there in front of you, and I refuse to let you throw that away. You've worked so damn hard to not end up with a life like this. Raising a child while you're still one yourself. You've spent your life caring for others, for your mother. You've never had a chance to be a kid all on your own. So I refuse to do this. I refuse to take away the small shot you have at a life so you can take care of another. I've seen what happens when someone so young is forced to raise a child before they are ready. I've seen my own daughter fall apart and crumble, ruining any shot she had at a future. And I forbid for that to be your story. I forbid you to toss away your shot at a future." He had tears in his eyes, and his words cracked as they fell from his mouth.

I'd never seen Big Paw so emotional, and I knew the words he spoke came from the deepest part of his soul.

He sniffled a bit, and I stood there, stunned, as I looked on the giant who'd worked so hard to stay strong.

"Big Paw . . . ," I softly said, shaking my head. "With all due respect, I'm not your daughter. I wouldn't fall into the role of parenthood and run from it. I wouldn't abandon you or my sister. I would be here completely committed to this. I know that me finding my way is important, and I'll work toward that—I swear. But there's one thing I've always wanted."

"And what's that?"

"A family."

Holly frowned. "But sweetheart, you're so young."

"By age, not experience. Please, you two. Just help me figure this out somehow. Help me at least see if this is a possibility. Otherwise, I'll spend the rest of my life thinking about how I didn't do everything in my power to keep the small bit of family I had left."

They were quiet for some time, shooting glances back and forth. The two of them had such a powerful way of communicating with one another without using any words. Big Paw tapped a fist against his lips, and Holly rubbed her palm against her cheek.

"I won't make any promises," Big Paw grumbled, finally turning back to me. "I've never gone through anything like this, and I know there will be a lot of hoops that we'll have to jump through."

"That's fine," I eagerly replied, swallowing up the slim idea that Big Paw was on board with trying to get the baby into my custody. I'd do anything to make it happen. I'd leap over every hurdle and through every hoop if it meant I'd have a shot at raising my sister.

"And you still have to look into college, because no matter what, you are getting a degree down the line."

"I can do online classes," I swore. "I'll do whatever it takes. I swear, Big Paw."

He scowled, but I knew the only reason he was doing that was due to the fact that he was going to let me try to figure it all out. "You women are going to be the death of me," he muttered.

I rushed him, wrapping my arms around his body, and I held on so tight, probably squeezing all of the air from his lungs. "Thank you, Big Paw."

"Don't thank me. I haven't done anything yet."

"But still, thank you. For everything you've done for me."

He gave me a half smile, and I swore that was the first time I'd seen his lips do such a thing to anyone outside of Holly. "If by the grace of God we pull this off, I refuse to change any diapers."

"Oh, Harry. You're going to change whatever we tell you to change," Holly said.

Big Paw grumbled some more, because he knew she was right. He sat back down in his chair and gestured toward the hallway. "Go check on your sister. We'll be over there in a few."

I did as they said and disappeared down the hallway. Before going into the NICU, I washed my hands thoroughly. My sister had been moved to a new space in the NICU. She wasn't hooked up to as many machines, and there were holes in her incubator, which allowed people to reach in and hold her hands.

After I was done scrubbing myself clean, I walked over to her and smiled as she lay there resting. She was so small but so fierce, so strong. Such a fighter.

I slid my hand into the incubator and placed my finger in her palm so she could grip it. Her fingers were chilled, and I did my best to warm them up. I sniffled a bit as she wiggled around and made the quietest sounds. So many babies in the NICU cried for hours on end, but not my sister. She hardly made a peep. If I didn't know better, I might've missed that there was even a baby in front of me.

"Hey, sweetheart," I whispered, looking down at the angel. "I know you don't know me, but you will so very soon. You see, I'm your big sister. I'm the one who's going to be looking after you from here on out. I know this probably isn't what you signed up for. Lord knows this wasn't how I saw my life going, but that's the thing about life: sometimes it just shifts without our permission. But that's why we have to stick together, okay? Because when life shifts, it's easier if you have someone to hold on to, so hold on to me, sis. I got you." It may have been my imagination, but I swore it felt as if her grip around my finger tightened a little bit. As I held on to her hand, she finally opened up her eyes for me. I'd been waiting days for her to look my way, for her to give me her stare.

Her beautiful, beautiful hazel eyes.

"She's stunning like her sister," a voice said, making me tense up as I pulled my hand away from the incubator. His voice was deep and smoky and mine.

My mouth fell open and a hand flew to my chest as I turned to see Ian standing there. His eyes had bags beneath them, and his hair was wild, as if he hadn't pushed a brush through it in days. He stood tall with a relaxed appearance. His eyes sparkled as he looked my way with his hands stuffed into his jeans pockets, and the smallest smile sat against his lips.

A heavy feeling sat in my stomach as my heartbeat raced. "What are you doing here?"

"Come on, Haze," he softly said, walking toward me. He wrapped his arms around me and pulled me into an embrace. "I think you know the answer to that."

I melted into his touch as if he were the sun and I were an ice cube. My hands fell against his chest, and I kept praying I wasn't daydreaming his presence.

"You're really here?" I asked.

"I'm really here." He kissed my forehead, and I fell that much more in love. "Sorry I'm late."

"But how, though? I thought your schedule was packed for quite some time."

"I found a bit of wiggle room."

"Ian—" I felt deflated, thinking that he'd chosen me over his music. That was what I was most worried about, him losing sight of his dreams because I was blurring his vision.

"Shh, Haze. It's fine. Trust me. I figured it out. We had a free day, and I took a flight back home. I leave tonight on a red-eye, but I couldn't imagine not being here for you when you needed me."

"You're only here for a few hours?" I asked. "You must be so exhausted."

"Yeah. But it's worth it. Now come on. Introduce me to your sister." He started walking toward her, but I stepped in front of him like an overprotective mama bear.

"Wait! You have to wash your hands before you can touch her."

He smirked and held his hands up in the air. "I already did. The nurse notified me before I came in. Go ahead, HCT me."

I leaned in close to his hands and sniffed, smelling the hospital soap against his skin. I smiled. "Okay, carry on."

We each took a side of the incubator and put our hands inside. Ian took her left hand, and I held her right. It almost looked as if she were smiling too. Sure, I knew that was probably not a smile, and she might've had gas or something, but her lips were curved up, and that made me feel happy. At peace after a very nonpeaceful few days.

"I want to yell at you for being here, but I also want to kiss you for being here too," I whispered to Ian as we lay in the hotel room. Big Paw, Holly, and I had been staying at a hotel for the past few days in order to be close to the hospital in case anything went awry. They were back in their hotel room doing research while I was soaking up every single second of my time with Ian.

He'd be leaving in about two hours, and all I wanted to do was wrap myself around him and not let go.

"Go with the kissing option. That's the better one."

I smiled, which in turn made him smile.

"I missed that, Haze. I missed your smile. I'm not going to lie—you scared me when we talked the other night. About how my life was moving forward and yours was frozen. It sounded like you had all these doubts, and it freaked me the hell out."

"I know, and I'm sorry about that. But I still feel that way, if I'm honest. And with everything going on with my sister, my life will be tossed upside down if I get to take care of her. I know that's not something you signed up for, Ian, and I don't want that to somehow get in the way of your dreams. You can't slow down right now. You're about to take off."

"Just give me a chance to prove that we can make this work, okay? Don't give up on us too soon, Hazel. I know there's a way for this to happen."

The butterflies in my stomach swirled as he clasped his hands with mine. "I'm not running, Ian. I swear, I'm here. I'm just being cautious and realistic."

"Well, stop that," he laughed, kissing the palms of my hands. "Just dream a little dream with me for a while."

I wanted to argue with him that we couldn't live in a dreamworld, but in a few short hours he'd be gone again, and I didn't want to leave him feeling unsettled about what we were. So I kissed his lips.

He kissed me back and arched an eyebrow. "So . . . about you screaming my name . . . ," he commented with a sly grin.

"Okay." I snickered. "Take off your clothes."

We made love in the hotel room that night, and for those few hours, I allowed myself to dream of a world where he was him and I was me and that was more than enough.

The next day, Big Paw, Holly, and I drove back to Eres. Even though I felt awful leaving my sister's side, we had to go and collect more information. Big Paw told me we'd be better off if we could get Charlie to agree to signing custody over to me, but I felt like that was a big shot in the dark. Charlie would never come around to that idea. Even though he was still locked up, I knew the last thing he'd want would be to give the girl who was responsible for that something of his.

Still, I was going to try all avenues that I could think of before giving up.

As we drove home that afternoon, the radio played a song by the Wreckage, and all three of us freaked out in excitement.

"Well, I'll be damned," Big Paw exclaimed, slapping his hand against his leg. "Ian's out there really doing something big, huh?"

"Yes, he is." Holly beamed ear to ear.

Big Paw cranked the music up, and I sang every lyric to the song as if the words were tattooed in my mind. Hearing his voice on the radio gave me an odd sense of hope that maybe Ian and Holly were right. Maybe, at the end of the day, everything would work out; everything would be fine. If it looked as if things weren't working out, then it probably wasn't the end just yet. I'd had enough faith to get me through yesterday, and I'd have enough to get me through tomorrow.

Patience was the name of the game, and I had every plan to be the best player.

27

HAZEL

Hazel: Confession time: I've been listening to your songs on repeat.

Ian: Confession time: Every time I sing a love song, I'm singing it for you.

I'd been working closely with Big Paw and Holly to figure out how to get my sister home to us. Luckily, a lot of the laws said they preferred to put the child into the home of a family member, and seeing as how it was my little sister, that made things a bit more hopeful.

Still, I had to get more information from people who hadn't had much desire for me to be in their lives anymore.

The look in Garrett's eyes told me that he was getting pretty fed up with me asking him questions, but I didn't know who else I could've gone to in order to get more information on Charlie. I knew he was in communication with him, and I needed to figure out a way to get Charlie to agree to me having the little girl.

"Listen, Hazel, I've given you more than you deserved already, and I'm getting pretty sick of you showing up and making demands." Whiskey wafted off his tongue, and his eyes were bloodshot red. It was clear he was drunk, based on the way he stumbled side to side, and he was obviously high on some kind of drug. The more things changed, the more they stayed the same.

"It's not a demand, Garrett; it's a request. I want you to try to convince Charlie to let me keep my sister with me. I couldn't imagine her going to grow up in a stranger's home when she has family right here."

"You ain't got shit to offer that kid. An adoption family could, though. You're being selfish."

"Maybe, but it wouldn't just be me. Big Paw and Holly are planning to help too. We have a whole family unit ready to back up this little girl, and she deserves to stay with family."

"Just let it go, Hazel. Drop this whole thing," he muttered, turning to walk back into his house.

I reached out and grabbed him by the arm. "Garrett, wait. Please. I don't get it. I know you hate me for all your reasons, and I get it. But I know you also know me. You know how important family is to me. If you could just reach out to Charlie—"

"It won't help," he snapped.

"It might."

"Trust me, it won't. Charlie can't do shit for that kid."

I narrowed my eyes. "Of course he can. As the father—"

"Jesus, Hazel! Use your fucking context clues, will you?" I stepped back, completely astonished by Garrett snapping. "It's not his fucking kid. Okay? Drop it. Let the kid go. Just leave it alone."

My stomach tightened as I was struck by an unbelievably strong sense of fear. "What did you just say?"

"I said drop it."

"No." I paused, raking my hands through my hair. "You said Charlie wasn't the father."

He lowered his brows and brushed his thumb against his nose. "What? No, I didn't." The crinkle in his nose showed his perplexed thoughts.

"Yes, you did. You said Charlie isn't the father."

"Shit," he muttered, rubbing his hands over his face. "Listen, you have to go, Haze." He went to close the door, but I stuck my foot in the way.

"Garrett," I begged. "Please."

He sighed, tossing his hands in the air. "You're not going to be fucking happy about this."

"It's okay. I just want to know what's going on."

He grumbled and stuffed his hands into his pockets as he leaned against the doorframe. "Charlie can't have kids. He had a surgery years ago to keep it from being a thing. He said he couldn't run his business if he had little shits running around. He always said you were already too much of a headache."

What?

"Then who is the father?"

His bottom lip twitched, and he shook his head. "Listen, Hazel, I get why you think you want to know this, but—"

"Tell me."

His head lowered, and he muttered out, "It's me." Those words flipped the whole situation upside down. "Why do you think I cared so much about checking in on your mom these past few months?"

My chest tightened as the wind was knocked out of me, and I stumbled back a few steps. "What?"

"I didn't mean for that shit to happen, all right? One night, your mom and I were getting high together. You were at the library studying or some shit, and well, one thing led to another. And then another and . . ." His words trailed off, and to be honest I couldn't keep up with the thoughts shooting through my mind. That was the last thing I'd expected him to say.

My mother had slept with my ex-boyfriend.

If that wasn't beyond disturbing, I didn't know what was, but there was a silver lining in all of this mess. Charlie wasn't the father. I didn't need his approval at all over my sister. I needed Garrett's.

Even though rage rushed through my soul and I had the desire to punch him in his jaw, I held my composure, because I still needed his help.

"You don't want to keep the kid?" I asked through gritted teeth.

"Shit, Hazel. There isn't anything about my life that has room for a kid. My mom wanted me to take her in, because, well, responsibility and crap. But your mom and I decided the real responsible thing would be to give this kid an actual chance at life."

"With me," I said, holding my hand to my chest. "She could have a real shot at life with me, Garrett. I don't just want her—I need her. She's my family."

He lowered his head and kicked his shoes around. I knew he was drunk and high, but there had to be a part of him that understood how I was the right choice for her.

"I don't do drugs. I hardly drink and won't anymore. I took care of my mom all my life. I took care of you when you couldn't, Garrett. I've always been there for you, even when I shouldn't have, because that's what I do. I take care of the things I love. I'll take care of her forever."

He brushed his hand beneath his nose and shrugged his shoulders back. "You really want this, huh?"

"I do."

He squinted one eye shut as the sun beamed straight into his face. "And you don't hate me for what I did?"

"Oh, trust me, I hate you. But . . . this isn't about you and me. This is about her, and I can't let my feelings for you get in the way of me caring for her."

He blew out a cloud of smoke and nodded. "Fine. Whatever. Just tell me what I have to do."

I didn't know my heart could be so broken and healed from so few words. "You'll have to do a DNA test and stuff, and we'll have to get this all on paper."

"Sure. Whatever. Just let me know what to do and when to do it."

I nodded and thanked him. As I began to walk away, Garrett called after me.

He looked strung out, like so many people we'd grown up surrounded by. His hair was thinning, his teeth were stained yellow, and he was walking down a road toward the life I never wanted for us. He looked so much older than his young age, and for a split second, I felt bad for him.

There were so many years when all I'd wanted to do was save Garrett from his own destruction, but I was learning quick that you couldn't save people who didn't want to be rescued. All you could do was leave the porch light on in hopes that they'd save themselves and find their way home.

"Rosie," he said as he brushed his fallen, greasy hair out of his face. "My grandmother's name was Rosie."

I nodded once, knowing exactly what he was getting at. "Thanks, Garrett. Take care of yourself."

He didn't say anything else to me, and I walked to Ian's truck and drove home.

Home to the place that would soon be the home to my little sister. Little Miss Rosie.

Once we completed all the paperwork and met with a handful of social workers, we were able to bring Rosie home. There was still so much more that had to happen in court. So many hurdles we'd have to jump, so many court dates and procedures we'd have to cross off the list down the line, but for the time being, Rosie was home with us.

Her crib sat in my bedroom, and even though she didn't cry a lot at the hospital, that little girl discovered her lungs once she made it to her new home. The first few days and nights were almost unbearable. I'd tried my best to mentally prepare myself for the fact that I was going to be nineteen and raising a newborn, but truth was you couldn't prepare yourself for having a child.

I could've read every baby book on the planet. I could've gone to every pregnancy class, but none of that mattered, really. It turned out raising a child was a one-step-at-a-time process. It was overwhelming, and sometimes I'd find myself sitting on the toilet just for five minutes of rest as tears fell from my eyes.

So much guilt sat in my chest as the tears fell, because maybe Garrett was right. Maybe I was being selfish taking Rosie in. Maybe she would've been better off with another family. But I needed her. I needed her maybe more than she needed me.

And then each day she'd do something that would light up my world. Smile, chuckle, sleep. Oh, I loved watching her sleep as her chest rose and fell in a calming pattern.

It also helped that Big Paw and Holly were more than willing to come over and take shifts with Rosie. They loved on her as if she were their own grandchild. Also, seeing big ol' Big Paw holding a tiny baby in his giant hands was the most adorable thing in the world.

I'd missed so many calls from Ian. In the morning and at night. Whenever I received a second to breathe, I was knocked out, and otherwise I was catering to Rosie and her needs.

Ian: Missing you. Missing your voice. We're in NYC this week, and all I can think was how I wished I was back in Eres with you.

Hazel: I'm sorry my life is a mess.

Ian: I'd love to get messy with you.

I didn't understand him. I didn't get why he was being so understanding and patient with me. The Wreckage was exploding on the scene, and they were in the studio nonstop working on their album release for early next year, and he still managed to make time to call me every morning and every night.

I didn't deserve his love when all I'd been able to give to him were crumbs.

I googled him more often than I probably should've, looking up news articles on the band. Reading everything possible about what the world was thinking about the Wreckage.

During one of Rosie's 4:00 a.m. feedings, I was flipping through some of those news articles out of habit when my eyes fell on an article with the tagline, *Music's newest bachelor, Ian Parker, is single and ready to melt your panties off with his voice.*

I closed the article quickly, wanting to read no more about it.

Single and ready to melt your panties off.

Jeez. If that wasn't a kick-to-the-vagina kind of headline, then I didn't know what was.

I tried my best to shake off the nerves, but it didn't help that I signed into Instagram and saw the massive amount of females that showed up at the meet and greet for the guys. Beautiful, tall, slim girls who were throwing themselves all over Ian Parker.

I knew I had to make more of an effort with Ian if I was going to keep our budding story growing into all that it could be. I wasn't ready to let go of him, of us. It was my job to show him that I was completely committed to our relationship, no matter how complicated and complex it had become. I needed to prove to him that I was all in.

Even if that meant less sleep and more calls. I was juggling my life in front of me. There were so many pieces to my puzzle. Raising a newborn. Searching for online colleges. Falling deeper in love from a distance. Working at the ranch. Each one of those things was important to me. So I did what I had to do to make time for them all.

28

IAN

The band and I had been going nonstop for weeks, it seemed. When November rolled in, I hardly knew what day and time zone we were in. Plus, I missed Hazel more than fucking words, and I hated the guilt that hit me from seeing those fake articles about me being single.

"All right, small-town boy, here you go," Max said, walking over to me with paperwork in his hand. We'd started our week in NYC, and now we were back in Los Angeles spending day after day in the studio.

The guys and I were burned out. Autumn was flying by, and we hardly had any time to enjoy it. Everything in our lives was moving so fast it felt as if it were all a blur. We were exhausted yet happy. Tired but blessed.

"What is this?" I asked.

"Your tickets home for the holiday. I had Amy clear the weekend schedule for you guys. I got you all first-class tickets to go back to Eres. I figured you could need a bit of time out of the wildness of this world. It's a lot to be tossed into. Plus, I was hoping I could head home, too, to meet with my family. My wife is chewing my ass out for planning to miss another Thanksgiving." He reached into his bag and popped a few pills into his mouth. "If only she knew those missed holidays paid for those mansions she loves."

I stared at the tickets and felt a knot in my chest as his words settled in. "Seriously? You're giving us a break?"

"Well, seeing as how your single hit the Billboard Hot 100 charts, I figured we can give you a few days off. I know it's not much, but—"

"No, no. It's more than enough. Thanks, Max. You have no clue how much we need this. I appreciate this and everything you've done for us. Before I tell the guys, Max, I have a question. I was scrolling through the internet reading articles about the band—"

He shook his head. "Rookie mistake number one. Don't read that shit. It's toxic and will ruin your mood for years to come."

"Yeah, but it was one of the interviews we did. The headline read that I was single and something about panties. I never said I was single, so that just rubbed me the wrong way."

He shook his head. "I'm sure Amy told the interviewer that to up your sex appeal."

Amy was in charge of making us appear as this badass band that women craved. I understood her job, but that felt as if she was crossing a line.

"I don't want to send off the wrong idea, though. I have a girlfriend, someone I really care about, and I don't want her seeing that kind of shit when we're already struggling with long distance."

"Right, of course. I hear you. I'll talk to Amy about that. But for now, make it clear to your girl that tabloids run on lies. It's just the name of the game, and clickbait is the easiest way to score points. Now, go ahead and pack."

I did as he said, and for a minute I thought about calling Hazel and letting her know that I was coming home, but I stopped myself. I wanted to surprise her. I couldn't wait to have my arms wrapped around her and her lips against mine again.

I knew she'd been feeling awful for being so overwhelmed and exhausted lately, but I didn't think any less of her for it. If anything, it made me fall for her even more. She was the definition of giving. She always gave herself to others tenfold. It was one of her best qualities to me. Though, at the same time, I wished she would give to herself as much as she surrendered for others. She deserved the stars and the moon, yet she acted as if even a spark of light on her was too much attention.

When I arrived home the day before Thanksgiving, Hazel was passed out in her bed. Her hair was in a wild bun, and her T-shirt looked as if it had a milk-vomit stain on it, and she was still fucking beautiful.

Rosie was in her crib, staring at me wide eyed. She looked just like Hazel with those large eyes.

Rosie began to fuss in the crib, and when she started to holler, I was quick to pick her up.

Hazel leaped up from her sleep, alert and alarmed. "I got her; I got her," she muttered, rubbing the sleep from her eyes.

"It's okay; we're good," I said, soothing the baby, who was calming down a bit as I bounced her around.

As realization set in for Hazel that I was standing in her bedroom, tears filled her eyes. I didn't know if they were from happiness or exhaustion, but she rushed over to me quickly and hugged me from behind as Rosie lay in my arms.

"I feel like every time you come back to me, I'm going to fall apart," she whispered into my neck, gently kissing my skin.

"I feel like every time I come back to you, I'm not going to want to leave."

Rosie fussed a bit more in my arms, and Hazel frowned a little. "She's probably hungry. I can take her from you and go warm up a bottle for her."

"It's fine. I'll hold on to her. You can go get the bottle. We'll wait here."

She hesitated as if she was going to argue, but instead she murmured a thank-you and hurried out of the room. When she came back up with the bottle in her hand, Rosie and I were sitting in the gliding chair, finding a nice rhythm.

Hazel smiled our way. "It looks like she's comfortable with you."

"I like kids. I used to help watch James and Leah's little sister when she was a newborn. Kind of comes naturally for me."

"Well, I wish I could say the same," she joked. "Trying to get her to calm down when she's hollering is a new kind of hell. Do you want me to feed her?"

"I can do it." I reached for the bottle, and once I started feeding Rosie, she began eating like a champion. It was crazy how the first time I saw her, she'd looked so small and broken in that incubator, but now she was growing so fast, making a big turnover from her rocky start at life.

Hazel sat on the floor in front of us and looked with wonderment in her eyes. "I want to ask why you're here, but honestly, I really don't care. I'm just so glad you're home."

I smirked. "Me too. Max surprised the band with tickets home for a small holiday break. He said it was a gift for us hitting the Billboard charts. Which . . . by the way, we hit the Billboard charts."

She grinned cheek to cheek. "Yeah, I know. I read about that early this morning." She picked up her phone and showed it to me. "I sent you a text message about it but obviously was too out of it to remember to hit send."

"Ha. No worries. You have good reason to be exhausted."

"Yeah, but still, I'm so proud of you. Not to sound like a complete creep, but I kind of stalk you guys on the internet like it's a drug habit."

"Careful. You can't trust everything you read online."

She raised an eyebrow. "That's funny, because before you said believe everything on the internet."

"Yeah, well, that was before I saw the dark sides of it."

"You mean your single bachelor lifestyle and panty-melting skills?"

I cringed as those words left her mouth. "I was hoping you didn't read that article."

"That's the problem with being your biggest fan. I read every article."

Rosie finished eating, and I moved her to my shoulder to burp her as I kept gliding in the chair. "Listen, Hazel, that whole article was my publicist's doing. We hadn't even known it was going to be run that way until it was up. I talked to Max about it and told him it was uncool. I want the world to know about us."

She shook her head. "I'm fine with it being this way. I get that part of being a rock star is having the sex appeal that makes women melt. In the words of the All-American Rejects, I'm fine with being your dirty little secret."

I groaned. "But I don't want you to be my dirty little secret. I want you to be my dirty little public girl."

A wicked grin fell against her lips as she leaned forward. "I can do a lot of dirty things privately and publicly."

"Don't say things you don't mean."

"Trust me. I mean it. The minute Rosie goes down, I'll show you."

Well, that didn't sound too awful. As I held Rosie on my shoulder, I felt a wetness moving down my back as realization set in that the baby had thrown up all over my shoulder.

I held her away from me, and Hazel was quick to grab her. "Sorry about that. Gosh, she's been spitting up like crazy after eating."

"It's really no trouble. Vomit happens. How about this. How about you try to get her back to sleep. I'll go take a quick shower from the long flight, and then we'll talk about those dirty little secrets you mentioned before."

She smiled and nodded. "I'll be here waiting."

I dashed out of her bedroom and hopped into the shower. My hands moved all over my body, washing up as quick as possible, so I could hurry and get back to Hazel, wishing, praying, and hoping that Rosie was sleeping already.

I headed back over to Hazel's room, ready to do things I'd only been able to imagine for the past few weeks, and all hope died the moment I saw her lying in her bed, completely passed out while Rosie slept in her crib.

Well then, this is a new hurdle to the relationship.

Instead of bothering to wake her, I crawled into bed beside her, and without thought, she curled her body against mine, just like the good ol' days. In that moment, I was happy to have something that made me feel like I was officially home again.

"I figured she could wear this," Big Paw grumbled as he stood on the front porch of my house the night before Thanksgiving. He held a turkey onesie for Rosie in his hands, and he looked so mad about it, but the fact that he even was holding a onesie made him look that much gentler. "I saw it at the store when I went out of town to get some supplies. Figured the girl should have a first-Thanksgiving outfit."

"I'll make sure to pass it on to Hazel," I promised, taking it from him.

He scratched at his beard and muttered a bit before looking back up toward me. "Saw you and the boys on TV the other night. You sounded good. Real good."

What was that? A compliment from Big Paw?

Little Rosie must've been making him soft.

"But don't let it go to your damn head. You aren't that good, boy."

Ah, that sounded more like the grandfather I knew and loved.

"You, Hazel, and Rosie should come over to our place tonight to help Grams with some food prep. Plus, she cooked a meal for you being back in town."

"I'm actually feeling a bit tired, Big Paw. I was hoping to crash for a few hours."

"If you can perform for strangers, you can show up for your grandmother," he said. "We'll see you in a few."

He turned around and walked off, not giving me much of a choice. Then again, he was right. I hadn't been able to connect with my grandparents much over the past few months, and I'd missed them.

Sleep could come later; family was always first.

It didn't take much to convince Hazel to come with me, and an hour later, we were on our way. The moment I walked in the door, it smelled like Thanksgiving. The warmth of the season filled my grandparents' house, and I welcomed it. I'd missed them. I'd missed home. After traveling and working nonstop for the past few months, I felt pretty damn homesick.

"Sweetheart!" Grams said, grinning ear to ear as she walked over to me wearing her turkey apron. She was covered in flour and moving a bit slower than I remembered, but when she hugged me, I felt her love.

Gosh, I missed Grams's hugs.

As she let me go, I rolled up my sleeves. "How can I help you?" I asked.

She snickered. "Oh, sweetie, I think we are safer with you not in the kitchen."

I knew she had to be overwhelmed with cooking.

Thanksgiving in Eres wasn't a small event for my grandparents. Just as they did with everything, they thought about the town's overall enjoyment. Therefore, the barn house was set up with over two hundred chairs for people to show up and enjoy a meal. It worked mostly as a potluck where everyone brought a signature dish to pass around.

"Are you sure you don't want me to make my grand slam sloppy joe sliders?" I joked.

She shivered. "No, no. Sliders aren't made for Thanksgiving."

Brittainy Cherry

"They can be. I'll even add a few slices of cheese to make them fancy."

She shot that down fast.

What a shame—a nice can of sloppy joe could go a long way.

Just then, Hazel popped her head into the room. "Do you need any help in here, Holly? Big Paw is holding Rosie for a while."

Grams reacted completely differently to Hazel's request to help. She beamed ear to ear and waved Hazel into the kitchen. "Yes, yes, honey. I'd love the help. Please, come on in."

Hazel wandered into the room, and Grams gave her tasks instantly, and I felt personally attacked. "Are you kidding? I can help!"

"You're better helping Big Paw," Hazel said. "He's requesting your presence in his office."

I headed toward Big Paw's office, and when I walked inside, I snickered a little at the image of him holding little Rosie in his hands.

"That's a good look for you, Big Paw," I joked, but he didn't laugh.

He nodded toward the seat across from him. "Take a seat, Ian."

"What is this? A godfather moment?" I joked.

"Sit your ass down," he ordered.

I swallowed hard at his tone and took my seat. The sternness of his voice threw me for a loop and shot me back to my high school days when he used to scold me for being a dumbass kid.

He cradled Rosie in his arms—and to be clear, it was still hilarious to watch—and he narrowed his eyes toward me. "What are your intentions with Hazel?"

I chuckled, completely thrown off by his words. "What? What do you mean?"

"I mean exactly what I said, boy. What are your intentions? Do you see a future of some kind with her, or are you just playing the field out there on the road? Because that's a good girl with a hard work ethic who is raising her sister, and so help me, if you hurt her, I will kick your ass so hard you'll become a soprano."

236

"What the heck, Big Paw? I'm your grandson, not the other way around. Shouldn't you be giving Hazel this talk about her intentions for me?"

"I already did," he stated matter-of-factly. "She's a good girl who sees a future with you. But I can't have you out there playing with her emotions. She's a great human being, Ian. This world doesn't get many great human beings, and she's already been through a lot in her short lifetime, so if this isn't something you see yourself going with, if your career is the main focus for you right now, that's fine. But if that's so, let her go now before she falls deeper. Don't drag her along if you don't want something more. So I ask you again—what are your intentions?"

I clasped my hands together and leaned back in my chair, looking straight into my grandfather's eyes. "It's the kind of thing you have with Grams," I said, feeling it deep in my gut. I wanted to make a million memories with Hazel. I wanted our grandchildren to witness our love story firsthand as we grew older with one another down the line. I wanted her to sass me for the rest of forever.

I wanted to grow old with that girl who'd helped me open up my heart.

"All right, then." Big Paw smiled with the corner of his mouth, and he nodded once and only once. "No matter the fame and success you find, you keep holding on to that girl, all right? No matter what, you don't let her go."

29

HAZEL

"Please tell me that you got the godfather talk from Big Paw, too, and he wasn't just saying he gave it to you?" Ian asked as we drove back home late that evening from helping his grandparents.

"Oh, I received the talk and the threats that went along with it." I glanced back to Rosie sleeping in her car seat. If there was anything I could count on, it was Rosie falling asleep on car rides. Lately, when she was too overwhelmed, I'd pack us up in Ian's truck and drive around for as long as it took to soothe her. "The threats from Big Paw seem a little tamer when he's going gaga over Rosie, though."

"He's obsessed with her, huh? It's funny seeing him that way. Who knew it would take a baby to make him gentle? I thought only Grams could do that."

"There's not a day that he's not checking in on her. I swear, he comes to the ranch a lot more now that Rosie is around. She's a special thing, my little sister."

"She must take after you."

I smiled toward him as I laid my head against the headrest. "Can I tell you a secret?"

"You can tell me all your secrets."

"I worry a little about your grandparents working so hard at their age. They do too much for others, and they should really ease back. Holly is still working day in and day out at the Farmhouse, and Big Paw is pretty much running the town. It can't be good for their health. Plus, when I was cooking with Holly tonight, she seemed to get winded quite fast."

"I know. I've been telling them to slow down for the past few years, but they don't listen. It's as if they don't know how to take breaks from the grind of it all. They've done so much for this town. It's time they take a step back. I don't know what it will take for them to pull back any. They aren't really the type to take help—they are more into giving it."

"That makes me sad for them. They deserve a break, time for themselves."

"Says the girl who doesn't take time for herself."

I laughed. "I know it sounds crazy, but I feel more like myself than ever since I started working at the ranch. I never thought I'd be able to say that I loved a job like this, but I do. For so long I've been thinking about running away from this place, and the more time that passes, the more I think about how nice it would be to stay and teach Rosie about the ranch when she's old enough."

"Big Paw was telling me how good of a worker you are. It's hard to impress that man, so you should be proud of yourself."

"I am. I mean, it's hard, especially with Rosie, but somehow I'm keeping my head above water. I'm remembering to swim."

He put the truck in park in front of the house and shut off the engine. "I guess this isn't the point I should ask you to come on tour with me for a few weeks, huh? In my mind it sounded like a great idea, but now that I see how much you're loving your life, I'd feel awful pulling you away from everything."

"I don't know if the team can handle me leaving for a long period of time. After losing the Wreckage on the ranch, we've been trying to train new guys to be as good as you four were."

He smirked. "Good luck with that."

"I do want to see you in concert, though. I want to see you in your new world. It just might take a while for me to be able to get there with Rosie and all."

"She's always welcome to come, you know."

"Soon," I agreed, taking his hand into mine. "I promise we'll come see you soon."

Just then, Rosie started crying, and I glanced back to her. "Do you think we can do once around the dirt roads to get her back to sleep?" I asked.

Ian turned on the truck and put it into drive. Within five minutes, Rosie was sleeping again.

"Did you ever see yourself raising a baby at nineteen?" Ian asked. His right hand was still laced with mine, and I loved the warmth his touch sent through me.

"I actually fought really hard for this to not be my reality, and yet here we are. Truthfully, I don't regret it. Rosie is one of the best things that's ever happened to me. If you'd asked me if I would be dating one of the biggest up-and-coming musicians, I would've called you crazy too. But I guess that's the thing about life—it just happens."

He pulled my hand to his lips and kissed it, sending me waves of comfort.

And sometimes what happens in life is better than one could've ever imagined.

Thanksgiving dinner was filled with laughter, comfort, and tears in the barn house. I was seated at the table with the Wreckage as Rosie played with one of the many toys that the boys had brought back with them for her.

Eric, James, and Marcus were all smitten with the little girl in her turkey onesie, and it seemed that all of Eres was smitten with the Wreckage.

"I'm sorry to interrupt your Thanksgiving dinner, but I was wondering if me and my friend could get a picture?" a young girl said, shaking as she walked over to our table. Her friend stood back a little, trembling. They couldn't have been over fifteen, and the stars in their eyes were so bright and filled with hope.

When Ian and the guys agreed to the photograph, the girls jumped around with glee. The photographs with fanatics didn't stop until Big Paw made an announcement, forcing the crowds to stop storming the guys.

"How weird are your lives?" I asked them all, smiling. I loved the attention they were getting, because I knew how hard they'd worked to receive it.

"Pretty damn weird," Marcus replied, shoving food into his mouth. "But it's a good weird."

"Based on the number in our bank accounts, it's a really good weird," Eric sang, grinning ear to ear.

"And speaking of numbers in bank accounts," Ian said, reaching into his suit pocket. He pulled out an envelope and handed it over to me. "This is for you from us."

I raised an eyebrow. "What is that?"

"Open it and you'll see," James said.

Slowly I opened the envelope, and the moment I saw what was inside, I shut it and tossed it onto the table. "What the hell is that?" I breathed out.

"It's a check. You have seen a check before, right?" Ian joked.

"Not a check with that many zeroes, and was that a comma after two numbers? Commas don't come after two numbers on checks!" I exclaimed. My heart was pounding against my chest from simply touching that in my hand.

Ten thousand dollars.

The guys had handed me a check for $10,000 as if it were the easiest thing in the world. I remembered a few months back Marcus and Eric had fought over who was paying for their twenty-dollar Chinese-food bill. Now, they were handing out $10,000 checks.

Funny how fast someone's world could change.

"I can't take that," I told them.

Ian picked up the check and placed it back in my hand. "You can and you will. If it wasn't for your help with the lyrics, we would've never been discovered, and the more we take off, the more we'll thank you. This is just the beginning."

"Ian—"

"No," he cut in. "Don't fight this, Haze. You deserve this. You do so much for others without getting anything in return. It's about time you get rewarded for what you do."

"And there's more where that comes from!" Eric bellowed, swiping Ian's dinner roll from his plate.

As realization settled in, a wave of comfort began to wash over me. That money was going to help me more than they knew. I could do more for Rosie and me. I could start saving for a future I'd never thought I could have. I could breathe a bit easier.

"Thank you, guys. You have no clue how massive this is for me."

"Well, seeing as how you've been kicking it with our boy Ian, I'm sure you're used to seeing massive things," Marcus joked, nudging me in the side.

My face turned redder than the gelatin mold Mary Sue had made for the dinner.

"Stop embarrassing her, you ass!" Eric said, shoving his brother.

"What? I'm not! It's not like this whole town doesn't know about Ian's massive cock," Marcus argued. "Plus, I'd be happy as a dog eating a turkey bone if my girl was proud as day about my massive cock."

"Stop saying 'massive cock,'" Eric groaned, slapping his hand to his forehead.

"Maaassive cooock," Marcus dragged out, looking to drive his younger brother up the wall.

"Massive what?" a voice said from behind us.

We all looked over our shoulders to see Holly standing there, sweet as ever, with a raised eyebrow.

Now it was Marcus's turn to match the gelatin mold. "Uh, nothing, Grams," he said, shaking his head. I loved how all of the guys called Holly "Grams," as if they were her grandchildren too. Based on how she was with everyone in town, it was as if she were all of Eres's grandmother.

"No, go ahead and tell her what you were saying," Eric egged on. Marcus must've slammed his foot hard on Eric's beneath the table, because Eric screamed like a person doing the polar plunge on New Year's Day.

Holly kept smiling and waved a hand. "Oh, you boys and your humor. The dessert table is open. Go ahead and get you some pie."

James's eyes lit up from the mention of pie. "Did you make your homemade apple?"

Holly nodded. "Made an extra so you can get your own. Plus, there's custard in the freezer to go with it."

That made him and the brothers shoot up from their seats and hurry away. Ian kept staring at his grandmother with a somber look in his eyes. "What about you, Grams? Did you eat yet?"

She waved him off. "Oh no. Not yet. I'll get to it, though. I just want to make sure that everyone else's bellies are full before diving in."

"Everyone's pretty self-sufficient now, I think. Go ahead, Grams. Eat."

She shushed him before walking over to him and placing her hands against his cheeks. Holly leaned in and kissed Ian's forehead. "I'm so happy you're back in town. I couldn't imagine not spending the holiday with you. I miss you."

Ian gave her a lopsided smile. "I miss you too, Grams. And I'm sorry I haven't called enough. I'll make sure to remedy that."

"Whenever I get a call from you, I'm grateful. But don't feel like you have to go out of your way to ring me and Big Paw. We know you're busy becoming the next Elvis."

I smiled at their interaction and somewhat envied it. I'd never known my grandparents, and watching the love that lived between Holly and Ian was beautiful.

"Now, go on, go on. Get yourself some pie. I'm going to notify the other tables that it's ready," Holly said.

"I can just stand up and shout that dessert's a go," Ian offered, but she shook her head.

"No, no. I want to greet everyone and let them know that I'm grateful for them being here." She looked over to me and reached her hand out toward me. I took it in mine, and she gave me that smile that warmed me. "I'm so grateful for you being here, Hazel."

My eyes must've watered, because she ordered me to not cry before she headed off to the other tables.

"Gosh, she's a gem." I sniffled, wiping at the few tears falling from my eyes.

"Come on, Haze," Ian said, nudging me. "She said don't cry."

"I know, I know. I'm just so happy. This whole get-together is beyond amazing. I hadn't celebrated Thanksgiving over the past few years. Even when I did celebrate, it was mainly just my mom and me eating a store-bought chicken."

He raised an eyebrow. "My grandparents have been hosting this event since before I was born, and it's been free to all in town. Why didn't you come here?"

"Charlie didn't want us getting mixed into town events. He said it would bring up too many opportunities for nosy people to get in his way." He frowned, and I hated that. I hated when Ian looked sad for my past. I patted his knee. "But I'm here now, and that's all that matters."

"If I could go back in time, I would've never treated you the way that I did, Haze. I know time has passed since our first meeting, but damn. I still hate myself a little for being such an ass to you."

I chuckled a little. "Well, you've more than made up for that fact, that's for sure. Plus, the ten thousand dollars covers all rude comments of the past," I joked.

He stayed somber, and I missed the happiness that lay on his lips. "What is it, Ian?"

"I just miss you. I miss this," he said, gesturing toward the crowd. "I never thought I'd miss home so much until I left it."

"What do you miss the most?" I asked.

He breathed out a cloud of hot air. "Hell, everything. The stupid bumpy dirt roads. The bonfires. The animals on the farm. Dottie kicking me with her hooves. You. I miss you."

I leaned in and kissed his lips. "Well, I'm here right now."

"I'm thankful for that."

"I'm thankful for you."

His smile crept back to his lips, and he kissed me once more. As his lips lay against mine, he whispered to me, "Can I make love to you until the morning?"

"Yes," I replied, biting his bottom lip. "Or at least until Rosie needs a diaper change."

30

IAN

The short trip home came and went faster than I would've liked, but I was thankful for every second I'd been able to spend with my family and loved ones. When it came time to pack up my bags, Big Paw, Grams, and Hazel were waiting outside the house again like the first time I'd left. The only difference this time around was Rosie lying in Big Paw's arms.

"We really need to stop parting this way," Grams joked, kissing my cheek.

"I'll hopefully be back sooner than later."

"For Christmas?" she said, hopefully.

I frowned, knowing that we'd be gone doing Christmas shows. Never in my life had I missed Christmas with my grandparents. Perhaps Max would give us some kind of Christmas miracle. "I hope so, Grams." I kissed her cheek.

Big Paw waved me off and told me not to do the sad send-off again. I kissed Rosie's forehead and shook my grandfather's hand. "Do good out there, Ian. Then come home."

"Yes, sir."

Then I moved over to Hazel, who was holding a box in her hands. I dreaded saying goodbye to her. A part of me wanted to beg her to join me on tour, but I knew that was selfish. She was making a life for herself on the ranch, and I couldn't expect her to give up something she loved so much just so I could wake up with her every single day.

But dammit if I didn't want to wake up with her every single day.

"This is for you," she said, holding the box out toward me.

I raised an eyebrow and opened the box. As I studied the pieces inside, I felt as if my chest were going to explode with happiness. Funny how I'd left home to find happiness, but it had been sitting right there beside me all this time.

"It's a piece of home," she explained, digging through the box for me. "This is a jar filled with the old dirt road. There's a bonfire-scented candle and a few photographs of all of us. I even took pictures of the animals around the ranch. Also, Holly made a dozen of her kitchen-sink cookies for you, and I made a few loaves of banana bread. Just something to remind you of us whenever you need it."

I loved her so damn much, more and more each day. I hadn't known love could keep growing, but every time I was around Hazel, my grinch heart grew three sizes.

"You're perfect," I told her, putting the box down and pulling her into an embrace. "I'll see you soon, all right?"

"But not too soon," she ordered. "First your dreams need to come true."

"Trust me." I kissed her forehead. "They already did."

"You're my best friend, Ian Parker."

"You're my best friend, Hazel Stone."

"Go make your music, and then come back to us, okay? Don't worry—we'll leave the porch light on for your return," she said, kissing my cheek.

I put the box into my rental van and said my final goodbye. I stopped by the other guys' places to pick them up, and then we headed for the airport. As we sat in the terminal waiting to board our flight, I kept flipping through the pictures that Hazel had given me. It was clear as day that home wasn't a place—it was people, and I was the lucky asshole who'd never be homeless ever in my life.

"Is that from Hazel?" James asked, nodding toward the photographs.

"Yup, she made me a comfort package, and you know what?"

"What?"

"I'm going to marry the hell out of that girl someday."

When the guys and I got back on the road, it was a nonstop swirl of performances. We'd been given the opportunities to open for megastars across the country and then still work on preparing for our official album drop coming the following year.

Oftentimes, I thought Eric was going to have a heart attack as he watched our social media numbers climb to surreal heights. "One fucking million Instagram followers!" he shouted on the tour bus as we were on our way to Richmond, Virginia, for a show. "We just reached over one million followers!"

We all celebrated as if we'd won a damn Grammy. It felt good knowing that people were taking notice of us. That was the biggest reward to me—having people connect to the work we were putting out.

It felt as if we were in an avalanche of success. Each show we performed, more and more people would show up chanting our names. Fans would find out which hotels we were staying in. It became harder and harder to walk the streets without being recognized.

We were becoming everything Max Fucking Rider had promised to us—we were becoming famous, and it was all happening in a blink of an eye.

I was thankful for the connection I still had back home. I was thankful for my calls with Hazel because she kept me grounded.

After a mind-blowingly good show in Richmond, I tossed on a winter coat and walked outside late into the night for some fresh air and a conversation with Hazel.

"I can't believe you opened for Shawn Mendes and I wasn't there to see it," Hazel sighed, probably sadder about missing Shawn than missing me.

"I'm kind of glad you weren't here, because he looks better in person and sings better in person, and he's just a good fucking person. I don't need you leaving me for Shawn."

"You're right," she agreed. "I would've been begging him to have my babies."

I smirked. "The only one ever putting a baby in you is going to be me." My phone got quiet, and I realized what I'd said. "I mean, someday far, far away. I mean, shit. That came out pretty heavy handed. Pretend I didn't say that."

"No, it's fine. Really. I just didn't know you wanted kids someday."

I rubbed my forehead. I supposed that wasn't something we'd talked about before. "Well, yeah. Someday. Not anytime soon, of course. But I could see a few Ian Juniors running around. I think seeing Rosie really enforced that for me. She's cute as ever, and it got me thinking about it."

"She has that effect on people."

"What about you?" I asked, with a knot in my stomach. "Do you want kids down the road?"

"Oh yes. Two or three, at least. Even four or five. I want a big family filled with laughter. I grew up with not a lot of connections, other than my mom. I want to build a big family."

Me too, Haze.

I want to build that big-ass family with you.

I didn't say that, obviously. It seemed a little too forward.

"Excuse me! Excuse me! Are you Ian Parker?" a voice said from behind me.

Shit.

I kept walking. Max had instructed us that if we were ever seen in public and not interested in being approached, we were to keep walking at a normal speed and act as if we weren't who we were.

"Did someone spot you?" Hazel asked.

"Yeah, but I'm going to play it cool and loop around back to the hotel. It's fine."

"Excuse me! Please! You're Ian Parker, right?" another voice said. This time it was a male's voice. Most of the time it was women who called out to us, so the deep manly tone threw me for a loop.

"Nope, not Ian," I called out, keeping my pace.

"It is you!" the woman said. "It's Ian! I can tell. Ian Carter, it's us."

I paused my steps as my middle name rolled off the woman's tongue.

That was a new one to me. The last person who had called me Ian Carter was my—

I turned around to see the two people following me, and I felt as if I'd been sucker punched the moment I locked eyes with them both.

"I'm going to have to call you back, Hazel," I murmured, hanging up the phone. My lips parted as shock rocked throughout my whole body. "Mom? Dad?"

They looked broken down and tattered, but it was them. Her eyes matched my eyes; his frown matched my frown.

Mom raked her hands through her thinning hair, gave me a bright smile, and said two words as if she hadn't been missing from my life for the past fourteen fucking years. "Hey, baby."

31

IAN

Hey, baby.

Out of all the words I'd thought I'd hear my mother say after fourteen goddamn years, *Hey, baby* weren't among them. Maybe *Hey, Ian. Sorry for abandoning you and, oh, I don't know, fucking up your mind for fourteen years.* Or *Hey, son. Sorry about missing those fourteen birthdays.* Or *Hey, son. Still a fan of those Dallas Cowboys?*

Honestly, I'd thought I'd hear anything else in the whole fucking world other than those two words.

I didn't know how it happened, but somehow the three of us ended up sitting inside a diner down the street. It was as if I were moving on autopilot—too stunned to realize what exactly was happening before me. The two of them went ahead and ordered pretty much everything on the menu and stuffed their faces as if they hadn't eaten in years.

I hadn't an appetite at all.

"We just wanted to thank you for meeting with us tonight, son," Dad said, tossing a few fries into his mouth. His foot tapped repeatedly against the tiled floor. He wore a worn-down winter coat with holes in it and a winter hat. He had a beard that hadn't been trimmed in God knew how long, and he couldn't stop . . . fidgeting. I didn't even know if he knew he was fidgeting so much, but he hadn't stopped.

Mom was the same way, but her movements were not as intense as Dad's.

They looked . . . fucking awful.

As if they'd left Eres and had been riding the shit train ever since.

It was clear they were still using, and that broke my heart. I'd figured one of two things had happened since they'd left: (a) they'd overdosed and lost their lives, or (b) they'd found their way to living a happy, clean life and just left me in the past.

Obviously, option B made it easier for me to sleep at night.

But finding out that there was an option C—they were still as fucked up as before—broke my heart.

"We'd been meaning to reach out for so long, but I doubt Big Paw would've wanted us to come back like this," Mom said, shivering as if she were cold, but sweating at the same time. I tossed off my jacket and wrapped it around her shoulders. She smiled. "Looks like they ended up raising a southern gentleman," she commented, nudging Dad in the side. "I told you he'd turn out to be great, didn't I, Ray?"

"She sure did say that," he agreed, sipping at his cola.

"What are you doing here? How did you find me?"

"Oh, you're an easy one to spot. We saw you were performing in town tonight, and your face has been broadcast all over the internet and magazines and television. I don't know if you know it, son, but you're kind of a big deal around these parts."

I gave him a tight smile. If only he knew the uneasiness he gave me by calling me "son."

I hadn't been their son in years.

"But why are you here?" I asked again. "What do you want?"

I saw how taken aback Mom was by those words, but I didn't know how else to ask. I'd envisioned the two of them and me reuniting many times before, but unfortunately, I'd hoped it would've been before fame came— not after. Now that I was on the path of making something of myself, it came off as quite suspicious that they were approaching me for a family reunion.

Mom reached out toward me and placed her hand on top of mine, and fuck, it felt good to hold her hand. I hated how good it felt. Even though her hands were ice cold, her touch was enough to warm up the chilled parts of my soul.

"We wanted to see you, Ian; that's all. To make sure that you are doing okay."

"You could've checked in a long time ago to make sure of that. My address hasn't changed. You knew where I was."

"Yes, but we didn't have the money to travel back down to Nebraska," Dad argued.

"I'm guessing you didn't have money for a pay phone either. Grams and Big Paw's number has been the same since the nineties."

Dad's brows lowered, and a coldness washed across his stare. "What are you trying to say? We didn't try hard enough to get in contact?"

"That's exactly what I'm trying to say," I said straight out. "It's just odd that you happen to reappear after all this time now that you saw me on TV. It's fucked up."

"Watch your tongue, boy!" Dad barked, pointing a stern finger in my direction, causing people to glance over to our table.

Mom reached out and lowered his arm, shushing him. "Calm down, Ray."

He grumbled. "I just don't like what he's getting at."

"Why, because I'm right?" I asked. I pulled out my wallet and began thumbing through the bills. "So what are we thinking? How much do you need? I mean, you are after money, right? It's clear we aren't here to reconnect and share memories."

Mom's head lowered, and she shook it. "We did want to see you, Ian. I swear, but it's just . . . we've fell on some hard times and were wondering if you could help us out."

The regret I got from allowing my heart to beat again after all these years came storming back toward me. The problem with beating hearts was that they could break in an instant.

I pulled out the cash in my wallet and set it in front of me. Their eyes glazed over in wonderment as they looked at it, showing me that the money was exactly what they were after. "I got five hundred."

"Bullshit," Dad—no, Ray—snapped. "You're a damn superstar. You can give us more than that."

"What in the hell makes you think I owe you anything?"

"We're your parents," he said, his voice dripping with anger. He was probably high out of his fucking mind.

"You're not anything to me. Here's the thing. You take the five hundred dollars now, or you take no money, and we can figure out if we can have a relationship down the line. But if we do, I'm not giving you a dime ever. You take the five hundred dollars, or you get your son back. The choice is yours."

I felt like a damn idiot.

As the seconds ticked by, my heart, my stupid bruised and battered heart, was crying out like the eight-year-old child I used to be, asking—no, begging—his parents to pick him. I wanted them to pick me, to choose me, to want me.

They glanced toward one another, then to the cash, never looking back toward me. In one quick movement, Ray scooped up the money and stuffed it into his pocket.

And my stupid bruised and battered beating heart?

It fucking shattered.

They left that night with $500 in their hands to continue to chase their high as I was left alone in the diner, looking like a damn fool.

"What's going on? What happened?" Hazel asked as I lay in the hotel room with the phone pressed against my ear. She'd left me dozens of text messages and called multiple times, leaving me voice messages filled with worry.

I'd finally built up enough nerve to call her back around one in the morning. "Just some bullshit," I murmured. It took a lot for me to break out the whiskey, but I was sipping away at a glass as I sat in bed. I was drunk by the time I'd called her, and that probably wasn't a good thing.

Whiskey normally made me sad, but that didn't matter—seeing as how I was already crushed.

"Was it someone who ran into you? A fan? Paparazzi?"

"No." I shook my head as if she could see me. "Even worse. It was my parents."

Hazel gasped through the receiver. "Oh my gosh, what?"

"I guess they saw me on TV. Wanted to catch up, and by 'catch up,' I mean they wanted money."

"Oh my gosh, Ian. I can't believe that. What did you do?"

"I gave them an option—five hundred bucks or a relationship with me."

She sighed, almost as if she knew what they'd chosen. "They took the money?"

"Yeah." I chuckled, the back of my throat burning from the whiskey and the pain of the night. "They took the fucking money."

"Idiots," she whispered. "I hate them. I know I shouldn't hate your parents, but I do. I really freaking hate them."

"Yeah. It's not like they made the wrong choice," I drunkenly said, tossing the whiskey back, before walking over to the bar to pour myself another glass. "I wouldn't have chosen me either."

"Don't say that. You aren't the mistake in this, Ian. They are. They are the flawed ones, not you."

I stayed quiet and placed a hand on the bar to stabilize myself as my mind spun from the whiskey and the heartache.

"What do you need?" she asked, her voice alert and stern. "Tell me what you need."

I swallowed hard and cleared my throat. "My best friend," I muttered. "I need my best friend."

"Okay. I'm on my way."

32

IAN

"What the fuck is this?" Max hollered as he stormed toward me in the hotel lobby the next morning. We had two more shows in Richmond, and I couldn't help but want to go home. But as they said, the show had to go on.

The guys and I were waiting in the lobby to head off to a few interviews, and the sound of Max's high-pitched voice felt like nails on a fucking chalkboard to my hangover.

I pinched the bridge of my nose as he stopped in front of me. I was sporting the nice sunglasses and dark apparel, and all I wanted was a few ibuprofen and deep-fried foods.

"What's what?" I grumbled, not wanting to deal with my manager that morning. Did he make our dreams come true? Yes. Did he drive me insane at times? Double yes.

"This," he said, shoving the phone into my hands.

I stared at the screen, and a knot formed in my stomach. It was a tabloid image of me sitting in the diner with my parents, and it captured me handing money over to the two of them. From the outside looking in, it looked shady as fuck.

Okay, regardless, it was shady, but the tabloids made it look fucking awful. Now I understood Max's panic.

"What is it?" James asked, taking the phone from my hand. The moment he saw it, his mouth dropped open. "Holy shit. Is that . . . ?" he asked.

I nodded. "Yup."

Max snatched the phone back from my hands, completely unaware of who I was sitting across from in that picture. And he obviously didn't care.

He sat on the coffee table directly across from me and clasped his hands together. "Are you on drugs?"

"What?" I blurted out. "No, I'm not on drugs."

"Don't fucking lie to me, Ian. If you are, I just have to know what kind. Cocaine? I can do. Molly? Sure. A few pills and cough syrup on a Saturday night? Sure, why not? But this—this picture looks like two people on fucking meth. And I don't fuck with artists who are doing meth," he bellowed with his nose flaring. "So did you meet up with those meth heads to join their party?"

James's jaw clenched, and he lowered his brows. "You don't know what you're talking about, Max," my friend said.

"No offense, Yoda, but I'm talking to my star right now. A star who is about to throw away everything we have going for him. So please, mind your own business."

James parted his mouth to give Max a piece of his mind, but I held a hand up to stop him. James's face was bright red with anger, and it took a lot to get him to that level. I knew if he snapped on Max, there would be no going back from it.

When James grew upset—which hardly ever happened—he turned into the Incredible Hulk, and he would've smashed things. Like Max's face.

"They are my parents," I said, knowing there was no reason to lie. "They haven't been in my life for years, due to their drug problem, and when they found out about my success, they came around looking for money."

Max sighed and rolled a hand against his face. "Please don't tell me you gave them money; please don't tell me you gave them money," he begged.

"I did, but I told them they couldn't come back for more. It's over."

"God dammit!" Max said, standing from his sitting position and stomping around like a damn child. "No! No. You never give addict family members money. You know why, Ian?"

"Enlighten me," I grumbled, annoyed by my manager.

"Because they never fucking go away! If you give a druggie a penny, they come back again asking for a dime. This is shit. This is fucking shit." Max dug into his fanny pack–type bag, pulled out his prescription pills, and popped them into his mouth. He took a deep breath and tried to ground himself. "Okay. Okay. That's fine. I'll fix this. But in the meantime—don't go around handing out any more money to anyone, okay? Your career is just starting, and I really don't want it to end because some meth-head parents decide they want to get rich quick and write a tell-all story about Ian Parker."

"They have nothing to tell. They haven't known me for years."

"People don't care if they are telling the truth! They just want drama!" he shouted.

Before I could reply, he was already making calls and storming off.

The guys all looked at me with the most sincere looks on their faces. It was clear they were more concerned about my well-being than Max was, but I wasn't in the mood to talk about it.

"Not now, you guys," I muttered, leaning back against the chair. "I can't talk about it now."

"I get it, man," Marcus said, patting me on the back. "But when you're ready to talk, we're here to listen."

That night's performance was probably one of the hardest ones I'd had to put on, but I followed through, and when it was time to get off stage, I dashed to my dressing room. I wanted nothing more than to avoid all human contact, go crash in my hotel room, and live in my self-pity.

As I opened the dressing room, I noticed a person sitting in the chair near my mirror with their back to me.

"Uh, excuse me?"

"You know, you have to be more careful about these dressing rooms having better security." Hazel swung around in the chair and gave me her smile. The smile that fixed things. "Otherwise any fangirl could come in here and try to touch your butt."

I didn't reply to her sassy comment. I just beelined toward her and pulled her in for a hug. I held her tighter than ever.

"I'm sorry I'm late," she whispered, nudging her head against my chest.

"You're right on time. Where's Rosie?"

"Big Paw and Holly are watching her for the next two days, with the help of Leah, until I get back to town." She pulled back a little and placed her palm against my cheek. Her dilated eyes pierced me. "Are you okay?"

I shook my head.

She hugged me tighter. "Okay."

Just then, the dressing room door swung open, and Max came barging into the room. "Ian, we need to—" He stopped. He arched an eyebrow and eyed Hazel up and down. "Oh. Uh, sorry, I didn't know you were with company."

I stepped away from Hazel and gestured toward Max. "Haze, this is Max, my manager. Max, this is my girlfriend, Hazel." It felt good introducing her that way to people—as my girlfriend.

Max's eyes began to study Hazel a little more, and for the first time since I'd been working with him, I realized what he looked like. He looked like a rat, always studying things to see if he could get something from them.

He pushed out a smile, walked over to Hazel, and offered her a handshake. "Max Rider. Nice to meet you. So you're the one taking up a lot of Ian's focus, huh?"

Hazel grinned. "Guilty as charged."

Max kept his lips pressed together tightly and traced his eyes over Hazel once again. "What's your last name, Hazel?"

She cocked an eyebrow but answered. "Stone."

Max whistled. "Hazel Stone and Ian Parker. It has a good ring to it. Anyway, I don't want to take up too much of your time. I just wanted to remind you of the party tonight with some big names, Ian."

I cringed and shook my head. "I was hoping to lay low tonight with Hazel. It's been a crazy twenty-four hours."

"Who are you telling? I know. I've been in charge of damage control, remember?"

Hazel cocked another eyebrow toward Max's tone, and I could tell she was bothered by him. She must've been trying really hard to bite her tongue. I could imagine the sassy responses flying through her brain.

"Yeah, I know. But I just need a night off."

"Not now," he argued. "Now is the time you get out there and showcase that you aren't on drugs. You be charming and funny and the persona we are creating Ian Parker to be."

"I don't feel like being charming and funny."

"That's why it's called acting."

"I'm a musician, not an actor."

He laughed. "All musicians are actors. The only difference is musicians can sing better. Anyhoo, I'll text you the details."

He hurried out of the room and slammed the door behind him before I could respond.

"So that's the amazing Max Fucking Rider, huh?" Hazel said, rolling her eyes so hard I thought she'd never see straight again. "He does know that at the end of the day, he works for you, right?"

I gave a lazy smile. "I doubt he knows that. Sorry you had to witness that. I was hoping we could talk and chill, but I think I have to make an appearance tonight, for damage control and all."

"Who's handling the damage control on your heart?" she asked.

I wrapped an arm around her and pulled her in close. "You are." I pressed my lips to her forehead. "I know you didn't come out here to come to a party, but I'd love to have you by my side to keep me levelheaded."

"Where you lead, I'll follow. Whatever you need from me over these next thirty hours, I'm yours."

33

HAZEL

Max Fucking Rider.

More like Max Fucking Dickhead.

I couldn't believe he was so cocky for such a little, little man. Max was a bald-headed guy, probably in his forties, but he dressed like he was in his twenties. He was obviously trying too hard to stay relevant, and it was coming off exactly as that—a middle-aged man trying too hard. Plus, he had a large amount of chest hair curling out of the top of his shirt.

If a penis and a gorilla had a child, it would be Max Fucking Rider.

If it weren't for Ian and the band, I would've told Max where he could shove it. But instead, I was a good southern belle. I smiled and charmed and kept my extremely unpleasant thoughts about the man to myself.

Then I went to the hotel with Ian to get ready for the party.

"I have nothing to wear for a party," I confessed, combing through the few items of clothing sitting in my suitcase.

"Whatever you have is fine. You could wear what you have on now, and that will be fine," Ian said.

I laughed and looked down at my oversize hoodie and leggings. "Really? Is this what people wear to meet celebrities nowadays?" I frowned, feeling a bit defeated as I saw the fancy clothes that Ian was changing into. I doubt the women who were surrounding the Wreckage on the daily looked the way I did. They probably wore formfitting dresses and high heels.

I looked down to my Adidas.

Definitely not Christian Louboutin.

"Don't do that, Hazel," he warned.

"Do what?"

"Think you have to change for this world I'm in. These parties, these fancy clothes—this isn't real."

"And what is real?"

"Old dirt roads. Bonfires. Grams's cooking." He smiled at me and walked over to scoop me into his arms. "You. Me. Us. We're real. Everything else is just an act. Whatever you wear is good enough."

The comfort those words gave me eased my troubled heart. I couldn't help but fall more in love with the man standing beside me. "Is it too soon for me to ask how you're doing with seeing your parents? Or do you want to get through tonight first?"

"Let's get through tonight; then we can talk until morning."

"Perfect."

"And Haze?"

"Yes?"

"I also want you to tell me all your thoughts on Max."

I snickered. "Trust me, they aren't nice."

"I know." He nodded. "That's why I want to hear them all."

When we arrived at the nightclub, I was completely out of my element. Yet still, Ian kept my hand wrapped in his as we wandered through the club. People were packed in like sardines. Everyone and their mama were in that place for the night, chatting it up and kissing the asses of the boys of the Wreckage, singing their praises. It was so strange seeing how much people loved the band. It was . . . powerful.

The guys all interacted as if they belonged too. Even though Eric was underage, there must've been an "I am becoming famous" clause, because he was allowed into the club too. Plus, I was allowed in because I was on Ian's arm.

"I'm going to run to the bathroom," I said to Ian, giving his hand a squeeze. He hadn't let go of me since we'd walked inside, and I was so happy for his touch. He gave me the comfort I hadn't known I needed.

"I'll wait here," he said, stepping to the side of the bathroom.

"You can wander. I'll find you."

He grinned. "I'll wait here."

I headed to the bathroom to refocus my mind, because I truly felt as if I'd stepped into the twilight zone.

As I walked into the bathroom, I noticed two women—twins, it appeared—reapplying their lipstick. "Did you see that Ian Parker is here?" one asked.

"Yes. And holy crap, is he hot," her twin echoed.

"Dibs!" the other said.

"Not fair," the other pouted. "Then again, the drummer is hot. I could go for him too."

She pushed her boobs together and smirked before looking toward me with a confused look.

"Um, can I help you?" she questioned, looking me up and down like I didn't belong. Then again, she might've been looking at me so strangely because I was being a complete creeper and staring at them in the bathroom as I eavesdropped on their conversation about my boyfriend.

"Oh, uh, no. Sorry. Are you in line?" I asked, pointing to the bathroom stalls. The completely empty bathroom stalls. I wanted to crawl into a ball and rock in a corner because of how awkward I was.

"Um, no, sweetheart. It's all yours."

I hurried into the stall and shut the door. I pounded my hand against my forehead, feeling ridiculous. How humiliating.

After I heard them leave, I took a few deep breaths and walked out of the stall. I stared into the mirror and tried to erase how beautiful those women were. "Dirt roads, bonfires, Holly's cooking," I murmured, reminding myself what was real and what truly mattered.

The moment I stepped outside of the bathroom, an uneasy feeling rushed through me as I noticed Ian was missing. My eyes danced around the space in search of him, and as I began to walk off to find him, I heard my name being called. I turned around to see Max Fucking Dickhead in an overpriced suit.

I raised an eyebrow. "Yes?"

"I thought that was you. It's nice to see you again."

"It's nice to see you too," I lied, giving him a small, fake smile. "I'm sorry, I was just off to find Ian," I started, stepping off.

He held his hand out and pointed across the room. "Oh, he's right there, talking to the Romper twins. They're up-and-coming vocalists. Just as hot on the scene as the Wreckage."

I looked up to see the two beauties from the bathroom, and my stomach dropped.

They were flirting with Ian, touching his shoulders and tossing their heads back in laughter, as Ian kept his hands to himself with a small, uncomfortable smile.

"I sent him off to chat with them. You know, networking and all," Max explained. He stuffed his hands into his tailored pants and swayed back and forth. "I'm glad I bumped into you, actually. I was hoping to get to know more about Ms. Hazel Stone."

"There's not much to know, actually."

He chuckled. "Humble, huh? That's nice. You don't run across a lot of humble people where I come from. I must admit, I almost feel as if I know you from the amount of times that Ian brings you up. You two must've been dating for ages."

"Not that long, actually. We connected over the summer, and we actually only made it official right before Ian went out to Los Angeles to work with you."

"Oh? That's surprising. So it's not too much of a serious relationship," he remarked. I didn't like the way he said those words.

"I disagree with that. We are very close. We mean the world to one another."

"Yeah, I'm sure that's true. Young love and all. I just worry about how that's going to shape the future of his career, you know, having him be with someone like you."

"Excuse me? Someone like me?"

"You know: a single mother. You *do* have a child, right?"

I remained quiet and didn't find the tone of his question to be to my liking. And obviously, he knew things about me.

He gave me another smile. I didn't return the gesture this time.

"I have to ask, is the kid Ian's? Just from a marketing point of view, these things are important to know."

"No, it's not, but it is a pretty private situation that I don't feel comfortable talking about. Now, if you'd excuse me—" I pushed past him but froze in place when he spoke again.

"I just worry about the headlines that your relationship with Ian could bring to the forefront. Like the fact that your mother is in prison for running a meth lab."

"You're crossing so many lines right now," I barked toward him, barging back in front of his face. "I don't know how you know about my mother, but it is truly none of your business."

"But it is. With a quick Google search, you can find out everything there is to know about anyone on this planet. How do you think it will look when people get ahold of the fact that Ian is in a relationship with a meth addict?"

"What? No. I've never used drugs. I don't have a problem. I'm not my mother."

"But what does that matter? The internet will make you your mother. They will twist the story and spin a web of lies. They will make it seem as if Ian, too, is a drug addict. They will shut down his flame before he even has a minute to burn, and for what? For a girl he hadn't even been serious about before the beginning of the summer? Is that what you want for him? Do you really want to kill his chance at fame for a love story that might not even be everlasting?"

My mouth parted to speak, but no words came out. It was as if Max had stolen every ounce of courage from my bones as he stared my way. What I hated most was how there was so much truth to his words. Those same thoughts had been flying through my mind for weeks now. How would it look if I were on Ian's arm, especially now with Rosie in the picture? What would people say? How would people judge us?

What would happen to his career?

"I can tell that it's sinking in. I can tell you're putting the pieces together in your mind. I'm not trying to be the bad guy, but if that's how I'm coming off, so be it. I'll take that bullet in order to make sure that these guys get the best shot at a career. I've been doing my job for a long time, and I know what it looks like when people have the 'it' factor. Ian Parker has it in waves. All I'm asking is that you don't weigh him down. You have to let him fly. They are getting ready to soar. Break it to him sooner than later. It will be harder if you drag it. I mean, I get it."

"You don't," I snapped.

"Trust me, I do. You both are from the same world. His parents are druggies, and yours are too."

"That's not the reason I connect with him. You have no clue."

Dirt roads. Bonfires. Holly's cooking.

"Sweetheart, it is. You're from the same world, but Ian? He's on his way to a whole new planet. I mean, look at him," he said, gesturing again toward the twins and Ian. "That's his future. Those are the kind of women he needs on his arm. Just be content with being a part of his past. It will end up being a good story to tell your grandkids someday, that you dated Ian Parker, the superstar, for a short period of time."

I didn't say another word to Max.

Max Fucking Dickhead.

The man who spoke the truth even when my heart didn't want to hear it.

I walked away from him and headed straight in Ian's direction. The nerves that were shooting through me eased as he looked up toward me and gave me his smile. Not his famous Ian Parker smile but his real grin. The one that he saved only for me.

That's real. We're real.

I stepped in front of the twins, and Ian held his hand out toward me. I took it into mine, and I felt at home once more. Sure, I didn't look like the ladies surrounding me, but Ian looked my way as if I were the most beautiful woman alive.

He pulled me into his side and gave me a tight squeeze. More comfort. "Erin and Trina, this is Hazel, my girlfriend."

They looked at me as if I were trash, and I couldn't help but smile. I held my hand out toward them for handshakes. "Nice to meet you," I said.

"Same," they replied in unison.

Ian leaned into me and whispered against my ear. "Can we get the hell out of here, put on pajamas, and order room service?"

"You're speaking my language."

We excused ourselves from the conversation, and I swore the twins were left dazed and confused. Ian had a car waiting for him out back, and when we stepped outside, he looked deep in thought as he studied the sky.

My fingers fidgeted together as Max's words played over and over again in my head. I wanted to tune them out and allow my feelings for Ian to be the strongest thing in the world, but it was impossible not to feel an ache in my heart.

If Max had been able to find out that information about my past in a short period of time, I was certain others could too.

Ian and I had happened so fast. We hadn't even had a chance to fully wrap our heads around the idea of us being together before he'd been off to Los Angeles. Then, after that, everything with Rosie had happened, which had added another wrench to our situation.

We were still so fresh, so new to the possibility of our love story, that we hadn't had a chance to really be concrete about it all.

Ian kept looking up at the sky, and I kept looking at him. "You know . . . every night since I've been gone, I'd go outside and look up at the moon. I'd sit there for a while staring at it in all its phases, and I'd feel a weird sense of comfort. Los Angeles is different, Haze. It's a land of its own, and there's so many people, but it's as if no one really knows or cares for each other. It's not personal. It's stiff. Don't get me wrong—I'm happy for what I've been given. The opportunities have been out of this world. But it gets lonely, and I miss home. So when I look up to the moon, I feel a little bit better. Because I know you're staring at the same thing back in Eres."

He didn't have a clue how much comfort his words gave to me.

We'd crawled into bed after stuffing our faces with deep-fried foods. It was the first time we'd been able to truly talk about everything that had happened with his parents. I didn't want to push him, but I was happy when he brought it up all on his own.

"I want to pretend that it didn't fuck with my head, but it did. I want to pretend I didn't pray they'd choose me, but I did. I want to pretend I didn't drink to get through the show tonight, but I did. I'm a mess, Haze, and seeing them in the shape that they were screwed with my head so much. I just want to stop for a while and not be forced to act happy like I had to at the party tonight. I don't want to do shows feeling miserable, but I have to do it. If I didn't, I'm not only fucking myself over, but I'm screwing the guys up too. This isn't just my dream—it's theirs, and I can't pull back because it would affect so many more people than just me."

"The guys will understand, Ian. If anything, those three get it the most."

He grimaced. "But then there's Max."

"Screw him," I bellowed, feeling my skin crawl at the mention of him. "Like I said before, he works for you. He makes your life easier, not the other way around."

Still, Ian didn't seem convinced, so I dropped that angle. "Well, at least for tonight, you don't have to act happy or be 'on.' You can be whatever you need to be, and I'll be here for you. I'm not going anywhere."

"Promise?" he whispered with a crack in his voice. He sounded so heartbroken. "Promise me you won't abandon me too?"

"I promise."

He held me close and fell apart against me that night.

I stayed close enough to make sure I was able to pick up his broken pieces. And when we made love, I hoped he felt forever against my lips.

34

HAZEL

The moment I landed back in Nebraska, I drove the few hours to make it to Eres, and I headed straight to Big Paw and Holly's to pick up Rosie. I knew it had only been two days, but gosh, I missed that little girl. It felt like I had a big hole in me.

"Thank you for watching her," I told Big Paw as I took Rosie into my arms. Holly stood nearby with that sweet smile on her face.

"Anytime," Big Paw said, grumbling. "Even if she threw up in my face."

I laughed. "She has a way of doing that. I was hoping I could talk to you both about Ian . . . I'm a little worried."

Those words made his grandparents' eyes widen with worry.

"What is it?" Holly asked. "What's wrong with him?"

"He ran into his parents; that's why he wanted me to come out there. They used him and asked him for money. I think he's really struggling right now, trying to figure all those things out."

"Son of a bitch," Big Paw grumbled, taking off his hat and slapping it against his leg. "See, Holly! This is what I said would happen! I said the moment that boy found success, those two would come trying to claim some of it."

Holly frowned and nodded knowingly. "How's our boy doing?" she asked, her brows low. I saw the worry in her eyes, and I couldn't blame her.

"He's struggling," I explained. "But he's strong. He'll be okay."

"I don't get why they couldn't just let him be," Big Paw huffed. "He was doing good on his own. They didn't need to come and piss on his parade."

"Yeah. I feel the same way. If only we could control the choices of others, life would be easier." I soothed a fussy Rosie in my arms as Big Paw kept frowning.

"Get that girl home, and get her a bottle. And hold her up a bit higher; it makes her stop fussing so much."

I did as he said, and like magic, Rosie calmed down.

Who would've ever thought?

Big Paw—the baby whisperer.

Rosie and I headed home, and when I unlocked the front door, I placed Rosie's car seat down on the ground to turn on the lights.

"Oh my gosh!" I gasped as the room filled with light. In the middle of the living room was a battered and bruised Garrett, hunched over. "Garrett, what happened to you?" I hurried to his side to help him up but stopped the moment I heard another voice.

"He didn't listen—that's what happened to him."

I turned around to see Charlie standing next to Rosie's car seat.

Every hair on my body stood up as he bent down and lifted Rosie into his arms.

"Put her down," I ordered, charging toward him, and he released a sinister laugh.

"What makes you think you can tell me what to do?" he hissed. "After the shit you pulled, getting me locked up for all that time, making my business suffer, you think you can order me around?"

I tried to control my trembling, but watching him hold Rosie sent a wave of panic through me.

"Looks like you built yourself a nice life out here," Charlie commented. "Living the dream, are we? I heard rumors about you dating Eres's own rock star too. That must be great."

"What do you want?" I asked, wanting him to get to the point. Rosie began crying, and Charlie sat down on the couch with her and began bouncing her on his knee.

"What do you think I want? What's mine. I lost thousands of dollars because of that stunt you pulled. I lost clients. I got the uppers chewing my ass out because of you. If it wasn't for your mom, I'd still be locked up. So I'm here to collect. Every cent you have is mine. Every paycheck that you get from this lame-ass job comes to me. And your happy ending you think you got? The love story with your rock star? That comes to an end."

"Leave Ian out of this."

"Oh, no way. You see, my other half is locked up because of you for the next two years. Why should you get a love story when I don't get mine?"

"You don't love my mother," I barked. "You never did. You loved controlling her, just like you love controlling everything. I mean, look at what you did to your own nephew!"

"He betrayed me!" Charlie shouted, standing up and gesturing toward Garrett with one hand and holding my screaming sister in the other. "The asshole betrayed me when he helped you get Rosie, and he's going to be paying for it each day until he proves I can trust him again."

"He did the right thing."

"Fuck the right thing. Do I seem like someone who cares about the right thing?" he argued. He took a deep breath and sat back down. "Sorry. Sometimes my temper gets the best of me. I took a meditation class while I was locked up—I'm working on my breathing techniques. Anyway, as I was saying. You break things off with that boyfriend of yours."

"Why are you being so cruel?"

He snickered. "Because I think you're right. I think I like controlling things."

"I won't do it," I said. "I won't break things off with him."

"That's too bad. You know what else would be too bad?" he asked. "If this nice old ranch burned down. Or even worse, if something happened to this little sister of yours."

I knew he said those things as threats, but I also knew that Charlie's threats normally ended up as promises.

"So here's what we are going to do. You're going to give me money every two weeks, you are going to break up with your superstar, and you are going to live a miserable fucking life, because you don't deserve to be happy. You got it?"

"Just say yes, Hazel," Garrett choked out.

"How about you learn to shut the hell up," Charlie called out toward his nephew. "The grown-ups are having a meeting. So Hazel, what do you say? Do we have a deal?"

I nodded slowly as tears slipped from my eyes.

He walked over to me and placed a finger beneath my chin. He raised my head until I locked eyes with his. "I need a verbal agreement, sweetheart."

"Yes, we have a deal," I said, shaking from his touch.

"Now, pull out that cell phone of yours, and make a call to the guy, and let him know you're over."

"What? Can't I—" I started to argue, but the fire in Charlie's eyes was enough to terrify me. I pulled my phone out of my back pocket and dialed Ian's number.

Please don't answer; please don't answer; please don't—

"Hello?"

"Hey, Ian, it's me," I said with a shaky voice.

"Good. You made it home?"

"Yup, I'm here safe and sound. There's just one thing . . . I, um, I . . . I . . ." My words fumbled against my tongue as I covered my mouth with my hand to conceal my tears.

"Haze? What is it?" Ian asked, growing concerned.

"Spit that shit out," Charlie ordered in a low tone.

"I—it was great seeing you, Ian. Truly, it was, but after seeing the world you're creating out there, I realize that there's not much space for me in it anymore."

"Wait . . . what?"

"I just think it's best if we end it now, before your career takes off. I'm sorry. I just can't be with you anymore. I can't be in this relationship."

"What the fuck are you talking about, Hazel? We're good. We're so fucking good. We made love this morning, and everything was fine. You left and said you loved me. Tell me what's happening here. What's really going on?"

"Nothing. I just had a lot of time to reflect on the flight home, and it's clear we're going two different ways. My life is here on the ranch, and yours is out there in the world. It's best that we end it now."

"You can't say this," Ian started.

"Hang up," Charlie said, shoving me in the arm, making me tremble even more.

I can't, I mouthed.

"Hang up now, or I walk out with your sister," he threatened.

With a pained heart, I clicked the phone off as Ian was still begging for answers to my sudden change of heart.

"Good girl," Charlie whispered, rubbing his hand against my neck, sending chills down my spine. "Here. Take this bitch," he said, handing Rosie over to me. "It's been nice doing business with you. Garrett, get your ass up, and let's go."

Garrett did as his uncle said and stumbled toward the front door.

Charlie turned back to glance at me, and then he looked down at the carpet. "Half a cup of warm water mixed with one tablespoon of ammonia. That will get the bloodstain out of your nice carpet."

Then he left, leaving me there sobbing against Rosie. Our tears intermixed as she howled in sadness.

My phone kept ringing with Ian's name popping up on the screen, but I didn't dare answer it. Even if all I wanted was to hear his voice.

Three days later, Ian was back in Eres, standing in front of me with confusion and heartache in his eyes. "Did Max say something to you? Did he try to push you away?" he asked as we stood near the shed late that evening.

Oh, Ian . . .

Please don't make this harder than it has to be.

"It's not that," I said. "I just feel like we aren't right for each other."

"No one's more right for one another, Haze. It's us. But I'm so confused. I feel like you're talking as if you don't believe in us anymore. As if you don't think we can figure this out."

I closed my eyes and shook my head. "That's because I don't think we can. I'm sorry, Ian. My life shifted, and I need to learn to accept the way it is shaping up. I'm coming to terms that my responsibility in life now is to look after my sister. And I'm coming to terms that you and me can't be—"

"Don't," he begged, shaking his head. "Don't say it."

"Ian. We can't do this anymore. I can't be yours, and you can't be mine."

"You're running away before you even give us a fair chance. I know things have been crazy lately, and I know we haven't found our footing yet, but we just need more time."

"You're right. We need time to let go of the idea of us. You're an amazing person, Ian Parker, and you have so many outstanding things coming your way. But I refuse to be the girl who gets in the way of your dreams. I know you say I won't, but I know I will. Especially with Rosie. So I'm ending this. I'm breaking up with you because I care too much about you to keep this going."

"You promised," he said, shaking his head in disbelief. "You promised you wouldn't leave. You promised you wouldn't abandon me."

That felt like a knife to my soul. I knew of his struggles. I knew how he feared being left behind, but what choice did I have? I couldn't be with him, because not only did it put his family's ranch in danger, but it put Rosie in harm's way, and I couldn't let anything happen to her. I couldn't let her get hurt because I selfishly wanted to be with Ian.

I didn't respond to his comment, and that was the hardest thing I'd ever had to do, because I wasn't trying to abandon him. If I had a say in the matter, I'd easily love him forever.

He lowered his head. "I want to push you, but it feels like you've already made up your mind."

"I have, and I'm sorry. It's better this way. I know you can't see it right now, but it truly is better. I am so sorry for hurting you, but it's better to do it now than years down the line."

Tears flooded my eyes, but I did my best to blink them away. I didn't want to cry, because I was certain he'd want to wipe my tears away.

I saw the moment it happened, the moment his shell began to harden. His eyes flashed with that same hatred he'd held for me when we first met. His jaw clenched, and he stuffed his hands into his jeans pockets . . .

"Ian . . . I'm sorry, please don't . . ."

Hate me.

Please don't hate me.

"Keep the damn house. Keep the job. Keep everything, Hazel. But I don't want to hear from you again."

He didn't say another word. As he began to walk away, my mind started spinning as panic began to settle in my gut. He was leaving, he was hurting, and he was building up his wall again—all because of me. "Ian, wait."

He looked back toward me, and a flash of hope moved across his eyes.

I swallowed hard. "Maybe we can still be friends?"

"Friends?" The hope sizzled from his irises, and his stare became stone cold. "Fuck you and your friendship, Hazel Stone."

35

IAN

Maybe we can still be friends.

Was she fucking joking? Those words felt like the biggest slap in the face after everything we'd been through.

She hadn't even tried to find a middle ground for our love. She hadn't given me a chance to showcase how things could've worked. She'd simply cut the cord and left without even trying. It had been weeks since Hazel had called it quits for us, but she'd reached out and kept saying she hoped we could be friends like before.

Yeah, fucking right.

I didn't know how to be her friend anymore, and I didn't want to be her friend. I wanted to be her forever.

At least, I'd thought I did when I'd thought I knew who the hell she was. It turned out she was nothing worth chasing. She'd abandoned me, because that was what people did. They fucking left.

I sat in the airport, waiting to board the plane to our next show. I kept flipping through Hazel's Instagram, where she had pictures of her and Rosie grinning ear to ear. I didn't know why I kept scrolling through the photographs, looking at them all as if it weren't killing me every single second, but I couldn't stop myself.

She looked happy.

How had she looked so happy after ripping my fucking heart out and stomping it into the ground?

I didn't understand. I'd thought we had something real, something that we both craved from this world—real love.

But maybe I'd been dreaming. Maybe there wasn't anything real about us. Maybe we were just a temporary love story.

I should've known. All good things had a way of leaving.

"You all right, man?" James asked as he nudged me in the arm.

I shut off my phone and slid it into my pocket. "Yeah. I'm good."

He frowned, knowing better than to believe me. "You know, I don't think Hazel did what she did out of not having feelings for you. I think she honestly was trying to protect you."

I huffed. "Protect me from what?"

"From you giving up your biggest dream to have her in your life."

"I wouldn't have given up my dream. I've been doing it, haven't I? I've been showing up and performing and putting one hundred percent into this music, James. So fuck that excuse. I'm not buying it. I even invited her out here with Rosie to join us. I went out of my way to bring them into our world."

"Yeah, I know, but you can't believe that's for the best. Not really."

"What do you mean?"

James grimaced and patted my shoulder. "Ian, Rosie is only four months old, and Hazel is just now getting a grip on some kind of normalcy. Do you really think it would be wise to bring a kid as young as Rosie on the road? What kind of life would that be for her? For Hazel? You're asking them to uproot their world to come into yours, and that's not fair."

I hated that he was right, and I hated that I was being so selfish, but I didn't care. I wanted them there, with me, so Hazel and I could try to see whatever it was we could've become. It was stupid; I knew that. I could hardly imagine me being on the road for months, traveling city to city, hotel to hotel, with no sense of normalcy. It was messed up for me to even offer up such an idea to Hazel. But still . . . I'd tried.

"Shit," I murmured, rubbing my hands against my face.

"I know it sucks, man, and I know you really care about her, the same way she cares about you, but the best thing you could do for yourself is handle these next few weeks and remember why we started this all. It's all about the music. It's always been about the music."

Yes, that was true. It had been all about the music before I'd known that there was more to the world.

I gave him a half grin. "I'll be fine. Don't worry about me. Just got to get through the first few weeks of this change, and I'll be back to my normal self again."

Bullshit.

Bullshit, bullshit, bullshit.

He gave me another pat on the back before heading off to talk to the other guys. Probably to inform them that I wasn't going completely off my rocker and I'd be able to be committed to the next few months of our lives. I would be committed too. *Until forever* still rang true when it came to my bandmates, even though I'd been slipping a little as of late.

They were busting their asses day in and day out, and what had I done? Given them reasons to doubt our shot at fame because my heart ached for something that wasn't mine to have anymore?

The walls I'd been working so hard to knock down over the past months were beginning to build again as reality set in—I'd never fucking known who Hazel Stone really was.

I had to shut it off. Shut off my feelings, shut off my heart, shut off my emotions.

I unfollowed her on social media. I deleted all of our previous text messages. I let her go as much as I could, and then I boarded the plane and found the whiskey.

I prided myself on being able to be fully invested in our performances no matter how heavy my heart felt. It became easier when we were standing under those bright lights and a sold-out crowd was singing our lyrics back to us.

Every single day, I thanked God for our fans and for having the ability to meet them. To perform for them. There were so many hard parts of the job, so many things I hated and wished I didn't have to partake in. Having meet and greets with the fans wasn't one of those things. If anything, it was the highlight of my career. It was because of those people that I was able to live the life I lived. It was due to their undying love and support that I was allowed to do what I loved doing: create music.

The lines grew more and more each show, which felt surreal to me. Everything was happening in superspeed. I wondered if this was what boy bands felt like. One day, they were performing at high schools, and the next, boom. Millions of fans.

The fans came in droves, hundreds of people spending way too much money to meet me and my gang for the amount of time it took me to scribble my name and snap a photograph. There wasn't much time for conversation, but there were tears.

The fact that people cried over me and my bandmates baffled me.

It all felt like a dream. Days blended into nights, and weeks transformed into months.

And still, every now and again, Hazel Stone would cross my mind. I tried to brush her away from my thoughts, but it was almost impossible to do so. When I called home to chat with Grams and Big Paw, it took everything for me to not ask how Hazel was doing. Sometimes I'd hear Rosie crying in the background, and I'd want to rush home to hold her.

So stupid, I thought to myself. *It's not even your kid, and you miss her.*

Whenever Hazel would cross my mind, I'd let her linger there for a while before moving on and focusing back on the music. Max Fucking Rider told me I just had to find a hot model to bang to get Hazel out of my head, but that was the last thing I wanted. Luckily, Marcus was more than willing to take the models off my hands.

I hadn't come on that tour for sex, drugs, and rock and roll. I'd come for only one reason: to share my music with the masses, and that was exactly what we were doing.

Still, oddly enough, even though I was surrounded by thousands of fans chanting my name, never in my life had I ever felt so alone.

If you'd asked me years ago if I would miss Eres, I would've laughed in your face. Still, there were days I would've rather been in the pigpen, hauling hay and staring at Hazel Stone as she told me her confessions.

No matter how much I'd tried to shut off my heart, I couldn't. It was as if after Hazel had awakened it, I couldn't turn it back off. And it hurt. It hurt so fucking bad some days all I wanted to do was stay in bed and sleep.

Since I couldn't do that, I used whiskey to cope.

I drank more than I should've every day to keep my heart from shattering. The guys mentioned it every so often when I'd show up with sunglasses on to the meet and greets, but I didn't have the energy to explain myself to them. I was fucked up and needed the whiskey to keep me going.

I never missed a show.

That should've been all they were concerned about—I always showed up.

Three months had passed since Hazel and I had ended the relationship. The band and I were officially heading back to Los Angeles to finish the tracks on our first album. After the album launched, I knew our lives were only going to grow busier.

One night after our last meet and greet before heading back to LA, James pulled me to the side. He must've smelled the whiskey on my breath, the same way he had all the nights before.

He lowered his brows. "Be honest, Ian. Are you happy?"

I snickered. "What does happiness have to do with anything? We're getting famous," I sarcastically remarked. He went to argue with my words, but I stopped him. After all, the show must go on.

It amazed me how it could seem that all your dreams had come true, yet still, it wasn't what you'd thought it would be like.

I'd been having nightmares. Some involving my parents, others involving Hazel. I didn't remember all of the pieces of them, but at the end of each dream, I'd be falling down what felt like an endless black hole. I'd scream out for help, and everyone would stand around me on the outskirts, watching me spiral, watching me fall, and yet no one would reach out to me to give me their hand to hold. Instead, I'd keep free-falling with no hope of finding my way back to solid ground.

When I'd awake, I'd sit up in the darkness of my room and then fall back to sleep, hoping the dreams wouldn't come back.

36

HAZEL

"James said Ian has been miserable," Leah mentioned during our girls' night, which was now a weekly event. We'd been bingeing Netflix, doing face masks, and eating crappy food as Rosie rolled around in her playpen. Leah had become a best friend to me, and I couldn't have thanked her enough for stepping in to help care for Rosie when I had online exams to complete.

My chest tightened as I sat on the sofa, eating popcorn. The last thing I wanted to hear was that Ian was struggling with our split. I'd had a strange hope that he'd be able to move on from thinking about me due to his career taking off.

"I wish you would've brought me a better update," I muttered. Guilt had been eating me alive lately, along with loneliness. I missed Ian more than words could ever express. My sleep had been affected by everything that had happened over the past few weeks too. My nightmares had come back, only this time they were dreams about Charlie harming Rosie—my worst fear in the world.

The hardest part about the nightmares? When I'd awaken, I couldn't roll over and have Ian hold me. I couldn't pick up my phone and find calmness with his voice. I couldn't go to him for comfort.

Leah frowned at me as her clay mask began to harden. "I wish I had a better update, too, but truthfully, James is pretty worried. He said Ian has been drinking a lot more too. The guys thought the music and concerts would've helped Ian, but his heart just isn't in it at all anymore. You know why I think that is?"

"Why?"

She reached across and placed her hands against mine. "Because you are his muse, and he doesn't have that anymore. He misses you, Hazel."

I lowered my head as tears filled my eyes. "I know."

"And you miss him. I can tell. You haven't been yourself, either, and if I'm honest, I just don't understand why you broke things off with him. You two were as perfect as Big Paw and Holly—meant to be together. I wish I had what you and Ian had. Is it because of the distance? Or, like, those women hanging around the band? Because they are just in it for clout."

"I don't know what clout is," I commented.

She laughed. "Of course you don't, my sweet, sweet Hazel. All I'm saying is Ian would never betray you by hooking up with another woman, if those are your fears."

"I wish that was it, but it's so much more complicated than that, Leah. There's just so much more at risk with me being with Ian that I'm not willing to put up with."

Her eyes narrowed, and a baffled look landed on her face. "That sounds really telenovela of you," she nervously joked. "What in the world could be at risk with you and Ian being a couple?"

I swallowed hard and shook my head as tears filled my eyes. Just thinking about Charlie's threats made me emotional. The way he'd talked about causing issues to the ranch and, worse, to Rosie terrified me.

"Hazel," Leah sighed, her eyes watering just from seeing me grow emotional. "What is it?"

"I . . . I shouldn't tell anyone. The more people who know, the bigger risk there is for trouble."

"You have my word that I won't tell a soul, I promise. Besides, whatever is eating you up shouldn't be solely on your shoulders. Hazel, you've done so much to help others. You're literally nineteen years old and raising your newborn sister. You deserve help. Let me help you. Let me take some weight off your shoulders."

I took a deep inhalation as tears began rolling down my cheeks. "It's Charlie. He's back in town."

She raised an eyebrow. "Charlie? Who's Charlie?"

That unleashed a sea of information to catch Leah up on the wildness that was my life. The more details I gave her, the lower her jaw dropped in horror and complete shock. When I finished, she plopped back against the sofa in disbelief.

"Holy balls. You are a telenovela," she exclaimed, completely distressed. "Oh my gosh, Hazel. And you've been dealing with this all on your own?"

"I didn't have anyone I could tell. I had to do it on my own; it was my only choice."

"No," she disagreed, shaking her head. "Maybe in the past you had to handle things by yourself, but you don't have to do that anymore. You have a family now. People you can lean on for help or at least comfort."

I gave her a half grin as I wiped the tears falling from my eyes. "Thank you, Leah."

"Of course. It all makes sense now, too, why you pushed Ian away. If it makes you feel better, I would've done the same exact thing—especially if that psychopath threatened Rosie. You made the right choice. Even though I know it crushes you."

"It really does, Leah. All I can do is think about Ian and hate myself for hurting him. I know he had abandonment issues, and for it to happen right after he crossed paths with his parents makes it even worse. I wish I could explain things to him, but that is too risky. I just hope he's able to move on and find his happiness again."

"I'm sure the guys will make sure to look after him. I have no doubt about that. But as far as you go, I'm here to make sure you find your happiness again. That's what friends are for."

I thanked her as she leaned in and gave me the tightest hug in history, and she promised me that everything would be okay someday.

I wished I could believe that to be true, but knowing that Charlie was out of prison was enough to leave me always on edge. What if he snapped and decided to harm Rosie and me, simply because he could? Charlie was a madman whose actions never truly made any sense whatsoever. At least he couldn't get to Ian and harm him. There was some comfort in that knowledge.

Later that night, I awakened from a nightmare due to a crying Rosie. I scooped her up in my arms and tried to soothe her back to sleep; then I took her outside into the darkness of the night and rocked her in the chair on the porch. I looked up at the stars sparkling throughout the sky, and I made a few wishes.

I first wished for my sister to be safe from any harm. If anything ever happened to that little girl, the little girl who'd had a chance of being adopted by a family who wouldn't have put her life in danger, I would never forgive myself.

Then I wished for Ian's happiness, praying that someway, somehow, he'd find himself another muse. I wished for him to move on from me and for his battered heart to heal over time. I wished for him to not give up on love and close himself off once more. He'd worked so hard to tap into his feelings, and I'd hate for him to lose that connection to himself again.

Lastly, I made a wish for myself. I wished for the ability to stay strong even during the darkest of times and for my heart to keep beating every day, even though each beat hurt more and more as time passed without Ian by my side.

If those wishes could come true, I'd never have to wish upon another star in the sky.

37

IAN

"Are you kidding me?" Eric blurted out during our meeting with the record label. We all sat there in full disbelief as we spoke to the team of people in charge of our first album launch. "How does something like this even happen? I mean, you do have a solid team behind you making sure this doesn't happen, right? I mean, you're Mindset Records, for goodness' sake. How did this even happen?"

Eric was angry, which didn't happen often, but he had every damn reason to be pissed off.

Hell, we all did.

Our first album—the album we'd poured our blood, sweat, and tears into—had been leaked across the internet.

Max sat at the table, checking his two cell phones repeatedly, appearing to try to do damage control on the situation at hand. Donnie Schmitz, the head of Mindset Records, sat at the head of the table, with his hands clasped together. "We'll be honest; this is a major mistake on our part. What's worse is we are still two months out from the launch of the album. Which means we have to make some choices. We can't push out an album that has already been leaked, so we must shift. We need new material, and we need to get you in the recording studio as soon as possible."

"What?" I huffed out. "Are you kidding me? It took us months to nail those songs down! We can't just pump out a new album out of nowhere."

"Now, I know how this can sound daunting," Donnie began.

"I think the words you're looking for are *fucking impossible*," Marcus corrected with a grimace.

Donnie continued, "But we have a list of tracks that are already fully developed. All you need to do is get in the studio and do your magic."

"What do you mean, fully developed tracks?" James asked.

"We called in some of the best songwriters in the industry," Max cut in, nodding my way. "It's the greatest news. Warren Lee wrote the tracks."

I raised an eyebrow. "Warren Lee?"

"Yes." Max nodded. Warren was one of the best writers in the industry, if not the best. Working with him meant Grammys and money. Everything he touched turned to platinum records. But what did using his songs mean for us?

It wasn't authentic. It wasn't ours.

"We create our own music," Marcus said, with his hands clasped together and a determined look on his face.

"Yes, but you don't have the time to create your own music. You said it yourself. It took you forever to create those tracks. So we took the hard part out of your job. Now, you just go in the studio and do what we tell you."

"We aren't robots." Eric sighed, taking off his glasses and pinching his nose. "We don't just do that cookie-cutter bullshit."

"Yeah, didn't we tell you that from day one, Max? We wanted to be us—the Wreckage. Not some bullshit manufactured band that doesn't have a voice of their own," James added in.

I sat there quiet, unsure of what to say, because one: I was a tad bit drunk. And two: I couldn't come to grips with the fact that all of those months of our work were gone. Everything we'd sacrificed to create that album meant nothing.

All the time I could've been back in Eres with Hazel, growing our connection . . .

What?

No.

Whiskey was supposed to drown out my thoughts of Hazel, not make them heavier.

But still, the lost time creating music that ended up being worthless hurt.

Fuck. What was the point of it all?

"That was before this leak happened. Look, you guys, I'm pissed off too. You think I wanted this to happen? Of course not. But this is where we are. This is the place we are sitting, and we can moan and whine about it all damn day, or we can get to fucking work. Besides, Warren Lee makes superstars, and you are going to be superstars if you get out of your own fucking way."

The mood of the whole space was pretty damn disheartening. My bandmates looked as if they'd been hit by a semitruck. Eric kept going on and on about how he didn't understand how something so major could happen with the record company's security system.

How did a whole album just get fucking leaked?

"And if we refuse to use Warren's songs?" I asked.

Donnie pushed his lips together and gave me a hard look. "Listen, you signed a contract with Mindset Records, and we know this issue wasn't a fault of yours, but to put it frankly, you owe us music. Time is ticking, and I don't want to have to bring in the legal department on this."

Of course.

We were being pushed in a corner, forced to create something that wasn't authentic, something that wasn't ours.

It was literally an artist's worst nightmare.

Why did it feel as if the world was crashing around us? Why did it feel as if our dream was slowly but surely shifting into something that wasn't ours to hold anymore?

We were in the hands of a record label that had the power to control our every move with the threats of lawsuits—lawsuits that I was certain we'd lose in a heartbeat.

I cleared my throat. "Can we have a minute to talk with the band alone?"

"Sure. But don't waste too much time trying to figure out a way around this," Donnie mentioned as he stood, along with the lemmings who followed after him. "We don't have time for diva artists."

Diva artists.

I didn't know it made someone a diva to want to speak their own truths.

They all left the room as the guys and I sat at the table.

The guys and Max.

We all glanced his way with confused looks. He looked around with a cocked eyebrow.

"What?"

"We were hoping to talk alone," Marcus mentioned.

"I'm your manager. I need to be here for these meetings."

James shook his head. "This is more of a band-only conversation. We'll notify you once we get our thoughts together."

Max sighed and brushed his hand over his mouth. He muttered something under his breath, and I was happy I didn't hear him. He was probably calling us spoiled brats or something.

He picked up a folder and slid it our way. "These are some of Warren's songs for you. Look them over. These have Grammys written all over them. Don't be stupid about this, you guys. Make the right choice."

With that, he left, closing the door behind him. The moment that door clicked, Marcus flew to his feet. "Are you fucking kidding me?" he exclaimed, waving his hands around like a madman.

"There's no way we can do this," Eric said, flipping through the songs. "I mean, I'm sure these tracks by Warren are great, but they aren't us. And we've built our whole social aspect around being us. People don't want songs from Warren; they want songs from us."

"It's impossible to create a brand-new album in that amount of time. We can't do it," Marcus said, sounding defeated. "Plus, I'm sure they'll fuck us with law fees, and we'd end up broker than we were before we left Eres."

"We can try," James offered. "We can try to make our own music over the next few months. I know it will be hard as hell, but we can work our asses off to make it happen."

The three of them began going back and forth—arguing about what would work and what wouldn't. The more they argued, the more my chest felt as if it were on fire.

I picked up the pages on the table and began flipping through the songs Warren Lee had written.

I zoned out as I read the lyrics. Lyrics that meant nothing to me. Lyrics that were cookie cutter and mainstream. Lyrics that belonged to someone else.

And I was going to be forced to sing those songs.

"We're taking Warren's songs," I said, pushing myself to stand up.

"What? No. Dude, we can't do that. We can't sell out like this," James said.

"He's right, Ian. I know we are in a hard spot, but we can't just throw away everything we've worked for," Marcus agreed.

"We have a limited amount of time, and we can't waste time trying to create new songs," I explained.

"But . . ." Eric sighed, but he didn't finish his thought.

Probably because he knew I was right.

"I can't let us all go into major debt and lawsuits because of this, you guys. We can't go backward. We have to move forward."

"Even if that means selling out our souls to mainstream music?" Marcus asked.

"Let's be honest; we did that the moment we signed the contracts. If we wanted to stay small, we should've walked away at the beginning. We signed a contract, you guys, and there's no way to get out of it. I'm going to go tell Max we're taking Warren's songs, and we'll get in the studio tomorrow to get going."

I walked out of the room and only stopped when James came chasing after me.

"Ian, wait up. What's going on, man?"

"What do you mean?"

He narrowed his eyes as if he were staring at a stranger. "You don't even want to fight to try to create our own music again? You don't want to try?"

"I've tried my whole life, James. I tried with my parents, I tried with Hazel, and I tried with our music. Trying doesn't work. We might as well just go with what they want us to do. It will be easier that way."

"Just because it's easy doesn't mean it's worth it. You don't mean what you're saying. You just feel defeated, but you can't let your pain weigh you down so much."

"I don't feel pain," I said, shrugging my shoulders. "I don't feel nothing."

"Don't you think that's a problem?" he asked.

Maybe it was.

But I was too tired to really fucking care.

I lay in the darkest form of night. Even when I opened my eyes, I felt as though I were still staring into the blackness of my eyelids. How long had I been lying in the shadows? How long had I been in my current state of affairs? I shifted a bit, and my lower back stung. My whole body ached from head to toe, as if I'd been hit by a semitruck. What the hell had I done yesterday? Run a marathon? Fought a grizzly?

Oh yeah, I'd gotten drunk as hell after leaving the meeting at Mindset Records.

I rubbed the palms of my hands against my eyes, completely dazed and confused as I tried to piece together the last few hours of my life.

Dammit, Ian. How did you get here?

I didn't mean that in a superdeep, profound, meaningful way. What I meant was, How the hell had I fucking gotten here? And where, exactly, was *here*?

My head pounded at a vomit-worthy speed as I tried to swallow down the crashing memories of the meeting at Mindset Records.

I pinched the bridge of my nose, and before I could sit up, two pairs of arms wrapped around my body in the darkness.

Two big, strong pairs of arms lifted me up from my bed. As I went to holler, someone covered my mouth with one hand and my eyes with the other as the arms carried me away. I began kicking and trying to shout as I was hauled to the hallway of the hotel, in a complete panic as these men carried me away.

Was this some kind of fanatic kidnapping? Was someone going for me because of my money?

I bit the hand that was covering my mouth and heard a shout of pain. "Dude! What the fuck?"

"Shut the fuck up, will you?" the other hissed.

"He fucking bit me!"

That voice . . . was that . . . Eric?

"I don't care if he fucking bit you. We aren't supposed to talk!"

"Well, you weren't the one who was freaking bit!"

"I told you to duct-tape his mouth!"

"I'm not some freaking psychopath! I wasn't going to duct-tape his mouth!"

"That's why you got bit, you idiot!"

Eric and Marcus?

I'd know that bickering from miles away.

"What the fuck is going on?" I yelled now that my mouth was uncovered.

The hands dropped my body to the hallway floor, and when I was allowed to look up, I saw my three bandmates dressed in all black like fucking ninjas. What in the ever-loving hell was going on?

"What the hell is going on?" I blurted out, rubbing the back of my head, which had smacked hard against the floor.

"Sorry, Ian, we were, er—we thought—" James started, looking guilty as fuck.

"We're fucking kidnapping you, dude," Marcus exclaimed, without a second of guilt in his tone.

"What?"

He didn't explain any more. He nodded toward me. "Come on, guys. Grab him."

The bandmates did as Marcus said, and before I could yell, Eric pulled out a roll of duct tape and slapped a piece against my mouth. "Sorry, Ian. But this is for your own good."

What in the hell? Where the hell was security? Didn't they see me on camera being dragged out of my hotel room by three men in black? This had to look suspicious as fuck.

When we got outside, going through the back entrance of the hotel, there was a black van parked near us. They hurried me over, tossed me inside, and scrambled in themselves.

Marcus hopped behind the steering wheel and began driving off.

I ripped the tape off my mouth and hollered, "What the fuck is wrong with you psychopaths?"

"Sorry, man," James said as he calmly put on his seat belt. "We just didn't think you'd come easily of your own accord. But to be completely clear, the ninja kidnapping was Marcus's idea."

"And a damn good idea, if you ask me! I always wanted to do, like, an underground kidnapping. For fun, obviously—I'm not a damn crazed human. And it was going great until Bozo the Clown over here yelled."

"He fucking bit me!" Eric exclaimed once more. "I think I'm bleeding. He hit a vein."

"Don't be a fucking baby, or I'll tell Mom to start changing your diapers again."

"Fuck you, Marcus!"

"Fuck you too, little brother."

"Fuck you both!" I added in, still feeling dazed, confused, and drunk as fuck. "What the hell is going on?"

James leaned over my waist and buckled my seat belt like the damn caring guy he had always been. I would've thanked him, too, if he hadn't just kidnapped me.

"Listen, Ian. I've been up all night doing some deep computer-nerd digging," Eric explained. "I didn't feel settled enough knowing that our album was leaked somehow but the record company hadn't a clue how it happened. So I did some work. And you won't believe what I found. It was—"

"Max Fucking Rider!" Marcus blurted out as he drove down the road.

"Dude, what the hell?" Eric snapped, smacking his brother in the arm. "That was my massive reveal."

"Will you get over yourself and continue the story?" Marcus ordered.

Eric sighed at his brother and raked his hands through his hair. "It was Max Fucking Rider. I tracked the hack back to a server that led us straight to his laptop. Then, for extra confirmation—because if you're going to geek out, you're going to geek out all the way—I hacked his emails and his social media and his everything. He had emails back and forth with Donnie from weeks ago. They went on and on about how the music we created wasn't mainstream enough and they needed to make a big shift before the release."

What?

"They set us up, dude!" Marcus said. "They fucked us in the asshole and then sat in front of us and called us divas for being pissed about it."

"Holy shit," I muttered, sitting back in my seat, finally letting the shock of being kidnapped disappear as the shock of being fucked up the ass began to hit me. "Why would they do that?"

"Money, probably. Everything's about money to these people," James said. "And can you imagine the buzz we're getting with our tracks being released? Now, people are watching us more closely than ever to see what we do next."

It made sense.

It was messed up, but it made sense from their evil standpoint.

"That doesn't change the fact that we are still screwed by the contract we signed. We're still screwed," I explained.

"Maybe, but we aren't going to be screwed in Los Angeles. Especially with you in the headspace that you are," James said.

"What's that supposed to mean? Where the hell are we going?"

"Look, Ian. We know these past few months have been hard on you. From your parents, to Hazel, and now to the record being fucked over. But we, as your best friends, cannot allow you to lose your light. You can't give up on everything."

"I didn't give up on everything." Everything had given up on me.

Fuck. Did I even hear myself? How much more emo could my ass be?

"No offense, dude, but you're drunk all the time," Marcus said, his voice low and filled with care. "And I don't fault you for it, because I'd be the same way if I went through half the shit you went through. That's why we allowed it for so long. What happened to you was fucked up, man. You were dealt a shitty hand, and you were playing it the best you could, but it's time to realize that you don't have to play alone. We're your best buds. So we kidnapped you to give you the detox your body and soul need."

"Detox? And where the hell is this detox taking place?" I barked, still annoyed as fuck about being kidnapped from my drunken daze and dropped in a damn hallway.

"Eres," Eric said, glancing back at me from the passenger seat. "So sit back, relax, and enjoy the twenty-hour drive. We're taking you home, Ian."

38

IAN

The guys forced me to drive with them for the whole twenty hours. Whenever we stopped, I couldn't even figure out a way to get away and back to Los Angeles. They hadn't brought my phone or my wallet. I had no way of escaping my friends kidnapping me.

What an odd situation.

I couldn't stop thinking about what Eric had uncovered about Max Fucking Rider and Donnie Fucking Schmitz. I wished I could've said I was surprised, but it turned out dreams didn't come without their own set of troubles. Max had had red flags from the beginning, but we'd chosen to ignore them, because we wanted our dream so fucking bad it ached.

Now, we were left in a shitty situation because we'd trusted the wrong people. We'd trusted the people who didn't give a damn about us as individuals. They only cared about the money being brought into their bank accounts.

The moment we pulled up to the old dirt roads of Eres, I felt a lump in my throat. The guys drove me to my house—correction: now Hazel's house—and before I could argue with them, they tossed me out of the car and drove away.

It was the middle of the night, and I had no desire to walk inside to see Hazel.

Okay, that was a lie. I had every desire to do exactly that, but I didn't. Instead, I grumbled like a damn child and stomped off to the shed.

I'd sleep there until morning, when I'd go to my grandparents' house and beg Big Paw for a bed to sleep in for a few hours before I figured out how to get myself back to Los Angeles and face reality.

I grumbled, tossing and turning in my sleep. I was having that dream again. I was falling deeper and deeper into the bottomless pit of darkness, shouting for someone to give me a hand. Begging for help. My parents reached down, and right before I was about to grab ahold of them, they snatched their hands back, and they began laughing hysterically as they stared my way. Then everyone else began laughing too. Big Paw, Grams, the guys. Everyone began pointing at me, laughing their heads off, as I kept falling deeper and deeper.

Everyone except Hazel.

She locked eyes with me and moved her mouth to speak. I couldn't hear her, though.

"What?" I called out.

She kept moving her lips.

"What?" I shouted.

"Wake," she whispered.

"I can't hear you!"

"Up," she said. "Wake up, wake up, wake up!"

I shot up from my nightmare, drenched in sweat and panic. My eyes bugged out as I looked around, trying to piece together my whereabouts, and when I looked to my left, I froze.

Those green eyes were piercing me.

Those eyes that I'd missed.

Those eyes that I still stupidly loved.

Those fucking green eyes.

"What are you doing?" I demanded, feeling flustered and completely thrown off. I felt as if half of me was still in the dream state as the other half was awake and wanting to wrap my arms around Hazel and fucking beg her to love me again.

I didn't do that.

I sat still as a brick wall.

"I heard shouting in here and came to check it out." She tilted her head, seemingly confused. "What are you doing back in town, Ian?"

My hand brushed against my temple, and I groaned. "Been asking myself the same damn thing. Don't worry; I'll get out of your hair."

I got to my feet, and she shifted in her shoes.

Those black Adidas.

God, I hated that she still wore those black Adidas, and by *hated* I meant *loved*, and holy shit, I'd missed her.

"Wait, no. You're not in my hair. You're . . . I'm just . . . you being here . . ." Her words stumbled and fumbled against her tongue. "How are you?" she asked.

After all these months of silence, that was all she had to say to me? All she could muster up was *How are you?*

Not good enough for me.

I turned and walked out of the shed as the morning sun beamed down on me.

I wasn't in the mood for the walk to Big Paw's house, but I knew that was the only place I could go.

I brushed my hand against my forehead and turned to Hazel. "Can I use your cell phone?"

She hesitated as if I'd said the most obscure thing in the whole world. "I, uh, you, um—"

"Words, Hazel," I griped. "Use words."

301

"You can't use my phone."

"And why not?"

"I was instructed to not let you use it."

I lifted a brow. "By who?"

"By your friends."

Fine.

I'd use the phone in the offices.

I started walking off, annoyed as ever, and I heard Hazel call after me. "Wait! Ian. You're wasting your time if you're heading to the offices. The phones have been disconnected there."

What in the hell?

"And why's that?"

"So you can't call out to get away from here."

"Why would I want to stay on this damn ranch, huh? Why in the fuck would I want to be here?" I was coming off sounding like a big dick, but I couldn't help it, because even though I'd tried to shut off my heart again, it kept fucking beating and breaking every day since my parents and Hazel had stomped it into the ground, and it hurt. It hurt so fucking bad standing there in front of her. It hurt so fucking bad being in the same space as her. It hurt so fucking bad that I wanted to rip my heart out of my damn chest in order to stop feeling.

I wished I'd never started feeling again at all.

"Because this is your home," she said, her words throwing me for a loop. Did she mean she was my home or the ranch was my home?

Didn't matter.

I was still leaving.

"I'll just go to Big Paw's and call," I muttered as I began walking again.

"That won't help you, seeing as how Big Paw and Holly are waiting inside the house over here, along with the band."

"Why are they there?"

"They want to talk to you. They want to make sure you're okay."

"Like an intervention? Not interested."

"Ian, you're not okay . . ."

"I'm fine!" I snapped at her.

"You're not," she replied, calmly as ever.

"And what exactly do you know about me, Hazel Stone?"

"Everything," she said so matter-of-factly it made me want to crawl into a ball and cry like a little bitch. She gave me a half smile and shrugged her shoulders. "I know everything, Ian. You're my best friend."

"Then why did you leave me?" I asked, sounding desperate. A flash of sadness washed over Hazel's face. I shook my head and turned in the direction of the house. "Don't answer that."

I didn't need her answer, because it didn't matter why she'd left me. It only mattered that she'd left—easy as that.

I should've learned a long time ago that when people left you behind, it was best that you never asked why. You'd always be disappointed with their reasoning.

The moment I stepped foot into the ranch house, I felt my nerves start to skyrocket. Everyone was sitting in the living room with doomed expressions on their faces, as if they'd lost their best friend, and I couldn't help but feel ridiculous about their dramatic looks.

"What is this?" I demanded. "Why are you guys holding me hostage here?"

"Don't come in here with that damn tone, boy. You don't get to be nasty toward people because they care about your well-being," Big Paw snapped. "Now bring your butt over here and sit down."

I wanted to argue with him, but I knew that wouldn't lead to any place good.

I sat down in the armchair, not happy about it at all. "So. What do you want?"

"We want you to stop acting like a damn stubborn child," Big Paw hollered.

"Harry, be easy," Grams said, placing her hand on his knee.

"No. Easy doesn't work with this blockhead. We need to break through to him. Ian, your bandmates have told me you've been drinking each night. Is that true?"

Snitches.

"I've had a few drinks," I murmured, readjusting myself in the chair.

"He's been wasted every night for more than a month," Marcus added.

What a fucking asshole. "I've done my job," I said. "I've showed up and never missed a show, so what does it matter if I have a drink or two—"

"Or five," Eric quipped, making the anger grow inside of me.

Who did these people think they were, talking about me like that? I was supposed to be their friend, and this was how they showed their love?

Fuck love and all its twisted fairy tales.

"This isn't you, Ian," Grams said in her gentle tones. I'd missed her. I'd slipped up on calling her to check in every week, and seeing her brought that guilt back to me instantly. I hadn't been a good grandson lately, and I wasn't that shocked.

I hadn't been a good person as of late.

"People change, Grams. Maybe this is who I am now."

"No." Big Paw shook his head. "This isn't you, dammit. You aren't some drunk."

I shrugged. "My parents weren't always meth heads, but they changed too. Maybe I just take after my parents a little more than usual."

"Shut it, you damn idiot!" Big Paw shouted, shooting up from his chair. He paced back and forth, slapping his hands together in anger— or maybe disappointment? Maybe sadness?

When he looked up at me with tears flooding his eyes, my messed-up heart cracked even more. I'd never seen Big Paw cry in all my life, and watching him stand there before me with tears rolling down his cheeks made me want to kick my own ass for being difficult.

"You don't know what it's like," he whispered, his voice cracking. "You don't know what it feels like knowing you're losing everything around you. You don't know what we've been going through back here, Ian, and you have the nerve to throw away your life like it doesn't matter. You're selfish—just like your parents. You're goddamn selfish, and you can't pull your head out of your own ass to see how much your actions are hurting others."

Grams stood up and walked over to Big Paw. "Harry, calm down . . ."

"No. I'm done. If he wants to be a drunk, then by all means. Die the same miserable way that my father did. But don't do it here. If you want to ruin yourself, go back to LA, and do it surrounded by people who don't give a damn about you. I refuse to watch another person I love lose themselves. It was too hard the first time, and I'm tired." He brushed his tears away and stormed out of the house. Grams chased after him, leaving me with the guys, who all looked guilty as ever.

I scrubbed my hands over my face and released a weighted sigh.

James grimaced. "I'd never seen Big Paw cry," he muttered.

"Me either," I replied.

Marcus raked his hands through his hair. "Look, Ian. We weren't trying to gang up on you bringing you back to Eres. I know you have a lot of shit going on, and I thought being back where we'd fallen in love with music would help. Getting back to our roots. But if you want to go back to LA and record those tracks from Warren Lee, then we'll do that. Because when we said 'until forever,' we didn't mean until things got messy. We fucking meant until forever. Always. We got your back regardless."

I couldn't believe the jerk I'd been lately. I couldn't believe the way I'd lost myself on the road to success or how I'd let my heartache swallow me whole. I didn't want to be like this. I didn't want to be so damn broken, but I couldn't help it. I was drowning, and my family and friends were trying their hardest to pull me up for air.

Unlike in my dream, they were reaching out. I was simply being too stubborn to give them my hand.

"I'm sorry, you guys, for . . . everything. I'm not doing too great after everything that went down. I'm going to do better and work on getting back on track. I know we have to decide what to do for the music, and you need answers from me on what we should do sooner than later."

"Take the next day to regroup and focus on yourself, man. Minus the booze, of course," Eric said. "Then we'll come back together and take a group vote on it all."

"Although we'd already have our votes, so realistically, whatever you decide will be vetoed," Marcus joked. "Really, though, take your time, Ian. We'll be around seeing our families and stuff. Just give us a call."

The guys headed out, and I sighed as I rolled my hands over my face. I felt exhausted in all ways—physically, mentally, and emotionally burned out.

When a knock landed on the door, I got up and headed over to find Hazel standing there.

"Why are you knocking on your own door?" I asked.

"It was your door before it was mine."

I didn't know what to say to her next, even though there were a million things that I felt needed to be said.

I scratched at the back of my neck. "Don't worry; I'll stay in the shed again tonight. You don't have to worry about me getting in your way."

"I'm not worried about that. I . . ." Her eyes glazed over, and it appeared as if she, too, had a million things that needed to be said.

Say it, Haze. Fucking say it to me, and I'll say my words back.

Her rosy lips parted, and I almost leaned in to taste them; then she shut them. Sealed them up tightly and gave me a pathetic smile that wasn't a smile at all.

Even though her lips turned up, I saw the sadness in the curve.

"I, um, you should probably go check on your grandparents," she said, shifting her stare away from mine. It was as if looking me in the eyes was too hard for her to do. "They've been going through some things and could probably use your company."

"What kind of things?"

"Just . . . they need you, Ian."

The way she said those words made my gut tighten with nerves.

"Can I use your truck to get over there?" I asked.

She tossed me the keys. "It's actually your truck—I've just been borrowing it."

I nodded once before turning away from her and heading toward the car.

I wondered when I'd get to the point where I didn't want to look back at Hazel in hopes that she was still looking my way.

When I glanced over my shoulder and saw her still staring, I almost smiled. Then I remembered that she'd broken my fucking heart, so I kept my smile to myself.

"Your grandfather went off to clear his head for a little bit. Come on in. I'll make you a sandwich. You're looking pretty slim lately."

"Touring and performing has a way of doing that."

"Still, you need to eat more. Now, get to the kitchen," Grams instructed as she waved me inside the house. She slowly moved toward the kitchen, and I followed behind her.

I sat down on the barstool in front of the kitchen island and clasped my hands together. "I've never seen him that upset," I said, speaking about Big Paw.

She nodded as she grabbed items out of the fridge. "He's been having a tough time lately. And he worries about you after everything that went down with your parents and Hazel. We both do, sweetheart. We worry about your heart."

I shrugged. "I'm okay."

"You're not happy."

I didn't reply, because I couldn't lie to Grams. She could see a lie from a mile away.

"Your dreams are supposed to make you happy," she commented.

"I think somewhere along the way, the dreams I had shifted into something else."

"And what are your true dreams? What do you want?"

I grimaced. "I think Hazel is my dream."

"Okay. Then go out and get her."

"It's not that easy, Grams. I can't have someone who doesn't want me back."

"Oh, Ian," she soothed as she placed two pieces of bread on a plate. "You know well enough that that girl loves you."

"No. I don't. She broke up with me, Grams, after the hardest days of my life with seeing my parents. That's not love."

"Based on everything you know about Hazel, does that seem out of character of her? For her to do something like that?"

Of course it seemed out of character.

I'd been blindsided by her actions. We'd made love the morning she'd left, and it had felt like the realest, most powerful experience of my life, and then I'd been hit with whiplash as she'd decided that she didn't want to be with me any longer.

"She loves you, Ian. There's something keeping her from being able to show you that love. I know it. So please, fight for her. Push her. Poke her. Make her open up to you. I have the feeling she needs you the same way you need her. She's scared of something, so make sure she knows she doesn't have to be scared alone. Do you think your grandfather and I made it this far without being afraid? Of course not. I've been so scared that I've pushed him away, and he's been too stubborn to allow me to do it. You know what I've learned over time?"

"What's that?"

"The most important things in life are worth fighting for. No matter what fear says."

She set my sandwich in front of me and sat on the barstool beside me. I thanked her for the sandwich but didn't pick it up.

"Is everything good here? Are you and Big Paw doing okay? I'm sorry I dropped the ball on calling weekly."

"Oh, sweetheart, it's okay. I know you're busy."

"No. I'm just selfish. I should've called more. But you two are okay?"

She gave me a tight smile and placed her hand on mine and patted it. "No matter what happens, everything is going to be okay."

What the hell was that supposed to mean?

"Grams," I said, gripping her hands in mine. My eyes narrowed and I tilted my head. "What's going on?"

39

HAZEL

Later that night, I glanced out of my front window and saw somebody standing at the end of the driveway, staring up at the sky in the pouring rain. As I opened the door, I noticed it was Ian. His back was to me, but I knew him well enough to know who it was.

"Ian?" I called out.

He turned to face me. His white T-shirt clung to his chest from the pouring rain, and the water from his eyes wasn't due to the raindrops. He looked as if every ounce of happiness had been stripped away from his soul.

"Ian, what is it?" I asked. Alarm shot through my gut as I stepped onto the porch.

"She's sick," he choked out as his body shook from the cold and his nerves. His head lowered as he slid his hands into his pockets. "Grams is sick, Haze."

The moment the words left his mouth, I stepped down into the rainfall, headed toward him, and wrapped my arms around him. He melted into me as if our bodies were always meant to be one, and he proceeded to fall apart as I tried my best to catch his broken pieces.

The rain hammered against our bodies as Ian's sadness hammered against my heart.

I brought him inside once he was able to collect his emotions.

"Here's some towels to dry off, and of course, you still have some of your clothes in your bedroom, if you want to change."

"Thanks," he murmured as he stared down at his clenched hands.

"Where's your mind?" I asked.

"Lost." He raked his hands through his hair. "It's ironic, you know? Grams has the biggest heart in this world. She gives herself to anyone and everyone in need. She holds no grudges, no judgments, and no resentment. Yet somehow she ends up with a broken heart. How does that even happen? How does the kindest woman on this earth end up with a heart that doesn't work correctly?"

"Life's not fair."

"Maybe she loved too much."

"That's an impossible thing to do. The world should fight to love the way Holly Parker loves. We need more humans like her."

"We need *her*." He sighed. He pressed the palms of his hands against his eyes. "I don't know what I'd do without her."

"Luckily, she's still here. As long as she's here, we should stay thankful."

"Did you know? Did you know she was sick?"

I looked toward him, and guilt hit me. "Yes."

"And you didn't think to tell me?"

"I wanted to, Ian. Really, I did, but your grandparents made me promise not to tell you until they were ready. They didn't want to put guilt on you or make you feel as if you needed to come home to care for them."

"I would've come home," he muttered, wrapping the towel around himself. He then placed his hands against his face and sighed. "I haven't even been calling to check in on them enough."

"They don't blame you. They know you were busy."

"Busy being a little shit."

"Ian, they love you so much, and they don't hold anything against you. Trust me; they love you. They just didn't want to ruin your career right as it was taking off."

"Seems that everyone thinks I care more about this shit career than the actual people in my life," he huffed. "Isn't that why you broke up with me, after all? Because of my job?"

I hesitated to answer. I saw the pained expression in his eyes and the way he was dealing with so many unanswered questions. I wanted to pour out the truth. I wanted to tell him about Charlie and the threats he'd made against me. I wanted to tell him about the struggles I'd been going through with not being able to be with him. I wanted to tell him that I loved him, that I missed him, that I'd worried about him every single day since we'd gone our separate ways.

But nothing had changed. Charlie was still a threat to me, to Rosie, and to Ian's family's ranch, and I couldn't imagine putting more pressure and pain onto Grams and Big Paw, seeing as how they were going through so much already. The last thing they needed was Charlie coming around and destroying everything they'd spent their whole lives building.

"It's not that easy, Ian," I said.

He walked over to the couch and sat down. "It seemed that easy when you pushed me away."

"I know." I dropped my head and sat next to him. "I know it doesn't make any sense, seeing as how everything seemed good between us. I know I probably confused you and the breakup came out of left field. I wish I could explain it to you."

He tilted his head in my direction with the most sincere look. "Explain it, then."

I parted my lips, but my throat dried up. I didn't know what to say, what to do, or how to react. He must've been able to tell, because he took my hands into his and slightly squeezed. "Do you still love me?" he whispered like a gentle breeze passing across my heart.

"Yes," I said, knowing I was completely unable to lie to him about that one thing.

"Then why aren't we together?"

"Because we can't be."

"And why's that?"

I swallowed hard and looked down at our hands, linked ever so perfectly. "Because I'll hurt you."

"Nothing you could do could ever hurt me to the point of no return, Haze."

I nodded. "Yes, but it wouldn't just hurt you; it would hurt your family and mine. It . . ." I shut my eyes and took a deep inhale.

He pulled me into him and placed his lips near my ear and spoke softly. "What are you so afraid of?"

"Losing everything."

"I've been there. I know that fear. I'm living it right now, and that's why I can't lose you too, Hazel. My whole life has been about building a wall to keep people away. I worked hard to keep people at a distance, and you had the nerve to break me down. To teach me what love is. So please," he begged, his breaths hot against my skin, sending a wave of energy to the pit of my stomach. "Stay with me."

I felt his tears falling against my skin, and I was certain he felt mine against his. I began crying harder as I held on to his shirt. "I'm sorry, I'm sorry," I kept repeating.

"What's hurting you, Haze?" he asked so softly. "What's doing this to you?" He wrapped his grip around me and pulled me in tighter. "It's okay. I got you. I got you."

I hated that I'd begun falling apart when he was the one who should've been broken after finding out the news about Holly. Yet there I was, holding on to him and crying as if he were nothing more than a dream and if I let him go, he'd slip away.

He held on to me as long as he could, until reality set in that I couldn't do this. I couldn't hold him close to me. If Charlie found out . . .

I pulled away. I sniffled and brushed my hands against my eyes. "I should really go check on Rosie."

He looked so perplexed by me pulling away, but he stood to his feet and gave me a nod. "Of course."

"I am really sorry, Ian . . . about Holly."

He gave me a broken smile. "She's still here. So I'm going to stay thankful for that."

Good.

"Okay, well, good night. Let me know if you need anything."

"You," he replied so quickly I was almost unsure he'd said that word.

"What?"

"I need you," he swore. He stuffed his hands into his wet slacks and cleared his throat. "I get it. Something happened, and you're scared. You're afraid to share whatever happened to you, and I get that, but that doesn't mean I don't want or need you, Hazel. I think you need me too. You know how Grams made you promise not to tell me about what was going on?" he asked.

"Yes."

"Well, she had me make her a promise too. She made me promise to fight for what I love—so no matter what, I'm fighting for you. I'm not running away, Hazel. I'm not building my wall back up. I'm staying in town, and not only am I going to work on myself, but I'm going to work on us. Even if that means just being too damn much in your business. I'm fighting for you whether you like it or not, Hazel Stone. Our love song isn't over. We're just getting to the chorus, and I'm going to sing for you, for us, until forever."

Ian wasn't kidding—he stayed in town and stayed very much in my business.

He and the band didn't get on an airplane to head back to Los Angeles to record their rushed album. Instead, they went back to the basics of recording their own tracks in the barn house as they made a plan to tackle their record label.

I hadn't a clue how they were going to pump out a complete album in such a short period of time, but I also knew if anyone could do it, it was the Wreckage. They were determined to prove to Max Fucking Dickhead that he couldn't control them.

When Ian wasn't with his grandparents or recording with the band, he was on the ranch, giving me a run for my money.

Big Paw put me in charge of giving Ian his tasks, and it was as if we'd come full circle.

As he was cleaning out the pigpens, I stopped in to check if he was getting the work done. Also, I simply liked checking in on him, because I couldn't help but want to be around him.

"How's it going?" I asked.

"Oddly enough, it's not too bad. I missed this literal shit storm," he said, putting his pitchfork down. "I'm a bit slower than I used to be."

"Yeah, you are," I joked. I clapped my hands together. "Get it together, or you'll be here all night."

"If only I had someone to help me." He smiled. Gosh, I loved that smile.

"If only."

"Come on, Haze." He gestured toward another pitchfork and one of the messy pens. "One more for old times' sake?"

I narrowed my eyes. "Are you trying to get out of doing your job?"

"No. I just like being around you."

Butterflies.

So many butterflies.

315

I took a deep inhale and released it through my lips. Even if Charlie did walk in on Ian and me, it wasn't as if we were doing anything outside of the normal. We were working; that was all.

At least that was all I thought was going on.

As I began shoveling the soiled hay, Ian spoke. "Confessions?"

I shook my head. "I'm not sure I'm up for it."

"Why?" He narrowed his eyes. "Afraid of what might be said?"

"Exactly."

He didn't let up, though. "Confession: I miss you."

"Ian . . ."

"Confession: you're my best friend."

"Please stop."

"Confession: if you gave me the chance, I'd love you until forever."

I swallowed hard as I watched him walk toward me. I was standing right in the middle of pig manure, doing the most disgusting job, looking as if I hadn't slept in days, and Ian Parker was telling me how he wanted to love me forever.

He continued on. "Confession: you are my sun, my moon, and my stars. Confession: whatever's hurting you, we can fix together. Confession: I'm never going to give up on this."

I didn't know how it happened. I didn't know how my hands found his or how our bodies became pressed together. I didn't know how his forehead fell to mine or how my heartbeats increased erratically.

I didn't know how his lips fell so close to mine or how his exhalations became my inhalations.

But there we were, seconds away from our lips locking together, and me falling into a drunkenness that I'd never be able to recover from. If I started kissing Ian, I knew I'd never be able to stop.

He was it for me.

He was the hook, the bridge, and the melody.

"I feel it in your body shakes," he breathed. "I feel it as I hold you. I feel the love that's there, so tell me, Hazel. Tell me what's keeping us from being us. Give me your confession, and I'll make it all right."

"Charlie," I whispered, my voice shaky and unsure if I was doing the right thing. "It's Charlie."

He pulled away from me and raised an eyebrow. "What do you mean, it's Charlie?"

Feeling an overwhelming amount of dread sitting in my chest, I began pouring everything out of me. I told him about how Charlie was out of prison, about how he'd threatened me and forced me to break things off with Ian. How he'd threatened the ranch as a whole. How he'd threatened my little sister.

"He said he would hurt Rosie. You see? I had no choice. I had to break things off with you, Ian. He put me in a corner, and I didn't have any other choice."

Ian's face turned bright red as his hands formed fists. "He said he would hurt Rosie?"

"Yes." I nodded, hating the memories that came rushing back to me of Charlie holding Rosie in his arms.

"He's going to die for that. I'm going to fucking kill him."

"No." I shook my head. "You can't do that. You can't go after him, Ian. You can't do that. People don't get Charlie. He gets people. Trust me, I've tried to get him put away, and it all backfired. Plus, you're in the public eye. Max was right about that—you can't be getting involved in my mess when you're on the road to massive success."

"Max said something to you too?" he hissed as his nose flared. "What the hell?"

"It's really okay. He worried about your image and what it would be like being with someone with so much ugliness to my past. I understood that a bit."

"No. Fuck that, and fuck Max. And fuck Charlie. And fuck!" he shouted, pacing the barn. "We can't just let Charlie get away with this. You can't spend the rest of your life under his chains."

"I have no choice."

"There's always a choice and always a way."

I wished I could believe that, but I knew how Charlie worked. I knew the number of times he'd dragged my mother back into his world of despair. I knew he could ruin my life and Rosie's with a snap of his fingers. I'd never feared anyone other than that madman. Charlie was a monster—and he wasn't afraid of hurting anyone who got in the way of his destruction.

"I'm sorry, Ian. I just . . . we . . ." I sighed. "We can't be together."

"I don't accept that."

"Well, you should. There's no way to make this work."

"Just you wait," he promised, taking my hands into his and kissing my palms. "We're going to get our happily ever after. But first, allow me to ruin this asshole's life."

40

IAN

I'd spent the whole night trying to figure out how to help Hazel, and when it became too hard and I felt as if I were running in circles, I went to the only person I could think of who could help me. The person I always turned to during the hardest moments.

Big Paw sat in his office chair with his wrinkles deepening into a frown as I told him everything Hazel had unfolded to me the previous night.

"I always hated that Charlie Riley. He's a toxic creature to this here town, and it's about time we get rid of him."

"How? Hazel said there's no way. His presence here is too big, and even when people get one step forward, he pushes them two steps back."

"Not this time. He doesn't get to push my loved ones into a corner."

"But that's what he's doing, and there's no way we can push back against him."

"Yes, there is. When you are pushed in a corner, you put on your boxing gloves, and you fight back, Ian. You think I've never faced hard times? Of course I have, but do you know how I've made it through those tough periods?"

"How?"

"I didn't give up, I kept fighting, and when I needed it the most, I reached out to others to help me. We don't have to face every battle alone. Sometimes, all of the time, we're stronger together." He reached out toward me and placed his hand against mine. "I'm glad you came to me with this. Now, get to work today, and be up bright and early tomorrow. We have a long drive to take tomorrow."

"A drive to where?"

"To the one person who is Charlie's blind spot. We're going to see Hazel's mother."

"What? How? She's in prison, and she won't even see Hazel. She hasn't seen her in months."

"She doesn't have to see Hazel. She has to see me, and seeing as how I'm already on her visitor list, it won't be a big deal. I was going up there tomorrow, anyway. The only difference is I'm bringing you along with me this time around."

I had so many questions for him. Questions about why he'd been visiting Hazel's mother. Questions about why we were going to visit her in the first place and how she could help the Charlie situation. Questions about . . . everything.

But the way Big Paw smiled my way showed me that I was supposed to just trust him.

Therefore, I did.

As we headed toward the prison, my stomach sat knotted up with the thought of seeing Hazel's mom, Jean. When you thought about meeting your girlfriend's mother, you didn't assume it would be in a prison. Talk about unorthodox.

"Now, let me do a bit of the talking first to get the conversation moving," Big Paw ordered. "I don't want you making any trouble by saying something offbeat."

We walked inside and went through all of the security procedures before being led to a table to wait for Jean to come out.

When she did, she looked surprised to see me sitting at the table with Big Paw.

"You brought a guest," she said, looking him dead in the eyes as she took her seat. "Where's Holly?"

Wait, what?

Jean knew Big Paw *and* Grams? How was that possible?

"She wasn't feeling too well today. She couldn't make the drive," he told her.

I shifted around in my chair, trying to get comfortable but knowing it was impossible. Jean had a heavy sadness about her whole persona. It was pretty hard to witness. You could tell she'd been through a lot of hard shit in her life just by looking into her eyes. She gave me a sideways grin, and it disappeared quickly before her eyes shifted to her clasped hands.

"I got you some pictures," Big Paw mentioned, pulling out a stack of photographs. He held each photo up for Jean to witness, and tears began falling down her cheeks as she took in the photographs of Rosie that Big Paw was sharing with her.

"She's getting big," she commented.

"Yes," I agreed. "She looks so much like you."

"She looks like Hazel," she corrected, fiddling with her hands. "When Hazel was a baby, she had those big eyes too."

"Wait, so how do you and Big Paw know each other?" I asked, bewildered.

"Holly and I've been visiting her quite a bit over the past few months," he explained.

"Yeah, he's been a pain in my ass," Jean joked.

"And she's been a pain in mine, always has throughout the years."

"Years?" I asked.

Jean nodded. "We'd crossed paths many moons ago, when I was a teenager. I was pregnant with Hazel and on my own when I came to Eres. I was running from a troubled childhood, and when I got here, Holly and Big Paw took me in with arms wide open."

"It seems to be what they do," I said.

"Yeah, but I didn't make it easy for them. I got involved with your mother and father, and I made a few choices I shouldn't have after Hazel was born. I started hanging out with Sarah and Ray, and they introduced me to Charlie, and we all know how that ended up." She gestured around her and frowned.

All this time I'd blamed Hazel's mother for the beast that Charlie was, but it seemed as if my parents were the ones responsible for bringing Charlie and Jean together.

"You can only go up from here," I said, hoping to give her a splash of hope.

She rubbed her hand up and down her arm nervously. "I want to do right; that's all."

"Which is why we're here," Big Paw said. "We need your help."

She snickered. "No offense, Big Paw, but I'm not really able to help people much with my current situation." She gestured around her again.

"But you can do what you can from where you are," he said, clasping his hands together. "He threatened your daughters."

Jean's eyes widened, and she gave Big Paw a panicked look. "How so?"

"He's forcing Hazel to give him all of her income, controlling her relationships, saying he'll burn down the ranch, and threatening to do harm to her and Rosie if she doesn't obey. He's been beating up Garrett, too, pretty bad."

Tears filled her eyes, and she shook her head. "I got her in a terrible place. I should've never gotten involved with Charlie. He shouldn't be able to hurt my girl, but that's how he is." She wiped a few tears from her eyes and swallowed hard. "I don't get how I can help, though."

"That's easy," Big Paw said. "If there's one person who knows Charlie, it's you. You know how his messed-up brain works. You know his plans, his drops, his . . . everything. So I need you to tell us some things to help catch him. We need to get him locked up, and this time, he won't have anyone to take the fall for him. This time, he's on his own, and this time, we'll make sure it sticks."

A moment of silence passed by as Jean lowered her brows. She clasped her hands together and nodded once. "I'll tell you anything you need to know."

And she did exactly that.

She gave us all that she could until it was time for her to leave the space. As she stood up from her chair, she looked my way. "You love my daughter?"

"Yes, ma'am, I do."

"Can you do me a favor and treat her well? She deserves someone who treats her well."

"I promise," I told her. "And thank you for your help. You have no clue how much this means to us."

"I've been a terrible mother. I've been messed up more than I've been clean, but getting off drugs in here has made me very clear minded. I want to do what's right. If I can help you, I'll do whatever I can. If it keeps my girls safe, I'll do anything. If you could tell Hazel I'm sorry— for everything—that would mean a lot to me."

"You really love your daughters, don't you?"

"I do. I've never been a good mother, but I've always had the most amazing girl. I just couldn't realize it when my head was fogged. Please tell her I'm sorry."

"You should reach out to her yourself."

"I doubt she'd want anything to do with me after I cut her off all those months ago."

"She will," I swore. "She is Hazel, after all . . . she loves unconditionally."

Jean nodded once before her stare moved to Big Paw. "Please send Holly my well-wishes. I'm sorry for what she's going through, and I'm sorry that you are struggling too."

As Big Paw and I walked outside, I asked him the one question that had been sitting in my head all this time. "Do you blame yourself for what happened to her? As if her living with you was the cause of her meeting Charlie?"

"Every single day."

"And that's why you wanted to give Hazel the job all those months ago?"

He nodded. "Just looking for a little bit of redemption."

"Trust me, Big Paw. You've been redeemed."

The moment we made it back to Eres, I told Hazel what the plan was going to be. Even though she was hesitant, there was a splash of hope in her eyes.

I wished I could've said there was some super-blockbuster-movie moment that happened when Big Paw and I set Charlie up, but there wasn't. He was caught at one of his drop-off locations, and he was arrested once more. This time, it would stick, because he no longer had Jean to take the rap for him. Plus, he'd been in and out of prison so much that there was no way he'd be able to walk away clean.

When I got the word from Big Paw that Charlie was in handcuffs, I headed to the house to see Hazel. When I got there, she was already in bed, and I woke her up from her slumber.

"Hey," she whispered, rubbing the sleep from her eyes. "What's going on?"

"It's over."

Those were the only words I said, and they were enough to get her to sit up in bed. "It's over? Really? They got Charlie?"

"Yes, and he's not getting out anytime soon. Garrett even said he'd testify against him in court. It's really over, Haze. It's over."

She released the biggest sigh of relief and fell into my arms. "It's over," she whispered.

That night I made love to my love, and everything felt right.

41

IAN

"That's perfect, perfect, perfect!" Hazel clapped her hands together as she sat in the barn house with the band and me, helping shape up the lyrics to a few of the tracks we'd been creating.

We'd been working day and night, trying to pull this album out of our ass, and as the days moved by, it was appearing more and more unlikely.

Lately, all of our phones had blown up with dozens of text messages from Max, ordering us to return as quickly as possible to get the album up and running with Warren Lee's tracks.

"Ignore him," Eric told me. "Max Fucking Rider will be okay for a while. Our biggest concern right now is our music, not him."

I thanked him for reminding me what was important.

"I think they are beautiful," Hazel said, grinning ear to ear. She'd been nothing but an asset to the songs, taking my vision and making it soar. We worked together so effortlessly, and I was glad to get back to the basics of the music. It was beginning to feel like fun again.

Leah had been attending our rehearsals with Hazel, and I was thankful that she'd become such a big part of Hazel's life. Hazel needed a friend in town, and I knew Leah was a loyal one. Watching them grow closer each day was the best damn thing to see.

"Not to make your egos bigger than they already are, but that was beyond amazing," Leah said. "And believe me, it kills me to give my brother a compliment, but it was magical."

"I agree with Hazel. That was amazing!" Grams exclaimed, sitting in a chair beside Big Paw. Since we weren't able to perform or post anything about the new music, the only people we could share the tracks with were people we could really trust.

"I think that you really tapped into—" Grams's words trailed off as she stood from her chair. Her hand fell to her chest, and she took in deep inhalations. Everything felt as if it were moving in slow motion from that point on. I dropped the microphone from my grip as Grams's legs began to buckle. Big Paw flew up from his seat, Hazel shot toward her, and the bandmates dashed too.

But it was too late. Grams hit the ground with a hard thump, and in an instant, I'd forgotten how to breathe.

We headed straight to the hospital from the barn house. Big Paw and Grams were picked up by an ambulance, and everyone else was following closely behind. For the most part, the trip was driven in complete silence. Finally, Marcus took control and turned on the radio. After two songs, ours came on the station and blasted through the speakers.

"Jeez," James sighed, shaking his head. "I'm never going to get used to that. I'm never going to wrap my head around the fact that we're on the radio."

"Life's crazy," I muttered, chewing on my thumbnail as I stared out toward the dirt roads we were approaching.

We pulled up to the hospital, and I shot out of the car and hurried inside. I walked up to the receptionist's desk to ask about Grams but was cut off.

"Ian."

I turned around to see Big Paw standing behind us.

"Hey, what's going on?"

"They think she might need a pacemaker put in. But first, they have to go in and repair a vessel," he explained. "They are prepping her for surgery now."

Surgery?

Fuck.

"Can you believe that bullshit?" Big Paw grimaced. "These SOBs want to cut into my Holly's heart." His voice cracked, and tears fell down his cheeks. "How wrong is that?"

I walked over to Big Paw and patted him on the back. "Don't worry. Everything is going to be okay."

"How can you say that? You don't know that for sure," he argued.

"Yeah, I know, but that's what Grams would say, isn't it? She'd say that everything always works out. If it doesn't work out, it's not the end of the story."

He huffed, wiping his overworked hands against his face. "That's just some mumbo jumbo bullshit she says. That woman is going to be the death of me. I can't believe she's doing this to me." His tears began falling faster and faster. "How can she go in there and let those people cut into her?"

"I don't think she has a choice, Big Paw, but I'm sure these doctors are good at what they do. They are great at their jobs. They are going to take care of Grams; I know it. You just have to have a little faith."

"I can't. Holly was the one with faith. I'm the old fart who doesn't believe in any of that shit. It's funny, actually," he said with such a somber tone. "They are cutting into her heart, but it's mine that's breaking."

I pulled him into a hug and held on tight, trying to help his troubled heart, but I knew nothing would help him until the love of his life was coming through the other side of surgery.

We all sat in the waiting room while Grams was in surgery. My band-mates and I shut off our phones, because the nonstop messages from Max were starting to drive us up a wall. My grandmother's life was on the line, and all Max cared about were the numbers and the dollar figures he was losing out on. It was as if we were nothing more than robots in his money machine.

I sat with my hands clasped together, tapping my feet against the carpeted floor, unable to steady my movements. The idea of Grams not making it out of surgery and not being okay shook me to my core. I couldn't stop thinking about all the time I'd spent away from home, chasing a dream, while my grandmother's health was failing.

Who knew how much time I had left with them? I should've been home. I should've been helping them around the ranch. Hell, Big Paw shouldn't have been working still.

Rosie sat in her car seat, sleeping, and I was jealous of the amount of peacefulness that baby had. I wished life was that easy and peaceful. A hand slipped over mine, and I looked up to see Hazel standing over me. She gave me that small smile that I loved so much, and she sat down in the chair next to me. She held my hand, even though I hadn't asked her to. She held on tight, and I was thankful for that. I needed a hand to hold. I needed something to stop the nerves from taking over my whole system, and a simple touch from that girl calmed the wildest parts of my soul.

"Thank you," I murmured so quietly I wasn't even certain she heard my words.

At that point, she held on tighter.

When the doctor came out, he didn't look as ecstatic about the surgery as we would've liked. We all shot to our feet, Big Paw standing more quickly than anyone, and we approached him.

"What's going on?" he barked at the doctor, sounding grumpier and more annoyed than ever before. "I don't get why nobody has been out here to update us on my Holly! What kind of goddamn place is being run here, anyway? Is it run by apes? This is madness."

I stepped closer to the doctor, who looked taken aback by Big Paw's strong opinion. I gave the doctor a half grin. "Hey, sorry about that. My grandfather is just worried about his wife."

The doctor tried to keep his composure, even though I was certain he had a few choice words for Big Paw. "It is okay. There were a few issues with the surgery, and we weren't able to get in the way we'd hoped we could. There was a lot of fluid around the lungs, and we didn't feel comfortable doing the surgery before we were able to drain some of that."

"Are you fucking kidding me?" Big Paw huffed. "You're telling me you all been back there all this time and haven't even done anything?"

"I'm sorry, Mr. Parker, but we had to determine the best route to take for your wife's safety. We didn't want to cause more damage by opening her up on the table when she wasn't physically strong enough to handle it. We're going to work over the next few days and make sure that we get her to a stable place, and then we will revisit the surgery option."

"Thank you," I spat out before Big Paw could chew the doctor a new one. Judging by the fire in my grandfather's eyes, he had a few choice words he would've likely used. "Can we see her?"

"She's being transported back to her room. A nurse will notify you when you can go in."

I thanked him again, and he stood there, almost seeming dumbfounded. I cocked an eyebrow. "Is there something else . . . ?"

"Uh, well, yes and no. Not about your grandmother, but . . ." He scratched at the side of his head. "You're Ian Parker, right? You guys are the Wreckage? My daughter is the biggest fan of you all. Would it be completely inappropriate to ask for a photograph?"

"Yes," Hazel cut in, stepping a few feet in front of me, blocking me from the doctor as if she were my bodyguard. "That would be highly inappropriate and extremely unprofessional."

The doctor grimaced and walked away.

"What a piece of work." Big Paw blew out, still shaking his head. "The things these people are putting Holly through is driving me crazy," he said, sitting back down in his chair. "I just want to take my girl home with me."

It shattered my heart watching how broken Big Paw was becoming. It was as if he hadn't a clue how to exist without Grams by his side. Without her, Big Paw could hardly breathe.

"It's going to be okay, Big Paw," I echoed once again, hoping I wasn't telling a lie. But I knew that was what Grams would want me to say.

Everything's going to be all right.

42

IAN

"Can I get you anything?" Hazel asked as she held Rosie in her arms. It was wild to me how big the little girl had gotten over the past few months. "I was going to go to the cafeteria and see if I could find a coffee or something."

I grimaced. "I'm good."

James cleared his throat. "Maybe you could go with her, Ian, and grab us chums some food. I'm starving. Hazel, we can watch Rosie for you if you want." James cocked an eyebrow toward me as if telling me to go with Hazel unless I wanted to continue being a dumbass for the rest of my life.

"Are you sure?" Hazel asked. "She can be quite a handful."

"Lucky for me, I have big hands." He stood up to grab Rosie from Hazel, and she thanked him for the help.

I stood up from my chair and stuffed my hands into my pockets as I began walking down the long hallway with Hazel. God, even with all the time that had passed, she still drove me crazy whenever she was near me. She made my heart beat erratically every single time she stole a glance my way. I noticed every time she looked, too, because I hadn't been able to pull my eyes away from her.

We were both quiet, but I felt her nerves filling the space. Or perhaps it was my own nervous energy. I couldn't tell anymore whose feelings were whose. She rubbed her hand up and down her arm as she gave me a small smile. "I know you're probably worried about your grandmother, but you don't have to be. She's a fighter. And you were right when you told Big Paw that if it's not okay, it's not the end. I think he needed to hear that. I think it's true too."

I clasped and unclasped my hands repeatedly as I kept walking down the hall. Holy hell, where was this cafeteria? On the other side of the planet?

"Can we talk about anything other than Grams right now? It's too heavy and hard."

She nodded. "What do you want to talk about?"

"Us. Let's talk about us. What was the hardest part of being apart to you?"

"The hardest thing in the world was not being able to reach out to you when I had a bad day. Or talk to you when things went well. I missed you so much, Ian, and for a long time I convinced myself my missing you was one sided. I convinced myself that you were happy and living your dreams to the fullest. I needed to do that in order to keep myself from reaching out. But I've written you a million messages in my notepad, updating you on things. Letting you know what was going on in my world."

"I still want to know everything, and this time, I'm not going to let you go. We will have our forever kind of love story. The kind of love Big Paw and Grams share. I'm going to grow old with you, Hazel Stone."

She stood there completely still, her lips parted as if she were stunned by what I'd just said. I knew it would probably take her some time to wrap her head around it all. I knew she'd need time to let it settle in, but I didn't care.

She was going to be my happy ending, and I was going to be hers. I didn't have plans on going anywhere anytime soon.

"Hey, you guys," a voice said, snapping us from our conversation. We looked down the hall to see James holding a sleeping Rosie in his arms. "Holly's awake if you want to go see her."

"Okay." I nodded, and before we started heading in the direction of Grams, I lightly placed my hand on Hazel's forearm. "Just to be clear, Hazel, you're beautiful. You're so beautiful it makes my chest ache. I love you. Fully, hopelessly, greedily."

Her lips parted, and a small sound escaped her. "I love you too."

"I'm doing okay," Grams said repeatedly as we all stood over her hospital bed. She looked so tired and weak. It broke my heart seeing her in such a state. But the nurses informed us that it was good that she was talking. Even though she wavered in and out of sleep.

"You don't have to lie. If you're not good, say it, and I'll get these doctors to do their damn jobs," Big Paw grumbled, sitting close to Grams's bed as he held her hand in his.

Grams smirked and looked my way. "Please don't tell me this old fart has been giving all these kind folks at this hospital hell."

"You know Big Paw. All bark and some bite," I joked.

"Well, I heard the nurse saying you've all been here all day. Go home and get some food and rest. Lord knows you're tired."

"I'm not leaving your side, Holly Renee," Big Paw argued.

"Yes, you are. Go home and get some sleep. I can tell by your bags you haven't slept in days. And take a damn shower. I could smell you from down the hall earlier," she joked; then she had a coughing fit, making everyone alarmed. "Really, you guys. I'm in good hands here. Just go get some rest. Please. That will make me feel better. I can't get better if I'm worrying about Harry's health."

He frowned and pressed his lips to her hand. "You're too good for this world, Holly. Too good for me."

"I know." She smiled. "Now, go home and listen to your wife."

"Eric and I will stay with her while you guys go get some rest," Marcus offered.

"I'll stay too," James added in. The three of them were like grandsons to Grams. Of course they'd offer to watch over her.

"See, Harry? I have a slew of people looking after me. Go get some rest, and come back by morning."

"I love—" he said, leaning in and rubbing his nose against hers.

"You," she finished, rubbing her nose back against his.

Hazel and Rosie headed out with Big Paw and me back to Big Paw's house. As we pulled up, Hazel took control, making sure everyone was fed and cared for and making sure Big Paw got into the shower and headed to bed. She was so good at the mothering role. It came so naturally to her—the same way it came to Grams.

We stayed in Big Paw's guest room that night, because I didn't want him to be left alone. The guest room had been set up with a crib for Rosie, who was now down for the night.

After I took a shower of my own, I headed back to the guest room, where Hazel was sitting at the desk, studying.

"When do you take a break?" I asked.

She snickered and yawned. "From studying or from life? Because the answer to both of those questions is never."

"Maybe take one now?"

She looked over to me and bit her bottom lip. "Okay."

"Meet me in my old bedroom so we can talk without waking Rosie?"

"Will do. Let me grab the baby monitor, and I'll be right over."

"Sounds good. And Hazel?"

"Yeah?"

"Check your Instagram."

43

HAZEL

After Ian left my bedroom, I hurried over to my cell phone to open Instagram. My heart was flying at a million miles per hour, wondering what it was that I was supposed to be witnessing. Then I saw it. Ian's newest post.

A post of me.

I'd never seen the picture before. He had to have taken it when Rosie was in the NICU without me knowing my photograph was being snapped. I was looking down on Rosie with the biggest smile against my lips as I stared at my little sister. It was a simple shot. Nothing out of this world, but the one thing that could be taken away from the picture was love. There was so much love shining through as I studied my little sister's heartbeats.

The likes on the post were skyrocketing right before my eyes. Hundreds. Then thousands. Then hundreds of thousands. I was officially going viral on Ian's Instagram page.

My hands fell to my chest as I went to read the caption that accompanied the photograph.

This woman controls my heartbeats. Every love lyric I sing each night is made for her. Every melody chases her heartbeat, and every chorus begs for her love. It has been brought to my attention that a few people on my management team have chosen to approach the love of my life and tell her that she wasn't good for my image. Due to her looks and the past she had no say in creating, they said she wasn't good enough. It's true, we grew up in the same town, but that didn't mean our home lives were built on the same steady foundation. I was blessed enough to never know struggle. This girl had to fight tooth and nail for everything she was given. She sacrificed her own youth, because she didn't want her little sister to go into the foster system. She gave up love, in order for me to go chase my dreams. She gives and gives in order to make others happy, because that's the person she is.

She's the most beautiful human being alive, and for anyone—especially people who are supposed to be in my corner—to say differently disgusts me to my core. I am not a robot. I hurt, I ache, I love, and I cry. And it breaks me to live in a world where I have to be afraid of showing who I really am in order to gain followers.

So if you don't like this fact—that I am not single and that I am hopelessly in love—then that's fine. If I lose fans over this, I'm okay with that. I will make every sacrifice in the world from this point on in order to give my love fully to the woman who has given more than she ever should've had to give. I love you, Haze. From the new moon to the fullest. From now until forever.

He'd made a public declaration of love for me. Giving his manager the biggest middle finger in the whole world. My hands trembled as I reread his words a dozen times. Then I heard him call out to me.

"Haze? Are you coming?"

I took a sharp inhalation and hit like on the post before placing my phone down on the dresser. "Yes. I'm coming."

The moment I stepped into his room, I didn't give him a chance to offer me any words. My lips crashed against his as he wrapped his arms around my body. Our kiss was so much more intense than ever before. It was as if we were making up for the lost time, for all the kisses that had gone missing due to Charlie.

His tongue danced with mine, and I greedily sucked at his bottom lip whenever I received the chance. We made love that night, rocking our bodies together, fitting our pieces back into their rightful places. He owned every inch of my body and every piece of my soul. Every time he slid into me, I moaned for more. Every time he thrust deeper, I dug my nails into his back.

"Forever," he whispered into my neck before swiping his tongue against my skin.

"Forever," I breathed out, thrusting my hips toward him.

We made love three more times that night, each time more passionate than the last. And when I fell asleep in his arms, I knew I was home.

I awakened to the loud sounds of banging. I sat up in bed, looking around as confusion hit me.

Bang, bang, bang!

What in the world?

I glanced over to the left side of the bed, where Ian had been before, but he was missing. My hand swept over his spot, and a chill raced over me as I missed his warmth.

Bang, bang, bang!

I shot up to my feet and grabbed my robe, tossing it on quickly. I checked in on Rosie to make sure she was all right, but thankfully, she was still sleeping peacefully.

I hurried down the steps and paused when I'd almost reached the bottom. The whole living room was in complete disarray, as the wooden panels of the floor were being pulled up. Big Paw was taking a hammer to them, and Ian stood beside him, pulling up his own pieces.

It was still pitch black outside, and I, for the life of me, couldn't figure out if I was still dreaming or not.

"What's going on here?"

Big Paw didn't look up. He kept hammering and hammering non-stop into the floor.

Ian looked up to me and gave me a sloppy, broken smile. "He's been promising Grams that he'd fix these floors for the past twenty-five years. I came down and saw him hammering at it, so I joined in to help."

"She shouldn't have to come home to this squeaky mess," Big Paw murmured, wiping away the tears that kept falling from his eyes. "I'm the asshole who didn't do it when she asked."

He was beating himself up because he was scared for his wife. His mind must've been terrified that he wasn't able to fix her, to make her better. So he did what he'd spent the past eighty years of his life doing—manual labor to show his love. He hammered into the floor, and Ian stayed directly next to his grandfather, being the rock that kept him steady. Working as hard as he could to help tear up the floor. I wasn't sure if what they were doing made any kind of sense. Maybe it was just an outlet to let their worries release from their souls.

Truth was, it didn't matter why they were doing it. All that mattered was they were doing it together.

I grabbed a hammer and joined in, because that was what family did. We stood by each other's side through all of the ups and downs.

———— ☙❦❧ ————

A week later, Holly's lungs were doing better, and the pacemaker surgery was performed. Thankfully, the operation was quick and without complications. Her recovery process would require a lot of care and attention, but she had a good army behind her to make sure everything went as smoothly as it possibly could.

All of the guys pitched in to help finish the flooring in Big Paw's house before Holly came home.

"The biggest concern is making sure Holly is all right," Eric said one night as we all gathered in the barn house. "The music isn't going anywhere."

"I still feel bad for all of this, you guys. Max has been coming down hard on us all since I put up that post about Hazel, and I feel bad that I didn't come to you all about it first," Ian said.

"Are you fucking kidding me? Max Fucking Rider crossed every line saying that to Haze! He had a lot of nerve, and if I had known, I would've never let that fly. I'm glad you posted that shit. It's about time someone spoke the truth," Marcus exclaimed. "And another thing: he also fucked us over with our album! Fuck Max Fucking Rider in the fucking ass."

James sat on the stage where the band used to put on all of its shows. His fingers ran across the wooden platform, and a crooked smile sat on his lips. "I miss this place. I never really thought I'd say that, but I do. I miss the way we used to love the music. Don't get me wrong: I know we're blessed, and I wouldn't give up this world for anything, but it feels like it's so far out of our control sometimes, and I feel like if we don't put a stop to some of these crazy demands, we'll lose ourselves down the line."

"I say we take a vote," Eric commented, dancing his fingers across his keyboard. "All in favor of sitting down with Max and Donnie and having a real fucking talk about who we are and what we want to do with this career of ours, say aye."

"Aye." The room echoed, and I smiled at them. The four boys who had dreams that they were taking control of once again.

Ian held his hand out. "Until forever."

Each of the guys walked over to him and placed a hand on top of his. "Until forever."

They all looked over to me with cocked eyebrows, perplexed. "Oh, sorry. I didn't mean to crash your moment. I can let you guys—"

"Hazel, if you don't bring your hand over here right this second, I will have to force you over," Marcus threatened.

I laughed and walked over, placing my hand on top of theirs. "Until forever," I agreed.

"Speaking of Max and Donnie"—Eric smiled wide as he pushed his thumb against his nose—"I think I know the best way of tackling our issue."

"And how's that?" Ian asked.

"Let me show you." Eric walked over to his backpack near his keyboard and pulled out his laptop. As he powered it up, we all crowded around him. "You all know how I'm a professional at always recording videos and stuff, even when people don't know it."

"Yeah, speed up to your point," Marcus harassed his brother.

Eric pulled up a video and hit play. "I've been making a nice home video of situations with Max and Donnie since we met them. Times we'd been at parties and Max popped pills or did lines of coke. Times both of the very married men were seen with women on their arms. Times when they've had aggressive conversations. Everything. We have enough to nail these assholes."

"But we can't. This stuff would never hold up in court," James argued. "It was illegally recorded."

"That's not the point. We don't even have to take it to court. The point is we threaten to show their wives unless they allow us to get out of the messed-up contract."

"You think showing their wives will matter? These are assholes, Eric. They don't care about their wives' feelings."

"Yes, you're right. But I'm sure the wives will be interested in seeing what these men have been up to. Plus, they've been with their wives since before they found fame. And you know what that means?"

"What?" Ian asked.

"No prenups. Which means if their wives left them, they'd leave with pretty much half their shit."

A small smile formed on everyone's face as realization began to set in. That plan was brilliant and might actually work. I was certain the guys would fine-tune it before approaching Max and Donnie, but there seemed to be a light at the end of a very long and dark tunnel for the Wreckage.

The rest of the night, we stayed in the barn house, with Rosie joining in when she awakened from her nap, and the guys played music with all of their hearts and every ounce of their passion. They returned to their roots and sounded better than ever before. I loved that they weren't afraid to speak up for their wants, for their needs as musicians. It couldn't have been easy to go against men like Donnie and Max, but they weren't doing it solo. They would be walking into that meeting with their heads held high as a complete unit.

No matter what happened when they met with the record label, I knew everything would work out exactly as it was supposed to. The Wreckage would end up exactly where they were meant to go, because they had each other's backs through thick and thin. There was no getting around the fact that when they said "until forever," they truly meant those words.

I stayed there listening to the lyrics rolling off Ian's tongue as he sang, his voice melting into every inch of my soul.

And that evening, I knew those lyrics were being sung solely for me.

44

IAN

"Please tell me you're joking, because every demand you are making is out of the realm of possibility. Furthermore, for you to go off the grid as long as you did without reaching out is beyond unprofessional. You've missed ample studio time, and now you have no damn album to showcase. But now you have the nerve to come sit in the conference room of the biggest record label ever, with Donnie Schmitz, the CE-fucking-O of Mindset Records, to tell us that we owe you a fucking apology?" Max spat at us in a complete state of shock.

It was funny how much had changed since we'd sat across from Max for the first time. We were so naive back then and happy to just be given a chance. We were so happy that someone as big as Max took notice of us that we didn't even consider what exactly someone like him noticing us meant.

"You all are in for a hell of a lawsuit," Donnie grumbled, clasping his hands together with a threatening look on his face.

I clasped my hands together in the same fashion and sat up straighter. "I doubt we have to get lawyers involved. We just want a few things from you, and we'll get out of your hair."

Donnie huffed. "You want something from us? We gave you everything!"

"Yes, even the kindness of you both leaking our album earlier in order to force us to play your mainstream music," I explained.

Donnie and Max both glanced at one another before Max shook his head. "What in the hell are you talking about?"

"We have our own geek squad," James said, nodding toward Eric. "He figured out where the leaked records came from. Don't play dumb; it's not a cute look on you."

Donnie grimaced as he rolled his hands through his grayed hair. "Yes, well, you hacking into our emails isn't going to look swell for you. That's an illegal act."

"Yes, which is why we aren't taking the emails to the feds. We are, instead, sending these videos to your wives," Marcus said matter-of-factly. He pulled out his cell phone and emailed Donnie. "Mr. Schmitz, if you would please check your email."

Donnie opened his email to a very, very inappropriate video. After Eric had revealed his plan to us, we'd been able to reach out to some of the girls in the videos with Max and Donnie, and they were fans of our music. They'd been eager to send us videos of their private affairs with Donnie and Max, and let's just say a lot of weird shit had happened with grapefruits and dicks. Max raced over to Donnie to see what video was being played, and I watched the exact moment the color drained from his face.

Donnie sat up in his chair. "Where did you get this?"

"It doesn't matter, but if you were smarter, you would've had those women sign NDAs. But seeing as how you didn't, I wonder if your wives would be interested in seeing these videos. Also, if you were smarter, you would've probably had prenups put in place before marriage. But instead, it seems that your wives might be able to take a good chunk of change from you."

"They are bluffing," Max spat out. "I know these guys. They don't have the balls to—"

"Shut the fuck up, Max," Donnie barked, silencing Max in mere seconds. Donnie's brow knitted, and he lowered his eyes as he kept replaying the video. His lips were pressed together so tightly the vein in his neck throbbed.

When he was finished staring, he finally placed his phone down and locked eyes with me. "What are your requests?"

"Are you kidding?" Max sighed. "You can't really—"

Donnie held a silencing hand up to Max, and he instantly shut up. *Good puppy.*

"We want three more months to create a new album. You'll push the release date back. We'll release our music—our real fucking music—and then, once that's done, we're freed from our contract with you. We don't owe you any other albums down the line, and everything we agreed to is null and void. We're free to walk with our hands clean after this album releases."

There was a thickness to the air as Donnie contemplated his choices. He cleared his throat. "I'll have a new contract drafted up over the next few days."

"Are you shitting me?" Max hollered. "You're really going to allow these small-town dicks to push you in a corner?"

Donnie leaned forward toward the conference telephone and hit a button. "Laura, please have security come up front and remove Max Rider from the building."

"What? What? You're joking, right?" Max said, looking panicked. "You can't kick me out of here."

"Yes, I can, and I am. I should've never taken you up on the idea of leaking that album, and that is something I'll have to live with. But for now, you are no longer allowed at Mindset Records."

"This—this is all because of you dicks!" Max hollered, gesturing toward the band and me. "You idiots ruined your only shot at fame. I discovered you! I fucking made you what you are! You are shooting yourself in the fucking foot. You're stupid and making a million mistakes. You staying with that girl is a scandal waiting to happen. Your stupid fucking indie music is a train wreck. You won't take off without me. Don't you know who I am? I'm Max Fucking Rider! I make stars!"

He hollered those last lines on repeat as security dragged him out of the building.

As we gathered our things, Donnie looked our way with a frown against his lips. "So about that video. Do you think you can get rid of it?"

"Oh, Donnie." I shook my head. "I think we both know that we can't remove it until after the new contracts are in place."

"Fair enough." He nodded in understanding. "Max said you small-town boys weren't the brightest, but it seems you proved him wrong. It seems you can indeed hold your own. We'll be in touch shortly."

We all agreed, and as we walked away, Donnie said, "The grapefruit thing was worth it. It felt great against my dick as the girls worked their mouths."

Marcus groaned as we left the room. "And just like that, I can never eat grapefruit again."

I felt a bit of unease about the choice we'd made in the conference room that afternoon, but I knew it was the right one. We'd be able to release our album and our music on our terms. Sure, perhaps we'd never be able to have the superstar success we'd dreamed of without a huge company backing us, but at least we'd have our music—which was what it was all about in the first place.

Eric patted me on the back. "Good job, leader."

"Yeah, that was great and all, but also why do I feel like my balls just dropped and I want to vomit?" Marcus semijoked. "Did we just tell Max Fucking Rider and the head of Mindset Records to fuck off? Is that the end of our careers?"

"Nah, I think we're going to be fine. You know what they say: if it's not okay, it's not the end of the story. I think the Wreckage will live to see another day," James said. "And if not, I'm sure we can get our jobs back at the ranch."

Back to the pigpens and Hazel Stone.

Didn't sound so awful to me.

Then again, I knew we couldn't give up on the music. We were going to figure it out one way or another. Only this time, we were going to do it our way.

"So you threatened Max Fucking Rider and the head of Mindset Records, and you lived to tell the story," Hazel said as we sat inside of the shed as the sun began to set. The guys and I had been back in Eres for about thirty minutes, and I'd already found my way to the shed to sit beside Hazel and stare up at the sky.

"I think we lived to tell the story. We'll see after the nauseous feeling subsides," I joked. "I don't know what happens next with us, but I guess we start with trying to find a new manager. We have a meeting at the record label next week to see the new contract. We're going to have our lawyers comb through it nonstop to make sure Donnie isn't trying to screw us over somehow."

She snickered. "Your lawyers. What a crazy thing to even say. You have your own set of lawyers. Who would've thought this was how your life would turn out?"

"Wild, right?"

"In the best way. I, for one, think you guys are making the right choice searching for a new manager. Not just because I hate every piece of Max's soul but also because you need someone behind you who believes in the same things that you do. Someone who believes in your dreams and will help you get to them. Someone who will stand up for you. I'm sure that manager is out there. Just give it time. You'll find them."

"You think so?"

"I know so."

She rested her head on my shoulder, and we looked up at the darkening sky. The moon was full, and a part of me thought about howling toward it. I leaned down and kissed Hazel's forehead.

"You know what I've been thinking?" I asked.

"What's that?"

"That you should probably marry me someday. Soon."

She lifted her head up from my shoulder and twisted it in my direction. "What?"

I snickered. "Don't worry, I'm not asking you now, but I do plan on asking you someday, and when I do, I hope you'll say yes to me. Because the idea of having you as mine until forever means more than you'll ever know to me."

She leaned in with a smile and kissed my lips. "I'd say yes, you know. Over and over again, I'd say yes."

My chest tightened as realization set in. I was in love with a girl who loved me back. What could've been greater than that? No fame, no fortune, nothing. We were lucky to have found one another, lucky enough to not have given up when things got heavy.

Hazel Stone had changed me. She'd showed me what ultimate strength looked like. She'd showed me unconditional love, and I hoped to do the same for her for the rest of our lives.

As we lay there inside the shed looking up at the sky, I felt a fullness wash over me.

Hazel Stone was my best friend, my darling, my melody, my song.

And damn . . .

She sounded so good.

Epilogue

HAZEL

One Year Later

The barn house was packed as people danced in circles all night long. Rosie was on the dance floor with Marcus, and the two hopped up and down wildly as a Bruno Mars song blasted from the speakers. There were tables set up with the most stunning bouquets of roses as the centerpieces, and people sat at the tables eating the most yummy cake known to mankind.

I stood back from all of the action, taking it in from afar as happiness glowed throughout all of Eres.

A hand wrapped around my waist, and Ian pulled me in close to his body. His mouth brushed against my earlobe, and he whispered, "How's Mrs. Parker doing?" He kissed me gently up and down my neck.

I giggled. "I told you, you're not allowed to call me that until after we actually get married." True, the celebration we were watching wasn't our own, even though Ian had proposed to me over a year ago in the shed as we'd stared up at the moon.

We were in the wedding-planning territory, but we still had a few years before we'd officially walk down the aisle. The Wreckage had just released their sophomore album, which had shot up the charts, landing them their first number one album. After the fallout with Max, they'd found a manager named Andrew Still, who understood their dreams and was willing to do whatever it took to make them come true. They were heading off for the first leg of their new tour in a week. I was going to miss him dearly, but Rosie and I already had plans to meet up with them for a few shows over in Europe during the summer once my classes were done.

I was two years into my business degree, and I couldn't have been prouder of myself. I knew I couldn't have done it without Ian's family helping me through it all.

"Are you sure you don't want to run off to Vegas and just elope? I hear Elvis is alive and well down there and willing to tie the knot for us," Ian offered for the umpteenth time.

I laughed at the request and turned to face him. "There's no rush. We have the rest of our lives to be together."

"I know, but I want that," he said, nodding toward the dance floor. The occasion of the night was Big Paw and Holly's sixty-fifth anniversary. The two were out there swaying back and forth, giggling with one another as if they were teenage kids who were falling in love for the first time.

"We'll get that," I swore. "We're going to dance at every wedding and be the last couple standing."

"Speaking of dancing," Ian said, holding his hand out toward me. I placed my hand in his, and he moved us to the dance floor. We began swaying back and forth, his hand resting on my lower back, my head sitting against his shoulder.

It amazed me how far we'd come. How we'd grown into a love so strong. I'd been nineteen years old when I'd known my heart beat for Ian Parker, and I'd be late into my nineties with my heart still beating for that man.

Even though we were young, I knew that the future was going to be bright for us. We were going to bring babies into this world; we were going to use our gifts for good; we were going to give to those in need. We were going to love each other and nourish that love year after year.

And no matter what, we were going to spend the rest of our lives dancing under the moonlight.

Three Years Later

"Are you sure you don't want to work in the restaurant?" I asked, sitting at my desk. Across from me was my mother in her best clothing. She looked so much better than she had years before, and seeing her smiling across from me made me the happiest daughter alive.

There was a long time when I'd thought I'd lost her for good. A part of my life when I'd thought Mama was too far gone with her demons.

After she'd gotten out of prison, she'd been afraid she'd fall back into her old patterns, so when Ian had offered her a chance to go to an amazing rehab center, she'd taken him up on it. Mama had put in the hard work to turn her life around, and while she'd done that, Ian and I had always kept the porch light on, in case she ever wanted to return to us.

When she'd been ready, she'd come back, and now she was looking for work on the ranch.

"Oh no, no. You already know I don't belong in the kitchen. I think I can do some of the work around here, even if it's just cleaning up some messes. I mean, if you think there's room . . ." She fiddled with her fingers and gave me a half grin. "I'll do anything to just keep myself busy. Plus, Rosie said she wanted me to be working around the horses with her."

"Sounds about right." My little sister loved Dottie as much as I did. If she was ever missing, you could always find her in those stables. "We can get you started Monday. But don't think I'm going to take it easy on you since you're my mother," I sternly stated.

She nodded. "I wouldn't expect you to. I'm going to put in the hard work, Hazel. I promise you, I'm not going to let you down."

"There is one more stipulation to the job, Mama."

"And what's that?"

"You go to college."

Her face lost a bit of color, and she shook her head back and forth. "Oh no. No. I can't, Hazel. I don't even have a GED. College isn't something I could do."

"A long time ago, Big Paw told me you used to dream about going to college. Isn't that true?"

She fiddled with her hands, and embarrassment fell across her face. "Yes, but that was a long time ago. I'm not smart enough for any of that, and I'm old and worn out . . ."

"You're smart, Mama. You've always been smart, and I won't take no for an answer. We'll get you your GED and then work toward getting you into some college courses. You're never too old to achieve your goals. You can do it."

When she looked up to me, she had tears in her eyes. "You really think so?"

"I know so. We'll figure out all the details down the road, but enough about all of these things," I said, smiling as I stood. "We need to get to Thanksgiving dinner before Big Paw chews both of us out. You'll start next Monday."

Her eyes filled with tears as I pulled her into a tight hug. "Thank you, Hazel."

"I love you, Mama, and I'm so proud of the work you've done to turn your life around."

"You're going to make a great mother," she commented, placing her hands against my growing belly. I was mere weeks away from delivering my first child, and needless to say, I was terrified.

I wasn't even supposed to be working anymore, seeing as how the doctors had put me on bed rest, but I couldn't let anyone else interview Mama. Even though I said she wouldn't get special treatment, I knew she was going to get special treatment.

Family perks and all.

Since Rosie had been born, she'd lived with Ian and me, but once Mama had gotten herself together, she'd moved in with us too. I knew it was important for her and Rosie to form a connection as soon as possible. She might not have been able to be there for Rosie in her beginning stages, but Mama had every hope she would be there until the very end. Even Garrett was stopping by every now and again to visit Rosie. He'd never seen himself as a father figure, and he thought it was best that Rosie not see him in that role, but that little girl loved crawling all over Garrett, and she loved calling him her friend.

We walked over to the barn house—well, Mama walked; I waddled—where Thanksgiving dinner was taking place, and I smiled as I saw the room packed with people. It was my second year being in charge of the Thanksgiving feast, and I was so thankful for the townspeople helping me with creating a magical event. I hoped Grams was watching from the heavens above, smiling ear to ear at how it had all turned out.

She'd passed away a little over a year ago, but those last few years of her life had been lived to the fullest. She and Big Paw had finally taken time away from work and spent Grams's last days loving each other fully.

Big Paw had struggled with it for quite some time, but he had his lucky star, Rosie, to keep him on his toes. I swore he smiled so much due to my sister, and he called her the reason he was still around.

Brittainy Cherry

"She can't be getting in the mischief all by her lonesome. She needs me to make some trouble with her too," he'd told me.

Even though Grams had passed away, Big Paw still left the front porch light on so her spirit could always find her way home to him every morning and night.

"Mama! Mama!" Rosie yelled, hurrying over to our sides. She tugged on Mama's arm. "Mama, our seats are over here. Come on! Before Big Paw eats all the pie!"

"I ain't going to eat all the pie, you tattletale!" Big Paw yipped, shooting Rosie a sharp glare.

Rosie stuck her tongue out at him, and he stuck his out at her. Then she rushed over to him and pulled him into a hug, and he kissed her forehead. That summed up their connection perfectly.

Mama hurried over to join Rosie and Big Paw. Seeing Mama with Rosie felt like a gift for us all. She was finally clean and clearheaded enough to be the mother Rosie deserved, and I was more than happy to slip into the sisterly role.

Besides, I had my own bundle of joy coming my way sooner than later.

"Ready for some heartburn?"

Two arms wrapped around me from the back, and I snuggled in as I felt Ian's body against mine.

"Oh yes. Bring on the bad foods and the antacid," I joked.

He turned me around to face him, and he kissed my forehead and then my belly. If there was anyone more excited than me about my pregnancy, it was Ian. He was already going to be the father of the century based on how he cared for me and our child.

Each night, even when he was traveling, he'd have me place my phone against my stomach so he could sing the baby lullabies.

I hadn't known I could love him more each day.

"Everything's going to change once she comes, isn't it?" I asked, snuggling up against him.

"In ways, but we'll still always have this," he said, gesturing around. "We'll have our dirt roads, our ranch, and our happiness forever. And we'll have each other forever. We're just adding a little more love to our song, and I couldn't have wished for anything more."

I couldn't wait for our bundle of joy to join us.

Holly Renee Parker—she'd be named after our favorite angel.

Ian brushed his lips against mine and kissed me gently. "I love you, darling."

"I love you too, best friend. Forever."

Until forever.

ACKNOWLEDGMENTS

First and foremost, thank you to each and every reader who took the time to read Ian and Hazel's story. I hope they made you smile as much as they made my heart soar. Without all of you readers, I am just a girl with words written down on paper. You are the reason those words take flight.

Next up is my amazing team over at Montlake Publishing. Without the amazing support from my editors, Alison and Holly, this book wouldn't be the magic that it is today. Thank you for all of the hard work and dedication you've given to this project. To the amazing team that helped shape this story—from the cover designers to the copyeditors—THANK YOU! To the publicists and the social media teams, THANK YOU! The team over at Montlake goes above and beyond to make our author dreams come true, and I cannot adequately express my gratitude.

To my outstanding agent, Flavia, over at Bookcase Agency: Thank you for always being in my corner, pushing for my dreams to come true. You are an earth angel to me. I'm honored to work with you and your brilliant mind.

To Mama: Thank you for always pushing us kids to chase our dreams and never losing faith in me when I lost my way. You're my best friend, and without your love, I'd die.

To Papa: Thank you for instilling in all of us kids the importance of hard work and dedication to our crafts. You're the definition of a hardworking man.

To my siblings: You all are my inspiration. I'm so proud of what you're showing this world, and I am always going to be your biggest cheerleader.

To my love: Thank you for holding my hand throughout every up and down of this crazy ride. Your support and love and cheerleading push me through each day.

Once again, thank you to every reader who keeps showing up for me and my words day in and day out. I'm honored to have a chance to share my stories with you in such a special way.

Until forever,

BCherry

ABOUT THE AUTHOR

Brittainy Cherry has been in love with words since she took her first breath. She graduated from Carroll University with a bachelor's degree in theater arts and a minor in creative writing. She loves to take part in writing screenplays, acting, and dancing—poorly, of course. Coffee, chai tea, and wine are three things that she thinks every person should partake in. Cherry lives in Milwaukee, Wisconsin, with her family. When she's not running a million errands and crafting stories, she's probably playing with her adorable pets.